Bad II t.

Anton Marks

A rock I can always depend on — Many thanks for the support you and cian have given me over the years.

Marksman Studios
London, United Kingdom

Anton Marks (signature)

Marksman Studios
Marksmanstudios1@gmail.com
www.anton-marks.com

Publisher's Note: This is a work of fiction. Names, characters, places, and incidents are a product of the author's imagination. Locales and public names are sometimes used for atmospheric purposes. Any resemblance to actual people, living or dead, or to businesses, companies, events, institutions, or locales is completely coincidental.

Book Layout & Design ©2013 - BookDesignTemplates.com

Ordering Information:
Quantity sales. Special discounts are available on quantity purchases by corporations, associations, and others. For details, contact the "Special Sales Department" at the e-mail address above.

Bad II the Bone/ Anton Marks - 1st edition.
ISBN-978-0-9562660-0-2

Printed and bound in the UK by
PublishPoint from KnowledgePoint Limited, Reading

A woman and a katana are two of the most beautiful elegant and dangerous things on earth; love and respect them both equally.

Anonymous

In Dedication to All the Mothers around the world who are real life Guardians of the Light

Prologue

What are the chances that in our vast solar system the planet we call home sits at the perfect orbital distance from our sun so that life could begin and flourish? I mean think about that for a moment. A few hundred thousand miles both ways and the Earth as we know it could be a smoldering lump of revolving magma or a spherical block of ice in the expanse of outer space.

I mean, what are the chances of you beating off the competition from a million sperm cells all jostling to reach your mother's egg?

One in a million, one in five million?

Or was it fate, coincidence or happenstance that you are here?

More like destiny if you think about it, ordination even.

Three years ago, London is in the grip of a solar occultation, the first total eclipse in the city for decades. Three minutes where the moon positions itself between the sun and the earth, transforming day into eerie twilight. While the city is awestruck by the astronomical phenomenon a robbery has been planned. Its intent is to use the eclipses power to sway the cities focus from its routine, just long enough for the heist to take place. And it would have worked too if the three young women going about their business in their local bank had not been marked by destiny's hand, foiling the robbery and single-handedly overpowering professional gun men, thugs for hire who prided themselves on viciousness and results, beaten and humbled by pedestrians.

It seemed the celestial event was a sign. And our gifted heroines were the recipients of the message.

Yvonne 'Y' Sinclair is a tall dark-skinned beauty with a sharp mind and equally sharp skills with a samurai sword. Gifted with the ability to channel her life force into the steel, she is their leader and not one to be trifled with. Susan 'Suzy Wong' Young - an empath of exotic Chinese and Jamaican mix, wise and lethal in the art of Wusu martial arts, she is there moral compass. Then there is Ramona 'Patra' Jones – hood chick, statuesque, stunningly attractive with a gift of confounding the laws of probability and blessed with a sweet right hook Mohamed Ali would be proud of. Patra's unquenching love for life keeps them moving forward always to the next challenge.

They are three friends who are reluctant warriors in a war that has raged for millennia. They have been chosen as protectors, inseparable sisters who were predestined to be together, their destinies entwined by forces beyond their understanding, set with a purpose in the grand scheme of earth running's that even they could not fully comprehend. You see the powers that be, masquerading as coincidence, had chosen them as agents to maintain the balance in the eternal struggle for dominance between good and evil.

When Bad II the Bone - a multi-tiered beauty, hair, fashion and fitness salon they had dreamt of opening, was violently snatched from them fate strolled into their lives to test their worthiness on other matters of metaphysical importance.

Why them?

God does not endow you with a gift that in the fullness of time you won't be press-ganged into using to accomplish its grand scheme of balance.

So soon they would find themselves toppling over an abyss into the unknown, locking horns with an adversary of unbelievable power and embarking on an adventure they could never have imagined, even after one too many pulls on a Westmoreland blunt.

And so it all begins with a situation that had been brewing long before they ever met, involving powerfully evil people they never knew, who held dark secrets that were best kept that way.

Secrets that could cost you your sanity as well as your life

1.

South London, Five years ago

The life blood was draining from Jimmy's bullet-riddled body, drenching Spokes in crimson and all he could do was rock his best friend on his lap murmuring ineffectual prayers as if it would soothe his injuries. But he knew, even if instinct was trying to obscure the truth, his spar's last moments on earth would be right here.

"Jesus Christ," he muttered. "Jeeesus Christ."

His breddrin was dying in his arms on the most ignoble of death beds and nothing in Big Jim's Scrap Yard, including Spokes' subdued wailing, would change that inevitable fact.

He was numb, he was confused.

Huddled together in shadows cast over them by the rusting architecture of cars and vans - rising from grease-stained soil as if it was the master work of some L'enfant terrible of the art world – Spokes was sensing everything around him with what seemed like hyper clarity. The smells of rust were intense, the groans of contracting metal from the afternoon sun acute. He was sweating and trembling at the same time as the unfamiliar symptoms of shock played havoc on his senses. He was finding it difficult to remember even the journey here.

Damn, it was that fucking phone call.

His memory was like film stock being yanked through a cinema projector violently.

All the commotion in the background, Jimmy's voice pitched with desperation, a car backfiring multiple times that now he realised were gunshots and a crazy expectancy for a shout of, "Cut!" from a director pissed off that Jimmy had stumbled onto his film set. But when the disgruntled shouts did not come he should have prepared himself for the worst?

It wasn't his idea to meet up at some decrepit scrap yard in North London just after lunchtime. That suggestion left him brimming with questions and frantic with worry but this was Jimmy Éclair we were talking about. Jimmy Éclair a slick dresser, a smooth talker, a cunning mind under a neat fade that would be suited for defence lawyer duties if sales weren't his passion. The same Jimmy Éclair who had never forgotten their roots from their mountainside village in St James, Jamaica and who had welcomed him to the UK seven years ago. Jimmy, who had never guided him wrongly and looked out for his welfare at every turn, now needed him.

And he was there for him no matter what the situation but maybe, just maybe, Spokes should have been looking out for his welfare much sooner.

What did it take for him to realise something was not quite right?

The changes were subtle at first but still changes.

Sudden deviations from how *dem use to rest.*

Jimmy's dinner meetings and power breakfasts became gatherings and sittings. The mundane language of finance was replaced with esoteric symbols and secret handshakes. His business partners became brothers and apprentices and communication was mainly done face to face, leaving his precious Blackberry to gather dust.

Brother Enoch became a name he used with as much reverence as he once reserved for his bank manager. The man Jimmy ascribed his success to was a mystery at first. A name Spokes had grown to mistrust and even fear as this self-confessed obeah man subtly snuck into the life of his friend without introduction or fanfare, appointing Jimmy his financial advisor and his go-to-guy.

Then that goddamn call today.

Spokes was grouting a wall at the Catacombs nightclub, a gig he had fortuitously acquired from - a cash strapped client who was willing to profit share with him after his previous contractor left him high and dry. The icy fear in his friend's voice, how he tried to force the words down the phone line with urgency but modulating his tone so as not to alert anyone around him. Then, in moments, his breathless speech, cut short with sounds of mayhem and gunfire.

The line suddenly went dead and no manner of frantic call backs could establish the connection again. He acted on what he had heard and came here.

Jimmy spluttered, thick streams of arterial blood from his mouth and Spokes daubed it with his shirt. He was no physician, barely competent with first aid if it came to it, but he knew his pardy had suffered appalling internal damage from three bullet wounds to his stomach region. He knew something had compelled him to drive a 4 ton truck across town, bleeding, delirious and miraculously untouched by *Beast in blue* to this point.

Travelling all this way to die in his arms but why?

What deh rass happened? Spokes' question stuck in his throat like an errant herring bone bent set on choking him to death. And the only way he could breathe was not to leave any burning question unanswered.

He had fished a key from the bunch Jimmy had left beside him on the passenger seat. He undid the big padlock at the back of the van and nudged it up. Assaulting him first was an ominous feeling of unease, like old car oil floating above effluent water, separating itself from this bad situation with the prospect of something worst to come.

And he wasn't the only one who recognized it either. Rats were scurrying away from the van, in a squeeking grey mass. They flowed like multiple tributaries through the wrecks. A throbbing, confused river of red eyes and sharp teeth with only one intention.

And that was to get away.

He shuddered and opened the shutter half way.

Old smells, smells of prehistory and privilege, rushed him then the undercurrents of leather, mingled with a tinge of Victorian chemistry and the faint rawness of desiccated decay. Then the overpowering overtones of twenty first century assaulted him with a bouquet of plastics, paper and metals.

Fully extending the shutter to the top, Spokes, with eyes wide, stood looking before he switched on his mobile for illumination and entered.

It was a veritable treasure trove of the ancient, the modern and everything in-between. Aluminum cases stuffed neatly with different denominations, combination locks helpfully set at ooo, lined every side of the panel van, with gilded containers, silk bags embroidered with gold, antique puzzles and crates of obviously valuable artifacts and heirlooms that Spokes felt with certainty belonged to Brother Enoch.

Somehow, somewhere, Jimmy had been ambushed.

He let the theory settle.

Jimmy had driven across London bleeding profusely; his will to live was uncannily strong. Spokes could see it in the set of his jaw. The intense muddy brown of his eyes, held an almost manic determination that seemed to be improved by the obsessive flexing of the fingers of his right hand into a fist. His arm was catching an unhealthy blue tinge through the surface of his caramel skin as if a rapid infection had taken hold. Spokes reached down to rub his fingers calmingly over his pardy's arm, coaxing him into relaxing his fingers and the incessant flexing but he wouldn't stop, he just switched rhythms. Gently Spokes clasped his hands around Jimmy's hand.

"Easy mi breddah." He raised Jimmy's hand up to his chest and watched intriguingly as the squeezing action of his fingers copied the beat of his own heart. Blood oozed from his palm as his nails bit into the soft flesh of his hand. Prying his fingers open one at a time was the only way for Spokes to help relieve the pain his friend must be needlessly inflicting on himself. Once his fingers were spread wide Spokes turned his hand over to see the depth of the wounds.

The bristling buzz like an angry bee startled him.

"Almighty father..."

He looked down and jerked backwards almost throwing Jimmy's hand from his. Nestled grotesquely into the life lines of his friends palm, was a huge glistening black wasp, partially cocooned with a symmetrical red diamond shape on its thorax, its bloody wings fluttering protectively, lying in a nest of crusty and congealed blood, almost as if it was giving something to his host or taking something away. The arthropod's underside throbbed grotesquely and the hairs on its appendages bristled with annoyance. It had obviously gnawed its way through Jimmy's epidermis and was partially buried into the raw and exposed flesh. An uncontrollable shiver racked Spokes frame.neck.

"Kiss mi muma...", he whispered his fingers over his mouth.

Immediately he remembered the Jamaican urban myth about being bitten by a Galla Wasp and not letting it get to open water before you kill it or you would die instead and suddenly he was not sure it was an old wives tale after all.

Jimmy's fingers reflexively closed around the wasp like a bear trap and Spokes began to wonder if that thing was helping to keep his spar alive somehow.

He absently made the sign of the cross.

Spokes could not take his eyes off the abomination that was concealed in his fingers and even if Jimmy was able to prolong his life with dark science, even with his exposure to the secret knowledge Brother Enoch possessed, no miracles would be performed today. Spokes was looking through tear-blurred eyes, on his knees cradling his spar and shivering in the sunlight. A heady mix of fear and bewilderment was attempting to cloud his judgment but he held fast.

D Lawrence, Obeah, dark science. Wha deh rass had Jimmy got himself involved in?

Spokes was surprised by his own mental clarity but was still unable to pull himself free from the anchor of panic that rooted him to the spot.

You try to put that into rassclaat words for his wife

and kids, he thought. Try attempting to explain to the kids their father wouldn't be coming back home ever. He had been murdered in what seemed to be a botched robbery, protecting items from some demented obeah man who was much more than he seemed.

Spokes was watching the life force ebb from the man who had welcomed him to London with open arms seven years ago, the man who had taken him in and allowed him to break bread with his family. A spar that was a constant source of encouragement and a font of knowledge now lying on his lap dying.

It felt pointless, fucking useless to *blouse an' skirt* but Spokes undid his friend's tie and wriggled him out of his jacket. His white shirt was soaked through with crimson and blood was congealing around the entry wounds. He still didn't speak, maybe exchanging his remaining power with that fucking *sumting* in his hand that had preserved his life so far. Maintaining eye contact at all times, Spokes murmured a mantra of relief that was supposed to counteract the pain, something his old lady would have done when he hurt himself back–a-yard. Yet with every rise and fall of his chest Jimmy was losing the battle. His eyes were unfocused, his lips were chapped and blistered from fevered chewing in his agony but they still released whispers of sounds that made no sense to him but he chose to interpret them as pleas.

As his life's candle flickered, it was if Jimmy was pleading with him to snap out of his stupor and take action. He hadn't fought his injuries to be here for him to then be a useless tool in this unfolding crisis.

There were five aluminium attaché cases stacked with the cash and an assortment of artefacts, precious stones and books that looked old and expensive. The Wheels of Construction, his day to day heavy haulage van stood almost accusingly wondering when he would realize he could only do on thing. Who knows if he was followed here by the bandits? Who even knew if the police were involved? A bullet to the brain or a stretch at Her Majesty's Pleasure was not an acceptable outcome to this? He wasn't built for prison food, so he had to shift into gear now.

Transfer the money and stuff to his van and take Jimmy with him.

Back in the real world, he had a schedule to keep.
The refurbishment contract he had acquired demanded he be back there to meet the night club owner. Everything had to seem normal so he had to be there. Spokes could do nothing to arouse suspicion and would go about him business same way. It would fit into his lifestyle like a tailor-made suit.

Jimmy's words again.

Spokes stared down at him, the memory of his words not matching the pathetic figure on his lap. But that pathetic figure had power enough to be insistent in screaming its urgency. It was telling him to move now – *don't worry about me, time fi dat later.*

Go!

With the imaginary voice of reason freaking him out, Spokes struggled to his feet and dragged his dying brethren to the van. He had work to do.

2.

Present Day
Ealing Broadway, West London
Thursday, July 4th
10.45am

How could Y have known that today she would be thrust headlong into a life changing situation through the most mundane of doorways, that of her local bank.

Why else would she be here, it wasn't as if this was one of her favorite places to visit? A usual haunt, somewhere she would hang out with her sisters for drinks. Besides a hospital, a bank would be the most unlikely place she would turn up on a whim or an emergency to think of it. But then it wasn't everyday she was driven by a weird compulsion to check on their freedom fund. The realm of unexplained whim's and fancy was Suzy, her sister's forte. Y had been given the dubious honour of having their combined savings in an account for which she was the main account holder and withdrawal of funds required at least two signatures. Not that in the last four years that ever happened. This account was as tight as Aunt Millie's purse. It received funds period, and a withdrawal was for the day they, or she more specifically, gave up being a wage slave and took her financial destiny in her own hands. She wondered now how easy it would have been to use her smartphone to check the account but today she felt strangely different, hands on. It was almost as if something had shifted in the framework of her life. A subtle change in the status quo of things she couldn't quite put her finger on.

Y entered a gallery of ATVM's, her poise dented slightly from her aversion for banking institutions and found one of the machines vacant. She cautiously fed her plastic into the slot and punched in her PIN number. A harsh voice at the cashiers desk, made her look around. She fidgeted uncomfortably and looked back at the screen showing her account balance. Y took a step back, smoothing down the front of her uniform as she did so then her arms were stiff and straight at her side. Her expression hardened and with what seemed like a concerted effort she approached the ATVM again. This time she did a printout. She lifted it up to her eyes.

A moan escaped her lips.

Under the circumstances Y's response was ice cool, a testament to the measure of her self control.

"Closed?" She asked, her voice measured, her emotions sealed in a strongbox of calm.

"That's right Miss Sinclair, your account has been closed. In fact the entire sum was withdrawn...today."

Magdalene Patten smiled through the reinforced glass, pleased she had answered the query to the customer's satisfaction and sat eagerly awaiting any other questions like an attentive puppy waiting for its favourite stick to be thrown.

The stoic look on the face of the young woman in the pristine white uniform spoke of a mind numbed by her customer service rhetoric or so she thought. The teller prattled on unconcerned.

"Because you are one of our most dedicated customers, I'd like give you the opportunity to obtain our Gold Card. There will be no application forms just a few simple questions and we will be able to process your details from between seven and ten days. The benefits are excellent, so..."

Y felt the restraints she had mentally lashed around her feelings begin to snap. The hollow droning of the customer service rep's voice continued and the unravelling continued unabated. She could almost hear the ping of rivets violently snapping apart from her mental construct.

Y's eyes blazed.

"Shut up!" Y snapped.

The customer service rep's well rehearsed sales speech had rudely been ripped from her mouth, crumpled up and thrown into the neat waste paper basket in the corner and flame throwered.

"Did I hear you right? My account is closed, the balance withdrawn?" Y asked the questions with kind of calm precision that had a sting in its tail.

The teller shook her head, the shatterproof glass separating both women now not as reassuring as she had first imagined.

"Check your records again." The cashier felt the chill from Y's voice, almost expecting the glass to frost.

Y was shaken; the emerging sense of fear she was trying to control was taking hold. She gritted her teeth. Yet still she allowed the objective part of her mind to fall into the background concluding nothing, allowing what was taking place here to conclude itself. She forced herself again to look down at the paper that had been spat at her from the ATM outside and scrutinised, the zeros at the column that said account balance. She looked back up slowly and placed her hands on the counter to stop them from shaking and watched her reflection with surprise.

Stay loose, girl.

Y ran her fingers through her short styled hair and straightened the body hugging uniform, striking a more appropriate pose for the confident, no-nonsense type of person she was supposed to be.

But she could feel pieces of her armor cracking and falling away from its battlements.

Allow the situation to conclude itself.

Furitavely, she checked the fob watch attached to her pristine white uniform.

Late for work for the third time in two weeks and she didn't give a shit. Another day of hauling her ass into work, inwardly miserable but doing what she was paid to do.

This had been a compulsion. And she told herself it was the kind of thing she needed to lift her spirits, to remind her that there was a way out of this and that she was doing something about it. But that maggot of disquiet was burrowing into her flesh now and regret was a consequence.

Imagine this was a split second choice to make a detour because she needed a motivational shot in the arm before she ended up at the 'forced labour camp', that was the beauty salon. Nothing could make her feel it was all worthwhile except seeing those five figures all neatly layed out on her bank statement.

So why did a sudden urge to rearrange the cashiers well proportioned face with a training weapon of choice materializes in her thoughts.

The poor girl had nothing to do with this. It was a serious computer error and that's all it can be.

Pure and simple.

An army of apprehension continued to storm her defences and she kept them at bay for now. Master Azimoko taught her that everything you think is not necessarily so. Pain is pain only if you consider it to be. A bank account with a questionable statement is only that if you see it as that, right? Absently she used her painted fingernails to draw imaginary circles on the counter then, as if struck by an inspiration, she looked up.

The bank teller's eyes had nervously shifted from the articulated screen to check on her customer's mood and realised it had hardened.

The embossed smile Magdalene had nurtured over her five year customer service career fell away from her lips like a piece of tissue being flushed down the toilet. She punched nervously at her keyboard and waited. Whatever data appeared on the VDU that instant didn't please her. Staring at the screen blankly, she pecked away some more and then her hands fell to her sides in defeat. The look on her face did not inspire confidence. Y could see the apology drifting up from the muscles of the teller's neck to her small mouth.

"I'm sorry Ms Sinclair, our records still say your account is closed and that you made a cash withdrawal of the entire sum today using our telephone banking service."

"A week ago my account had nineteen thousand four hundred and eighty two pounds and sixty two pence. I haven't made a withdrawal from the account since I set it up, two years ago."

Instinctively Y used the mobile phone around her neck to call Tyrone. Nothing unusual about

wanting to share your ups and downs with someone you care for, right? Then the strangest thing
occurred. It was if that sentiment directed to her
boyfriend was an abhorrent antithesis of the truth
that her mind was rebiling against. A rush of
awareness contradicting everything she held dear
about her boyfriend buffeted her as if she had been
unceremoiniosly dumped into a wind tunnel. Y
caught her breath and the realization suddenly
stood stark and obvious.

*Tyrone's work-pass left slung on the bedroom door
that he never returned for, his guitar not leaning in the
corner beside the bed, a bottle of Johnnie Walker Blue not
in its pride of place in the kitchen, a small crate that
housed a collection of vintage reggae vinyl's also not in its
usual spot, his toothbrush not in their his and hers cup....*

"He took it." Y's words were said with a cold certainty. "The bastard found a way to take our money."

Her ears popped as if she was unexpectantly losing altitude and the veil that had obscured her vision, lifted. Her heart slowed, her world slowed too
as if everything she loved and believed in was about
to implode. Y lowered her head trying to deny a
reality that was just too much for her to accept at
that moment and all she could see was the disappointment in the eyes of her sisters and the empty
loss of something they all held dear. Y's features
hardened as she bit into her lips, drawing a stream
of blood which she daubed with her tongue, tasting
its sharpness. Her whole body, trained as it was to

react immediately to a threat, was ready to protect itself from an unknown protagonist.

Her eyes burned with held back tears that felt like droplets of molten magma behind her eyelids and under the counter her fists flexed. The surge of energy to her clenched fists made her fingers go warm, that weird thing she was able to do, focussing her chi into things when she felt threatened. She spun away from the counter, dissipating the energy with a thought, got a grip on her almost out-of-control anger and turned to face the teller again, her intensity making the young woman shuffle uncomfortably backwards.

Magdalene diverted her eyes, knowing a storm was coming.

"Get your fucking manager out here now," Y growled, the tears finally breaking from her glistening eyes. "And they better have some answers for me!"

Brixton High Street
McDonald's
10.45am

"Baby, what's up?" Suzy asked concerned.

Y's voice over the mobile sounded dark and foreboding, an almost alien monotone delivered with uncharacteristic hopelessness that caught Suzy unaware as she listened. Immediately her intuitive nature – that weird sister ESP thing they shared - knew something was disastrously wrong. Suzy tried to maintain her focus on the iPhone stuck to her ear but the cold dread leeching into her core was impossible to ignore. She wasn't sure whether Y's immediate trauma had her on edge or the situation that was developing on Y's side of the phone was the cause of her patience to drain away.

"It's not good sis," Y continued, her voice unsteady.

"What nuh good babe?" Suzy asked.

"Everything, our plans, our dreams, up in smoke," she lamented from a place of despondency Suzy had never experienced Y come from before. "I need to see you, we all need to talk."

"Who the fuck yuh talking to, chiny gal?" The Mouth that brashly flung the question, interrupting Suzy's heart to heart, sounded offended the focus was not on him.

"That's bad manners." He said. "You know I ain't done dealing wid you yet."

Suzy's thin brows twitched upwards and her

eyes narrowed while she watched The Mouth and his cronies invading her personal space with the manufactured menace that should have her concerned but didn't.

"Everything okay?" Y asked at the other end.

"Mi cool baby. Let me call yuh back. I'm on deh clock an' have a pressing situation I need to resolve. I'll call Patra when mi deal wid dis."

"You're sure things okay?"

"Tings criss sis. Relax, we will talk later."

If Suzy had worn a short sleeve shirt to work today maybe she could have defused the animosity she sensed immediately directed to her as she walked into the restaurant. If they could see the dragon shaped burn that stretched from her shoulder to her wrist that she'd had a master tattoo artist render to resemble the glorious colours and viciousness of T'eng-she – the Chinese flying dragon – maybe she could have deflected their intention.

Bad gal, don't test.

But that wasn't going to happen. The Mouth and his crew were the focus of this bad vibe maelstrom that not just coloured her psychic senses but her pedestrian perception had to put up with it as well. And if that wasn't enough, her mind interpreted their radiating bad intentions as a smell of vegetation rot, a chlorophyll tinged stink issuing from the boys only she could smell. Suzy slid the housing on her mobile shut and tucked it into her belt holster, her intense brown eyes sweeping over the boys.

That's right bwoys.

The Mouth was in his early twenties maybe, quite good looking, a solid physique with an attitude that had been nurtured without a reality check by friends, film and music. He wore an Averix leather jacket with a white T-shirt underneath. His black jeans were loosely slung low under his ass held in place by a prayer and an appreciation for belt tension. Suzy knew his type well, whether they were in Kingston or London their life spans were short and sometimes as gloriously self destructive as meteorite burning on entry into the Earth's atmosphere.

Suzy Wong shook her head and thought of ways to diffuse this – practise some of what she preached. Maybe now was the ideal time to stop allowing her outdated sense of justice to be more of a hindrance than a virtue but that was just not how she rolled.

She could take what they issued and walk away. The problem was Suzy would not stand by while an innocent was being mistreated.

Suzy had only come through the Golden Arches for a cold drink and burger, a treat while the boys were in the armoured Securicor van on double yellow's arguing about the Arsenal loss the night before.

The Mouth and his posse had entered moments after, joined the queue beside her and on reaching

the cash till began a tirade of abuse on an unsuspecting cashier. The ugly duckling with corrective
glasses, braces, acne and a clumsy demeanour
seemed to have developed a thick skin to callous
predators like these. But Suzy knew the truth. You
never truly got used to the jibes, your feelings were
so deeply buried that even you had no access to
them after a while. The cashier emanated the vibrations of pink, milk chocolate, cuddly teddy bears
and chalk. Suzy smiled as she absorbed a snapshot
of her with the empathetic talents and let the accompanying feelings of hurt and the fear wash over
her too. Suzy just could not bring herself to watch
the injustice play out against a good soul.

Anger balled up in her chest in a volatile concoction that the trio seemed gleefully willing to ignite.

The three stood scowling at her interpreting her
silence as submission.

What more could it be?

Hair knotted into a pony tail, a face of smooth
flowing contours and a lithe body hidden by her
neat uniform.

As was usual the male ego immediately disre-
garded her as a threat.

Beauty equated with being soft and compliant in
their world.

"You ain't got nuthin' to say all of a sudden,
chiny gal." He turned to his boys. "She was running
off her lip a moment ago blood. I think she's
scared." He mocked.

Suzy breathed deeply trying to calm herself and said.

"Why don't yuh just take yuh food and leave while yuh can?"

The threat mixed with the grating patios of Kingston, Jamaica, took them by surprise especially as it was coming from a petite oriental girl but that was for only a moment. And as the questions formed behind their eyes, Suzy slowly placed the helmet she had under her arm on the counter and brazenly matched their glares with equal ferocity.

"Deh girl have some fight in her, blood." The Mouth laughed. "But people get hurt by poking dem nose into tings that don't concern them. Get messed up, yuh si me?" He took a sip from his Coke, twirling the contents in his mouth as if he was testing it for body and bouquet. "Now mind yuh fucking business."

He threw the ice cold contents of his cup into Suzy's chest and backed away from the spray, laughing.

"Oops.........!" He said.

Suzy gasped.

The stream of soda hit her square in the chest and seemed to explode in every direction, soaking her from neck to mid section. The Coke left a dirty brown stain on her navy blue shirt and dripped on-to her trousers. The material stuck to her breasts showing her lace bra, ice cubes lodged in her cleav-age, melting against her skin and she felt the hun-dreds of carbonated bubbles bursting on her stomach as the liquid evaporated.

Calm gal! She told herself.

The words of cool reason slowly sunk under a bubbling geyser of hot vengeance. Suzy felt nothing, reasoned nothing. This was all instinct. She walked into the midst of boisterous laughter and congratulations as if the battle was a foregone conclusion and placed a slender but firm hand on The Mouth's shoulder.

Turning, he saw the Chiny Gal gracefully leap into the air as if gravity had reversed itself, à la Matrix, heard the rustle of her clothes, felt the air part as her right leg hurtled towards his jaw in a perfect flying roundhouse kick.

His recollections ended abruptly.

The force of the blow lifted him off his feet, twisting his body in mid-air and deposited him head first between a cash register and perspex charity box. His tense arms tangled around the leads of the monitor, tearing it out of its housing and bringing it down with him to the ground with paper napkins and straws.

Suzy watched him slide limply out of sight and turned to look at his friends-in-arms her wusu stance loose but no less effective. They backed away ever so slowly only giving a fleeting look of concern over to The Mouth bleeding and battered on the other side of the counter before they scuttled away.

"Yuh bitch, yuh!" was one outspoken sentiment

from an old lady who sat watching her grandson eating. Some swore incredulously; a small smattering of applause spread around the restaurant and voices of support for her actions grew.

Contrary to what you would expect, the adulation did not improve Suzy's frame of mind. She lowered her head and cursed herself.

Turning away amidst the confusion she collected her helmet and her Fillet-o-Fish and disappeared.

Gridlock, Tottenham Court Road
10.45am

Ramona *Cleopatra* Jones, Patra to her sisters gave the Kawasaki Ninja some revs and punched the warm fuel tank between her legs with a gloved fist. The Bluetooth wireless rig in her ear blinked as she spat the words with venom.

"Can you believe this bullshit?"

It was Suzy on the other end of the line and she sounded excited and concerned but not as excited and concerned as Patra was at this very moment. She stood helplessly on her kick stand and surveyed the gridlocked traffic of Oxford Street, the fallout from a 24 hour Tube Strike. In front of her was a winding construct of multi-coloured steel made from vans, buses, cars and trucks, undulating their way along like a sun drunk sidewinder, its multiple exhaust haze distorting the buildings in the West End's commercial centre as it went along.

"You did what? That nigga deserved every bruise his ass got," Patra nodded her head and belted out her signature laugh. "I'd loved to have seen that beat down. Y's trippin you say, whaddup?"

The earpiece that hugged her earlobe blinked with the comment and a flurry of high pitched mobilespeak that made sense only close up, made her shrug leather clad shoulders and nod in agreement, her focus firmly engaged in the traffic madness of the West End.

"Okay, okay I'll be there but her ass better be on fire 'cos I'm bringing the water, yuh heard me."
Patra looked behind her and realised every degree of a three hundred and sixty rotation was tight, the sun was reflecting off bonnets and obscuring her view but the blaring horns and the shimmering heat curtain being flung into the sky said it all.

Motherfucking gridlock.

"Gotta go Suzy but I'll be there, I promise sugahh."

Pulling the helmet onto her head, Patra glanced at her carrier unit and knew this delivery was going to be tight, if not impossible but savoured the odds.

As fate would have it though, the outcome of this particular ride would decide the future of all female despatch riders who joined the chicken shit outfit of Pathos Couriers.

By 1.45 she should have been regretting her outburst of indignant wrath but the snide comments, the disrespect and the downright sexism had gone beyond male banter to victimisation. By accident, Patra had walked into the midday drivers' coven. Their little fantasy session was in full swing, describing her as a horny bitch best suited to be riding cock instead of a motorbike. In a fist fight she could take these pansy ass faggots without breaking a sweat but she had to learn to approach challenges without resorting to physical conflict. She was a woman after all and she was blessed with a brain and the guile to use it. So in the heat of the moment, her mouth getting in the way of her brain or so she would have them think, she threw down an unusual gauntlet.

"So you niggas think you can handle this?" She twirled and grabbed a butt cheek, her anger simmering. Wild agreement from the cave men was spontaneous and enthusiastic.

"Okay, okay. Let's put your money where your motherfucking mouth is."

Just at that minute a priority request was made by one of their corporate clients that a record contract had to be collected from its headquarters in the sticks of Middlesex and delivered to a promotion company in the heart of Soho in a ridiculous time frame.

Patra didn't think and neither did that hollow yearning in her chest, that tingle at the base of her skull that flexed the laws of coincidence in her favour in many a tight scrape.

That was her gift and it was grinning from ear to ear.

"If any of you cocksuckers wants to take it, that's fine by me." She had proclaimed. "But I know I can collect and drop off the package in forty-five minutes. And I'll stake my ass literally on that shit."

It was a done deal as the words left her mouth and after the laughter died down she was dashing out the door with the clock ticking and the possibility of five salaries in her back pocket if she won. Losing on the other hand was not worth considering.

That's how she was brought up, to be a competitor.

Her memories of growing up with three brothers in Georgia, Alabama, fighting with them to gain every ounce of respect by doing what they could do and doing it better was what made her. Competition and adventure flowed through her veins and moulded her character. Telling her she couldn't do something was an invitation to conflict, something she revelled in. And with her talent of confounding probability - an above average lucky break quotient some would say - nothing much scared her.

The fact that they were chauvinistic morons whose centre of intelligence was in their gonads was a forgone conclusion. Her duty, and one that any woman from the Jones family in Alabama all upheld, was their pride of self and an unhealthy belief that whatever any man could do - biological restraints not withstanding – they were not just their equal but their betters.

Not the most endearing character trait, especially with prospective boyfriends, but it was the truth.

Running her fingers along her tight braids, sweat trickling down her brows, Patra had ten minutes to make the drop.

And it would be done by any means necessary.

It was about then she saw the motorcycle cop surveying the traffic situation.

Nothing had changed since her last profanity-riddled thought and Patra began to feel the uncomfortable emotion of panic as the seconds slipped away and failure loomed.

Boxed in on all sides, she didn't even have the luxury to snake her way through the gaps in the vehicles.

Trapped like a son-of-a-bitch.

She looked over to the cop who was in conversation on his radio.

This was bullshit. She had to do something now. Huffing, she swung her long legs off the saddle and proceeded to lower the Suzuki to the tarmac, with cars in front, behind and to the side of her. The driver of a BT van popped his head through the window totally bemused at what she was doing.

"Oi, what the fu...?" He shouted like he was lost for the right words.

Patra gave him the finger and reached for the package. Miraculously the vehicles in the left lane started to move at a steady pace.

There was still a slim window of opportunity.

Patra flew back on the Ninja's saddle making it

squeal as she fed it through the tightest of gaps. Wiggling her leather clad ass from left to right, shifting it's centre of gravity with every twist, she deftly manoeuvred herself away from another lane going nowhere and instead lurched onto the side walk.

Pedestrians stared open mouthed while Patra revved the motorbike threateningly and sped up the sidewalk parting the gawping tourists like farmyard chickens. Traffic lights loomed so she bumped back onto the main road and broke right, weaving her way through the stationary vehicles who might as well be sitting with their engines removed.

A sudden speakered wail and the unmistakable blue flash.

Five-O, they can get a piece of my ass later. She thought as another bottleneck hurtled towards her.

This time she didn't test the impossible.

Speeding up a cloistered lane, Patra grabbed the brakes, skidding the Ninja to a stop and unceremoniously flung the motorbike on its side. Reaching over she undid the latch from her carrier unit, snatched the package and started sprinting down Needle Street.

The sirens grew louder behind her and the strobing blue lights bounced off the glass walls and shiny metal but she kept ahead of any implied threat the familiar sound was supposed to instil in her.

Patra's mind was at the finish line.

She was shedding weight in mid flight.

Her gloves went first, savagely shaken off her hands, then her bulky jacket spiralled above her head and next her lipstick red helmet was tossed behind her, bouncing off the urine soaked walls and spinning to a stand.

Looking up she saw the neon lighted sign in the distance.

Razzmatazz Records.

Fifty metres in four minutes.

Piece of cake.

She sprinted forward.

Docklands, East London
Thursday, July 4th
23.45

Toppa yawned and arched his back, farting as his urine found the perfect trajectory into the toilet bowl. He wanted to applaud himself but he had one hand on his dick and the other propping himself up against the wall so instead he let out a sigh of contentment and that's when the scream messed up his reverie. A stream of piss splattered the wall and splashed on his hand as he jerked to attention.

"Rass!"

A scream, like nothing he had heard in a very long time and not one he would have ever expected from the present company. In his line work you become a conniouseur of screams. After hearing so many as he meted out ghetto retribution on orders from the boss you begin to appreciate their depth and meaning. It was an unmistakable sound of hopelessness and terror that sent chills of pleasure and uncertainty down his spine. This was not the sounds you would imagine to hear from the representatives of two of London's most notorious crime fraternities playing their monthly poker game.

Toppa had resisted any collaboration with these English *bwoys* but the monthly friendlies had fostered an understanding between the rivals who came to appreciate the need for a mutually beneficial arrangement in carving up London drug turfs. It wasn't something the Chinese or the Turks understood but the big boss Deacon was a forward thinking Yard man and the fruits of his smarts were paying off, well until now.

An attack, what else could it be? Toppa thought.

The hard men he sat around a poker table with once a month, would take a bullet or a knife, and accept their fate no screaming like a pussy, no beseeching to the higher powers like a bitch.

These nerve shredding screams were not characteristic of the thugs he knew and that paradox chilled him to the core.

No, this was something else. This was something bad.

Instinctively he clenched his ass, balls tingling, he cut his piss short and reached for the weapon in his shoulder holster. He pushed the toilet door open with the tip of his weapon and looked out.

The coast clear he buckled up and moved out into the hallway. The home of the East End mob enforcer was lavish but familiar to him as this was the second time the crew had been invited here. But Toppa had not reached the ripe old age of thirty five in this business without his innate sense of survival. As he hurried along the sweeping balcony he opened every door and peered in on his way downstairs, his ears peeled.

A cold claustrophobic silence met him as he descended, quickly spreading its gnarly fingers in the confines of this huge space. The air hung frigidly expectant of something's arrival, something dark and unwelcome. He shuddered and every candlelit story of the undead and ghosts from his past in Jamaica came back to torment him.

Toppa descended the stairs, his breath raspy and hoarse, the bones of his thoracic reverberated from his trip hammer heart and his mouth desert dry.

Cool nuh, he chided himself. *Just cool, star!* But the silence threatened him and with it some dread expectation, he could not put his finger on.

He flinched. More gunshots.

The 9mm rounds echoed off the walls and so did the blood curdling screams and the sounds of a frantic struggle – a desperate struggle for survival. The lights dimmed almost immediately after the screams, appliances humming with a power surge and then there was darkness.

"Bomboclaat!" Toppa spat, his breath plumes of cold condensation, his forehead slick with cold

sweat and his legs suddenly hesitant. Almost breathless with anticipation, he felt his way to the last step on the staircase, every instinct telling him to flee. Toppa just couldn't. He had to know, even when every nerve was compelling him otherwise, almost as if he was digging his heels in but being overridden by synapses hell bent on preserving his life. He held his weapon high, gripping it hard to prevent his hand from shaking and shuffled towards the drawing room, the horror of what was unfolding behind those mahogany doors sufficient motivation to allow himself another step. In a few seconds he knew that motivation would not be enough. A primal curiosity had taken hold of him, hell bent on proving the existence of our darkest fears. His rational mind wanted to turn tail and head back to South explaining his failure to Deacon's glaring inquisition.

Who deh fuck was he kidding?

Not after hearing what he had heard. These were sounds of grown men slamming into walls, crashing into furniture, guns going off, the guttural screams of hardened thugs unused to fear and its consequences. And then there were the screeches, savage animalistic, high pitched mewls, that itched his inner ear that only a force of will stopped him from scratching the irritation.

He tried to cover his ears when the smell assaulted him next.

It was seeping through the cracks, under the

flues, a stink of excrement and gut wrenching rawness of an abattoir. Toppa was frantic but controlled and was unable to tell whether the heat
issuing from behind the doors was real or imagined. He smelled the blood too before he saw it,
seeping from under the doors, literally pints of
gooey scarlet and chunks of body tissue adding its
bouquet to the foul stench already here. One by
one the screams stopped and Toppa stood still, ce-
mented to the floor boards. He stared at the sturdy
lacquered double doors that he had walked through
earlier as he headed upstairs to use the toilet. He
wondered why no one had rushed through it as a
means of escape. Why the manic twisting of the
handle from inside? And why the bone shattering
slamming of their own bodies against it had not
flung it open? A stream of questions rifled through
his mind with no accompanying answers that made
sense to him. He simply watched like a befuddled
spectator as his own hand reached for the door
handle.

Wha yuh a duh bwoy?
The cold now – whether in his mind or in reality –
was seeping through his skin, gnawing into his
bones and freezing his marrow as he reached out.
He was shivering uncontrollably, as his willpower
fought with an unexplained urge to commit suicide
because, instinctively, he knew if he opened that
door he would be dead.

The shrieks broke the spell. Not human and not
any animal he was familiar with. A hellish screech

spat from a multitude of triumphant hungry mouths making his ears prickle and burn. Toppa found himself on his ass scrambling backwards ineffectually emptying the clip of his Walther PPK into the door. A wave of depraved derision lifted up into the high ceilings of the house in an ear splitting bay from things redefining the impossible and answering his premature gun ejaculation with venom.

Toppa knew he had become their new focus of attention and he could hear the frenzied scrambling at the door, the scraping, the scratching, the ripping, the splintering of the old wood. The door shaking to its hinges, savagely being gnawed away by whatever nightmares were on the other side.

He had to get away was all the gangster could think as he stumbled through the confines of the darkened mansion, toppling furniture, slamming into walls, tripping down steps. Confusion condemned him to this maze that would turn out to be his mausoleum. He was at a door he could not open, his chest heaving and his heart threatening to explode out of his chest, his own screams muffled by the internal panic thumping in his head. The *shotta* were trapped and the things were coming up behind him pushing the darkness his way like stale air being forced through a tunnel and gibbering, screeching, mewing their way ever closer to him. Their sounds resonated with every nerve ending in his body. His senses heightened, Toppa could smell them, a wave of fetid stench and an overpowering mix of bile, shit and sulphur. His own pounding and screaming felt disembodied as if he was watching himself a million fruitless miles away. Trapped he turned slowly and even in the complete darkness Toppa saw them, silent almost admiring him. Their eyes were smouldering red like liquid magma pools holding a malevolent intelligence, the gaping maws of their mouth set with rows upon glistening rows of jagged sharp teeth luminescent in the darkness.

"*Mi ready, feh yuh,*" he croaked chambering a round in his Browning auto. He made the sign of the cross with the barrel of the weapon, his lower lip trembling.

"*All a yuh...,*" his voice was hesitant but getting louder, more defiant. "*...all a yuh, can guh suck yuh mumma!*"

His finger wrapped around the trigger as a dark snarling tsunami engulfed him, drowning out the gunshots and his screams.

"Goddamit!" Deacon swore.

When he could not contact his soldiers at the poker game by Walters' in Mitcham, he knew instinctively that Darkman had come calling. Calmly he handed the mobile to Minty, a look of inevitability tightening his features and tried to relax.

Not suh easy.

The crime boss stood naked in a marble tub, gesturing to the voodoo priest to continue pouring the foul smelling concoction of herbs, bush and exotic minerals over his head. He imagined marked out symbols with a chicken foot drawing unseen forces to him. The light skinned man performing the incantation was bare footed and dressed in white slacks, necktie, with a garland of pungent roots slung around his neck and a white shirt - miraculously kept in pristine condition although blood, plant extracts and other things he dared not think of were liberally being used in this protection spell. The Voudon whispered in a stream of rhythmic phrases, his tongue twanging like a stringed instrument. Deacon understood the words to be Haitian patios but spoken with such power, the words knitted together to form a tapestry not understood but felt.

The liquid was warm as it was poured over his head and he breathed through his mouth, declining to inhale the repugnant odour. It took a moment for a tingling sensation to begin spreading all over his body like a cloak of invincibility just taking effect or was his mind trying to conjure the effect to cement a reality that was preposterous to most but was as real as the marble tub he was standing in to him?

The things he had seen growing up in St Catherine, Jamaica. On the islands you learned to appreciate how gossamer thin were the boundaries between the worlds.

Yes this was real.

Deacon made sure every inch of him was tainted with the vile liquid, remembering the classical story of how Achilles was defeated because his mother had tried to make him invincible by dipping him in the River Styx not realising the ankles she held him by were never kissed by the river of the underworld and turned out to be his only weakness.

He wasn't just allowing high school stories to inform his decisions; Deacon was flowing with his instinct. He wiped liquid from his eyes and smeared it from his lips with the back of his hand, watching the shaman stand silently swaying ever so slightly mumbling with his arms at his side. The chicken foot had fallen out of his hand to the ground. Taking that as a sign the spell had been cast, Deacon stepped out of the marble basin and looked around the darkened room, his eyes becoming accustomed to the wave of flickering candles. Content that he was in the here and now, he chuckled to himself.

His life had increasingly become a part of a world where the impossible was made possible and from time to time he had to make sure his feet were firmly set in the correct portion of that divide. Minty stepped out of the shadows with a full length towel draped over his arm and that concerned look that was now a resident expression since his boss became one of the main players in the London underworld.

Minty and Deacon had grown up together in the

mean streets of South London. Deacon was a natural hustler with a violent streak only Minty seemed to be able to channel with wise words and street sense. So, together the boss from Grants Pen, Jamaica and Minty - born in Red Hills, Kingston but left for London in his teens - climbed the rungs to gangster infamy. One of South London's most violent gang wars had been orchestrated by these two men and ended on their say so. Small crews were obliterated, larger gangs got with the programme or they too ceased to exist and the established crime families brokered deals or dismantled themselves. Deacon swiftly established territory, distribution centres, drug routes and the brutal elimination of the ineffective bosses standing in the way of progress.

In five days it was all over and an iron fisted peace established.

They became known as artists in the mechanics of threat and menace, keeping their manor in check. This was what they knew and what had made them successful and what they had to deal with every hype-filled day of running their organisation.

Everything changed when one of Deacon's lieutenants was found nailed to an inverted cross of pine wood, eviscerated and left leaning against the wall of his wine bar in Seven Sisters. Casualties of war were expected but this was some Old Testament shit and it sent tremors through him. With every twisted murder of his soldiers his belief about what was possible was spat on, trampled and burned.

As the murders became more brazen and the messages less cryptic, he knew who he was up against. If it was anybody else Deacon would have the full force of his *dawgs* on them but much to his chagrin this was no ordinary man, no ordinary situation.

Darkman was perpetrating this fuckery from prison.

Deacon had funded a robbery that later he realised targeted a Jamaican Obeah man who had supposedly fleeced a small fortune from believers in his powers. A treasure trove of money, gold, precious stones and artefacts he was shipping back to Yard. Deacon saw it as his duty to relieve this dutty Sanfi man of his bounty for all the false promises and deceit he perpetrated and then punish the pussies who wanted to believe there was something more to their dull existences.

Darkman was a St Thomas bwoy whose influence had held Jamaica's poor in thrall but here in the UK he depended on parlour tricks and menace.

Easy money, right?

Every general throughout history has made a decision they regretted - Hannibal, Alexander the Great - and now Deacon. Underestimating your enemy is something Sun Tzu would have chastised him for. Underestimating someone like Darkman was unforgivable. Deacon found out the hard way that he was dealing with a power, the real deal, a force of nature that could not be exaggerated in any Anancy story told around a camp fire. He was a one man army able to marshal dark forces that could murder or punish the ill prepared.

How do you think Deacon stayed ahead of the non-believers? His success was mainly down to utilising every advantage he possessed including the unconventional - namely his belief that there was much more to our existence than what we can perceive with our five senses.

A fact that was saving his skin now.

Deacon finished drying himself and slipped into a terry gown and slippers offered to him by Minty.

"Is he alright?" Minty asked nodding over to the Voudun who was now on his knees with his forehead on the ground and his arms slung beside him, knuckles down.

"Don't worry 'bout him, roots. I head hunted dis bwoy personally from Haiti. A top shottas in the notorious Ton-Ton Macoutes link wi up. He swears by him powers. Anyway if me dead because of anyting he should have done or didn't do, you know deh programme star."

Minty touched the weapon strapped to his upper body in a Versace patterned leather holster.

"Brackam!" Deacon patterned a gun with his fingers, firing at the still genuflected witchdoctor. "As long as me and dis place is shielded everyting is everyting. Business as usual." He paused, his eyes losing their lustre and his mouth folding into a grimace.

"Any answer from Toppa phone?"

"Nothing."

"I need to find that treasure and done dat bloodclaat St Thomas Obeah bwoy. There is nothing more important, seen."

"He's picking off our best men one at a time and we can't stop him." Minty said. "Can our plan stand up to that?"

"This is a race for survival and it is drawing to a close for him. I want what I want and him want, what him want. Him think pure power will do dis. Mi grow up inna deh street Minty. And if it is one ting mi learn, it's punch above you weight but keep that secret close to yuh chest, yuh feel mi?"

"But what of this voodoo ting ..."

"Believe mi breddah, this is real. Him motivated by revenge and now we know jail can't hold him suh we have to adjust. He will stop at nothing but him nevah count on me, count on dis."

He pointed to his forehead.

"He is hurting us Deacon," Minty said levelly. "He's murdered five of our best soldiers in the space of two weeks and he's just disappeared into the mist without a trace. How do we deal with a duppy, especially one who can call on the darkness?"

"Same way we deal with any bwoy who tink dem can muscle inna wi business. It's deh same result Minty, just different tactics," he gestured to the doorway.

They both walked casually out of the room that Deacon had modified for arcane purposes and into a utility area that branched off into an expansive kitchen. Deacon headed for his wine rack and poured himself a brandy. "What have we learned from the network?" He asked.

Minty's eyes diverted to process the question and then in moments his gaze returned to the eyes of his friend.

"I don't want to raise your hopes up D but the informers have finally come up with a name to Driver X. If this is the same man who Jimmy left the van with before he died, then we are one step away from the treasure."

"Bomboclaat!" He said the swear word caressing every letter. "Wouldn't it have to be in the middle of a war that him finally decide to show himself? Three years of looking feh this man with no head nor tail of him, now suddenly him surface." Deacon paused for thought. "But it could work to our advantage still. Ketch Darkman napping. Put as many soldiers on it as possible, yuh hear mi. And mek sure you remind dem to wear deh amulets blessed by the witchdoctor. It could save dem life."

"They'll be ready."

"By the way, what do you call dis bwoy. Him real name." Deacon asked.

"We only have an alias, so far. They call him Spokes. When Jimmy escaped the ambush it seems this guy secured the money and the goods."

Deacon nodded with an impatient glint in his eyes.

"Then find him an' bring him rass to me."

Y's Crib, Acton, West London
Friday, July 5th
06.00

Phase one of Operation 'Wipe Tyrone's Memory from Existence' consisted of going through her flat with as much purpose as when she was spring cleaning and make sure nothing of him remained. Y stood in her modest lounge rubbing her fingers on the reinforced glass case and the fingerprint recognition lock that housed the daishō - Masamune katana and Wakizashi – her prized samurai swords. If the insurance company had not advised her of the precautions she needed to take before they would insure it, who knows she could be looking at an empty space right now? But Tyrone was aware of the small fortune Pops had spent on keeping it secure and steered clear.

Y opened the tempered glass case keying in the code to shut down the motion sensor and used her thumb print to unlock the securing rod that held the lid in place. She gently took the Katana from the environmentally controlled interior. Twice a year and sometimes when the mood took her she would practise with the six hundred year old sword.

Her Pops had given it to her when she was five years old, much to Y's mamma's incomprehension but Mas Lenny was that kind of man. As the story went in Lenny's first year in Japan he befriended a destitute old man who camped outside of the hostel he used to live in. The old man - he called him General because of his military background - spoke good English and they became close friends. While he discovered Tokyo in the day, in the evenings he would sit with the General and be told the many stories of the samurai. The old man died in his arms six months into their friendship and left him his prized possession of a katana forged by master sword smiths in 13th century feudal Japan. It turned out to be worth hundreds of thousands of pounds and when she was old enough an invaluable part of Japanese history was given to her.

Lenny had been travelling around the Far East for at least three years and by then he was adamant Y learned to use it one day. Y's friends took guitar and flute lessons while she learned kendo. It became an obsession of hers to master its use and in time she became proficient.

Y's father's philosophy of life was unique to only him, especially his unhealthy passion for all things oriental, but still a practical Jamaican who grew up in the ghettos of Kingston with an understanding of discipline and purpose. The relationship Pops had with Y's mother was doomed from the beginning. Lenny's wanderlust was fuelled by an opportunity to travel the world and after two years the union was in ruins. In letters that he sent to her every month from her tenth birthday onward he explained why he had to leave when he did. His charm and providence guided his fortunes and financially he was able to contribute to her upbringing. He wasn't physically there for her but through his exquisite letters – they talked over the phone but Lenny loved the intimacy of the written word - she learned so much about him. With time and maturity Y understood why he had to do what he had done. There was never a doubt that he loved her, his destiny just wasn't to be with her in the UK.

Lenny married a wonderful Japanese woman called Yushi and Y had two younger brothers whom she met and loved immediately.

Y slowly pulled the sword out of its scabbard and moved smoothly into Okimanzo strike, the blade perfectly balanced in her hands conflicting thoughts interfering with her focus.

What the hell, that couldn't be helped.

Y spun on the balls of her feet, a grimace pulling her lips tight. She lowered her centre of gravity, and whipping the sword with her as she moved as a blur every kata followed precisely and some were even created on the spur of the moment but all merging into a lethal ballet fuelled by her anger. The imaginary Tyrone did not stand a chance as she severed his arm and watched him fall to his knees screaming, arterial blood misting her with its warmth and then detaching his head with one upward stroke and as the body tumbled forward with her back to him she thrust the Katana under her arm and into his thorax, twisting the sword for maximum internal damage.

The imaginary bubble popped.

She held the position and felt a wave of satisfaction and disgust at the same time. Tyrone was scum and he had done what he had done, for reasons best known to him and Y had to live with it. But she did not have to be bitter. The virus of self doubt and hate that he had left behind like landmines set into the dirt of her subconscious need not be acted on.

After all she was the master of her state of mind. And Y just could not allow Tyrone to dictate her emotions in his absence. In that moment she let the thought of him dissolve away.

Finally all that was left was the sensation of the katana in her hand, a inhaling of breath in her nostrils, its whistling through her throat and the rise of her ribs and stomach. The turbulence inside subsided and nothing else mattered but her breathing and a feeling of calm. But for how long?

Y's Bedroom
Acton
20.31

"Are you just going to lie there staring at the ceiling or are you going to get mad, swear, trash the place or something?"

Y asked Suzy the question, the sigh in her voice showing how much of a relief it was that this twenty four hours was at an end. She was already numb from the day's events but was not supprised to hear that Suzy had been suspended from work pending an investigation into charges of grievous bodily harm.

Then like a bad omen, Patra was bailed for serious traffic offences. Only after Y's lengthy conversation with her arresting officers was she released on her own recognisance pending a day at the courts.

If Y didn't know better she would have thought someone somewhere was out to get them.

Suzy Wong remained silent and instead shuffled her petite but tightly toned body over the king sized bed to allow her sister some space to snuggle up beside her. She adjusted the Kiss my Ass PJ'S around her waist, her top, short below the waist, showed her muscled midriff and jade piercing through her belly button. A multicoloured and detailed dragon twisted around her left arm from shoulder to its magnificent head snapping at her wrists, successfully concealing her burn mark.

Everyone had turned up at Y's place with overnight bags and a sense of leaving their troubles outside the door. And that's why it seemed so alien for Y not to be relaxed in the one place she called home amongst the few people she called family.

Damn she should have known better.

"I should be the one feeling like you, don't you think? After all he took our savings from my account. I let him in and lowered my guard, loved the son-of-a-bitch, lived with him, was getting serious with him and that's what we got."

Y sat on the edge of the bed, her XXL 49er's linebacker top down to her thighs and her long dark legs crossed in front of her, looking absently through her bedroom door to the small landing beyond, her mind a swirl of hurt and anger. Detaching her focus, she reached over without looking back to the bottle of Asti that had sat in a bucket of ice for the last forty-five minutes on her small side table.

"You guys did tell me, hinted as friends would and I just didn't listen. Patra hated him, Suzy you were more diplomatic but I could see in your eyes you wanted to smack him around a bit but instead of finding out why I tried to make excuses."

Suzy, suddenly animated, gracefully rose from her prone position like a cat, gently grasping Y's hand and taking the bottle from her. Deftly Suzy undid the wire restraint and popped the cork. Three glasses were filled and allowed to settle before handing Y a glass. After a few moments her brown eyes lit up, her expression resolute.

"Patra weh yuh deh?" Suzy shouted out.

"Chill bitch, I'm here."

Cleopatra came around the corner in all her naked glory, the towel on her shoulder, her muscular body mainly dry with patches of sheen on her legs and shoulders.

Anyone would look at the statuesque figure, flawless skin - notwithstanding some bruising from her kickboxing classes - proportions that needed no modifications from the brush of an Old Master and an aura that smouldered with the intensity for life even when others around her thought she was *nuff*. From the aggressive sway of her hips when she walked, as if life was a catwalk and she was its model, to her honesty, was vintage Patra. She was the most real person they knew.

"For you," Suzy said offering her a glass.

"What are we toasting?" Patra asked. "I thought we just got our asses robbed."

"A new beginning," Suzy replied. "One we're forced feh accept whether we want to or not." The statement was free from malice or accusation as was Suzy's way.

Everyone raised their glasses.

"New beginnings." They chorused.

Y hesitated to take a sip having difficulty accepting Suzy's optimistic view on what could only be considered a disaster in anyone's eyes.

She brought the glass to her lips, a dark anger seething below the level of awareness and one that desperately required an outlet to be vented. Y wanted anger to be expressed not reasoned, something to justify what she had allowed to happen. A strong black woman who had given her heart and trust without the required cynicism a woman was trained to exhibit. That was a philosophy she never personally ascribed to but her openness hadn't just affected her but her family too.

Patra joined the huddle of women on the bed, her back to them, her butterfly tattoo at the base of her spine. She leaned on Suzy and Y, letting her head loll between their backs, smelling fresh and her skin cool to the touch.

"I'm feeling your pain babe and I know you feeling guilty about this shit but it could have happened to anyone of us. We don't blame you."

"Come on sis, yuh know Patra reasoning mek sense."

"I knew you two would react like this but you can't help me feeling guilty about it. Tyrone duped me, duped us and I'm pissed. That bastard took our dreams from us man, I can't be cool with that."

"We not cool sugahhh," Patra said. "But we gotta accept the facts. Motherfucker Tyrone took our money, played us like a ten dollar whore and I want his nuts between a vice, you feel me."

Y smiled at Patra's directness and the amusing package of her delicate high pitched voice. For those who didn't know her very well they were always surprised by her street lingo and profanity. They stereotypically expected those character traits from Y, the fit, feisty dark skinned one not the statuesque, light skinned sister with the twinkle in her eyes and butter couldn't melt in her mouth smile. After their initial shock - even with the sexy lilt from the southern states of the US - what they wouldn't know was how much of a good soul she was, kind, selfless and loyal. And Y knew the world did not have an abundance of such people.

Y squeezed Patra's hand.

"I just can't help thinking you blame me."

Suzy kissed her teeth loud and long.

"Yuh know that's not true gal. If yuh going to start thinking like that yuh might as well blame me for not being stronger."

"Yep," Patra nodded in agreement, the word flipping out of her mouth petulantly.

"I should have kicked that Motherfucker's ass as soon as he tried to flip shit and breakdown our friendship."

"Nip it rass, in deh, bud." Suzy added. "He felt odd, sis. His whole vibe, from day one but nothing screamed out about him. That alone was strange."

"Maybe we misunderstood him? He was unfamiliar, so you read him wrong."

Patra sighed, rolling her eyes.

"Don't let me pop you upside your head giiiirl. Tell me you didn't just try to make excuses for that thieving cocksucker?"

"I just thought..."

"No you didn't think queen bitch." Patra looked over to Suzy exasperated. "You tell her before I get tribal on her ass."

Y knew it was the frustration of people who cared; finishing her Asti she placed the empty flute on her side table.

"Yuh don't know the full story baby." Suzy said. "Him aura was vivid in mi face, not evil dark, just a conniving light blue. I smelt old money and grease, tasted steel and coffee. Me know him have a mischievous aura but that doesn't make him bad. I wanted to talk to you about it but you wouldn't have taken it seriously. We decided to spare yuh the details." Suzy said calmly.

"And now."

"Well at deh time we thought wi had your best interest at heart." Suzy said.

"You felt I couldn't accept that, after everything we've been through?"

Suzy nodded.

"You were happy babe."

"I was a fucking fool." Y said.

"Hindsight is a bitch sugahhh." Patra concluded. And we both know Suzy has the touch, she can sense shit. We need to give her gift more respect. Y nodded.

"We hope him, would show him colours to you and you would drop kick him rass but he was smarter than we gave him credit for."

"As I said we should have bum rushed his bitch ass."

"The worst feeling is that I was sleeping with this bastard and my instincts told me nothing. What does that say about my choice of men?"

"It stinks." Patra stated plainly.

"Coming from someone whose relationships last in deh region of hours at a time, dat's rich." Suzy said.

Patra shrugged and grinned.

"What now?" Y asked.

"What to do but carry on." Suzy said.

"With what?" Y sounded exasperated.

"We alive ain't we?" Patra jumped up, arms pointing to the ceiling. "Let me tell you what I'm going to do now. I'm going to update my Facebook profile, drop kick that chicken shit outfit called a courier company I work for and find someone who appreciates my hard working ass."

Y spluttered in the background.

Suzy sighed staring into the middle distance.

"I hand in mi uniform next week then start looking around feh something part time." She looked at her sisters with sad eyes. "I haven't told him yet."

"What do you think he's going to say?" Y asked.

"Is what Paul won't say that worries me. He will cover our mortgage wid out question. I'm just not sure whether him getting tired of me an my drama."

"You mean our drama." Patra corrected her.
Their rock and ghetto oracle sounded forlorn, not

something they saw often from Suzy and it was attacked with optimism from quarters where optimism wasn't second nature.

"It will work itself out," Y said.

Suzy agreed.

"It will work itself out. But nuh fret, Tyrone nah get away wid it. I promise you dat."

"Hell no! I told you I got plans for that motherfucker, recognise."

"You an' me both but nuh worry, him time a guh come."

"But why us Suzy?" Y asked. "Why now after all the hard work and graft to get to this point just to see it dragged from us?"

"It's a shift. It can't be anything but dat." Suzy said.

Patra, with the towel over her shoulder scratched her head playfully. Y gesticulated for Suzy to keep going.

"It's another life changing event, yuh know like the bank robbery. A turning point in all our lives dat brought us together."

"So we are the lucky ones again, the chosen ones."

"What the fuck did I do in a past life?" Patra piped up.

"C'mon girls, deh world is a big place. Yuh don't honestly believe we are the only people experiencing this. No way. But we will be the ones who will accept what has been given to us, rolling wid the blows and adapting. When our destiny presents itself we will accept it.

"Remind me, what is our destiny?" Y asked.

"Mi nuh know."

"Great."

"We are but tools and fate will use us how it sees fit." Suzy recited.

"Shakespeare?" Patra asked.

"No, Grandma Wong," Suzy laughed.

"Talking about fate, I left a message on John's mobile just after this shit started today. He hasn't returned my call yet."

"You don't mean Detective Inspector John 'the dick' Shaft of the Metropolitan Police Force?" Patra parodied the tones of a southern belle in some Gone with the Wind drama.

"Don't play," Y said seriously. "He's a gentleman."

"You can't blame a girl for trying. All I know when I see him I just want to bite a chunk out of that chocolate booty. That nigga is fine."

"Him nuh have eyes feh the likes of you miss hot stuff, he's sweet on Y."

"Don't even start with that 'we should be together' bit. John is a pro and he's got more pressing things on his mind than me."

"Pressing it may be baby but what's pressing is not on his mind," Suzy couldn't resist.

"All I know," Patra shuffled on the bed as if the mention of DI Shaft made her uncomfortable. "Is if any cat is glad that lame dick son-of-a-bitch Tyrone is gone, Shaft is that man. Every nigga deserves a chance sugahhh."

Y's silence only meant that the thought had crossed her mind before.

"Suh let's make another toast," Suzy announced. Y poured some more Asti into their empty glasses, watching the effervescence settle.

"To battles fought and won."

"Battles!"

Their glasses met in the gesture of a toast, crystal clinking and the sound resonating as they pulled away in unison to sip from their glasses. That's when they saw a weak glow connecting all three flutes. This wispy flutter of light became more intense as the girls looked on in hushed amazement, the hairs on their arms standing on end and their breaths caught in their throats. The glasses almost sang as they vibrated a beautiful varying pitch that made their arms tingle, maintaining the tone of the glasses song like a soprano in an opera. Not wanting to break the connection themselves they watched it as the overtones rose to a heady crescendo and slowly died out, dissipating as if it never existed. They lowered their glasses in incredulous silence.

Suzy grinned and said.

"Ladies I tink we've just been given a sign."

3.

Soho, West Central London
Friday, July 5th
03.20am

DI John *Shaft* MacFarlane parked the car at the north side of Old Compton Street. He arrived with no fanfare and only when he had turned off the engine did he slide his emergency light on the roof of the jag and let it flash for a moment without leaving the car.

He checked his mobile and swore. Y had tried to call him and somehow he had missed it. Y's calls never languished on his mobile phone for too long because, on a level he did not quite understand, her presence required his full attention. He loved talking to her but most importantly he loved listening to her speak. It was the way she massaged her words with her tongue as they left her mouth, a husky female backbeat that cloaked her sentences, delivering them into the world with erections almost. Y could be talking bullshit – she never did – and he could happily luxuriate in how she delivered it. Then there was this mystical warrior princess thing she had going on with her sexy friends that was definitely a turn on. To her credit she never demanded attention - directly or through implication - but he felt she deserved it. Strange thing was she had a live-in lover and he presumed she was happy but for reasons he would one day look into he didn't care. He decided to call her in the morning when he could give her his undivided attention.

Soho was as blunt and unpretentious as always and he loved it for that. He loved the tacky neon lights, the smell of cigarette smoke, the dingy upstairs apartments and the aromas of stale beer. For this kind of summer weather the Pubs had spilled out their patrons onto the narrow pavements, conversation and laughter were everywhere. No one knew or cared what had happened not too far away at Soho Square.

The party goes on.

Tonight, even under the circumstances, he was glad to be here - in fact as long as he was away from Wood Green and any skinny women called Marcia he would be happy anywhere.

The priority message he was acting on deserved his full attention even if he was on a date. This had been the only real day off he'd had in three weeks, a great excuse to ignore it but truth be told his mobile had saved him from a date worse than death.

For single men like him it was a jungle out there, inhabited by a menagerie of venomous female specimens who wanted to take a mate whether they wanted to participate in mating rituals or not.

He slid out of the black Jaguar saloon dressed in a grey Ralph Lauren polo neck, a dark Kenzo suit, Gucci loafers with no socks and adjusted the symmetry jacket. Shaft had a gifted sense of fashion and his quick glance in his rear view mirror, reminded him his standards remained high.

Operation Black Book was never a good place to find an ideal woman anyway unless introverted analysts who barely knew the difference between an Orc attacking them in World of Warcraft and an amorous advance in the real world was your thing. Romances at work had a tendency to end disastrously for him anyway.

He had tried.

So DI MacFarlane instead focussed his efforts in a small obscure section of the Scotland Yard Operation whose funding sidestepped the Metropolitan Police bureaucracy and was kept hidden almost by its specialist category. The crimes he investigated featured heavily on the uncategorised ethnic crime fringe. The top brass had been able to kill two birds with one stone by forcing him to take this gig and making sure he never darkened the crime scenes of DI's who do real police work ever again.

John McFarland was not so easily ignored. Shaft, as the boys from Operation Trident preferred to call him because of his more than passing resemblance to a young Richard Roundtree - without the chest hair and tash – did not roll over for anyone. With an IQ of 160 he was a trained anthropologist, ambitious and confident. Shaft blazed a trail from Hendon to the streets with a detour in Africa, making as many enemies as he could along the way and some well placed friends too. Operation Black Book was supposed to neuter his drive, frustrate the shit out of him with no resources, no cases and no satisfaction. Instead his department reconnoitred resources from Operation Trident who dealt in cases of black-on-black crime – and begged, borrowed or stealed what they needed. Who would take seriously a division that handled the unexplained, strange, religious and superstitious stuff – kinda like a ghetto X-Files.

Well he did and a few well positioned figures in the Met hierarchy did too. Over the years the major cities in the UK were being adversely affected by cult, ritualistic, voodoo and urban myth related crimes. The many unexplained cold cases that fell between the cracks of rational explanation and involved the ethnic demographic did not rest well with the rank and file of the Metropolitan Police force. Fingers were being pointed and the Met spin doctors were struggling to shrug off the institutional racism label, hence his small department and its specific remit. The official line was that Black Book did not exist and that was fine by him. If it protected the sacred institution of Scotland Yard from the ridicule of sanctioning the investigation of spooks, myths and curses then that was a public relation coup for them.

So with everything going on it was difficult keeping the dating game fun and the dates themselves regular - he didn't like the idea of prowling nightclubs with the other bachelors like pack animals either. This required him to relax his standards and adapt a new method of meeting suitable women. With his expertise of human interaction and the importance of the highly evolved mating ritual of the human animal, online dating did not sit well with him. And that was his problem. Shaft didn't see it as a means to an end; he viewed it as an anthropological blind alley. Not just another tool with its unique set of rules. Against all he believed in his savior was to be online dating and tonight had been his first face-to-face.

They met at a restaurant of her choosing - which makes the rest of the story even more surreal - and at

Wood Green of all places.

The woman who walked in and greeted him was the spitting image of Popeye's Olive Oyl and now he was beginning to understand why she never posted a photograph of herself in full cartoon glory, just choice snaps of her best bits.

Their compatability charts may have been in the high percentile but she ticked all the boxes for the wrong reasons. A woman with bigger feet than him was an immediate and unequivocal, 'Hell no!' But he must have been trapped in the moment because he gave her the benefit of the doubt. After all a woman who could write so well couldn't be all bad, could they?

Then she opened her mouth and spoke.

By this time his jaw was dragging on the floorboards. Marcia's vocal tone was an impressive high end basso.

Damn!

He must have been in shock because Shaft sidelined 'the voice ting' as a mere oddity and by now was holding his breath, expecting a reprieve in the form of just one pleasing character trait, to salvage the evening.

Please.

He waited to exhale.

Then all hell broke loose.

A clumsy waiter, spilt wine, stained dress and grievous bodily harm. Marcia may have been skeletal in frame but it took Shaft some doing to pry her off the waiter.

It was comforting to know the old edicts still applied and why Marcia was to be the object lesson in how our basal instincts still dominate even after mankind's complete domination of the planet and to a lesser degree why women with big feet throw him off his game.

Providence came to his rescue and his bleeper went off - not that it mattered because he would have been out of there before his colleagues in blue turned up.

A mobile phone call later and he was making his way to the West End, leaving his androgynous, anger challenged, Olive Oyl lookalike date far, far behind him.

Shaft breathed his third sigh of relief and buried tonight's incidents deeply in his mind. Ahead of him was the reason for his hasty arrival. The part of Soho Square near Frith and Greek Street was sealed off.

Taking his time to observe his surroundings, Shaft casually walked over to the police cordon allowing the vibe - the smells, the feel and the gathering crowd's reaction - to wash over him. He recognised the unmarked Astra's and the Sprint vans and knew this had attracted the usual clique of hotshot DCI's. Shaft's involvement usually occurred when they hit a brick wall or became uncomfortable with the direction a case was taking. A call so soon was unusual.

He began to step over the cordon and immediately he was approached by a uniformed officer.

He flashed his warrant card nonchalantly, stopping him dead in his tracks.

Shaft said.

"I'm Detective Inspector McFarlane, I need to see your SIO. A Detective John Duncan?"

The officer looked around the area behind him, his eyes picking through the milling investigating team all engrossed in their work and bathed in light from powerful halogen lamps.

He pointed to an area near the wrought iron fence that ran the perimeter.

"He's over there sir."

Shaft nodded, seeing only an outline at first smoking a cigarette. To his right was a lighted forensic tent with its flap pulled to one side. He could just see the CSI team, in their disposable Noddy suits, capturing as much evidence as possible around the body and blood splashed area. And the area was blood splashed. As if some crazed surrealist artist had thrown buckets of animal blood all over, creating a macabre sense of depth to his composition.

That couldn't have come from one man, surely.

Snatching his eyes away from the carnage, he looked back to the detective, in his pale blue disposable suit and hesitated. The sewer mist was clearing from a slight breeze that had developed and he could just see the high cheek bones, full lips and smooth white skin. John - or did they mean Joan? – Dawson brought the cigarette from his lips with far too much elegance for Shaft's liking.

Shit!

In a dancehall, all shadows and sparse lighting, you could forget yourself with this brother if you were inclined towards skinny women, except she, was a he. Recovery from the shock was slow, and trying not to make his bemusement apparent, he headed in the detectives direction, his curiosity well and truly whetted.

The area smelled of urine, cars glistened under a layer of condensation enhanced from the street lamps above. Sound from the traffic behind him dramatically diminished some ways along. An ideal place for murder he thought.

He eased past two uniforms talking to what he imagined were witnesses and came closer to the Detective who was standing alone, sniffling. Feeling as if he shouldn't penetrate his personal space for some inexplicable reason, Shaft stood there only to see him lift his head to look at him and watched the tears welling up in his eyes and trickling down his cheeks.

Shaft swallowed.

Was this a wind up or what?

He had left one zone of weird shit behind him earlier and had just walked into another twilight zone. Uncertain of what his reaction should be, he decided to ignore the glistening tears and introduced himself with an outstretched hand.

"I'm Detective Inspector McFarlane, Black Book."
He turned slightly into the shadows his expression even more maudlin and decided his attention should remain where it was and gave him his hand. The detective snapped off his gloves and shook his hand. It was cold but a solid grip.

"Detective Dawson," he said with an unusually cadence. "A waste of life."

"Excuse me?" Shaft said.

"A waste of life," Dawson repeated with more clarity.

"You know the victim?" Shaft asked.

"All life has significance, detective."

Shaft's speech was measured.

"Boss!" he started with care, "You may not realise this," he lied. "But you have just taken me away from a beautiful woman and a confirmed invitation for coffee with the possibility of breakfast. It's not for me to comment on your life philosophy, detective but just tell me why I'm here and if you get around to it, how you got my personal phone number?"

"Of course, of course," he said calmly, "I sometimes forget not everyone is as focussed on their work as I tend to be."

Shaft's nod of agreement seemed to lament the state of the Metropolitan Police Force personnel as Dawson did. He watched the detective's red lips annunciate his words.

"Have you ever realised too late that you were not fulfilling your vast capabilities, detective?" Shaft breathed in to answer but Dawson was already away.

"That was the predicament I found myself in. My true calling would have been with the Flying Squad."

Shaft just couldn't see it.

"Nothing can rival the cut and thrust of tracking down the perpetrators using sheer cunning. Analysing their motives, drives and snaring them because they are slaves to their impulses. Outwitted, outsmarted, outdone."

"Right!" Shaft said thinking what next and trying to sound as focussed and reasonable as possible. That didn't work, especially when you were standing in close proximity to a colleague who had a definite sexual thing going on with this investigation.

He casually stepped out of arm's reach. Dawson's orgasmic zeal withered and he shook his head.

"Instead for my sins, this..."

He motioned disdainfully to the forensic tent, the investigating teams and the intense halogen lamps. Shaft in the meantime was still looking for some of the boys from Operation Trident to leap out and start rolling around with laughter.

He was disappointed.

Dawson grinned.

"You'll need this." The DCI motioned to the Noddy suit with plastic booties to slip over his shoes and a dust guard for his mouth.

"To answer your question I made my duty more bearable by analysing cold cases from the Sweeney and a case of yours came up and held my interest."

Even if Dawson saw Shaft's impatience, he wasn't in the least concerned. He had trapped a captive audience and he had no intention of letting go.

"This case in point had the Flying Squad in particular, and Scotland Yard in general, very worried, indeed."

Shaft groaned, knowing he was about to be dumped on with facts and figures from a closed file he had more than enough knowledge about because he was the one who closed it.

"Eight jobs around the country, that we know of - four witnesses killed, netting them over five million pounds in antiquities and mystic curiosities, no leads and no arrests. Much later we realised it was all organised by the enigmatic figure of Enoch Lacombe, a Jamaican national, whose followers believed him to be a Voodoo priest of the highest order. A man we knew nothing about until someone in his own group set him up and only then by sheer accident you were able to corner him."

Dawson slipped his gloves back on.

"Enoch's right hand man – the one that turned on him – he acquired the team from the South London drug Don called Deacon. Two of that team, got twenty years a piece, Enoch himself the recipient of the sting received three concurrent life sentences and the other two who were instrumental in his capture turned Crown's evidence and took on the witness protection scheme. Deacon himself escaped conviction completely."

"And everybody lived happily ever after," said Shaft, injecting some sarcasm.

"Come now," Dawson snickered. "Endings like that would prove an anticlimax for historians. No, detective, your first witness protection candidate was found murdered a week ago in Poplar and what remains of this gentleman is, I believe, your fourth witness under our protection."

Shaft's expression of unconcern vanished, much to

Dawson's amusement. Head cocked to one side as if he was listening to the grating cogwheels of Shaft's mental processes change gear, he nodded to himself, pleased.

The report that had materialised on Shaft's desk last week didn't exactly surprise him. Eric *Magar* Tin Bateson was found floating face down in a posh gym in Poplar, his lips torn or sliced off from his face. His first conclusion was men like him couldn't stay out of trouble even after he was given the opportunity to start all over again with a new identity and a chance to right some of his wrongs.

And then again if you really got to know him as well as Shaft had over the period of the investigation, you could understand, even condone, his murder.

He was scum of the lowest order.

Like a dose of tapeworms that made you constantly scratch your ass to relieve the itch but nothing would until you shat the little parasite out was just an idea of how he felt while he was tracking the skinny bastard down. This untimely death was not peculiar unless you threw in the fact that Dawson's body was possibly another witness from case file 547/ar.

Two dead witnesses from a case that had been closed three and a half years ago, dying violently in the space of a week and he was still fighting the impulse of excitement telling him he had very interesting developments on his hands.

He brushed non-existant lint from his suit and looked back up to Dawson suspiciously.

"What makes you so certain this is one of my witnesses?"

He patted his head with his gloved hands and stared.

"I take it you still have doubts about my investigative skills. Allow me to show you how I've come to my conclusions."

Dawson paced away from him and then stopped suddenly, whipping out his handkerchief again.

Shaft tensed, expecting him to burst into spontaneous tears any minute but he spared him the embarrassment and plopped the dust guard over his mouth

Shaft shrugged and followed Dawson as he flung open the tent flaps. Even with the mouth protection the smell of sulphur and burnt flesh dilated his nostrils with such force he stepped back.

"Christ!" He gasped. A veil of fetid rankness rose up like an intervening wall blocking his entrance and making his eyes water.

"Are you all right, Inspector?" Dawson's muffled voice sounded concerned. A lumpy orange pool with still recognisable bits of king prawns, pork balls and ale spread across what was now the entrance. He didn't see it until it was too late.

"Rass!"

Shaft looked down at his feet, thankful his plastic booties protected his Gucci shoes and slowly extracted his foot from the reservoir of vomit.

"The body was discovered by a gentleman wandering down here after a meal," Dawson commented. "He decided to make his contribution to my crime scene."

An involuntary shiver ran up Shaft's spine.

"How goes it?" Dawson chirped.

The two examiners looked up from their grisly work like albino vultures feeding on carrion and shrugged.

At first glance, Shaft could not be certain what he was looking at, so contorted was the body. It took Dawson, who was moving bits of clothing away from recognisable parts of the corpse with his pencil, to give the dead body a sense of proportion. Crumpled beside the wrought iron fence and a car, the body had evidently not been moved from where it was dumped because of its odd position - legs broken and twisted and left propped on the metalwork of a Mercedes. It looked as if the victim had been planted head first into the ground with immense force. Closer inspection revealed a ragged pulp of flesh and bone where his head should have been.

No photo-fits possible here then Shaft thought breathing harshly through his mouth as he absorbed the horrific picture.

What the fuck could have done this?

"You recognise this don't you, Inspector?" Dawson asked.

Shaft nodded.

Dawson's roving pencil had lifted the man's sleeves to reveal a distinctive pattern of scar tissue on his forearm.

Silently Shaft stood there staring but not actually looking, his mind retracing the Enoch Lacombe case of four years ago. And experiencing the same feeling he had then, that more was to come.

It clung to him like the oppressive smell of decay, which would not go away no matter how you burned your clothes and washed your skin.

"Goddamit!" He muttered to himself.

This was not over and he knew it to his core.

4.

Y's Crib, Acton
Saturday, July 6th
10.20am

Phase two was a meticulous and emotional business even if you were as hell bent as Y to make it a perfunctory exercise. Trying to destroy the evidence of a one year long relationship was not as straightforward as she thought. A better part of yesterday and this morning was dedicated to throwing away underwear, T-shirts and burning old correspondences between them. But how did you eradicate his smell, his memory? Y had been tempted to bin everything he had attachment to, in a whirlwind of anger anchoring this moment to make it symbolic.

Y had started this exercise totally distraught, the obvious memories not easy to just ignore but as she continued it became easier.

This was the final - and not just symbolic - exorcism of the demon that was Tyrone.

A profound thought tried to sabotage the therapeutic nature of what she was doing and pointed out the futility of it all.

It seemed to her that no matter who you were, a man or woman, of high moral standing or a cesspit dweller like Tyrone, you touched lives as you traversed the journey, always leaving a part of yourself with or without your consent.

Y fingered her way through the clothes racks in her wardrobe and pulled out a case in point.

The Voodoo dress - as Tyrone had named it - and one of her real favourites, deserved to go into the flame if she was following that line of thinking but she couldn't. Cream coloured, body hugging with sections of the midriff missing which revealed portions of her stomach. Short at the back and at the front much longer covering some of her left leg but revealing most of her right.

Homeboy's eye candy as Patra would class it. Every time she wore it to an event they ended up not going out and making love instead.

The smile that formed on her lips was spontaneous and just as quickly she crushed it with a grimace.

The bonfire roared angrily making Y think maybe she was a bit too ambitious in its construction. Still it felt right. Arms folded, dressed in thick grey sweat bottoms worn low, showing the rim of her designer briefs and with a sweat top zipped up, a shocking red Tee just sneaking a peek over her zipper. She was intently watching the flames gather strength and start licking skywards like dragon tongues. She hunched her shoulders and flipped the hoodie over her short cropped hair although it was a sunny day, distributing her weight between both feet as she did - a habit she had when put in the spotlight or under stress.

Beside her alligator Puma's, flecked with wood chip and humus, was a saw, a hammer, an axe and lighter fluid. This was her attempt at incinerating a part of her past but not so with her memory. That already was scorched with this episode, never to be removed.

The physical reminders were different.

Tyrone's wardrobe of designer clothes formed the bed of the pyre; all his paper work, bills and magazines were at the top and for a long lasting burn were the hacked and shattered remnants of his favourite work chair and table.

The heat was getting uncomfortable and Y stepped back, only now wondering if it would affect her neighbours, hoping the blackened embers would not accidentally smear someone's washing. Then again she didn't care. She'd already been given a visit from the Housing Association bigwigs accusing her of running a business from her home – which she was, but denied with silky smooth reassurance that this was not the case.

Her caring neighbours expected high jinx from her anyway, so why disappoint. Y smiled, rocking on her feet as if the emotions and hurt were buffeting her body, her eyes stinging and her focus almost captivated by the dancing flames and their ferocity. Just for that moment she stopped dashing photographs into the eager conflagration and held onto the few left in her right hand.

She resisted.

Her thumb rubbed over the glossy surface of happier times - or was it false times and artificial happiness? It was as if all her insecurities had reared their collective heads, roaring her inadequacies to anyone who would listen. What did it take for someone to masquerade their affection for someone else for over a year? What kind of focus and hate did that take? Was anything in the past year real, anything at all?

Tyrone had appeared to be the kind of man she could spend her life with.

She was happy, he seemed happy.

Suzy had sensed something malevolent that Y had not. And it all became clearer as she thought about Tyrone's reluctance to be anywhere near them because he had sensed his masquerade had been discovered. Y was supposed to be the strategist, her ability to see how things could go wrong and mitigating against it was a part of her gift but in this instance her own affections shielded her perceptions and that sunk her even deeper into depression.

Did it mean every relationship she entered into with her eyes closed because her usual astute senses were ineffective? Could Y trust her own judgement in situations of the heart? The wave of pessimism that was lapping at her feet seemed to subside suddenly as an image of Detective Shaft appeared laughing good naturedly at the state she was putting her self into.

For a moment she felt better.

A set of four-by-six photographs twirled from her hands embedding themselves in the heart of the heat and imploding immediately. Y looked down at the remaining photographs in her hand and for a moment she was transported.

Y is lying on her stomach naked, the cool white cotton sheets casually strapped over her backside almost reminiscent of her derrière being sculpted from Sicilian marble and the artist capturing every crease and fold of the sheet around it. The ceiling fan above spins out a languid rhythm barely able to cool the room. Not that she cared as beads of sweat evaporated off her back in tantalising waves of cool, whipped up by the fans. At that moment she was satisfied as she stretched and moaned. Satisfied because the man holding the camera made her dripping wet between her legs at a touch, made her orgasm with his words over the phone, who filled her up when he entered her like a hand in a perfectly formed glove. Satisfied he could spar with her and know she was his superior but was okay with that. Satisfied she could be herself in his company. So Y was acting up for the camera like a prima donna but still posing for that telling portrait. Her sense of completeness sparkled from the exposure and even when that memory sliced through the air, leaving Y's outstretched fingers spinning into the bonfire, seized by the flames, blackening and curling as it melted into oblivion, the power of that memory remained. She hoped that sense of completeness would not be incinerated like the photographs, never to return.

That's when her thoughts were drawn back to last night's, toast and that light that bathed them with a feeling they would never be alone. There was a literal magic around them when they were together that couldn't be denied, something good and true. And that made Y feel there was some higher purpose to her life. She just couldn't help thinking that broken relationships would be the price she would have to pay for being special.

She sincerely hoped not.

Suzy's Apartment
Shepherds Bush
12.35

When *tings nah run* right Suzy's first port of call was home. The comfort of being able to pick up the phone and call her family, especially her father, had been a life line when she was establishing herself here in the UK. The Wong family had a haberdashery store in Parade, downtown Kingston, Jamaica for over sixty years. Through political upheaval, violence and economic uncertainty, Mr Wong would be there with Suzy's mum and two brothers servicing one of the toughest areas of Jamaica's capital. Mr Wong was respected and respectful of his home and fiercely patriotic. He came to Kingston when he was three years old with Suzy's grandparents from Montego Bay. Their parents had worked as indentured labourers in British Guiana, fighting against the odds to get to Jamaica for a better life. If any one had helped to create the fortunes of downtown's trading history he had. But she saw them beyond the titles of pioneers; most importantly they were her family that she loved dearly.

Mr Wong had taught her to grasp both her cultures and to be self reliant. He just never realised his lessons in freedom had led his daughter to want her own life in a new country just as his great grandparents had. As old school Chinese as he was, he still couldn't say no to her, even if it meant not having his little lotus flower around him.

Recovery from the pain of leaving her home and the comforting shoulder of her father was difficult but destiny had called and she was open to the adventure it had to offer her. Nothing could have prepared her to fully except the experience itself and even after everything she would do it all again.

Remembering Mr Wong's parting words, a tear trickled down her cheeks.

Deh answer to everything is always inside of you Lotus flower. Just step back an mek it come. Step back an let it in.

Suzy was keeping herself busy trying not to think about her future and making her world on the outside as orderly as possible, hoping its frequency would impact on the conflict inside. Lynton had just called to say he was twenty minutes away from home and this was her chance to break the bad news. Correction, Suzy chastised herself – a chance to explain the new path she was about to embark on. Suzy met Lynton in Jamaica, and if her family's wishes had gone to plan, Suzy would be married to a nice Chinese Jamaican boy who owned a thriving supermarket business. In no time she would be looking after kids and helping to run a Cash & Carry store somewhere in the corporate area. Instead, the flow of her personal history was dammed and redirected by a dark-skinned, caring, giant of a man. She had found a kindred spirit housed in the body of a Mandingo with a heart that drummed out the same rhythm as hers whenever they were together. Lynton had swept her off her feet and she had no choice - much to her father's derision - but to follow him back to the UK. It was meant to be.

Although her present lack of income could be challenging, that inner voice was calm and composed, almost optimistic. And when her inner voice emanated peace she stayed cool – *nuh fret, cah everyting set.* Even so Suzy couldn't just break the bad news of her job loss just *so-so suh.* He would be disarmed in a haze of aromatic oils and scented candles.

Her baby would be pampered, all of those rough kinks smoothed out after a night shift on the tracks, making sure that Network Rail's infrastructure was intact and that he made a living. He wouldn't be too suspicious of the treatment – he did receive TLC more regularly than most – and his male mind would be speculating on the possibility of pregnancy. Suzy would let him stew on that point though.

The lounge in their small, one bedroom flat had been transformed. Towels were spread on the floor with a single bed sized sponge wrapped in terry cloth with aromatic candles burning around the perimeter. The bath upstairs had been run and the bubbles from the orange blossom bath mousse formed rolling banks of foam just beckoning to a weary muscle fatigued body to come hither. Even as she turned off the faucets the aromas were lifting her mood in the process and Suzy just relaxed into an easy wave of optimism induced by the smells.

Step back an' let it in.

The door opened and her lover was home, his presence filling up their nest and spiking her libido like a Pavlovian trigger.

"Suzy baby?"

Tired or not, her mind ran rampant with the thoughts of making love to him as he stepped onto the threshold of home. Suzy would be manipulating all those stimuli she had stored away in her mind that she knew aroused her man and she would be withdrawing them all from her arsenal. The silk ruby long drop camisole was rocking and underneath she wore nothing. The subtle smell of Chanel Allure had misted her body and she let her long black hair tumble over her shoulders. With all of the boxes ticked poor Lynton was caught in this web with his actions mapped out before his own conscious thought could question.

What deh ...?

She'd give him no time to shower or change, stripping his six foot two frame and kissing his musky sweat dried chest. To her his griminess and perspiration was a heady concoction that turned her on even more than the muscular sight of him. She was just caught up in dragging down his FUBU shorts to his ankles. He was a big man and his erection was magnificent thing to behold.

She took every opportunity she got to hold it in her hand and accommodate its head around her lips and tongue, watching his eyes glaze over and those gruff moans of satisfaction leaving his lips.

Suzy let the fantasy slide, moving instead down the stairs to greet him. Her bare feet taking the steps with the grace and sensuality her training afforded her. Lynton did not stand a chance. He was standing at the foot of the stairs, arms folded, leaning on the post, a sly grin on his face that slowly unfurled into the hungry stare as he saw something he craved. And at that very moment an idea popped into her head. Maybe she didn't have to break the news to him just yet.

Pink Kitty Kat Strip Club
Central London
21.10

"Cleopatra darling, never thought I'd see you again. When Freddy said you were here I had to come down and see for myself."

"Damn straight Giles, in the flesh, baby."

"And in the flesh I might add you're looking better than ever." He held her hand and kissed it.

Giles Sinton, the seventy year old owner of one of the most sophisticated strip establishments in London. Porn elder statesman, old world gentleman, multi-millionaire and kindred spirit, hugged her warmly. They were in one of the Pink Kitty Kat's VIP areas with its own mini-bar, pole and poker table. Giles was dressed in his trade mark Egyptian cashmere jumper and slacks

"You're looking as handsome as ever you old coot," she whispered in his ear, his favourite aftershave just as understated as she remembered. "Have you stopped dating women one fifth your age yet, G?"

"Ssshhh!" he whispered, holding her by the shoulders to view her better, "That's the secret to my longevity amongst other things. Keep it close to your chest. So what are you doing back? I know you enjoyed the job but the spirit of adventure was beckoning to you, I was told."

"And I listened. I got some juicy ass stories to tell you over a cigar and brandy but I was enjoying myself so much I lowered my guard and got jacked. My sisters and I have got some catching up to do, some serious shit to smooth out. I thought of you."

"I'm glad. Do they dance too?"

"They're thick enough and sexy as hell too but this

ain't their style. Besides, the fun stuff I got that covered. I leave the boring ass shit to them. They've got their strengths and I got mine."

"It sounds like you finally found a family. I'm glad. So when do you want to start Cleo?"

Patra shrugged.

"I think we may have a hitch, OG."

"Don't be silly, there is no hitch. Just tell me when you want to come down and start?"

Patra rolls her eyes over to the blonde in the business suit who was silently watching the reunion.

Giles sighed audibly.

The woman's poise was confident but with her arms folded around her chest it was obvious she was expecting conflict and from that crooked half smile on her lips it was something she would enjoy. Detaching herself from the poker table she was leaning on, the gold stripes on her suit shimmering when she moved, the executive blonde took two strong steps in her black Jimmy Choo slingback shoes.

"As I was explaining to Ms Jones before you came in, Mr Sinton, the last remaining positions have been taken by Jade, Smooth and Topaz. We have her details on our records and as soon as there are any vacancies we will contact her."

Patra's gaze slowly drifted over to the three new recruits and felt the ice cold daggers of contempt directed her way.

Skanky ass bitches don't even know me, she thought.

"Did you know that she holds the title for the most gratuities offered to a dancer in my club, Laura?" Giles asked.

"I didn't but..."

"Twenty thousand pounds, that was a damn good

night," his eyes went misty with memory and he grinned in Patra's direction and she grinned back.

"Do we have a problem with my decision making Mr. Sinton?" Laura asked. "This is what you employed me to do, right?"

"Hey, it's cool," Patra interjected uncomfortable with where this was leading. "I've got other gigs lined up OG, it's no biggy." Patra was reaching over to grab her backpack when Giles looked over to her, eyes sparkling.

"Don't go yet Cleo." He signalled Laura over to him for a powwow and set about outlining some scheme he was hatching.

Patra was beginning to feel guilty about her insistence that Giles delegate large chunks of his empire to able lieutenants who could replicate his success, so he had more time to enjoy life. From the youthful glow and exuberance he was showing it was working. Now she had to come back into his life to complicate it some more. The trio who had been slinging visual shots her way had shuffled a bit closer to where Patra was lounging, for no other reason than for them to make their ire heard and goad her into reacting.

Who the fuck does she think she is?

A Yankee bitch, coming in here demanding work.

No working girls allowed, dike.

Patra felt the adrenaline rush of conflict. That heady chemical reaction that was exploding in her cells generating that endorphin rush of pleasure she had anchored into her psyche when shit got twisted.

Oh yeah, you beefing with the wrong bitch.

She let the adrenalin seep into her blood stream savouring its power to make her fearless and competitive. Casually, Patra looked over to the three strippers trying their utmost to psyche her out with their not-so-subtle comments and just thought how 'those dumb ass bitch-es' were playing into her hands without even knowing it.

Don't test me ladies, I was made for this competitive shit.

If Patra knew how to do anything it was how to win and she was equipped to do so with talents they could never imagine in their wildest dreams. The smile crept up onto her lips, self assured and with an edge of dark humour to it.

Bring it on, she thought.

"Cleo darling, I think we have a solution to our di-lemma. Laura..." Giles called over.

"We...I have decided that the best way to resolve this situation is for you to compete for the positions."

The groans from the penny section reverberated in unison and Patra unfurled her fists and grinned.

"Now that's what I'm talkin' 'bout." Patra mouthed the words to herself and met eyes with Giles who nodded sagely.

"Just one thing before you ladies start on the pole." Giles said. "Freddy, play that old track from Ludacris for me. 'Stand Up', I think it's called."

The DJ nodded.

Giles winked at Patra.

"You like Luda, Giles?" Patra laughed all the way to the changing room.

"Time to smoke some lame ass bitches," she said con-fidently and for all to hear.

Wormwood Scrubs Prison
West London
Three weeks ago

It was a rainy London day and Senior Prison Officer Wilson was looking forward to an uneventful evening on the blocks. That was until the HMS Prison Service iPad reminded him today was cell search for the prisoner they nicknamed Damian. Like an enema administered up the ass he had the whole day to look forward to that mouth watering prospect. His reluctance did not stop the event from happening much to his dismay.

Enoch Lacombe folded the flannel neatly and placed it on top of the other folded towels on his bunk in the spartan confines of his cell housed in the maximum security D Wing facility. With his head lowered he placed the Holy Bible with meticulous care on top of his fabric constructed tower of Babel, lifted it from the bed he had lain his head on for the last four years and turned to face three of D Wing's elite Prison Officers watching his casual ceremony.

"Take one step forward prisoner 699, remain stationary and keep your eyes to the ground," the Senior Prison Officer's voice boomed in the confined space, its power trailing away suddenly as if it did not have the same supremacy in this place. Looking as if he would prefer to be anywhere else but here, he motioned to his colleague.

The younger man took a deep breath and was surprised at how clean the cell smelt. Not fragranced to conceal the smell of shit and piss but an almost antiseptic reek, a morgue pong. He shivered involuntarily, his short stocky frame concealing the tremors breaking through his genitals and neck as he tentatively used his metal detector to skim the personal atmosphere around the prisoner, taking more care than was normal, making sure the detector did not have any contact with the Darkman's skin. The officer was sweating, a cold perspiration gathering around his lips and trickling down his back although the confines of the cell were cool. Hurriedly he shuffled his big frame backwards, his metal detector unresponsive and made as much space between prisoner and Prison Officer as possible. The senior Prison Officer, Wilson, followed him out of the confines of the small cell just as careful not to have even casual contact with the inmate. They congregated on the landing, shoulders showing a wave of relief they would not admit to anyone and stood with two K9 officers and their dogs.

Enoch Lacombe had not moved.

"Sniff him out, boys." He signalled the men to let the dogs do their job but they were hesitant.

"Come on girl, come on." Officer Jacobs coaxed his bitch into the cell to do her job but she was whining, her intelligent Alsatian eyes almost begging for a reprieve. Her colleague was even more perturbed by the prospect of going into the cell to sniff out prisoner 699. The Labrador stiffened, whimpered and started making some pitiful cries. And no amount of tugging on his lead would get him any closer to the prisoner. Then they both started a chorus of whimpering and there was nothing their masters could do to control their panic.

"I don't know what's up with them, Sarge."

"Jesus Christ. Okay, just take them back to the compound and we'll finish up without it. I came prepared anyway."

"Poxy fucking mongrels," he grumbled and opened up a reinforced plastic case that was leaning on the bars at his feet. He unpacked the E-Nose and let the Home Office's new toy do the job the canines refused to. In moments he was satisfied that he had not been in contact with contraband and led Enoch Lacombe by a wave of his hands on to the landing so they could clean up and return him to his cell. Darkman stood patiently between two physically imposing prison guards this time his head held high, words floated up from his upturned lips.

A silence fell over the landings. Darkman paused his former words resonating in the confines of D-Wing then his lips parted again and a final word exited. No one standing beside him understood what he was muttering; they only knew it had an Arabic brogue to it and that it almost crackled with a power they could all feel but could never understand.

How could they?

The force of the final piece of the incantation rippled from Darkman at its epi-centre and spread throughout the prison block. Everyone in the entire wing froze in position for a second, a subtle shift in perception as if something had switched off, held them in place, making the dogs who were obviously unaffected start whining nervously. Then as if nothing had happened the world resumed functioning and the warders closed the cell door, leading him along the landing away from his cell.

Obediently, inmate 699 revolved his neck, cracking the bones of his vertebrae and walked with the casual sway of the Caribbean sun and cricket as his warders silently lead him out of the secure wing without a thought as to why they were doing it.

Eyes in the depth of the cells that lined his path peered out. Desperate men who had not had yard time for 36 hours and others whose stint in solitary was just beginning, all followed his progress with mute relief or palpable fear. Murderers, armed robbers and gang members with nothing to lose, respecters of nothing, afraid of no one in heaven or on earth, remained dumb as inmate 699 made his way past them. For anyone bold enough to peer too closely through their shutters, just the merest flinch of Enoch Lacombe sent them scurrying away from his attention.

The prison population even as desensitised as they were to a world beyond their five senses felt that prisoner 699 was not someone to be trifled with. Three men overstepped the mark and died inexplicably, horribly. Unbeknownst to the rumour mill that created the Frankenstein monster of Enoch Lacombe, the reality of his awesome capabilities was far, far worse than their limited imagination could ever create.

Away from the inquisitive electronic eyes of the Prison Service surveillance system, Prison Guard Pete Jackson kissed the fingers of his master's hand while he genuflected. The ingredients for the spell had taken almost a year to gather while his acolyte had to do his part by replenishing the choice ingredients in the Totems scattered around Worm Wood Scrubs' structure. But the mind haze - a lingering hypnotic trance - would allow him to do what he needed to without the undue attention of the authorities and affected anyone who entered the institution. His 'prentis' would keep the efficacy of the spell until he was away from this place and back 'a yard' for good. Laying his hands on the Prison Officer as if giving him a blessing because his aid wouldn't be forgotten, Enoch Lacombe turned away and stepped casually through the reinforced door within the reinforced siege gates into the moisture laden atmosphere, pregnant with ozone and carbon monoxide, filling his lungs immediately with air free of the taint of guilty men.

The tall black man freed himself of the shadows flung from the building with an unhurried stride, almost scoffing with his casualness at the institution that had tried to hold him for a life sentence but succumbed, as most things did, to an Obeah man of his vast power. He stood on the edge of light and darkness and turned to face his home for four years, what was left of his worldly possessions stuffed into two black leather bags held by hard hands. He wore a dark striped suit and white shirt with no tie.

The black trilby on top of his head shielded a face whose skin was pulled tight over the contours of his skull but he wasn't repellent to look at by any means, his body was conservative, requiring him to be lean, shedding all fat in his frame leaving only the necessary reserves. His eyes were dark and deep set with eyebrows ridging them like bony canopies shielding a cunning mind. If you were sensitive enough you could discern the stink of corruption that enveloped him like the atmosphere of a dead star. Maybe even sense how he siphoned off the dark energies flowing in abundance from the brutality, corruption and depravity of the city, storing it in his wiry frame like a gross capacitor bending it to his will and intention as he saw fit.

His gift.

As the dark clouds swirled overhead eagerly preparing for a downpour, their innards lit by forks of lightning, the sounds of thunder reverberated through the heavens with the violence of what was to come.

The tall man looked down to the end of the road with certainty borne of expectation. His deep set eyes glazed for a moment and a grey tinted Volvo materialised from around the corner and drove up to the prison gates. Aware but unconcerned about the droplets of rain spearing into the forecourt and the car pulling up beside him, his focus was firmly set on three days hence. He had an errand to attend to back-a-yard in Jamaica. Then, and only then, would he be fully equipped to punish the ones who had betrayed him, recoup the trinkets he had acquired and reacquaint himself with the most important person in his life; his son. Until then, until he cut out their gallbladders and reduced them to dust under his feet, he had things to do.

But nuh fret, soon every knee shall bow an every tongue confess...

5.

Metal Works Gym
Sunday, July 7th
20.35

The downstairs bar at Metal Works Gym, Uxbridge Road was charged with the excitement of its clientele anticipating the evening ahead but you would be forgiven if you thought the bar-tender had just slipped some rum or whiskey into their fruit juices such was the exuberance. The regulars dotted around the modern floor plan, the professionals flexing their biceps every opportunity they had in front of their admiring fans and the other cliques in pensive or boisterous discussion.

Of course it was a Friday evening and the relief that they had left the drudgery of work and just completed their reps, jogs, lifts and tans was self evident.

As they gulped and slurped down the healthy living concoctions and live foods, they gave no thought to how soon they would be immersed in alcohol and nicotine at some night spot reversing all the good they had done for the week.

So who gives a shit?

Every table was high spirited...except this one.

Just behind the large central column, furthest from the entrance and cut off from the view of the main area was The Corner. This portion of the ground floor was lavishly roped with silk, set with plush seats, ornate carpets and equipped with state of the art electronic entertainment. Simply walking past the sign that read 'For VIP Use Only' meant the handsome - depending on your sexual persuasion - Georgio would be catering for your every need, making you soon believe trekking over to the bar for anything was a preoccupation for commoners.

Why then was the gloom around this table so thick and all consuming that it could be scooped up with a spoon and served with a side order of self pity?

Y, Patra and Suzy sat in the shadow, their fruit juices in front of them sweating profusely with a mixture of expressions on their faces that ranged from disgust to anger.

The lights were dimmed and Mary J Blige was in uncompromising vocal form. On the walls were pictures of Lady Saw in gangster mode, Lil Kim letting it all hang out, Pam Grier as Cleopatra Jones and the mouth watering abs and sundry assets of Tyson Beckford and LL Cool J, honourees in their fit body Rogues gallery.

Moments before they had been 'bussing a sweat' - as Suzy would fondly say – in their preferred martial arts disciplines.

Their sessions had been savage affairs, which forced their kickboxing instructor to make the decision that punching bags would be preferable to real life sparring

partners for fear of injury. He even stayed on the side-
lines to watch them take out their foul mood on the
punching bags and he was a third Degree black belt. It
was only after two hours of gruelling work that the instructor insisted they take a break and the posse ended
up downstairs.

Patra shuffled her Reebok-clad feet that had been well
and truly planted on the table since they had gathered
there. Her chair was on its two back legs rocking gently
to and fro as she nonchalantly broke the no smoking
regulations, puffing contemplatively on an aromatic cigarillo.

Suzy crossed her legs and slouched back, her blue
Adidas track suit making crisp ruffling sounds of newness with her hands behind her neck while Y sat pain-
fully upright as if she was about to announce that
something rather uncomfortable was sticking up under
her ass.

No need to speak if the situation didn't warrant
speech, right? The girls had to simply caste their minds
back and the emptiness of loss reminded them.

In one day they had their lives upturned and Y, feeling left out, rashly gave her boss the abridged version of
why she despised her and the nail technician job she
had been doing for the last two years with two choice
words.

Suzy attempted to lift the morose vibe.

"I drove by deh property, today," Suzy said, trying not
to show how painful it had been seeing their unfulfilled
aspirations wrapped up in the guise of bricks and mor-
tar.

Y and Patra responded with nods and grunts; they too
were obviously still raw with hurt and Suzy was beginning to regret mentioning it. What Suzy had failed to

mention was that she had pulled up to 123 Destiny Street - the name was an omen in itself - parked her old Peugeot 307 and sat staring at a dream that to all but her was dead. This is where it was all supposed to begin, where the magic would happen. Ground floor was supposed to be Y's and solely dedicated to Nails and Beauty. Y had plans of starting off with the basics offering them acrylic nails and nail art, manicure, pedicure, then upgrading her services to the more flashy skin treatments.

The first floor would be her baby of health and fitness and the second floor would be Patra's focus of fashion.

"We had that bitch worked out," Patra's words derailing Suzy's memories.

Suzy shook her head as if it was with some effort she could convince them that their aspirations weren't crumbling before their eyes.

"Yuh know I still can't shake deh feeling that this place was meant for us."

"I'm glad at least one of us is still holding on to the possibility because where I'm sitting from our situation looks hopeless." Y ran her fingers through her short cropped hair.

"No shit!" Patra added for emphasis. "We were supposed to give the landlady a deposit."

"And the lease agreement was to be signed next week."

"Suh there yuh go then sis. We still have two weeks to manifest something feh redeem us, after we explain tings to Mrs Benjamin, she will understand."

"That is so cute," Y smiled falsely.

"Mrs Benjamin, a hardnosed Jewish business woman, won't have the need or time to sit down and commiserate with us on our financial loss. There is no four month extension Sue and even if there were, where would we get thirty thousand pounds from?"

Suzy glided off her stool and made two steps towards Y shaking her head.

"Yuh just can't see it, can yuh? Do you really believe that Mrs Benjamin or even Tyrone can stand in the way of what will be? I can't explain it and I know your nature is asking for proof. Even after everyting you've seen and experienced yuh still unsure." Suzy considered a thought for a moment. "When I do have these feelings are they ever wrong?"

"No." said Y.
Suzy sat down with an air of justification.

"Okay, so what do we do now then?" Y asked.

"We guh about our business, of course. Still making plans but not worrying about Destiny Street. Who knows, something bigger and better could be waiting in the wings for us."

Y let the sarcasm slide from her tone recalling the many mysteries surrounding them together and as individuals. Their circumstances were far from ordinary.

"I'm just feeling like the control of my life is being wrestled from me."

With an unusual burst of the profound Patra said:

"We not losing control baby, we just going with the flow." She took a puff of her slim-line cigar and blew rings into the vents. "We ain't fighting the surf just letting it take us out to sea."

"Amen." Suzy said changing the subject. "I was reasoning wid Mas P when I arrived earlier today," Suzy said her manicured fingers touching her chin.

"How's he doing?" Patra asked.

"Him safe," Suzy said." We got to talking an' one ting led to another and he decided to help cheer us up."

"You told him then?" Y asked with a snarl.

"Of course mi tell him," Suzy matched her pitch, her eyes narrowing. "Deh man is almost like family. I know wi save him life but him guh above an' beyond feh wi many times in the past, just to say how much him appreciate what we did. Don't forget dat."

Y folded her arms and nodded with a contrite purse of her lips.

"Anyway, Mas P gracefully hook we up with three VIP tickets to the MOBO's this coming Friday night with limousine to and from deh location."

Y's eyes bulged.

Patra whistled.

"Damn! For an Indian playa he's got game, man."

"An' he's looking after his girls dem from him heart. Yuh have to love him feh dat?" Suzy was looking over to Y, whose facial muscles twitched, struggling to translate the messages signalling excitement and joy to her face.

"Sue, I'm sorry," Y said finally, "I'm just not handling this well. I can't get that calculating, spiteful shit out of my mind."

Y breathed out sharply.

Patra rolled the cigarillo in her mouth and licked at the tip lovingly. Y and Suzy smiled at each other as Patra went through her ritual. For someone who was about to break the no smoking in an enclosed building laws she looked suspiciously as if she was performing oral sex.

She lit up and blew smoke circles, again.

Y paced over to the smooth central column and leaned against it keeping their deliberations unseen from the rest of the gym.

"He's messing up every meditation session I have."

Y drifted, her shoulders and arms tensing on the concrete as if she was about to topple the temple of Dagon on the heathen.

Slowly she coaxed her focus away from some point in space, wiped her eyes and stared back at them.

"I can't help thinking I could have done more."

Patra shot a stream of smoke to the ceiling extractors.

"You taking this shit waaay too personal sugahh," she said coolly. "Motherfucker was a con artist pure and simple. Blaming yourself now ain't going to remedy shit. Focus on payback baby."

"That a deh truth," Suzy agreed. "I suppose yuh haven't talked to John bout this yet?" Suzy asked. "Maybe dat will give you some closure."

"Girl," Patra laughed. " And you know closure ain't the only thing he wants to give you."

Y kissed her teeth and made a face.

"I called and left a message and he hasn't got back to me yet. He must be really busy," said Y. "But I'm still not sure I should tell him though."

Strangely the innocent question had the effect of injecting this whole unfortunate situation with a ray of light for Y at least.

Detective Inspector Winston Shaft McFarlane was the type of man a healthy chunk of the female population would not think twice about suppressing any morals or shame they had and try by any means at their disposal to make him theirs, wholly.

As in body and soul.

He was in his mid thirties, one of the youngest Detective Inspectors in the country, handsome, intelligent and with an ass you dreamed of taking a long leisurely nibble off - not that she had but the thought had crossed her mind too many times not to mention it.

Winston was like the unofficial fourth part of the posse. He had been the investigating officer at the bank robbery which had created their friendship.

It was one of those memorable scenes that just stuck with you. Wearing shades and an expression that said 'stay cool, goddamn it' he walked onto the fresh crime scene. The employees frantic, the customers relieved and still trying to understand the incredible events that had taken place. The players were still in place when the cavalry had arrived. One of the robbers was unconscious at Suzy's feet, Patra nervously pointing a gun to one of the men's head swearing and Y holding another in a headlock, The Rock would have been proud of.

There was no expression of amazement, no sexist remarks just a caring concern for their well being after such a traumatic situation.

On that day a great deal of respect developed between them and they continued to see him outside of his professional sphere as a detective, Y more than anybody else.

"If anybody can give us some pointers on this cat, John can," Patra said. "Just make sure you hook up with him. And Y? Remember business first and the butt naked sex comes later, yeah."

"We're good friends," Y protested weakly.

"Whatever," Patra grinned.

They realised Suzy had gone mystic on them after they had finished teasing each other.

Waiting as they always did for her to rejoin them, Suzy opened her eyes slowly. Meditation was her way of keeping herself and the world in check.

"Someting will turn up for us, it won't end like this," Suzy looked at Y, her voice losing its cold edge.

"If we keep talking about this motherfucker, he would have won. And there's no way his raggedy ass is going to have shit over me." Patra smiled cunningly, her hi-lighted corn rows glowing under the lights. "If anybody can pull us out of this shit with a plan you can sugahh. We've done this before?"

"We have, haven't we," Y said smiling.

Y's posture noticeably changed, a wave of determina-tion snapping her into her former shape. The dejected slump in her shoulders corrected itself and a spark of optimism shone in her eyes. She walked back over to Suzy and Patra, hugging them in turn then making her-self comfortable in her chair.

"So where do we go from here?" Patra asked.

Her legs crossed, Y made semi-circular movements with her toes.

The girls needed hope and what could she offer them?

The nervous twist of Suzy's lips and the frustrated shake of her head, Patra fought the turmoil inside by being cool, her hand unsteady as she brought the cigaril-lo to her lips, Y felt as if she was carrying a hollow bur-den of despair, like a chunk of rock had been forced into her chest.

What in God's name could she say to them?

It was clear how much she owed the girls. How much they believed that together they could make a difference. This calamity was her fault and her responsibility and she wouldn't allow herself to forget it.

The rest of the posse looked on.

"The facts are straight-forward," Y said. "We're broke. Any ideas we had of leasing the property for our little business venture is dead. No deposit, no two months in advance, no cash for refurbishment, nuthin'. Even if there was more time, which there isn't, we still couldn't come up with the cash to save the deal. I have a feeling that how things are going just now, even the bank would gazump our ass, just for the hell of it. Bad II the Bone will not be a reality any time soon."

"Tell me something I don't know," Patra mumbled.

"Wha bout Mr Patel?" Suzy asked. "Money is no object for a Don like dat. Him would lend us cash without a murmur but I'm not sure how mi would feel about dat."

"After we helped to solve the problem he had with those Punjabi boys, he knows we have his back. He went out of his way to repay us, though. Free membership at the club, he virtually built the corner for our convenience. I just couldn't find it in my heart to borrow money from him, as well."

"I could." Patra quipped.

Y patted her on the shoulder.

"One of these days girlfriend, we'll have a long talk about having principles."

Patra shrugged while Y kept on.

"If we play our cards right we won't need to compromise our values to make this work. We depend on ourselves and focus on the goal one more time. If we can't then we start asking for help."

"Back on form, mi gal," Suzy taunted, realising the old ideas machine was starting to chug into action again.

"Don't keep us hanging, girl," Patra added. "What's happenin?"

"Discovery..." Y continued. "We will dig deep and find some creative means to make money. We'll be looking for things that are out of the ordinary to claw ourselves back at least to an even keel. I don't even want to think about the three years it took us to save what we just lost. Six months is all I'm giving ourselves to get back to where we were before all this happened, and believe me it will take some revolutionary thinking to achieve it.

Forget about what we did before, that got us here. To pull this off we're going to need some serious personal power," she paused for dramatic effect then frowned.

Y needed a rallying cry. Girl power was too tacky, a bit namby pamby, back in the day, for what she was looking for. She needed a battle cry, a call to arms that was raw and incisive.

Y beamed.

"The Pum-Pum Factor."

"I like the sound a dat," Suzy laughed.

"It has a bad-ass ring to it." Patra joined in.

They held hands.

"To the next six months then," Y announced. "And like the old Chinese saying, may we live in interesting times."

"Pum Pum Factor!" They chorused.

St Thomas, Jamaica
Two weeks ago

Enoch Lacombe stood statuesque in the clearing of the Lacombe family cemetery surrounded by drooping monkeypod trees obscuring the view and stared up at the cloud and hidden moon distastefully. He was alone and undisturbed. The army of dismembered duppies that roamed his land would deter the opportunist trespassers but held no sway for him. His father had personally trapped the souls of the many mutilated victims of the Kendal Crash of 1957 and allowed them the freedom to roam and terrorise. Their appearance and anguished moans held his attention for awhile but soon that too was unimpressive. It was his impatience showing again, which to his mind was justified especially after spending four years in prison, his art and his obligations forsaken. Maybe it was the excitement of being released a mere forty-eight hours ago and finding himself in Jamaica executing his plans of judgement and retribution that had kept him focused for all those years. For some it was too late. His father had died and the family land and property was deteriorating.

You needn't have any arcane knowledge to surmise all was not well on this land. The balance the normal man took for granted in nature had been thrown out of kilter here. Science definitely had been usurped by dark magic. The Lacombe great house cast an eerie shadow over the estate from where he stood. It was standing dark and foreboding like a gargantuan doorway to another world, sucking light and hope into its maw. In its heyday the post colonial residence was a sight to behold. Two storeys of old world splendour whose décor had not changed much over the generations. Now the stone foundations and plastered upper storeys, whose interior was once resplendent with wooden ceilings and mahogany floors from the trees of the island itself, was infected and crumbling. The walls buckled, the land underneath shifting, the roof collapsed and water damage was extensive to all two floors. Parasitic vines had infected the structure, crushing it almost, their suckers leeching nutrients and maybe from the disconcerting chill, sucking its very essence too. Every living thing on the fifty acre spread from fauna to flora was dead or corrupted.

When the John Crow stone was set in its place, in a region where ancient ley lines criss-crossed and where at its centre a subterranean portion of the Yallas River emerged to the surface, the land was the most fertile in St Thomas. There were Orange groves, breadfruit trees, ackee trees, watermelons, peppers, exotic fruits of all descriptions and grazing animals. Migrating birds favoured it and wildlife thrived there. In the middle of this paradise was the Lacombe ancestral home.

Now look at it rass.

It was an almost alien terrain of weeds, tree husks, stagnant ponds and crumbling structures. It was a barren land that sustained nothing but vermin. The talisman which was the John Crow stone was what kept the land fruitful and without it, the land's true form shone through.

Enoch had taken the stone five years ago to replenish its powers back in Africa but the entire unfortunate goings on in London had him losing his ancestors' treasures, charms and talismans. The memory was an acerbic one even now. His family land and the power that had been handed down for generations were in disarray. It would get worse until he was able to appease the Dark Gods of the continent as his father had done and his father before him.

Enoch had to make them pay, return the stone, make amends and fulfil something much greater.

His heir.

One son you may have, to carry your legacy. One son or your seed becomes history.

A situation he would resolve at all cost or he would lose it all.

So he stood, shirtless, barefoot with a pair of green camouflage trousers on, just under six feet tall, his skin a blue black, almost absorbing the night, only the sweat on his wiry frame, reflecting the silvery edges from the spears of the moonlight, making him stand out.

He swore in an ancient tongue that reverberated with unseen power with every syllable he pronounced and he glared skyward as if his curses would have an effect on the astral world. Brusquely, Enoch walked over to the inert body lying on top of the tomb of his great, great grandfather Ignatius Lacombe, a very practical old man whose family history was regarded with fondness for his foresight.

His forefather had built this sacrificial altar on top of his remains as a kind of reminder of his preference for human sacrifices. He prodded the inert body with his finger and rubbed his thumb along his bony thorax as he strolled to the head of the tomb. He stank even before he had used the Tanting Bush to drug him and stank some more as Enoch slit his throat and he voided his bowels. But that sweet perfume of excrement simply reminded him of the insanity inducing realities he had brief encounters with, the dark places he drew his energy from and the need to continue with his plans in haste.

The carcass was snugly set into a slight depression on the top of the grave. It was inclined slightly so the life giving fluid would run down along the grooves cut into the marble surface for that express reason for collecting the blood. A man or woman of average build and height would be positioned so their throat, arms, groin and legs were situated over the channels. His throat neatly cut, his blood had drained from him like gross tributaries running along the mason grooves coaxed down by gravity and ending at his feet to an extended lip. A ceramic pot, circled with fading Mayan cuneiform, rested underneath it and was already full but capturing the remaining drops of blood.

Dis crazy rass has finally done something noble inna him life.

The corpse, which in its former life was a lunatic street person wandering aimlessly in the suburbs of

Portland, shitting on the street and feeding on scraps, would not be missed. But most importantly would be acting as the catalyst in his plan to regain control. Enoch let the blowflies who had already discovered the traces of his stench in the air, perform their merry dance on him, supping in the decay and finding access to lay their eggs. If he didn't know better he would have said they shared the knowledge that he would fulfill a higher purpose for them both. He took up the warm ceramic pot reverently with both hands and swirled the crimson contents. He walked back over to the clearing with energetic steps bordering on impatience or just sheer eagerness and slowly lowered himself to his knees, scraping up a handful of loam in his hands. Enoch slashed a look to the lunar perambulations and grunted more at the stratus clouds obscuring its full brilliance than at the moon itself.

Patience my yout.

The clearing skies were interrupting an ancient ritual that needed to be performed at no other period but this. He knew it was the uncertainty of results that had him on edge. Conjuring the dark forces a Voudum had at his disposal was no trifling matter. Mercurial and fickle were the forces of nature he was invoking and the great Voodoo practitioners - the true masters of the art, who were so far ahead of the parlour tricks performed by the Obeah workers scattered across the island - were all patient men and women. They appreciated the fourth dimension of time as variable, to be subtly manipulated. But for the fast paced, information superhighway fuelled era he shared, to be effective you required haste. Unfortunately the mystery systems were governed by the ponderous pace nature took and it irritated him. He had come this far, had lost his freedom because of lack of preparation and regained it through the principles he was resisting.

Another moment would make no difference.

Standing again this time he made his way to the clearing's dead centre with the bowl in hand. He had scattered seeds of a rare but special plant and bordered it with an intricate design that he had fashioned from streams of cornmeal and rice earlier which had taken him mere moments to reproduce and he viewed his handiwork as a mechanic would a repair completed to his satisfaction. The Vévé, as these designs were called, required precise symmetry, a keen eye, patience and a steady hand but it had been rehearsed in his mind's eye for four years. He had made no mistakes. Like a key, it would open up a sliver of contact to the Gods who lurked in the shadow of the bush and the dank gnarly roots of the swamp, the ones who directed the growth of rot and fungi and oversaw the decay of life on the jungle floor. He whispered the name of one of the Dark Gods of Petro and kneeled outside the edges of the Vévé, lifting his eyes towards the moon as if he was a wolf. But instead of a howl, he willed the unhindered light on his incantations. Nature having its own agenda allowed the clouds to thin to nothingness.

Deh final ingredient.

Enoch smiled and began to chant words from the pit of his stomach, words that possessed the power to commune with primal forces that could alter reality and rewrite the natural laws if they willed it. Words a Bocor of his standing had committed to memory and spoke with the timbre of drums from his African ancestors.

His voice rose up into the cool night, reaching a frenzied pitch, charging the air around him as he sprinkled the blood on the soil and over the cornmeal pattern of the Vévé. His eyes were wild and frantic, his body in spasm where he kneeled, the forces sparking through him. The Mayan pot fell from his hands and Bocor Enoch collapsed to his elbows, his forehead bowed, almost touching the ground, sweat running off his lean frame.

Then nothing but his raspy breathing and a curtain of silence descending as if all had been told to hush by a higher power. If not for the absence of sound and the diminished chorus of blood rushing to his head, the popping sounds would have gone unnoticed. Lifting his head to peer at the area splattered with blood and the obscured Vévé and in his weakened state he bared his teeth in a parody of a smile. A multitude of black speckled shoots were breaking through the surface of the soil, their growth reminiscent of some B-movie creature features from the 50's with its jerky stop motion cinematography but speeded up to give the impression of normal movement. This was disconcertingly real as cellular growth unnaturally speeded up and overran the clearing with a thorny, gluttonous black and green vine, reeking of decomposition and a faint sickly sweet smell. Already its rapid metabolism had it flowering and a deceptive fruit it was. It had delicate snow white petals with flesh pink innards and a fluffy stamen like a fairy's wand, a complete antithesis to the repugnant vegetation writhing over the top soil. But that was the gift that Enoch required. The deceptively deadly and rare flower of the Demonius Sativum - Demon Weed.

With his satchel slung around his neck, Enoch knelt and carefully - the thorns were immensely poisonous - Enoch began to harvest the petals and fill his army satchel to the brim - his plans to bring holy retribution to London now in full swing.

Brixton Police Station
21.25

"Shit!"

The south London coroners had contacted Shaft in reference to the autopsy findings of the last murder. The call had been made in the early afternoon but Shaft had inadvertently left his personal mobile on his desk then completely forgot to check it for calls or messages on his return. This was not like him but unconsciously he knew the pathologist's findings would be inconclusive.

Darkman did not do ordinary.

His Macbook was open, his section of the office was dimly lit, smelling of damp cigarettes, old paper and Earl Grey tea. He massaged himself into his chair, listened as it creaked patiently waiting for him to slide his ass into the sweet spot that made him sigh. The light from his screen provided the final piece of the ambience he required for intense thought. The page on his high clarity screen was an enquiry tab that linked straight into HOLMES 2 – a data system used by the Force across the country to help correlate the vast amounts of information that are part and parcel of major enquires.

Shaft should not by rights have mobile access to such a crucial tool without him jumping through some major hoops. His rank alone should have seen to that but the perks of being the head of a department, even if it only had two full time staff plus an underlying need to keep him happy allowed him the access on par with the big boys.

He opened the case file and started to look through the associated notes he had entered three years ago and the present related data. Shaft realised he was a bystander to some major tremors rocking the criminal landscape, that was turning up corpses and necessitating the rats and snitches to be scurrying for cover while the names battened up hatches. And at this stage only he knew it was no ordinary disturbance.

Three weeks ago this was a closed case except for the Art and Antiquity unit still on the hunt for the stolen treasures and the Flying Squads continued search for cash in the value of approximately fifteen million pounds that was never retrieved. He had five murders in the space of two weeks, no real leads, some tenuous connections, a strong feeling it was all related and a conclusion that matched Black Books' remit but went against his scientific discipline.

What did Sherlock Holmes say?

When you have eliminated the impossible, whatever remains, however improbable, must be truth.

So there you have it then. Somehow Enoch Lacombe was orchestrating the savage murders of his enemies from behind bars and equally impressively he had some of the most hardened criminals in London's underbelly scurrying for cover.

How?

Shaft needed a touchstone of normalcy that would take his mind away from the oppressive darkness associated with this particular case. It had to be something that would redirect his attention to the ordinary.

He almost craved it.

Maybe that's why the temptation to call her was so irresistible.

Y had become like the end of day swirl of Courvoisier he treated himself to after work. She had the power to smooth out the kinks of a day from hell with her conversation. She was to be sipped and appreciated without haste. Shaft couldn't short change her with a lunch-time call that was rushed because he had to get back to a case?

No way.

Unfortunately there seemed to be no end in sight to how busy he'd become. He had even been able to scrounge some extra staff from the Commander who was gearing himself up against the backlash of this spate of murders within the Black community. Shaft could only hope she was doing okay – it must have been a social call or she would have left a voicemail - and as soon as an opportunity arose he could give her his full focus. Now he was too drained and needed to wind down but he had to see her soon, he needed it.

Almost instantly calming memories that instinctively understood how drained he was rushed in like antibodies to ease his stress.

Shaft let them engulf him and almost watched detachedly as he recounted the first time he had gotten close to Y. He wasn't sure if he was doing the right thing then - the asinine police programming kicking in, trying to tell him who he could and couldn't see according to Met protocol - but after their first game of squash he realised that this was one of the best choices he had made in a long time.

Y wore figure hugging shorts and a similar top that showed her mid-riff. He remembered commenting that her legs were wobbling after the exertion of their game and he was wondering if she had something else in that vitamin drink she was sipping. Y stumbled into his arms with laughter and he held her. Shaft never forgot how soft her skin was for someone with such a brutal martial arts regime. His fingers gripped her stomach firmly and he felt how smooth and accommodating she was. Enjoying how her rippling muscles felt in his hands when she moved, forming the stunning curves of her waist. A flash of wish fulfillment or lunacy – take your pick - had him kissing her sweat smeared stomach.

Back on her feet they both looked at each other with dopey grins plastered on their faces and felt that unspoken sentiment of attraction.

Shaft was overdue for another game of squash.

Y's crib, Acton, West London
13.40
Monday July 8th

Patra's mouth fell open slackly as she held up her ten fingers and nodded her head in deep appreciation.

The workmanship here just did not come any better.

Before they ever met and became friends she had experienced many talon technicians here and across the pond - Atlanta in particular - but Y was a true artist. A Whitney, hell no, an Aretha Franklin of nails. The end product, even with no nail polish applied, was immaculate enough to be worn as is, buffed and polished to perfection. Daaayum! If she hadn't seen her apply the tips herself with the acrylic overlay, she would have thought Y had patented some new super slick nail application procedure. But it was nothing as dramatic as that. This was the product of sheer skill, brilliance and genius.

Even her converted sitting room was created by someone with an eye for quality and detail. Y had moved about the contents of her lounge for maximum effect. The objet's d'art and any of her personal effects that did not match up with the image of how the work area should be were banished to her bedroom. Her trophy stand that contained all her Kendo awards was converted to displaying products; the photographs of the posse and family were replaced with product posters. Being severely limited with what could be done to the place didn't stop a keen appreciation for colour and space, transforming it from what it had been to the elegant beauty salon it now was.

After a few minutes of drooling admiration Patra placed both hands down on the work station her fingers outstretched.

"What colour do you think I should wear?" Patra asked.

"So you want consultation too?" Y gave an understanding nod. "That will be an extra ten pounds please."

Patra laughed.

"You money grabbing bitch, I'm paying you nearly double what some of these other salons charge and hell, you're not even a salon."

"I'm worth every penny. Aren't you satisfied with the quality of my work?" Y asked feigning shock. Patra nearly gave away the game with a knee jerk response 'of course I am boo' but held herself back at the last minute, wagging her finger accusingly to say she was not so easily duped.

Y grinned, took Patra's forefinger and used a large fluffy brush to flick particles of dust from it.

That was the price you paid – with corny clichés aside – for the best in the west. It had taken one of Y's old dumbass Jamaican adages 'Business and friendship don't mix' to keep things on the straight and narrow. Patra had been tempted on more than one occasion to play the friendship card to jump the long queues that were forming lately but she had to remain cool. It was her own fault most of the time anyway because a simple call or a reminder when they met for training would be enough for Y to block out a time slot for her. But obviously that lacked the element of challenge for Patra's sensibilities. As usual she paid the price for her risk taking mentality and that meant wading through Ebony, The Pride, assorted female magazines dedicated to dissecting the Black male while waiting for some old dear in a pearl necklace Um-ing and ah-ing over a perfectly formed eyebrow shape.

Inconveniences aside, it was worth every damn minute.

"Don't you think they're too long?" Y said after appraising them thoroughly.

"These?" Patra asked spreading her fingers again to take a better look herself. "No way, they're perfect." She then stared intently at Y. "You dissin' me?"

"Would I do that?" Y asked innocently. "Okay I know before they invented dishwashers you used to throw your plates in the bin and I suppose you can get away with riding your bike but how are you going to put on gloves and box without shattering them?"

Patra nodded, smiling slyly.

"Don't worry I've got it all worked out, sugahhh."

"Have you now?"

"As a matter of fact, yeah, I have. All my training for the next two weeks will be shadow boxing so they'll be safe. What's worrying me is being away from my baby for all that time. It's gonna be hard without all that power between my legs."

"I believe yuh." Y burst into raucous laughter. Patra's amorous references to her Kawasaki Ninja ZX would make a casual listener blush. "That brings me on to my next point. You not having a man for so long and by now forgetting what bit goes where, I can think of somewhere else those claws are going to be dangerous."

Patra's face brightened with a sense of understanding.

"Daaayum!" She emphasized. "You know, that just up an' slipped my mind. You'd better soak those babies off girlfriend because I want nothing to come between me an my clit."

Y couldn't contain herself as Patra's contrived deep south accent fizzled out.

"Try getting it on with those deadly weapons at the tips of your fingers. That could be messy." Y made a funny face and shivered.

"Nasty!" Patra emphasised then looked over to Y's hands. All neat and more importantly long.

"Hey bitch! Practise what you preach," Patra pointed accusingly at Y's fingers although not as long as her own but growing.

Y flinched.

"Si yah! I'm only making my real nails grow out, giving them a breather from the extensions."

"Yeah, right!" Patra shook her head and spoke to the ceiling. "She's fucking wid me and we're both in the same shit."

"Speak for yourself gal. I've got something stiff and black waiting for me later," Patra nearly fell off her swivel chair with the hilarity of that lying statement.

"It's waiting for you alright. Black, ten inches long and vibrating like a motherfucker."

"Shhhhh!" Y chided. "There are virgins present in the room."

"Where? I ain't seen none."

They laughed some more and then Y settled back to finish what she had started.

Armed with Patra's chosen design of the bust of Queen Nefertiti, she stood up and walked over to assorted pieces of equipment she stored beside the far wall.

On a trolley, neatly set on a fluffy towel was the air gun and its component parts. They sat there gleaming on a bed of white, like tools to be used by a punctilious surgeon in an operating room. She started to assemble her air gun where she stood and soon felt an uncharacteristic silence descend on what was before a boisterous vibe.

Y immediately involved her in a topic she knew she felt passionately about.

"I can bet Daddy must be feeling pleased his daughter has given up the idea of being a dispatch rider for the more glamorous world of modelling."

Patra kissed her teeth with unshielded disgust, a tableau of all the family conflicts boldly coming to the forefront of her mind.

"I've told my mama about my plans so I suppose he knows where I'm coming from. They sleep in the same bed. But I wasn't going to tell him, shit. Hey Pop's, let's have a father to daughter talk. What do you say? Shit man."

The dredged up angst was self evident in her voice and Y felt like pond scum for nudging the conversation in that direction but Patra didn't talk much about it. And Y being the person she was felt concerned about that.

Y walked back over to her work station with the air gun fully assembled and turned to face her again.

She asked her.

"Do you ever think he will ever accept you, for you?"

Patra shook her head.

"No fucking way. Unless I suddenly decide to complete my MA in Business Studies, find what he considers a respectable job, marry into a known family of good breeding in Atlanta and have two point five children he could dote on and doing that shit on my hands and knees, begging for forgiveness while I kiss his black ass, no way!"

Y leaned back into her chair and looked at the glow of resolve shining in her eyes and those firm set lips, understanding why this family feud would remain at stalemate. She was much more like her father than she would choose to admit and both being Taurians meant neither would give in without a fight.

Ms Ramona Cleopatra Jones left the US almost begging the UK for political asylum. The States were suffocating her with its conservative views on being a woman, in particular a Black woman with her own set of values that weren't considered acceptable. From what she had read before coming here about Europe's open mindedness and her thirst for adventure, Britain was a no brainer. It had become home very quickly and, although it broke her mama's heart to see her go, preacher Jones was relieved. Ever since then Patra was in a constant state of rebellion against everything her father stood for. When the posse sat and talked about their childhoods, the issue of Patra's preacher father's lack of love for her was expressed with anger and bitterness. The girls shared an empathy with her.

The entire direction that Patra's life took was meant to be the antithesis of everything her father believed in and represented.

Mr Ignatius Jones was a self-made millionaire who had emigrated from Barbados to the States in the days when it wasn't the fashionable thing to do. Over the years he had worked his way up to a level of prominence and as well as being a wealthy businessman, he was a Baptist lay preacher and community leader.

A goddamn hypocrite, were the words his daughter used to describe him and justifiably in her eyes. For a father to treat a child with such contempt through her formative years because of his grief that his only two sons were conceived still born was unforgivable. Yet on a fundamental level she was trying to forgive herself, for heaping the blame for her father's actions on her shoulders and not where they should have been. She was making it right for herself and nobody else. It just so happened that what made her feel genuinely free and alive were affronts to everything her father had worked hard to achieve. Thank God for Mama Jones.

Patra was never left in the dark concerning her family back in the States and she talked to her mother once a week at least. Only Mama Jones remained proud of her opinionated, adrenaline junky, bi-sexual daughter.

Regrets.

Hell no!

Patra wouldn't change a thing.

Y and Suzy were her family here and they accepted her for who she was. Back home they would have to deal with the naked truth or kiss her svelte Apple Bottom ass.

Y snapped on her face mask and took Patra's index finger and applied oil to its edges. Placing it gently on a plastic column, she held the template in place over the nail bed and made a sweeping blast with her air gun. The Kemetic Queen's image stood bold on Patras nail. Y nodded with satisfaction at the first stage and reached for another gun loaded with gold.

A loud slam on her front door made her pause in mid application.

Who the hell was that knocking on her door like they owned the damn place?

Usually the doorbell was used by most visitors; it was so outrageous and in your face - shaped like a hairy bum and the tune it played was rather tacky Hawaii-Five-O theme - no one ever thought of gaining her attention in any other way.

It had to be someone with no sense of humour, an inflated sense of their own self worth or someone believing their own hype. Mam's choice Jamaican colloquialism rang in Y's head, *smelling dem arm, an tink a charm.*

A second barrage of bangs from her Victorian knocker reverberated through the house.

Who is this?

Y stood up about to storm out to her hallway but decided before she did anything rash, like alienating a potential client in the process, to check her appointments. She activated her smartphone and her digital diary app. It was clear. No one was due for the next forty five minutes and that client was a regular who didn't like waiting around.

This was unannounced company.

Y excused herself, just as Patra's mobile went off and her friend expertly flipped it open and was away in verbal fourth gear as she left the room.

Y grabbed a jumper on her way out and slipped it quickly over her head, concealing most of her formal uniform. She looked through the peep hole first and saw the distant image of two men in suits peering in at her.

She opened the door part way and peered out.

"Can I help you...gentlemen?" She said icily. And it better be friggin' good, was the thought.

One of the men - slender, effeminate with an air of perceived superiority about him - stepped forward and said.

"Are you Ms Yvonne Sinclair, resident of this address?"

"Who wants to know?" Y asked.

One of the officials obviously told by some deluded female that he was smooth - worst of all he believed it - reached into his jacket pocket and ran his business card along her field of vision sarcastically.

Windsor Housing Association stood out in bold gold letters with his name and credentials.

Y said nothing while smooth bwoy consulted a clipboard he had taken from under his arm.

He tapped it with his pen and looked over to his colleague, who himself had moved closer to the doorway. Y's heart began to rattle against her rib cage as it dawned on her what was about to go down.

Smooth bwoy seemed to be satisfied that he was talking to the right person and proceeded.

"It has come to Windsor Housing Association's attention that you have contravened clause 114 in paragraph 14 of your contract relating to business enterprises functioning from your domicile address. With that said we are requesting access. So no further action will be taken against you, we will need to search your premises for proof for or against this claim."

"I don't know what you're talking about," Y said sweetly. "You must have the wrong address."

Y started shouldering the door shut before she had finished the sentence but to her frustration it was inexplicably jarred open.

She looked down.

A shiny yet fashionable steel tipped Dr Martens was wedged between the door frame and the door itself. Smooth bwoy's colleague had just performed what she imagined to be his sole purpose and grinned as its importance was made clear to yet another satisfied customer.

"I don't think so, ma'am," Smooth boy spat smugly and proceeded to leaf through legal documents which gave him the right to force his way into Y's life uninvited.

Her anger barometer nudged up two notches but Y's usual response was subdued not that the Housing Officers would realise that especially as she flung the door open and stepped out to face them. Already her half concocted story boasting a cast of two main villains in suits and casting herself as the innocent tenant was gaining traction in her mind. For anyone who would listen to her side of the story after the fallout it would be presented warm and sincere from the oven of her mind. Y smiled crookedly almost amused by her own hesitation to take action. This reluctance to act, considering her actions like a chess player was happening with annoying regularity and was usually accompanied with the nagging voice of good reason. Y took stock of her situation before acting.

Good thing!

Maybe she was beginning to understand the rules of this warped game of fate that was hell bent on challenging them every step of the way.

Just as Y stepped out to face the housing men, two uniformed police officers seemed to appear from the hedges and as her eyes wandered further afield her breath caught in her throat.

A very familiar green Range Rover sat at the far side of the road and Mrs Granger rocking her mother of pearl necklace and also her 12.45 appointment, was being helped into the car.

Strange, her appointment was in forty five minutes.

Y's eyes locked onto the scene in bewilderment as if it was a performance she had seen before but was still unclear about the outcome.

Her mouth partially open, she watched with intense interest while a younger woman courteously closed the passenger door shut for her client and then turned.

Then the penny dropped

Sandy Brewster her erstwhile part time boss, who had been none too pleased when Y resigned turning down a full time position on her team, smiled a smile that literally cut her snide face in half with the delight she felt.

Y blinked.

"You bad minded bitch!" Y growled.

Patra arrived just behind Y and caught the tail end of her outburst. Already making a succinct evaluation of the situation she was punching away on her electronic third ear for reinforcements.

Not that it mattered.

Suzy wouldn't get there in time and Y had brushed past the men in the suits and was approaching Sandy Brewster's 4x4 at a steady clip.

Patra could only see Y's movements from the door-way, the two men getting off the floor, Five-O on Y's tail and the SUV's tyres burning rubber as the panicked driver, emergency brakes still in place, tried to escape the approaching mad woman.

Patra knew this was serious but could do nothing more than laugh and feel genuinely sorry for whoever was in the vehicle. Then she wondered if Y would get off with a caution and that made her smile even more.

Odeon Leicester Square
Central London
21.00

Leroy 'Minty' Thelwell loved the lure of the big screen. Maybe it was those memorable Saturday matinees as a yout at the Carib in Kingston, Jamaica that had left such a lasting impression on him. It was the only place where he and his spars could vicariously share the violent thrills with the movie heroes they idolised while the political wars raged about them.

Deh good old days.

So that was why when 'runnings' permitted and Deacon could survive without him he would travel all the way from Peckham, reserving the best seat at the Odeon Leicester Square to *tek in* his love in all its glorious colour and surround sound.

Tonight was the grand opening of a new Alex Weh movie. High octane choreographed violence, lovingly directed by one of Hong Kong's masters of that art form.

Then there were the guns.

The sexy purveyors of death and destruction.

All big, all shiny and packing fire power that left him salivating at the film's end.

He smiled at the thought of asking his Cypriot contact to source one of those pieces being used by the star bwoy. Make the gun runner lose more of his already thinning hair line in its acquisition.

Minty watched the credits scrolling from the screen for a second more and rose from his seat as the lights came on dimly. He was glad he had decided to take a break away from Deacon and the operation today. Giving himself some space to relax and chill. He had achieved that and more this evening and that was one of the reasons why his eyes searched the hazy interior, making particular note of the sisters departing.

He wanted his time away from business to last a bit longer and he knew how.

Turning quickly from aisle to aisle he hoped the woman who had made his pulse race with her stunning good looks wouldn't just disappear in the ever dwindling rush of movie goers. But he saw nothing of her.

Disappointed, he was still buzzing as he stepped into the foyer. Some of the patrons hung around, chatting amongst the promotional posters and gimmicks like monkeys in a paper jungle. Wanting to step down from the staircase and join the exiting chaos, he realised a bottle neck had formed and he was unable to move. Minty maintained his cool looking over the slowly dwindling numbers and it was then he sensed it. A pin prick of heat that slowly spread from the nape of his neck, as if he had been injected with some fast acting anaesthesia that would engulf his whole body and render him immobile. His hand shot up to the point behind his neck feeling for the offending sting but instead coming away with a clear moistness between his fingers.

Then the tingling feeling subsided.

He turned slowly and met the woman in red with her smouldering brown eyes, flawless dark skin and lips that were succulent and red. His balls reacted before his mind did and shrank protectively but his manhood, well that told another story. One that did not care for what his hardwired early warning system had so eloquently alerted him to.

Her red dress alone demanded attention on its own merits. It was if the material was poured onto her like intelligent liquid chocolate that took on the design requested by it's creator and set as fabric with the perfect colour and texture. It made every luscious curve, from the mounds of her breasts to the symmetry of her thighs, even more appealing.

Every red blooded brother lucky enough to be in the cinema's foyer at that time seemed to be drawn to her like the gravitational pull of a stellar object.

What's more, she obviously had an unrivalled appreciation for class. No need to make the first move, enthrall her with his gangster exploits or his 'bad bwoy' contacts.

No talking was involved, just body language.

It was clear she recognised the aura of sophisticated menace he emanated and the connection between them was unquestioned. Earlier the beauty never took her eyes off him as he had stood purchasing a Coke from the concessionary. Unfortunately, before he could go over to her and get a number she was gone but from the ferocity of his erection, not forgotten.

An look now!

What will be, will be, because here she was, he told himself.

Minty was too experienced in the ways of these things to be surprised. He just knew a certain percentage of the world's pussy you didn't have to do any work to capture. Law of averages. He had bedded too many stray pum-pum not to know that as a statistical fact. So why did he feel that nothing about this woman obeyed the law of averages?

Fuck it!

Flashing a grin in her direction she winked and crooked her finger his way, beckoning him over to where she stood but the crowd was dense. As best as he could with some subtle hand movements he tried to tell her to 'hold tight' and proceeded to shoulder his way to the entrance. Two minutes tops to get to where she was standing and she was not there. Peering through the glass facade, he saw her turn right along the Haagen Daz promenade. Leroy broke into the fresh air wondering, *what the fuck, is she dealing wid*? He looked up to Piccadilly in the distance, easily distinguishing her short red dress amidst the street performers, artists and their audiences. She walked backward for a while still beckoning him with a smile and a curl of her finger.

She then turned left into Soho.

His scowl fell away.

A freaky chick, turned on by the chase and the excitement.

He could live with that.

Stepping up his pace he kept on the trail, impeded by the amounts of people just aimlessly milling around but gaining on her nonetheless. The streets looked somehow shinier up here. Like showers had been limited to just these streets. Mist was clinging to the shop fronts, drifting down the streets and mingling with the smells issuing from the restaurants. She disappeared in the bellowing fumes of a car exhaust for a moment, her image suddenly illuminated in a cocoon of hazy light. He made to cross over to the other side when a garbage truck drove across his line of sight, tickling his nose with its stench. Stooping, Leroy peered below the trucks under belly and caught sight again of those long stockinged legs, head down a side street he imagined could accommodate only two people shoulder to shoulder. He had a feeling this was where she wanted him.

Taking his time, he regulated his breathing, popped his collar then slowly walked down the alley.

Light filtered from the window of a restaurant, a grill, planted at street level, leaked pale mist and his shadow stretched ahead of him until it died into the gloom.

Through the thin curtains of mist, he could see the silhouette, an indistinct figure, half way along the length of the alley, with her back against the wall. A red glow hovered away from her mouth, followed by a stream of smoke.

Calmly walking over, re-enacting the swaying gait of one of his movie idols, Minty stopped abruptly like a 'B' actor who had forgotten his lines. He scrutinised her carefully, before he leaned forward, placing the palms of his hands on the wall at either side of her head. He drank in her smell of honeysuckle and those molten brown eyes had not lessened in intensity.

"This running up and down ting," he whispered, "Gets you wet don't?"

Her arms arched around his waist in reply pulling him closer.

With a sigh he interpreted as anticipation, he started caressing her thighs. His coarse hands slid along her stocking legs until he felt the silkiness of her panties. Minty gripped onto the sparse G-string and ripped it off. Inviting him further she lifted her skirt and parted her legs some more. Leroy undid his fly with one hand and released his spring loaded penis from his trousers with the other. Leaning up from the wall to fish into his pockets for Jimmies, he felt a sharp prick to his neck again.

He bunched his broad shoulders, the bite reminiscent of the one he felt in the foyer and briefly thought how strange that was while he fumbled with his erect member.

It got stranger.

Suddenly a cold chill razored across his shoulder blades almost making him feel as if he had been stripped naked. A mound of gooseflesh rose at the back of his head as he turned. His eyes registered the blur of motion some distance away and before he could complete a breath, a hand that felt like a steel vice, gripped his jaw and squeezed. He felt a tremendous power in the man, vibrating from inside like he was hiding some huge internal turbine under his dark clothes. The hand holding his jaw twisted his head this way and that as if examining him and he could vaguely see the lady in red sashaying away in the distance. With no effort he was lifted off his feet, the overpowering rawness of the sea in his nose and the cold clamminess of the man's touch on his skin. Minty squirmed; the sensation of his touch was strange. It was as if it had no true consistency, a semi solid, not certain if the state it existed in was really solid or liquid. He was struggling for breath, the man's hand covering his face and for the briefest of moments, he felt flesh breaking down, transforming like little viscous feelers crawling into his nose and mouth, gagging him. Minty tried to scream but instead bit down on what was invading him, the man's flesh coming away in his mouth.

A sour loathsome taste exploded over his palette.

Minty heaved, leaving a trail of dark fluid from his mouth just as a force he was hopeless to defend against sent him flying through the air and smashing into the opposite wall. He fell to a crumpled heap and ever so slowly raised himself to his knees, retching, expelling the foul tasting substance from his guts and mouth.

Strings of regurgitated food hung from his lips as he looked up to see the hazy figure of the lady in red, looking at him from a safe distance and then walking away.

Anger or survival spurred him on, making him try to crawl out of harm's way but the impact with the wall must have broken bones because every move was excruciatingly painful.

His pathetic attempts to flee ended violently.

To his numbed senses gravity began to react differently and he found himself floating above ground, not realising he had been lifted and pinned once more against the wall.

Minty was looking wide eyed and straight into the face of the person who had jumped him but for the life of him he could not discern his features. It was like looking into a black and white TV set filled with jagged static. His feet were dangling off the street, the man's hand was pressing against his chest with such force he felt like an insect pinned to a display board. The pressure was unbearable but he struggled to stay conscious.

He thrashed left and right, his nostrils flaring as he breathed in that distinctive rank marine odour of his assailant.

Minty tried to concentrate on the man's face but even at such close proximity, the only thing he could be sure of was the *fucker* was tall, wore a long black coat and a broad rimmed black trilby and his face was sunken into oily canvas of visual static. Minty feigned limpness, not wanting to alert him to his lucidness before he was ready but the smell was making him swoon.

"Deh drug running through your veins is called the demon weed, star. A real versatile mix that right about now is making you more open to my suggestion."

That voice.

God almighty!

Minty's innards froze as if freon was being pumped through his veins. His body stiffened in immediate shock.

"Yuh look surprised? No jail can hold me, pussy. No prison a guh keep me from you."

The voice from his past rebounded off the inner caverns of his skull like an errant echo.

Enoch? Darkman?

His panic could not be more complete.

Desperately his fingers foraged around the inside of his trouser waist, searching, ignoring the pain in his chest and the man's words.

"I heard......."

Survival.

Nothing more occupied Minty's tormented thoughts.

"... a little bird seh..."

His fingers kept reaching.

"...you where looking for me."

The muscles of his elbow extended and could stretch no more.

"I was looking for you too, pardy."

The pain shot through his hand as the pads of his finger tips touched the smooth handle of his switch blade.

"Glad I could mek your acquaintance."

With a bellow like some rabid animal, Minty ejected the switchblade free from its housing and plunged the six inch stiletto into the mad man's ribs.

A stray beam of light brought his face into view for a second.

The look of agony he expected was instead a smile. An abomination of a grin which was impossibly wide, his face, seal skin black wildly stretching and distorting as if it was a sheet of elastic, being kneaded out of shape by some powerful internal force.

"I have two questions feh you. Do you want to tell me about Deacon's plans while you are alive...?"

Minty screamed, his brain on the verge of overloading and his senses sharper than he ever knew they could be. He felt the stickiness of his fingers and with a soft tearing sound he pulled the knife out of Darkman's ribs.

An uncontrollable shiver of revulsion shook him.

He tried to stab him again.

"...or I can drag deh answers from yuh stinking corpse."

The Darkman's hands encircled his and squeezed. Leroy's fingers shattered.

Blood trickled along what remained of his knuckles and dripped to the pavement. Every neuron exploded simultaneously, blurring his vision with its suddenness. But even as he stiffened with shock, the sound of the broken blade falling to the street was clear as if that was all that existed.

A lonely isolated sound of defeat.

Minty knew he was dead.

The shock revelation of Darkman being here now, fully present, no drug trip but reality. The pain exploding all over his body like minute depth charges ripping him apart was real enough too and so was that aching despondency in his gut of regret. The talisman – that reeking concoction of herbs, pungent oils, animal carcasses and incantations, that talisman that he was meant to wear everywhere he went. The one he had left because he had reasoned the smell would turn off any interested females.

That had killed him.

Darkman clamped his hands over Leroy's wails, his tar skin starting to spread away from his fingers, pulsating black pseudo flesh like a giant unicellular organism engulfing his victim's skull. With his undamaged hand Leroy frantically groped at the man's flesh, trying to tear it from his face but it simply replaced itself, getting denser and tighter. Then the throbbing mass of oil slick coloured living matter began to constrict, tightening, filling every orifice, suffocating him. The sutures in his skull made gross popping sounds as his head caved in. His struggling became sporadic twitches as the life left him.

Darkman let him fall.

In mock reverence he took off his trilby, stooped beside him, Darkman's chiselled and gaunt features unshielded for the first time and whispered to the convulsing body of Leroy 'Minty' Thelwell.

"By an by, we will talk. Deh teeming dead hold no secrets from me Minty. You will tell me what I want to know."

He stood up and spat on the corpse. Then as if he never existed, he disappeared into the mist.

6.

Metal Works Gym
Tuesday, July 10th
12.15

"It can't get any worse can, it?" Y lamented.

"Shit, we alive ain't we?" Patra said.

But no matter how it was processed, either through Y's sense of black and white or Patra's optimism filter, it seemed life was conspiring against them, cracking some cosmic joke at their expense and maybe hoping they were evolved enough to appreciate the mirth.

Y was on the verge of either receiving a criminal record or a police caution and was facing a definite eviction from her home. She had been so eager to get to Sandy Brewster, her part time employer, who had shopped her to the Housing Association the two Housing officers in her way ended up with a fractured jaw and a sprained ankle. The Community Officers were also injured slightly, due more to their clumsiness – grabbing onto someone as supple as Y was fraught with dangers - but unfortunately that wasn't considered when the reports were handed in.

Patra was the only light amidst the forest of bullshit and had returned home early from a model shoot in Nice, not in the best of moods. She had a tendency to devolve to a more savage representation of herself when she was without a partner for extended periods of time. And for the dawg ugly shoot director and not one of the models to make a pass at her was just too much for her to bear. Her day job at the Pink Kitty Kat was far less challenging and that's how she preferred it.

Today the only person who was making any sense was Suzy, and she was quiet, allowing one of her profound philosophical solutions to emerge.

It was just after lunch time and the posse was as relaxed as possible in their lair at Metal Works. The smoke from Patra's lone cigarillo curled up to the ceiling extractors.

Eyes were blank, tired.

Y's voice was edged with sarcasm.

"So, you think we should forget about everything," she repeated. "Relax, enjoy ourselves, kick back for a week or two and return with a fresh perspective."

Suzy nodded.

"And how the fuck are we goin' to do that?" Y spat out. "We have limited cash and we're worrying about our situations. How?"

Y lowered her head and used her left hand to slowly massage her temples. A soft "sorry" drifted up from where she had leaned forward giving Suzy's inevitable response a chance.

Instead of saying anything, Suzy's eyes fell on Patra who, strangely, in view of the circumstances, had a smile on her face.

Patra shrugged.

"Okay! Great idea. Take a breather and chill for a while. Question is how and with what?"

Suzy threw an envelope into the middle of the table and said brightly.

"Dis is a start."

Y glared at it firstly then as if it was a gargantuan effort, reached over and took it up. Her action seemed to attract Patra's attention as she leaned forward too, curious.

Y opened it and slowly said.

"Three VIP tickets to the MOBO awards After Party."

"You're shitting me." Patra squealed.

"I shit you not." Y said as both their eyes converged on the tickets again then on Suzy.

"He remembered."

Suzy shook her head smiling.

"Come on, Mr P doesn't make idle promises. You know that." she said to their unanswered question. "He wanted to cheer us up. Oh! And by deh way him seh we can order a limousine of our choice on him."

"Man, that is one cool dude," Patra commented.

Mr Guresh Patel was an enigma in his own life-time or so the girls viewed him.

A Hindu multi-millionaire whose beginnings were shrouded in mystery to everyone other than maybe only his family and closest aides and who treated the girls with the respect he afforded his family. Ever since they had prevented a possible kidnapping attempt in the car lot of Metal Works, he had made sure whatever he could do to make life for them more trouble free he would - without his wife's knowledge that is.

His benevolence aside what made him much more than a middle-aged Asian businessman was his mysterious contacts in the music world. For a boy born in Mumbai he had knowledge of all the black music luminaries and referred to them with an uncanny sense of familiarity - as if he knew them very well.

Signed autographs of visiting superstars, backstage passes and front row seats at the most sought after concerts was his mystery sideline.

Now this.

These tickets were for the most prestigious music Awards ceremony in the UK and could easily change hands on eBay for five hundred pounds a pop. They'd all given up asking, "How the hell does he do that?"

Y was looking into middle distance as if she had been stunned into silence but she was actually groping for a relevant description of herself adequate enough to describe how childish she had been acting.

In her panic it had been easy to forget that the girls had as much to lose as she did. Their underlying motives were different but their commitment to their ideals and one another were solid. Y had to keep reminding herself, that with life, health and good friends the direction her life took was still under her control.

"I don't...." Y began as a prologue to an apology.

"Forget it!" Suzy pre-empted again. "I understand sis."

"Yeah she understands alright." Patra butted in with one of her less than subtle evaluations of human nature. "She understands you're tripping."

"Thanks for the vote of confidence," Y said.

"Hey, what are friends for?"

"I ask myself that sometimes."

"Then I think it's my place to remind you girlfriend, if you forgot. And yow! You must have forgotten because we are all in this bitch together. To-ge-ther. You feel me?" Patra was out of her seat staring wistfully at a poster of a water soaked and densely muscled body of Usain Bolt. She unconsciously licked her lips and walked over to Y, putting her hands on her shoulder and massaged it gently. "These last few months have been hell for all of us and even when I tend to say stuff like, 'Hey we're fucked', I'm mouthing off and you expect that from me, right? But if you start tripping and really meaning that shit, we screwed. Suzy can't take care of business by herself and you know me. Being subtle ain't my thing." Patra grinned. "We know we were meant to be, so why fight it. All this bullshit around us is nothing, it's all about getting some, and if it means we have to bust some balls along the way, hey, bring it on."

Y leaned forward and shook her head, smiling weakly. Recovering from the shock of Patra's impromptu pep talk took some minutes and she allowed the truth of what she said to sink in. Lifting her head from her slumped position she looked in Suzy's direction.

"One day at a time, Ms Wong?"

Suzy nodded and smiled.

Betsure Turf Office
Harlesden, North London
12.55am

The cherry red Aston Martin Virage had a gleam on it that could only be matched by the gold tooth grin of equal brilliance in the driver's mouth. If there was ever a man who enjoyed his wealth it was Spokes. He was in his late fifties – not that you could tell – well maintained from the luck of the genetic draw and his strenuous efforts to keep the temple of his body free from the rigors of modern living - he sported distinguished streaks of grey in his hair and neatly trimmed beard. He had a good sense of dress too and the ability to hold his own in any conversation with ambitions above the virtues of pussy, drugs and music.

Now add that to the natural attraction afforded to you when money was no object. How respect was given - although in many cases it was false and more akin to fear - and the perceived mystery he exuded that women especially found irresistible and which was merely an unhealthy respect for his achievements.

Spokes pulled into one of the three car park spaces and briefly lost his oral sparkle. The forecourt was busy with the listless regulars who conducted a daily pilgrimage to the gods of gambling and who had spotted his arrival. Loud, lewd and opportunistic like hyenas, they hung outside and in, their meagre offerings to Mammon already spent. Spokes' high performance car would provide another welcome distraction for them.

"Pussyclaat!" Spokes spat.

The leader of the pack – a man he knew as Goose – raised up an extra few inches like a meerkat – long neck, furtive eyes and scraggly hair in the twilight zone of not quite dread, not quite afro. The others in his mob responded in that animated mirroring fashion forged from too much time together, curious but wary as if they were waiting for Goose to deem the encounter safe. Goose nodded admiringly and his crew surrounded the car like it had the promise of insect larvae.

So why not the gambling establishments of Westminster, Chelsea or Knightsbridge, for a more refined gambling experience?

The Devil you know, dem seh.

He knew what to expect from some of the most idle, callous, desperate, money grabbing, vile and wanton dutty bungle, the Caribbean and the UK had shat out. The corrupted intentions that sat behind their eyes might as well be emblazoned on their foreheads.

Envy.

Hatred.

Contempt.

He understood, he just didn't condone it.

Spokes slid out of the car nimbly and closed the door with a satisfying thunk of class engineering.

"Raw George! Dem nuh call yuh Spokes for nothing, big man. You love yuh fast cars, star!"

A middle aged Rasta man approached him with his hands out-stretched, made the promoter smile. Spokes grasped it, a friendly and genuine face amidst the predators.

"Ras Michael, how tings champion?"

"Flat foot hustling same way, pardy. Flat foot hustling."

Ras Michael could turn up anywhere selling some of the best Sensi in London. A roving entrepreneur who by the blessings of the Father - the Rastaman's words not his - had never had a single run in with the police. Always smiling, always optimistic he was a constant breath of fresh air amidst the rough necks he seemed to gravitate to.

"Yuh fancy a horse, today?" The Rasta man asked.

"Yeah, yeah. I feel lucky. You have a tip for me?"

"Mi always have a tip breddrin' but not deh kind you would appreciate."

Spokes laughed and started making his way to the interior of the bookmakers, watching himself approach in the glass frontage. He also saw Goose stretching over his car, as if he wanted to pop the bonnet, his mob in rapt attention.

Spokes shot back without missing a stride.

"Touch mi rassclaat car and yuh dead!"

"Fucking cunt!"

A downpour of white paper flung into the air with such disgust that it fluttered to Spokes' feet like an artificial snow storm in a bottle just as the fourteen forty from Cheltenham came to an end and he was ten thousand pounds up. Lady luck and providence all rolled into one.

Damn, he was good. Unfortunately the man standing beside him – the one who inadvertently wanted to create a winter wonderland theme with his stubs, wasn't so lucky.

Ras Michael popped his head through the door patting his breast pocket and smiled.

"Collect yuh money and you can taste some of my Clarendon Sensi star. What yuh say?"

The snake head ring that encircled Spokes right index finger tingled. The fringes of his perception shrank and coloured to a warm mauve. A pleasant warmness engulfed him completely and his taste buds exploded with the flavour of peaches and cream. Ras Michael was a kind, hard working man with good intentions and Spokes knew it would be a pleasure to share a spliff with him. Evaluating people using magic was so far removed from what he had known four years ago it felt almost like another life. A life his spar had forced him to immerse himself in and one that for a boy from Trelawney had strangely become second nature. Who would have thought his calling would be this?

Spokes licked his lips and smiled at Ras Michael.

"That sounds good to me, pardy."

Spokes held on to his receipt firmly in his fist and approached the payout booth. The memory of his mortally wounded friend forcing the ring on his finger knowing the Mesopotamian artefact would keep him safe but unable to articulate it.

The cashiers booth was empty, he rapped on the thick glass that reminded him of a reinforced chicken coup that was designed to keep some mutant strain of fowl in. The managers of this branch were cynical enough by nature or from experience to realise their priorities lay in security not decor. There was a conspicuous prevalence of CCTV cameras, sprouting up like fungus. A twenty four hour tape of the operations of this place would be the wet dream of any officer on the drugs squad, Operation Trident or a plain old Community Support Officer.

He imagined a police raid in here.

Shit.

The thought of a possible stampede of innocent and felon alike made him chuckle to himself. He pressed the buzzer beside his elbow and waited. Quick to take your money but not so forthcoming when it came to paying out the winnings, he thought.

Seeing no sight of the cashier he unslung the Vertu mobile from around his neck and turned away from the counter before he started to key in a number.

Ras Michael was impatiently gesticulating that he was taking too long. Spokes raised his five fingers to him, punched a number and placed the receiver to his ear.

A conversation drifted over.

"I'm telling you man, ah him."

Spokes felt a chill erupt across the back of his neck without warning. His backbone twisted almost of its own volition for a better vantage point. And with sharp eyes he locked onto two men talking, his ears seemed like they were standing to attention as he concentrated on what they were saying. Spokes realised he was staring just before the men recognised his attention was fully focussed on them.

Slowly, he adjusted the phone to his ear, deftly cut the connection with his little finger and gave them his back to reinforce the pretence.

The men continued their tone lowered.

"I talked to him three days ago. Him was on top form." The voice sounded incredulous

"Dem fuck him up, bro."

"Mi hear, the swimming pool dem find him in was a scarlet soup of him bones and flesh. Chunks Super, yuh understand me?"

"If a man like Maaga Tin can get reach, nobody safe star, nobody."

"True..true. But even him nevah deserve that..."

They lowered their voices and shuffled uneasily away from earshot.

The two men, partially hidden away in a cubicle to his left had done enough to ruin a care-free day, etching worry grooves into Spokes' forehead. The area the men stood in, was a low tech alternative to a secure room that was used by punters with winnings that they needed to count in some degree of privacy. The conversation almost achieved its goal of being private in an environment of foam ceiling tiles and Perspex partitions keeping the participants' words satisfyingly low.

Secret agents these hustlers were not.

If they hadn't made so much out of it, he may not have paid them much attention. But it was just the way they had isolated themselves, invading each others' space to preserve the secrecy of what they were sharing as if it could seep past them without their closeness.

The coarse monotones of the main speaker could not be modulated below a whisper if his life depended on it. And Spokes decided this was a good thing. Without making his intentions obvious, he stood still peering in front of him, a fading but majestic photograph of Lester Piggott in full stride and concentrated on the sounds. A few slight re-adjustments of his head from time to time and he heard the almost one sided conversation and allowed his mind to fill in the gaps.

The men had obviously been privy to some facts – Maaga Tin's murder - but the details he guessed from experience were eighty percent street embellishments and twenty percent reality. And that said it did nothing to improve his frame of mind, a sudden sinking feeling in his gut.

He leaned back on the counter, his heart pounding in his chest, his head screaming for him to get out of there, lock himself away and stay there.

Hell an powder house!

Who was next?

Spokes was having a whole new respect for these dudes reporting skills. His Snakes Head ring had discerned the truth of what was being said and its accuracy he could feel by the emotional snapshots smearing his mind's eye like a Dakar Rally car flinging up mud onto its windshields. He could taste that astringent copper tang on his tongue and the splashes of crimson behind his eyes.

Spokes swallowed, to keep the contents of his stomach calm.

The abattoir smell of a slaughter house wrinkled his nostrils and for a moment he was almost there amidst the carnage.

He spun away to sever the connection only just interrupting his contracting abdominal muscles and the embarrassment of hurling on the betting shop floor.

Jesas!

The why, was simple really. The players in this Danse Macabre where being brought to book for what they had done four years ago.

The how, was something else entirely.

Could you really hold a force of nature behind bars indefinitely? Wasn't it just a matter of time before he found the means to escape? And how long did *he* have?

He kissed the snake head ring on his finger.

This had kept him invisible from any and all metaphysical snoopers wanting to know his whereabouts and would continue to do so, as long as he had a heart beat. And there lay the rub and the subject of his galloping pulse. Spokes was not invulnerable and nothing in Darkman's stolen and acquired artefacts and oddities that he had researched over the four years could endow you with that gift. Any day under God's hot sun, Darkman and his eyes ever made four – if they ever met each other in the flesh - he knew he would draw his last breath.

But how can you kill what you can't find.

Jimmy was the only link to him and it was unlikely he could be questioned about it. Even if he was a necroscope he needed a corpse to interrogate and the whereabouts of Jimmy's mortal remains would remain hidden.

Calm down, old man.

Just cool.

Somehow that did nothing to console him.

What did was the thought of leaving all this behind and starting a new life.

Just this one dance at his night club, The Crypt, and his worries would be over.

Just one dance.

With that thought, he strode out, placing the winning receipt firmly in Ras Michael's hands, ignoring his questions with a wave, jumping into his Virage and disappearing in a haze of burning rubber and exhaust.

7.

Suzy took the glass of water from the bartender and smiled, a smile that came from that peaceful place she had struggled to find after two days of chaos and miracles but finally she felt, she was there. When you had so many adoring males fawning over your every move – her boyfriend compliments were important but sweet reinforcement from strange men with no good on their minds put an extra shine on her good mood.

Suzy thought of Y.

She imagined being able to take Y emotionally by the hand and dragging her to where she was feeling good. Tonight would go some way in achieving that but, more importantly, it would do Patra and Y some good and all thanks to Mr Patel and his kindness. Her sisters stood around her, Patra rubber necking the male talent who were reciprocating in spades and Y, trying too hard to be unimpressed with the stars of screen and song, looking completely relaxed as they danced, socialised and drank around them.

Her excitement was slowly oozing through although she was trying to remain aloof.

"I didn't realise Stylus was so short," Y said. "Seeing him in the videos he looks so, so..."

"Fit," Suzy completed the thought for her. "Short ass bwoy tink him hot but him batty flat like a bun pan. Him have a good voice though, you have to give him dat."

Y laughed, swaying gently to the music.

"Why so hostile Suzy, you're usually the one with the good word to say about everyone."

"Normally I do babe but him brush past me earlier and I don't know why but something of his essence rub off." Her eyes clouded as she recalled. "Him have some mommy issues, beat him last girlfriend badly. Mi nuh appreciate dat."

"Motherfucker!" Patra said.

An uncomfortable silence punctuated her comment and Suzy was beginning to regret having voiced her opinion but Y didn't allow it to outwardly phase her.

"It's our make-up as women, I guess. Being able to deal with it I mean but never accepting it."

"Yuh sound like Miss P," she mimicked Patra's catch phrases. "We can take it bitch, and we will hand it out again too. Built to last baby!"

"You wearing out my name again, biaatch?" Patra asked with a straight face.

"Wi just using your pearls of wisdom to make a point babe."

Patra looked at Y with a mischievous smirk on her face.

"She playin with me, right?"

"Yeah," Y said, laughing. "She playin with you."

Patra gave Suzy the fuck you finger.

"So, any other celebrities in your bad books Suzy?"

Ms Wong looked around to make sure but the star power surrounding her was dazzling.

"I know that nigga is gonna get some love, tonight." Patra held up a glass of Southern Comfort and pointed her pinky finger in the direction of US Southern rapper Rox1.

"Now he is what you see on MTV, the real McCoy baby, accept no substitutes. Damn he's packing upfront too."

Rox1 was surrounded with his entourage who looked like they took the job of his personal protection too seriously. He was amongst friends but still they maintained the human cordon of menace and exaggerated importance that comes with manufactured fame.

"Him look good but a pity 'bout the baby sitters, though. You think they tuck him in at night?"

"I damn sure hope that's all they do."

Patra smiled at the picture forming in her head and cast an appraising eye over the clubbers. Her gaze fell on a group of young women adjusting themselves vigorously and giggling. Immediately the game began. It was a habit she had of categorising groups of women in less than flattering terms and using herself as the empirical standard of ghetto chic to make her judgements. It was more fun with the girls participation but what the hell. The fidgeting group were annoying the shit out of her.

Why didn't these bitches wear their size. Wiggling their booty's into designer jeans showing ass crack, smoothing down tight fitting tops showing titty or pulling down skirts that have been riding up and showing coochie. Compliment the shape God gave you, sugahhh or use the goddamn gym.

Her mental rant over, her eyes were elsewhere.

The DJ, J A Katana, was flipping the discs with practised ease. The mixes flowed smoothly as would be expected from a man at the top of his game and it was a matter of time before Patra squealed at a track that delighted her and required her presence on the dance floor.

"I've got to dance to this Young Jeezy joint, sugahh. You coming?"

Suzy shrugged and unfurled an aberrant hem of her short black and silver dress – a knock off of a Karl Lagerfeld creation – and stroked it back to perfection. She had dressed hurriedly at Patra's place, knowing her boyfriend would be screwing at the dress's suggestive cut so Suzy didn't attempt getting ready from home. Sweet of him being jealous of the attention of other men but this was her, confident and not afraid of how she looked.

Wha' eye nuh si, heart nuh leap.

Y looked just as comfortable in her sparse Spartan themed shimmery gold outfit. She moved with self assurance, unconcerned what anyone thought of her even after all she had gone through Patra was not to be out done in the sexiness stakes. Miss P's slinky Yves St. Laurent dress that was almost backless and plunged just a delectable whisper from her coccyx defied gravity with the material exhibiting unusual characteristics of adhesion to her skin. The outfit's front was hell bent on showing you enough but not too much for your imagination to have no need for sensual spec. Suzy was wondering how she kept it in place with only a strap around her neck.

"You two can go." She said.

Patra grabbed Y's hand and pulled her onto the dance floor. A multitude of hungry male eyes followed their rush into the swelling ranks of dancers. A smile broke on Suzy's calm demeanour and she settled into supping her sparkling water with a twist of lemon.

The music thumped through the THX powered speakers, Young Jeezy's swagger on point. The smells of expensive perfume broken up by revellers wading through it like an aromatic brook. Suzy remembered how years ago partying could mean coming home smelling like a damp ashtray. It had always left a feeling of uncleanness at the nights end a niggling anticlimax at the culmination of an otherwise exciting night. Regular smokers Suzy could abide in small doses – she called Patra a joker smoker, as her cigar habit was of little consequence, one stogie every two weeks or so. The prolific smokers she could not abide by.

Maybe these thoughts triggered a faint taste of nicotine that had suddenly appeared on her tongue and a creeping sense of expectancy slivering up her spine.

The call was coming and she could do nothing to stop it. Her taste buds exploded with the taste of tar and copper. Suzy had not felt it since the last time a situation presented itself to them. A compulsion she had no choice but to attend to.

You know what yuh got to do gal, don't fight it.

It was an almost primal urge, galvanising her into looking over her shoulder. She spun in her seat following an unseen flow and let it gently guide her to the area of a fire exit on her right. Suzy with her glass in hand sipped again, the bubbles popping on her nose, her eyes locked on two casually dressed men who were in easy conversation. As if to punctuate the importance of what was being communicated to her, time dialed itself down to a crawl. In that instance, deep in the shadow a stray glimmer of light, from the state of the art lighting rig, that only Suzy could see reflected off machined chrome and tempered steel. A revelation that in a fractured second showed an automatic weapon, casually caressed in a shoulder holster of one of the men and then concealed by a fine linen designer jacket, anonymous again as if it never was there.

Suzy absorbed the scene, time resuming its pace and knew without knowing that the men's intentions were not protection but chaos. She downed the rest of her water, the phantom nicotine taste making it difficult, and turned away. Patra was about five metres behind her, a cloud of male bodies orbiting from the power of her female gravity. Both women's eyes locked and whatever weird connection they possessed communicated concern. Miss P left the attention being showered on her and danced over to her sister's side. Suzy threw a gaze back over to the duo of gunmen and watched the body language shift from preparation to determination. Their intentions set between them, they set off from the fire exit with an inconspicuous gait.

"What's good, mami?" Patra questioned and without looking away from the men, Suzy spoke low and harsh.

"It's happenin. The call is here."

"You serious?" Patra asked.

Suzy nodded.

"Bring it on, baby." Patra hooted.

"Wi could walk away?" Suzy asked.

Patra's laugh was like a shower of broken glass.

"You trippin, bitch? You know better than me that when it hollas, we come running. No sense fighting it, embrace it baby.

"No sense." Suzy said and watched Patra's perfectly formed eyebrows arched enquiringly.

"Dem two guys in the linen suits, one with deh cane row, the other with a low cut fade an deh gangsta lean, strap up. Shottas."

"How them niggas taste?"

"Copper and tar."

"Damn, shit gonna pop off, then."

"It bound to."

"Son-of-a-bitch!" Patra laughed. "And I was beginning to feel this party."

"Let's deal wid this, first." Suzy said. "And hope we have a party to come back to."

They peeled from the bar with Suzy taking the lead and snaked through the revellers on an intercept course of the two men making an unhurried walk to the VIP area. Contrary to what you would think, Suzy's mind wasn't filled with action plans and scenarios. That wasn't how their gifts worked. They would place themselves in the wild, unpredictable currents of fate, destiny or pre-destination, the word wasn't important. What was important, was that they listened with there whole bodies dipped into the waters chaos and let it take them instinctively.

A veil of adrenalin blanketed Suzy's system in a warm hug that had the effect of jump starting her senses to the level required to do what she had to do. With every touch and every glance of contact as she glided through the pockets of revelry, her sense of preparedness ramped up like spark plugs firing from a high performance car.

Suzy reached an impasse quicker than she had thought and gracefully stopped, making an assessment of three men whose timing stank and who were preparing for some chit-chat as they blocked the path of one of the finest honeys in the place. Suzy regurgitated a smile with effort and was preparing to pull back and veer right when an upwind of Christina Aguilera perfume whisked by her. The forcefulness of Y's personality was enough to disperse the male ego's intent on playing boys' games at an inopportune moment.

Bwoy better know, Suzy thought.

They backed off.

Y's question was direct and unambiguous.

"Is it serious?"

"Is the call ever not? We have two shottas and dem intentions are not honourable." Suzy said.

"How the hell did they get past security?" Y asked aloud.

"They were invited in."

A simple, unequivocal truth.

Y looked over to the right to see Patra keeping step and winking at her sisters. The men had crossed one side of the dance space and were close to the other without much resistance. Their silhouettes merged amongst the invited guests and they even shimmied with a few women as they made their way to whoever was their target but Suzy's gaze never faltered, her irises tracking them like crosshairs of a sniper. The game was always the same. Knowing what their intentions were and beating them to it. That involved allowing her crisis senses to evaluate the situation and guide her movements. She allowed her reasoning self to step back and let intuition take hold and moved with a purpose that was still unclear. Now there was three sets of eyes attuned to the threat, processing the situation in three unique ways, filtering what was useful and what could be discarded, allowing a conclusion about all this to come to them while they took action.

Without missing a step Y's sweeping focus fell on the VIP lounge tucked away in the corner of the plush floor plan, all protruding ribbed glass making a statement of its importance and the suited bouncer on duty like an obsidian sentinel.

Then, like a flash of brilliant awareness, the shared puzzle slotted into place. The Grime Rapper Grudge is standing outside of the confines of the VIP space reasoning with the bouncer with his characteristic gesticulations and body language. The revelation made Y gasp as it became all so clear what was about to go down.

Y brashly took point and it was if instructions were being sent below their awareness to Patra and Suzy to follow her lead. Suzy naturally fell back as support and Patra ran interference. Any changes in what they were about to do would be communicated with body language and a finely honed sense of the group spatial dynamics they exhibited.

As was expected, a gaggle of honeys were holding vigil outside the entrance to the VIP lounge and the flash antics of Grudge playing up to his drooling groupies would make this confrontation interesting. The shottas were out of sight for a moment as they circumvented a thick chrome plated support pillar but the moment they swung around from that Grudge would be in their line of fire. She had to reach him before they did.

Spokes had a glass of brandy in his hand, head back slightly and propped up on the bar bathing himself in the aura of celebrity that was on show tonight. The

MOBO VIP lounge was getting busy and, as you would expect, the quota of women far surpassed the quota of men. And he suspected that was how it was supposed to be. He fitted in perfectly. Not just his look which was mature but street but his easy way and that underlying attitude he had that said he was deserving of everything that came his way. It was an understated belief that he was as good as anyone, from the hip hop superstar to the Premiership footballer. Look at him, dressed elegantly but with a contemporary flair and drove a top marquee sports Mercedes from a stable of super cars. His date for the night was thirty six years his junior and she was a freak in bed with a good heart. Money was not a problem for him and if he was allowed a free reign over his life he would be happy and content from this moment on until he was unable. As it was, over the last few days his sense of gratitude was being slowly eroded. He knew a storm was coming, he just didn't know exactly how to protect himself against it; but until then, life continued.

Spokes waited for his girlfriend to return from the WC and then made his way out of the VIP Room for a quick change of setting, leaving her comfortably waiting for him. He made his way through the dance floor, appreciating the music and the young nubile bodies swaying to the sounds. Smiling with some who obviously appreciated his style, he then just stood and watched. He was beside a young man at the VIP entrance who was rocking some urban flava and almost coated in young women. The bouncers watched him nervously making sure he was not at risk but Spokes thought it should be the other way around. Those poor young girls needed protection much more than he did. His ring told him so.

Grinning with the thought another more urgent jolt of awareness from his ring superceded everything else that was on his mind. His attention shifted from the svelte bodies at the VIP entrance to one, two, three women deftly making their way through the party goers to where he was. Somehow his perception had picked them out, highlighted them and reduced everything else into obscurity. His ring responded to them like nothing else he had ever experienced. The vibration was almost bone deep, a pleasant resonance that colored his vision mauve and filled his mouth with the taste of sweet almonds. In a six sense snapshot he felt their strength and righteousness, an unnerving experience that took his breath away for a moment - beautiful women needing to get somewhere in a hurry. Spokes stood his ground buffeted by people moving around him and watched spellbound.

These young women were going to be the answer to his problems he just knew it. They were coming his way so he would let them come, finish his drink and approach them.

The force was strong in dem.

He grinned.

The ring tingled again and this time his perceptions darkened as someone or something else entered the theatre of his pretenatural awareness - a familiar warning he knew that meant retreat. He did not see the two men heading his way guns drawn. Did not know that their intentions were to murder him and take the ring. Spokes followed its urging without further speculation or question, turned and re-entered the VIP lounge as quickly as he could.

Y slid in between an opening of bodies, ignoring the protests twittering from the groupies annoyed someone else was even more loose and obnoxious than they were – and planted a kiss firmly on Grudge's lips that carried the momentum of her advances sending them both into the Cristal Lounge and stumbling to the ground. Moments later the gun men had rounded the obstruction with weapons drawn and no target in sight only hysterical squeals from some fracas ahead of them. Their target was gone and instead there was a sea of disgruntled estrogen and raised voices in his place.

The bouncer's eyes left the irate group of women on the ground for a moment inadvertently settling on the men tucking the guns back into their jackets as they approached, the slinky flaps of their designer jackets falling back into body hugging place. The bouncer whose highly developed sense of self preservation told him it was better to be judged by the twelve than carried by the six. He slipped away from a possible blood bath, his duties forgotten.

That's when the script was rewritten.

Patra and Suzy brazenly walked in front of the men as they attempted to enter the VIP lounge.

The assassins' instead of being angry were amused. Their grins gurgled up from somewhere in their bellies like aberrant belches as they looked at each other with restrained amusement.

They tried to push by.

An experiment in an irresistible force meeting an immovable object.

The girls stood their ground, shrugging the men off.

Real professionals should have known better and underestimated no one. Gun out, double tap to the head and disappear in the confusion. Instead they hesitated, assessing the determined women blocking their way with amusement first then regret.

These bitches were not the targets. Get them out the way and proceed to the hit.

How bad could that be?

Real bad motherfucker, Patra would say, if asked. Real bad.

Patience went through the window as the men attacked in a quick flurry of fists but when the smoke cleared Patra and Suzy stood looking at them, bored and unimpressed. The realisation they had wasted seconds and lost the element of surprise galvanised the men into doing what they should have done to begin with.

They reached for their weapons.

The dude sporting the cane row was a fraction slower than his colleague as his hands snaked for his gun. Suzy didn't hesitate. With a blur of movement she was up in his face, striking the bundle of nerve endings in his wrist, making his fingers involuntarily spring open and the gun clatter to the ground as if he had butter fingers. Cane Row howled and swung windmill-like with the back of his hands, trying to catch her off guard but Suzy ducked under it and deftly swayed left. She fired her elbow into his thorax; her dance had left her facing him and her fists stabbed into his thigh and knees like stilettos.

He buckled.

She gave him her back.

And like a final 'fuck you' statement she had forgotten to deliver, Suzy executed an overhead kick of balletic exquisiteness, snapping her Jimmy Choo's and dropping cane row guy on his ass.

About the same time Patra had already tucked into her Muay Thai stance, her five foot nine frame weaving, her shoulders together, hunched and fists up, releasing the right hook like it had been spat from the barrel of a shotgun. The other gun-man was in a conundrum. Block her strike or go for his gun no matter what. He voted to parry the punch.

Damn, he nearly lost balance from the force of the blow. He regained his footing, frantically reaching for the gun this time but was unable to gain his bearings or his aim. He fired and the explosion was deafening in the confined space but for all its dramatic effect it went wide lodging into the ceiling.

"You shooting at me motherfucker?" Patra growled and piledrove her foot into his chest, lifting him off his feet, separating him from his gun and sending him tumbling backwards. Both men, in their separate oases of pain struggled to compose themselves, looking like two men who had just had their asses handed to them on a platter.

By this Patra and Suzy had acquired their guns and pointed the business ends in their direction with a sort of grim resolve the men did not want to test.

"Stay on your knees boys, I'm out of practise. I don't want my gun go off accidental like," Patra said menacingly then broke into a smile. "Man that felt gooood!"

"This is nuh skin teeth business Cleo. Dem bwoy yah came to murder."

Patra pushed on the temple of one of the men on his knees with the gun.

"You came to murder biaatch?"

The man said nothing.

Patra grinned again, looking at Suzy.

"I know, I know, but come on you know what I'm saying."

Suzy grinned as Patra went on.

"They quiet though. Not big on talking."

"You just beat the shit out of two two professionals gal, what do you want dem to seh."

"How about something like,'I've had some ass kicking in my time ladies but that was the best whooping I did ever get. Thank you, thank you'." Patra laughed and Suzy rolled her eyes.

"Where's Y at anyway?"

"She is in deh VIP room. She look cool."

Patra looked at Suzy with an appraising eye and lowered her voice.

"Hey sugahh, you ever use a gun before?" Patra asked.

"No." Suzy said.

"I thought all you Jamaican bitches, knew how to bust gun," she teased.

Suzy shook her head disparagingly.

"Don't get me twisted, you got the stance right girl, legs apart an' all but in the excitement you flipped the safety on. If you gonna bust a cap in a niggas ass, you need it off."

"Dat cool," Suzy said and flicked it off with her thumb like a seasoned pro. "Better."

"Better." Patra nodded.

By this time the girls had been surrounded by an ever-growing swarm of gawking revellers. You could see the nervous smiles of uncertainty as the reality, or lack of it, was taking effect. Bouncers started appearing bemused with what they were witnessing, wondering why they had not been informed about this stunt. However, the closer they came to this surreal scenario, the more they became convinced they were witnessing something real.

Y breezed into the frenzy just as the security supervisor turned up and as succinctly as possible glossed over the parts they would not accept as truth and fabricated the rest.

Y didn't start trembling until some time after.

The girls sat together on one of the circular VIP seats and stared absently out to the deserted entrance of the nightclub. The debris of a night well and truly partied was strewn on the floor and tables. Out of the ordinary were the police officers milling around the floor plan, a few witnesses being questioned by plain clothed officers and forensic personnel in their white booties carrying equipment cases. Suzy looked calm, Patra was more on edge from the grilling by a Detective Jenkins who - if they didn't know any better – was insinuating they were more than reacting to a bad situation but were somehow involved in the situation. Y was more focused; she sat with her arms around Suzy recording everything said to them by the overzealous DI just in case it was needed in the future and was milling over his words in the confines of her head.

That freeze frame was held for a moment and through the haze of their own thoughts, the fine figure of DI Winston Shaft McFarlane stepped into the crime scene, surveying the proceedings with enough self assured swagger as if he owned the place. Shoulders raised in recognition, frowns disappeared and finally smiles imprinted on their lips as the sisters waved at him and he jogged over to them.

Shaft wasn't superstitious by any accounts, not after achieving a Master of Science in Cultural Anthropology; because that would go against everything he understood about the scientific process. Take his final paper on Jung's Archetype's and how it related to belief. That was like a guiding doctrine to how he managed the cases that came across his desk initially. But Spokes wasn't ashamed to admit Black Book had immersed him in many investigative situations that had made him momentarily question some of his long standing beliefs about fate, destiny and what was possible.

And these girls where like his counterintuitive control group, discounting everything he believed to be the way of the world. He would have remained a non believer himself, if he hadn't been a witness to the bizarre circumstances that had forged their friendship in the first place.

Now this.

He had been first at the crime scene five years ago, where he had met them and he had taken their statements back at the station. The surreal memory of that interview had remained with him. Then, just to add to their personal mythology some mental patient - who they had ascertained later was originally from Africa - they had busted in leafy Hampstead pissing on the pavement, started ranting about them being ordained warriors and how privileged he was to be in their company. He had laughed good and hard but remembered the mad man's sudden lucidity and his words.

Watunza mwanga
Three warriors to strike fear in the heart of the evil.
Three warriors to restore the balance.
Three ways, one mind, one cause, one weapon.
Watunza mwanga

Over and over he ranted on his knees, bowing to three strangers as his colleagues tried to restrain him. Today after looking at this mess, it didn't seem so funny.

One mind, one weapon.

He went by the numbers, as was expected when he had to take over an investigation from the presiding detective. Most were cool but some, like Jenkins, were a pain in the ass even when he knew this was Shaft's gig until proven otherwise.

Jenkins was shaking his head in disbelief.

"I've got this Detective. Thanks for keeping the ball rolling. Black Book will finish up."

Jenkin's scowled.

"You know this is bollocks, right. Nothing about this warrants you fucking witchdoctors being here. This has operation Trident written all over it mate."

"Remind me to buy you a Blackstone Police Manual on Evidence and Procedure for Christmas."

"Fuck you McFarlane."

"In your dreams Detective. In the meantime, keep your hard on to yourself, I've a got an investigation to complete, excuse me."

Jenkins stormed off muttering something about ass lickers but his insults had already been relegated to the back of McFarlane's mind.

Shaft had other things to worry about.

If ever he developed the stones to be honest with them, he would admit that circumstances like this had him in awe of them. He almost expected the normal flow of events to be altered when these three came together. Like heavenly bodies distorting the normal laws of physics or reason.

He approached the excited girls and hugged them all in turn, stepping back to check for any damage or injury.

What was he talking about; police procedure?

His stare remained on Y longer than normal.

"You three okay?"

"Hell yeah. Ask the other guys that," Patra said.

"You didn't have to go through all of this to get my attention ladies. A call would do." Shaft smirked.

"The first time was circumstance remember," said Y.

"Second time was bad luck," Suzy added.

"Third time...",Patra paused. "...is a goddamn charm."

Shaft laughed and knew he shouldn't but couldn't help it. Trying to stay professionally detached from the girls was like dancing the tango with a new partner who knew the steps but wasn't certain of the new routine through lack of practise. They had danced this dance before and although it was familiar, it was nonetheless uncomfortable.

"So Y," Shaft began. "Tell me, what happened?" The joviality had departed from his tones and the practiced formality of police procedure slipped into place. The sisters huddled around him. Suzy and Patra looked over to Y who began, re-enacting the incident in her mind, trawling the mess of pictures and jumbled word associations floating behind her eyes and picked the right ones that would be more acceptable for his notes and making sure she downplayed the sense of relief that Shaft had arrived at the scene. Y was almost compelled to reach out and touch his arm but she resisted. Instead she watched him tap into his tablet, his shoulders square and his poise comfortable.

"I tried calling you," Y said pausing after completing her account of their recent misadventure.

"You mean just now?"

"No, six days ago. We had a bit of a situation."

"I have to apologise for that Y, ladies, the workload was intense. I was waiting for a window to call but you found a way to get my attention anyways. What happened?"

"Another story dat John, for another time."

"Fair enough, Miss Wong," Shaft looked over to Y again.

"We were depressed," she began. "Mr Patel thought this would be a great idea for us to re-energise."

"From what happened six days ago?"

They nodded.

Shaft started tapping the stylus on the touch screen and when he was done looked up as if he was inviting Y to continue.

Suzy continued.

"I saw the man dem first and then the guns."

"We been doing this a minute now and we know when shit is about to get grimy." Patra added.

"Did you know the men at all?"

They shook their heads.

"All we knew shit was going down and we stepped in."

"You sound apologetic, don't be. They were obviously in here targeting someone. Whoever it was doesn't realise you just saved their lives."

He tapped the stylus on his PDA and lowered his voice.

"I can't believe I'm saying this, but the compulsion you girls share to have a go in dangerous situations is amazing or stupid. I haven't decided yet. I just keep asking myself, especially after that bank episode Five years ago, that you girls attract circumstances like this. And the frightening thing is that you are more than capable of handling the fallout on your own."

"Just keep having our back," Patra said.

"I'll try."

Shaft motioned over to two female police officers then faced the girls again.

"I'm going to have to get your statements separately. So I'll continue with Y."

Patra and Suzy broke into spontaneous laughter.

"Sergeants Peacemaker and Summers will deal with you two troublemakers."

"Anything you say, Detective, sir," Patra teased parodying some silver screen actress from a nineteen forties B movie, leaving Shaft to shake his head in amusement.

"Just go before I cuff you both."

"Don't make promises you can't keep, Detective," Patra crooned, still in character.

8.

South Kensington Dojo
Saturday, July 13th
9.35am

Y heard the swish of the blade as it sliced the air to her midsection and only at the last minute did she block the stroke with her katana, spinning away from the parry and blocking the thrusting wakizashi from the nimble old man that seemed hell bent on piercing her carotid artery with the lethal dagger.

You tend to forget that Master Azimoko was seventy five years old especially when he was in combat mode. His movements were nimble and fluid. Like a chess master, each step, each strike of his katana constituted a pattern of katas that would lead to the defeat of his opponent. His expertise was hardwired into his diminutive frame from decades of practice, racial memory from ancestors who were also samurai and if Japanese mythology was to be believed the spirits of long dead masters inhabited the worthy.

None of this was on Y's mind as she deflected his thrust with her wakazashi and gracefully spun away from him, knowing as she came around that their blades would kiss and they did. Then she struck low expecting the force of impact and seeing the flash of surprise in the masters eyes as his reaction to the movement faltered. Y pulled back just enough for him to see she had incapacitated him.

That had never happened before.

They froze in position for seconds, their dazzling martial arts ballet ending after five minutes of intensity.

Y bowed to the old Japanese master, who reciprocated. She stepped back into a yaku stance and gripped the handle of her samurai sword sheathing it.

Grand Master Azimoko eyed the strong set of her legs, the measured deep breath and the controlled power with which she replaced the Masammune sword. He nodded as a way of ending their session and showing his pleasure at her progress.

From the penny section Suzy and Patra stood up and applauded loudly.

Y smiled over at them, cheeks flushed embarrassingly at their enthusiasm and bowed deeply in the direction of the greying, diminutive sometimes irascible master Azimoko. Having the opportunity to practise with him was not just about the honour of improving her kendo technique with a veritable legend but after many years of working with him she looked forward to his visits.

His lack of pretension and his eager quest to understand the 'unenlightened' westerners was ripe with comedic potential. And the grandmaster played it straight.

Even finding time to comment on Y's funky coloured nails before they began a kata session.

"A talented hawk hides its claws", he commented in passing leaving Y scratching her head at the meaning. Usually he was a straight talking little man who had a natural way of encouraging you to higher achievement while pointing out your weaknesses as steps or hindrances to achieving the ultimate goal of perfection.

The old man travelled to the UK from Seki province once a year to show his support to his satellite schools teaching his Kendo styles to the west while fulfilling his passion for Earl Grey tea, British history, Oprah and Judge Judy. Master Azimoko also had a similar relationship with five other students throughout the country who, through recommendations and other unusual circumstances over the years, he would personally meet with them and test their mettle against his expertise in a real competition.

Y's claim to fame wasn't just her natural prowess with a katana or improving on her technique but the katana itself. Pops, on his many jaunts to Japan and the Far East when he was younger, was bequeathed with a treasure, he immediately gave to his daughter. The katana was forged by the legendary master sword smith Masamune in 1302 in Japan, it was one of his finest works using a metallurgy technique he tried seven times and because of the inordinate complications in its process he decided never to try that method again. Legend says from it he created seven swords with Y's katana included. The ill fated process created a blade that was balanced, sharp, strong and very light. So it was one of seven masterpieces that were priceless, and in master Azimoko's estimation needed tempering with regular bouts of conflict. And so did the wielder of the blade. Y could expect a written report from him on traditional paper and ink in Japanese with a translated print out. Tucked away within its folds would be an invitation to au revoir lunch before the master left for home.

That she would not miss.

The teacher-student formalities out of the way Y walked over to the girls, her traditional samurai suki looking stiff and unyielding but worn by the right wearer allowing enough give and take for battle.

Patra arrived first to hug her, laughing.

"Damn girl you getting real good with that thing. I gotta be careful how I fuck with you now. Shit."

Suzy hugged them both, all three rocking together and smiling.

"Yuh did brilliant sis, We gonna need to practise with the Chinese wushu swords together sometime. See if yuh can tek me."

"That would be cool."

"Okay, now when you bitches have finished getting hot and sticky over your sword fetish, can we go get some breakfast or something? I'm hungry."

"I'm way ahead of you and I invited a guest to eat with us too."

"If she have big titties or a tight ass I'm cool wid it," Patra chirped.

"Not just a tight ass but a good heart."

"DI MacFarlane," Suzy concluded.

"None other."

"Isn't there some Brit law against a police officer making booty calls to suspects of a crime."

"I suppose."

"He doesn't seem to mind." Y said sharply.

"I'm just saying." Jokingly, Patra puts up her arms in a defensive posture. "Anyway we didn't do shit. We ain't suspects but concerned citizens who happened to put the beat down on two punk ass motherfuckers."

"Not sure if that makes a difference, in the eyes of the law."

"Fuck the law. If his fine ass wants to spend some time with us, who in the British judicial system can tell me we can't."

"Amen." Suzy grinned. "But don't get too hot under deh collar gal, you are not deh main attraction."

"So you keep reminding me." Patra muttered.

Suzy continued unaffected.

"Nuh get mi wrong sis, I'm glad to see him again, even after the other night but is this business or pleasure."

Y shrugged.

"A bit of both I guess. You know he worries about us."

"You 'specially." Suzy said.

"And he'll be even more worried if my sexy ass dies of starvation. Let's bounce, man. Where we headed anyway?" Patra inquired.

"Don't you worry your pretty little head about that, just bring your appetite and your sharp wit."

Six steps ahead of them in the direction of the exit Patra calls back.

"Two thing I never leave home without, sugahh."

Parkhurst Industrial Park
South East London

The silver Audi A6 trundled into the condemned industrial park with its inhabitants silent. Deacon sat back in the plush seats with his index fingers touching at the tips and placed contemplatively under his lower lip. He was wearing a black Ozwald Boateng suit, white shirt and black tie.

Minty's funeral was well attended by allies and enemies alike and as much as Deacon had demanded it to be a celebration he had come away from it with a dull ache of loss in his chest. His right hand man had been murdered by a ghost that walked amongst men. A duppy, which was decimating his numbers and laying waste to everything he had bled to achieve. There would be causalities, he knew but not his brethren, not Minty. Especially not after finally knowing how he could fight back and win.

Deacon sighed and leaned back into the seat, eyes closed. The soldier that sat beside him looked uncomfortable because this was not a routine assignment of protection as was usual and his nervousness was showing by the set of his thick lips and the no-nonsense ridges formed by eyebrows preparing for conflict. He looked straight ahead at the white upholstery which was the only calming visual cue he had to put his mind at ease, the smell of fine leather prepared him for nothing more sinister than a good, cussing.

The sedan pulled up into the shadows of a dilapidated warehouse and stopped. Mounds of disused equipment, concrete chunks, shredded metal, all caste off's from architecture that had been crushed beyond recognition, lay on both sides. Old bridge and jib cranes stood rusting, twisted and worn, looking like Decepticons who had battled for Earth dominance and lost spectacularly. Troy the driver switched off the engine.

Deacon sighed and leaned back into his seat. He loved the battle of wills with whoever was willing to compete with him. Silence was one of the most effective tools at his disposal and he was wielding it particularly effectively against this fuck up.

What this pussy didn't realise, although all the signs were pointing in that direction, was his tolerance for excuses was at an all time low today. If the soldier who sat beside him had two brain cells to rub together he would know that a dark psychotic temperament could foreshadow his boss's actions in periods of stress, resulting in explosive outbursts of violence. It had to be done to keep healthy Deacon told himself. Release the gases of frustration, anger, betrayal and disappointment steadily so as not to fall into sudden meltdown like a volcano erupting.

This was how he balanced the murderous currents that buffeted him inside. He was practising that now.

He had just buried his childhood friend, sole confidante and partner in crime. Deacon had thought long and hard, made plans, good plans, that would unerringly lead to Enoch Lacombe making a costly mistake, a mistake he would be witness to and one he would make sure he paid dearly for. But how was he to achieve this outcome, if his soldiers could not follow instructions.

Deacon loosened the black tie around his neck, glanced at the gold leafed funeral programme for Leroy 'Minty' Thelwell – he had spared no expense in sending off his friend in fine style and rested it on his lap. He looked down at his friends smiling face and grimaced that the funeral was a closed casket affair. Darkman had treated him brutal.

Next he took off his black fedora and placed it on top of that. Feeling more comfortable he leaned back into the seat.

Deacon wouldn't utter a word until the other man spoke, no matter how long it took. The award for duration went to a female; fifteen minutes of silence before she broke and then he broke her. He savored the peace and waited.

Troy the driver seemed to sense it could be a long wait, so he stepped outside for what could only be a cigarette but walking an inordinately long distance to light up. Troy needn't have worried, the cockroach in the dock spoke up.

Deacon checked his watch in disgust; Four minutes. Pussy.

"The operation didn't go to plan, Deacon. Three women step in and get involved then after that the whole operation went pear shaped."

"You don't say." Deacon spat. "You were told to bring this bwoy Spokes finger with the ring on it to me. You had two trigga man with you to accomplish the task and here you are giving me excuses about three women."

"Deacon, look I..."

Deacon's index finger snapped up to his lips and Prentiss went mute immediately.

"No ring, two of my best trigga man pan lock dung and you waltz in, smelling like a rose with excuses. That have me worried and you know what, I'm the distrusting sort from morning."

Deacon opened the door his elbow rested on and stepped out of the car as if he needed fresh air to continue talking.

He suddenly peered back in at him.

"You should have asked deh Babylon for witness protection."

He slammed the door shut and walked two paces away.

Prentiss did not move but instead stared straight ahead bug eyed, the muscles of his neck taut.

The time it took Deacon to reach into his jacket for his pre-rolled spliff and slip it into his parted lips, a silent shadow floated out of the industrial detritus on the other side of the Audi. A gloved hand gently touched the passenger side glass and Prentiss looked up from inside sensing he was being watched. Three silenced rounds punctured the glass in rapid succession, exploding the interior in a crimson shower. The assassin stood beside the car with the gun smoking in the chill morning, almost reverently looking at his handywork.

Deacon lit the spliff took a draw and glanced over to the passenger seat and then at Troy.

"Clean up dat piece a shit and bring me my replacement ride."

Troy spoke into his mobile and the massive shutter doors to their right clattered open and the roar of the V8 engined Silver Mercedes 400SL made its presence felt by idling up beside the blood spattered Audi and stopping. The driver opened up the door and literally jumped out in greasy overalls and a tool pan. The man had long shoulder length auburn hair, pale complexion, Ozzy Osbourne type dark shades and a brilliant smile that bellied his profession of a gangland fixer.

"I thought yuh were busy?" Deacon asked, taking an intake of smoke.

"I was but as one of my best customers I made the effort," he walked over to the Audi and opened the door.

"Nice bouquet. Can't accuse you Jamaican's of being boring. I think your man shit himself though Mr Deacon.

"I wouldn't expect anyting less from a pussy like him. When will I get my car back with all traces of his sorry rass gone?"

Ozzy scratched his head.

"No body work required, window repair, bullet retrieval, upholstery repair and cleaning. I'll bring it over tomorrow."

Deacon had already slipped into the Mercedes and his driver was pulling away as he recounted events in his head and weaved in new strategies into the tapestry of his ever evolving plans. Messr. Remy his Haitan Vodun had warned them about the powerful guard ring Spokes wore – he had recognised from a set of surveillance photograph's they had taken of him. Only then had Deacon started to understand why all of their attempts to capture him had failed. No torture sessions to extract what Spokes knew would be possible if they could not get close to him. It would take magic to give them a window of opportunity so they could render his charmed jewellery inert. The shottas had been rendered non-threatening to Spokes guard ring for literally one hundred heart beats by an elaborate spell Remy had conjured - time enough to relieve deh country bwoy of his finger. Instead the reports from a watcher he had planted in the club made it clear, that this would not be as straightforward as he had hoped because now there were three more roadblocks to having this situation resolved. Deacon swore again on his nine month old baby's life, that Minty's murder would be avenged and no manner of fuck ups or incompetence would be excused from today onward.

The women who had intervened were obviously working for Spokes. How they knew this was about to happen and how they so easily got the better of some seasoned hard men, were questions to be left unanswered for now. In another time, under other circumstances he would examine these three bitches in more detail. But unfortunately for them they had become just three more victims. Three more hindrances amongst the throng of informers and wanksters but what did his old lady say? *Deh hotter deh battle, deh sweeter deh victory.*

"Amen, to dat, mama." He murmured."Amen to dat."

Stockwell Locks, Housing Estate
23.35

The lone figure of Enoch Lacombe stood with his hands in his pockets, back against a street lamp that was flickering uncontrollably above him. In no hurry, he leaned up and moved away from his point of rest, immediately absorbed by darkness that cloaked him as the street lamp died with his departure. Enoch Lacombe was as much a part of the shadows as the shadows themselves. His favoured long black coat trailed behind him as if the darkness pulled on him like a dying star whose gravity held fast to everything in its vicinity. He cast his eyes over the concrete jungle that was Stockwell Locks Housing Estate, welcoming the onslaught of memories that ambushed him.

This was one of his ends, a bank of goodwill, favours and retribution had been deposited in the past and he had every intention of making a withdrawal sometime soon. But first he wanted to feel what the situation was, absorb the present circumstances into himself and then decide his course of actions.

Stepping onto the grass verge his broad black trilby concealing his features, his long coat moving with him as if it were alive, he let the sensations emanating from the drab grey buildings engulf him as he moved steadily amongst them. The flow of evil that he was more sensitive to than most was what excited him about this city. Like a potter, his clay was the ebb and flow of depravity that the city's inhabitants deposited like a sewer and which made his incantations so much easier to manifest.

"INFORMER MUS' DEAD!"

The shout from one of the flats held a note of menace. Some warning to a neighbour or a statement of relief after a murder committed. Noises came from all corners as if the concrete itself was joining in.

Laughter.

Manic and shrill.

A joke told to the madman's schizophrenic self that could have been shared, but the punch-line could only be understood if you were capable of entering the warped psyche.

He-he-he-he-he-he-he-he-he-he!

And so he continued annoying and persistent. His cackling needling its way into deep sleep or keeping the dreary eyed awake.

"SHUT THE FUCK UP YOU WANKER!" came the hoarse cry of desperation from a neighbouring block.

You were given the impression that it was just a matter of time before laughing boy would be found by a group of sleep deprived vigilantes and flung from the fourteenth floor.

"He-he-he-he-he-he-he-he!"

Splaaaat!

The man adjusted the coat around his shoulders and directed his piercing eyes to new sounds.

His heightened senses could feel the high rise buildings radiating tremors of Grime and Dancehall music along the building's framework. Four hundred watt speakers that were over equipped for an auditorium were throwing out seismic waves of sound in a ten-by-five bedsit.

Cats squealed, dogs barked and the sounds of faked orgasms - which to his ears may well have been fed through amplifiers - added to the mix.

This vibrancy would continue until exhaustion brought peace in the hours of dawn.

And then the cycle would begin again.

He appreciated the chaos, the confusion making his skin tingle and focused on what he had to do.

Darkman finally stopped and looked up at the lighted squares on a dark rectangular tableau that was Columbus House. He took the trilby off his head, and inhaled the spores of degeneracy and corruption like a wolf, tracking his prey.

He smiled hungrily.

Stockwell Locks, Housing Estate
Columbus House, Flat 915

"A wha wrong wid dis bloodclaat baby, man?" Chips pulled the bedroom door shut stifling the sounds of the child's sobs and continued to put crack crystals in small self seal bags.

Taking up a woman with another man's yout was not a habit he endorsed or wanted circulated around town but these were extraordinary circumstances. And if he said so himself, it was inspired genius. What was the best way to circumvent the arduous graft and considerable risk to life of establishing a notorious rep in the drugs business?

To be vouched for, of course, or by circulating the story that he was the caretaker of the child of one of the most feared men residing in London at the time - even if that awe was based on not just gangster exploits but by being an accomplished obeah worker, and the real McCoy. The very same man Chips had a hand in sending to prison for a very long time indeed.

He had never truly ascribed to his parents beliefs in the powers of the old ways but reliable sources, sceptics with greater doubt than himself swore that Enoch Lacombe was a necromancer of great power who also favoured the collection of old valuables, artistic and arcane artefacts. Stories leaked out about diamond encrusted crosses, chalices made from gold, African masks peppered with precious stones, manuscripts, books and crates filled with oddities, antiquities and hard cash. At that time the Witch Doctor was working his magic with Sandra, an ambitious and beautiful ghetto chick who had converted a part of her flat into a gambling den. Clean, warm and with Sandra acting as a hostess the news spread to all the gambling pros and hustlers that it was a Spot. Reggae artists, gangsters, hustlers would all pass through the doors and Darkman would over see it all from the wings.

At that time Chips was a weekend regular, meeting the notorious Darkman only once in his visits - and that was one time too many. You immediately knew there was something about him, something malevolent. Softly spoken, a firm handshake, soulless eyes that knew things no one else did with a whiff of controlled anger that was never expressed but you felt was being restrained from bursting forth Hulk style.

It wasn't personal and although Chips didn't like his air of superiority – of course he did not admit to himself that he was frightened of him too - it was his taste for valuables that decided his fate. Chips hatched the plan with this St Lucian kid who had worked closely with Darkman for some years expecting to be given secrets to wealth for his dedication but saw only hard work and promises ahead of him. The operation required re-sources, they did not have so that's how the drug lord Deacon got involved – a mistake in hindsight, Chips thought but it was what it was. Together they organised the shake down and the frame up that landed Enoch Lacombe in jail. What they did not expect was to come away from the whole sorry incident with nothing for their troubles, the treasure spirited away as if it never existed.

Enoch was sent down for racketeering, theft and murder – thirty years minimum – and that's when Chips embryonic plan began to show a keen interest in Sandra. He kept a low profile for weeks hedging his bets that maybe, just maybe the Darkman was capable of escaping from prison. Was this an elaborate part of the Darkman's grand plans? After all he was a gifted obeah man and smart too but that had never happened. And with all such things that the street elevated to cult status Darkman's power and mythology waned.

Chip's concluded he was a fake and felt even more justified setting him up in the first place. All that unnec-essary fear he had harboured.

What a waste!

His focus then became Sandra and his plan blos-somed to what it was now. She was a beautiful dark skinned woman with an air about her that was more suited to the middle classes than the ghetto classes that frequented her home. Then again some sisters were turned on by the danger and once they set along that path it was a trend that was difficult to break. Armed with all this and *nuff* discreet inquiries later he found out that the posing and the big timer lifestyle pre-Darkman had evaporated and she had fallen on hard times with a young child, living on the ninth floor.

Chips elected himself as her saviour.

He thought of it as standing on the shoulders of giants, some misinformation here and there, namely that Darkman had given his consent for Chips to look after his woman in his absence - a story that could not be confirmed or denied strangely enough. Darkman's high security prisoner status meant visitors were limited to family members, friends - at the discretion of the Warden and his legal team only. Chips had tried the procedure himself and was met with a really weird request. Darkman wanted to have no visitors family, friend or legal.

And that meant peace of mind and that his story was bullet proof. All he had to do now was keep the Spot a hit with the punters and find any clues to Darkman's treasure from the inside.

Unfortunately that mouth watering prospect came with its burdens.

A four year old juvenile from hell.

The incessant gurgling, screaming and exploratory destruction was bad and nappy changing was the worst. He farted and fired streams of milk-based shit with ballistic velocity in mid change, leaving the cloying stench of digested baby food permeating the air. For the sort of clientele that was attracting to the Spot he couldn't have that. Trying to transact a deal with a serious player and then wading through a mountain of nappies to get to your merchandise, was not cool.

The problem was Sandra loved the pickney dearly and trying to convince her adoption was the best option was not a good idea. Sandra's hatred of him plumbed new depths and he slowly sidelined the mother and her infant to the spare room. Any cross border movement had to be done with his mother in tow or there would be hell to pay.

It seemed to be working because she truly believed he hated the child due to fact it was Darkman's offspring. Chips wished it was that straight forward.

There was something not quite right about that child, something he could never quite put his finger on. It wasn't just a pathological dislike either. How could he hold a grudge against a child because of its parents? Not even he wad that callous.

That was some immature pickney business that he did not ascribe to. After all he was a grown ass man. But he couldn't ignore how his mood would take precipitous dives around the kid and he, seemed to have the same effect on the infant too. Can you see something of the father in a child so young? Chips was not one for deep inquiring thought but he couldn't help asking the question. And even now the hairs on the back of his neck stood on end.

A gurgling, shit smelling informer, whose sole purpose was to remind all suitors the true king to his mothers throne was locked away for life. He appreciated why the kings of yore on the History Channel would not just execute traitors but their whole families.

Little Rowan was evil.

Even the thought made his stomach knot and his knees go weak. Disquiet telegraphed through time and jangled his nervous system, transporting him back to the flat with that demon pickney asleep, passing the room with its crib, the door closed and listening to a child who could barely speak, annunciating words in an un-recognizable language, over and over again like scratched record in guttural inhuman tones that even he knew was impossible from the vocal chords of an infant.

As long as that child stayed the fuck away from him he was good.

More important to him right now was making sure the dollars kept flowing and as he eyed suspiciously the assorted clientele of gamblers, thieves and druggists, he snuggled into his favourite corner and made sure his old forty five was on his table, greased and ready to transact business if anyone felt the need to test him.

Sandra brushed away a strand of hair from her eyes and tested the warmth of the baby's feed by dotting some of the mixture on the back of her hand. The contents temperature was okay for Rowan's delicate palette and so she screwed the teat on and made for the sitting room.

It was if she was trapped in a bubble of tranquillity that would burst if she opened the door from the kitchen.

She hesitated for a moment and listened.

The sounds of the crisp cards being flicked by professional fingers like the harsh flight of cockroaches filtered in from the adjoining room.

Strange the places she felt comfortable in within her own home.

She looked at her surroundings with a detached almost otherworldly familiarity. As if all this time her essence had been elsewhere and she experienced everything through the eyes of this body that she was not familiar with.

Unwashed plates in the sink, glasses and greasy pots, cooking oil sprayed from a frying pan in constant use formed a sticky residue on the wall nearest the stove. The bin was full and smelling of spoilt food and ripe nappies.

Sighing, she gazed at the spectacle with eyes like a tired mountaineer who was wondering if she had taken on one insurmountable peak too many.

Another chore to complete.

She rested the bottle on the draining board and leaned back.

All of this was the sum total of the challenges life threw at her outside of raising her son, a therapeutic escape comprising of Fairy washing up liquid, soggy sponges and greasy plates, a doorway into herself, away from the frustration, the constant demands, sexual advances and worthless promises.

The pit was closing in on her but the response wasn't one of a desperate struggle to get out, instead it was making herself comfortable, in a state of complete acceptance. Succumbing to what felt like to her an overpowering force of apathy that held her fast while simultaneously sapping her of all impetus.

That was one way of explaining her eroding standards to herself. In another life almost, another place in time the kitchen would have been sparkling.

She bent down, tying the mouth of the black garbage bag filling the kitchen with its filthy bouquet. A face looked back at her from the polished metal surface of the toaster that she didn't recognise.

Look at me, she kept muttering to herself. Look at me.

Sandra was never plain looking even with the most conservative descriptions. Crude oil black skin, silky long eye lashes shading eyes like glistening dark pools, and her subtly strong features making her remember what Enoch used to call her, his Queen of Spades. Other than the changes in her body from pregnancy and the frown marks around her mouth she had not changed much physically. It was that aura of hopelessness that branded her, a stark statement of decline all could see that shuffled around with her like a colostomy bag. What she knew for sure was that her strength of will was dying and she did not seem to care.

The door bell began to ring and Sandra straightened herself and wiped her eyes.

Suddenly she zoned out for a moment, standing still as a tombstone as if expecting something else besides Rowan's frustrated wail.

"Sandra baby," Chips gruff voice grated on her nerves. "Answer deh door nuh. And on your way jus see to deh yout."

As she expected.

"You rang mi lord," she whispered to herself, cringing at his inability to call her son by name.

If only she had choices.

She grabbed the bottle and headed into the lounge, allowing her eyes to make no contact with anybody within the bull pen - the area where they sat, gambled and dealt drugs - and walked briskly down the corridor. Placing her palms on the cold metal of the reinforced doors, she peered through the peephole. Other than being exceptionally dark beyond, a small umbra of light leeching from under her door could not penetrate outwards very far - she guessed the feral kids had busted the corridor lights.

She could see no one.

Frowning, Sandra turned back to Rowan's screams that had scaled up a few decibels but five paces away and the bell rang again. She stopped, turned shaking her head and approached the entrance with less urgency. A foot away, she stretched on her tip toes, placing both her palms on either side and peered through the peep hole. Seeing nothing, her eyes came closer to the concave lens.

Giant eyes blinked back at her, making Sandra flinch, her breath caught in her throat. The magnified eyes receded and she sighed with relief.

It could only be one of those mysterious high rollers who brightened up the shit hole she called home with their smooth exploits and stories of life as a hustler. She undid the latches and bolts and swung open the door.

No one stood there.

She glanced both ways.

As she suspected, the line of fluorescent lights that stretched along the landing had all been smashed open like insect pupae and the contents of its illumination sucked dry.

Some fool playing stupid games with her.

She couldn't see any further than the light from inside the flat would permit. It had cut a section into a slab of darkness that for all intents and purposes was a solid thing.

Sandra was held there for some reason.

Listening, soft breathing from the darkness.

Smelling, a subtle aftershave that permeated the landing.

Her breath held.

There was someone there watching her, she could feel it. Someone nestled in the folds of darkness, comfortably unseen and completely at home.

She waited, foolishly expectant of something to come to her. Knowing on the periphery of her thoughts that she could dash back inside and slam the door shut leaving the presence where it was.

Instead Sandra stood her ground, the darkness inching closer to where she stood. What should have been terror that rooted her to the spot was a profound, longing.

"A who dat at deh door?" Chips' voice startled her. The spell broken she quickly looked away not noticing a playing card spin out of the darkness and flutter to the floor near the doorway. Looking back she saw it face down.

Shaking she bent to take it up.

Rowan screamed in the background.

"Sandra!" Chips bellowed, having not heard her since he hollered her name the first time.

She turned the playing card over in her hand, her eye widened at the sight of the Queen of Spades and in the next instance Sandra was on the floor being propped up by someone who smelt of Paco Rabanne and seeing Chips' bearded face in the background telling her she would be alright.

"Jus' relax baby, your good."

9.

Y's Mom's place, Acton
Sunday, July 14th
6.00 am

"Yeeeeeeeesssssss!"
The squeal that issued from the telephone's speaker made Y pull the mobile from her ears and wince. Only one person she knew showed her enthusiasm with such a lack of restraint so early in the morning.

"I'm glad somebody's on top of the world."

"Hell, yeah," Patra shouted. "And if you got any chutzpah left in your tired ass you would be too."

Patra grudgingly had Y's attention, and although she was trying to maintain a veneer of cool she was just as eager to find out what Patra was so upbeat about. The recent weeks had not been an example of how life was worth living.

"Have you read today's papers yet?"

Y frowned.

"Girl you know I don't read the tabloids. More fiction than fact. Anyway it's six in the morning, the shops aren't open yet."

"Say after me, tablet computing." Patra annunciated slowly as if Y was deaf and not technology challenged. "I got my digital copy already and that, girlfriend, makes you shit out of luck in experiencing the turning point in our lives. Don't be like, I never knew this was happening P because now you know."

Y stifled a snicker.

"You sure you're okay?"

"Bitch don't play." Patra dismissed the question. "And stop goddamn asking me if I'm fine. Now get your sexy black ass out of bed and mosey on down to your local newsagent and pick up a copy."

"I thought you were going to read the story to me."

"You tripping or you high?"

"Can't you at least give me some idea of what I should be looking for, what page is it on?"

"No fun in that, sugahh."

"Misses, it's six in the morning, it's too early for fun."

"Never too early or late for adventure girlfriend," she chirped.

"You killing me, here." Y said.

"Bitch, please."

And with that profound statement Cleopatra Jones hung up.

"You cow!" Y grimaced.

Y sat in her velour track suit and sipped an orange juice, the house to herself as her mom had gone to work. She had been to her Dojo this morning and performed some vigorous shiai with some other kendo practitioners. Edicts of respect aside, Y had cut a swath through her opponents and felt great about her improving skills.

She had stopped by the Outpost corner shop on her way home and bought the paper Patra recommended. Maybe it was her smile or the fact that she had openly expressed her dislike for the tabloid that made Mohammed the proprietor shake his head in disbelief.

Now it lay neatly on her breakfast bar beside which was an empty glass made opaque by the remains of a protein shake and a small dish with moist flakes of cereal still warm from her breakfast.

Patra knew that when it came to her dreams and their attainment she had no sense of humour at all. Combine that with a call so early in the morning and this was tantamount to cruel and unusual punishment.

This had better be momentous.

Y spread open the newspaper and proceeded to make her way through the articles grimacing as she read carefully through the news print, looking for the life changing reportage - she needn't have worried.

Y was turning over the sheets of newsprint onto page seven when she flung her hands off the table and gasped. The stool she was sitting on flew backwards and clattered to the floor. She jumped to her feet, hands planted on either side of the newspaper, her body taut, arms flexing and a mild current of excitement running up and down her spine.

"Wow!"

The AM/PM gossip columns were packed with celebrity photos and brief stories but in the centre of the panel was the gem of a shot.

It had three sexy women stepping out of the MOBO awards after party at the Q Club as if it was staged. They were caught just as they walked off the last step suspended in mid air, sexy fashion icons with eyes alert and focused ahead at the shadows. Ahead of them was the obscure image of a man. Underneath the image was the caption.

Personal Protection Has A New Sexy Image.

"Wooow!" She said again but this time with emphasis.

The short article went into enough detail and fabrication about what happened on the night to paint a portrait of glamorous fiction interspersed with truth.

Who are these beautiful bodyguards? That was the final question posed in the article.

"I can answer that," she murmured. "That's us but we don't exist, we're fiction."

Y reached down and picked up the stool and sat, calming herself.

Bodyguards? Where did that come from? But Y knew not to question how the die fell because from experience and with a certainty deep in her core it was significant to them.

Bad II the Bone had tripped up and fallen on their feet. Now she understood Patra's bleating about life changing shit.

Christ.

They must have made a hell of an impression that night, shifting the course of their destiny without being aware.

A Powwow had to be called as soon as possible. The meaning of all this needed to be discerned if there was meaning to be had. Already Y was constructing her cover story for the many questions her clients would inevitably be asking when they saw this.

Her vibrating phone did a merry little dance on the breakfast table. Moments later her landline started ringing too.

This she could not be asked to deal with.

If staying by her Mom was not stress enough, the fall out from the tabloids' news would send her Facebook and Twitter profiles at least bacterial if not viral.

Y sat tired, sweaty and horny and considered where they were being led this time. Whether she liked it or not a new chapter in her life was on the horizon.

She could hear Patra in her head.

"Be careful what you wish for bitches, it has a tendency of coming true."

Monday, July 15th
Mr Patel's private offices
10.35am

The girls sat in Mr Gauresh Patel's office facing him as he sat in front of his desk, computer on standby and his walls filled with photographs of celebrities who seemed to be pleased to be in his presence. All around him were the trappings of success and only an exquisitely painted mural of Shiva meditating on the wall above from where he sat, was set apart from the usual.

Patra had her pedicured feet on the edge of his desk, getting as comfortable as possible but as always lost for words as her mind tried to understand the geeky Hindu across the table who had so much ghetto shine, but who had nothing to do with the movie or music business. Well, as far as they knew at least, and that fact alone made him a cool enigma in Patra's mind. Broach the subject of Mr Patel in the girls company and it was nothing but love for him. But it was his business acumen that Suzy and Y were really impressed with. Who else could they go for expert advice in this surreal situation that they found themselves in?

They sat respectfully upright having listened to a business proposal that had sprung from the coincidence of the weekend. Really Mr Patel should have given the kudos for this business creation to the hacks who had jumped to conclusions as usual in the name of cutting edge journalism.

But capturing a good idea was one thing, being able to work out its feasibility for success in the market was a completely different beast. Mr Patel had a great eye for investments and his millionaire status wasn't a consequence of any financial legacy but a literal business eye he kept talking about. A five-star hotel, six, five-star gyms, seven restaurants and six real estate agencies and you begin to respect the power of this 'twitchy' eye of his.

Y was leaning forward without knowing as the usual taciturn Mr Patel enthused in his own understated way and let the girls into his prodigious business mind. He had thought of the angle and the marketing models he wanted to employ and was willing to back his faith in them with cold hard sterling. The idea had him so excited that the first line of his marketing copy was already written fully formed and on the table for the girls to see.

Bad II the Bone
Intimate Protection - The World's First Escort Protection Agency

"Damn, Mr P. Intimate Protection. I like." Patra enthused. "And the skull and cross bones, that is bad ass, right there."

"Bodyguards?" Y questioned. "What do we know about protection services?"

"Think about it," Mr Patel said sagely. "You've saved my life haven't you? How many times have you accompanied me to events looking out for my welfare? And who knows how many times you have done that with was a clear and present threat to my person without mentioning it to me. You are naturals and I have a good feeling about this."

Y nodded.

"It feels suh right," Suzy said. "In front a weh nose an' wi just nevah realise it."

"I feel the same Ms Wong." Mr Patel said. "I know this is new territory and you may have a million concerns and my job is to smooth the rough edges, no expenses will be spared for that," the entrepenuer stressed.

Patra whistled with a grin that threatened to crack her face in half and looked over to Suzy. Y's eyebrows had arched questioningly with her lips frayed in an effort to control her; we can't do this shit, reflex.

Patra had already read the doubts in her mind from her expression and discounted them before they hatched.

"We back baby." She proclaimed, punching to the ceiling. "Hoorah!"

All You Beauty Salon
West London
17.35

He has gifted hands Y thought and that was not all.

She watched his prowling movements through the mirrored walls as he shifted position around the table. Sumptuous lips, carefree eyes, his biceps bulged, his pecs solid and those thighs, that ass.

Wow!

But his hands were the real instruments. A man like him could boost her self esteem for twenty four blissful hours at least.

Such a pity he was gay.

She mentally shrugged.

Ah, well!

One woman's loss is another man's gain.

Her internal dialogue faded as her level of relaxation became even deeper.

Y recalled Suzy had said Antoine had trained in a special massage technique that worked on the body's meridians and manipulated the energies between them.

Normally she would have wanted to know more and question him while he worked but Y couldn't speak, much less embark in lively debate. This boy was giving her pleasure without so much as an erection or the flick of a tongue.

Was Suzy sure he was gay or was that her sly way of keeping his tight ass to herself?

Another smile but a mischievous one this time as she let his powerful hands glide down her back and under the towel that covered the mound of her backside.

The sensuous cooing sound that floated from her lips said it all.

And before anyone took exception to this treatment, she confirmed to her disparaging other self, she deserved every second of it.

Every tension-releasing stroke, every flurry of butterfly chops and every skin tingling knead were as if they were Y's birthright almost and no one could tell her otherwise. If the posse wanted tonight's promotional party to be a success, she had to release the strain she was under or there would be casualties. The other girls were excited about the prospects of Mr Patel's idea. Y hadn't been completely won over by it yet but was willing to go ahead and see how things developed. He wanted to show off his new product to the potential client base that would need their services - whatever that would end up being. To be a walking talking advert for the new and improved Bad II the Bone, Y required calm or else blood would flow on the dance floor and chances are it would be male in gene type.

Hence her top-to-toe treatment.

If she could walk to the next cubicle she would have a facial, hit the steam room and drive to Skettel Pauline's to have her hair done, bashment style.

With the way she felt now that was a big, big if.

A few minutes later Suzy and Y wrapped in towels sat with their backs to the pine panelling of the steam room. The silence wasn't to last as Patra strolled in Lady Godiva bare. She stood in front of them both with her arms akimbo and her buoyant but firm breasts bobbing suggestively. She was glistening from the oils of her massage and was completely shaven Brazilian style. Her right breast had a petite 9mm automatic tattoo on it, her right bicep was encircled with a cute wreath of flowers and butterflies and so was her left ankle.

The piercing through her clitoris glistened.

"Tell me you chilled, right?" She said with an expectant stare and laboured breath. Y shook her head while Suzy seemed not to care about Patra's state of undress.

"Goddamit Y man, after all that good shit you're still feeling uptight. You need to get laid bitch and fast."

"I'm feeling good actually," Y said smoothly. "But you,.." Y motioned to Patra with the sweep of her hands " ... you must be on top of the fucking world."

Patra grinned and then frowned in one fluid facial expression, letting her hands roam up from her ripped stomach to her firm breasts.

"Hey, you see this right here? This is the body perfect and I'm proud as hell about what I got. Anymore smart ass comments from the nickel and dime section and the treatment goes on both you all credit cards. You feel me?"

"Gal yuh deadly. Suppose another woman walked in?" Suzy asked.

"Boring," Patra said and yawned.

"A man and woman then?"

"Now you're talking, we can get an orgy going off in here."

"Yuh not right, up here." Suzy said pointing to her own head laughing. "Yuh just not right."

Patra gave them the fuck you finger and twisted it in the air for emphasis.

Y tried but just couldn't maintain a straight face.

Ms Cleopatra Jones played it straight ignoring her sisters taunts but feeling the tightness of their friendship and saying a heartfelt thank you amidst her stream of thought. So she wasn't the most level headed of people – Y handles that shit - but when you needed results

Patra had the knack of pulling a rabbit out of the hat, even under these circumstances.

Suzy had finally been dismissed from her job and was temping with some fly-by-night security firms who weren't that interested in references. Y was evicted by the Housing Association and was bunking by her Mom's place. The butt naked Amazon in front of them had landed her third modelling job from AM Agency in as many weeks without breaking a sweat. She was performing at The Pink Kitty Kat when she wanted variety and the punters loved her. Yet Patra still had enough enthusiasm mixed in with her usual lack of fear to be hyped about this new and improved Bad II the Bone.

Y wanted to hug her but instead called her a cow.

Suzy laughed.

"Dis must be a good sign. I couldn't tell the last time we were together smiling for a change. I'm looking forward to a good time out and to test Mr P's theory that we are onto something. Sing low and don't break deh spell, it feel too good."

"Yeah!" Patra said dismissively not wanting to show how much in agreement she was. "While you girlies stroke yourselves and get all wet and sticky I'll get on with some business. I've got the outfits to collect and sisters they are HOT. You wanted to be the centre of attention when we pull up in our nineteen forties whip - compliments of an ex-boo of mine - and you will. Heads will turn and jaws will drop, guaran-fucking-teed."

Only Patra held the exact mental picture of how they would look tonight and that she kept a secret, but it reigned in their imagination.

The mind movies were broken by Patra's piping "we outta here" and disappearing out of the steam room with a smile on her face and swish of her ass, knowing she had left them in a state of white hot anticipation.

10.

Greenwich Gardens Morgue
North London
Tuesday, July 17th
23.35

Darkman padded easily into the autopsy room completely naked and slowly closed the doors behind him. He stood motionless for a while feeling the chill seep in from the soles of his feet, sniffing the lingering antiseptics used to cleanse the stink of death and listened grimly to the faint ethereal cries of lives cut short and their sweet pleas of redemption only he could hear. Enoch Lacombe licked his lips at how they were so open to the suggestion of mischief. Anything for these entities to feel a connection with a world they were lost to but he had no need of wraiths *dis night yah*, his focus was elsewhere.

Enoch had hurriedly left a pressing engagement of bloodletting to give his attention to a past colleague he had not been able to question. So he entered the environs of the Westminister Public mortuary as if he was a regular visitor and prepared for his enquiry.

The night assistant - old boy, pepper grey hair with a London accent tinged with the flavour of the Caribbean - was still seated at his desk, head slumped on a pile of reports, a stream of blood trickling from his nose and mouth, the only indication that the Amazonian brain beetle had entered the orifice and began eating its way through his soft tissue en route to his brain. An oval Vévé with the patterns of mental confusion was sprinkled in rice grains at the entrance to the pathology suite discouraging any staff from entering while Enoch prepared to extract information from an old acquaintance and informer.

In the examination room the body that lay grey and waxen on a metal table equipped with gutters and stirrups was the uncovered corpse of the late Omar *Michigan* Smiley who, from the report on the desk outside, had died from heart failure, a massive overload of his circulatory system. Enoch wished he had something more substantial to do with it but unfortunately *deh bwoy* had died in hiding before he was able to sit and reason with his living soul but there were other means at his disposal to elicit what he required from him.

Other more eosoteric avenues.

Omar would have his undivided attention behind that sublime veil of life and death. For the minutes that Enoch would commune with him, Omar would perceive them as seconds and Enoch would be the centre of his universe beyond the grave; his dark sun that he would supplicate to with the hope that he would stay awhile, sharing his eternal darkness. But for Darkman this was unpleasant business, not because of the process but because of the man.

In his life before prison, Omar worked as his messenger boy picking up and delivering items as and when his services were required. He was keen and could be moulded, doing what he was told without question especially after he realised he was working for someone who could literally make his dreams become reality. He saw how Enoch revived flagging companies, made law suits go away and old enemies disappear all by coercion or manipulating forces that frightened and enthralled him. The St Lucian remained committed and focused to stay in Enoch's good graces and to see more of what the master Voudon's power revealed. But fear did not keep him circumspect, instead it fuelled Omar's ambition and his greed, thinking he was the Darkman's equal in guile.

For a moment he must have thought he was right.

Look at him now.

Enoch still had a hard time believing it had been this same *yout* who had been integral in organising the theft of his arcane collection, this same *yout* had arranged the ghetto thugs to steal it and tipped off the authorities about some of the valuable items he had bought, stolen or murdered for. Enoch paid for his underestimation of the small island cockroach and paid again with the loss of his precious collectables, four years in prison and the almost irreversible destruction of his family heritage. Revenge was not enough. He wanted to shred them and scatter their remains across the city and paint an inspired mural with their guts and blood. But first of all the lynch pin, Mas Smiley.

He thought about all this as he stood naked, eyes closed, arms hanging at his sides, his thin but solid frame gleaming from perspiration even in the chill surroundings. As if prompted he opened his eyes slowly, blinked and revolved his locked shoulders. Breathing deeply but rhythmically, Enoch almost glided over to the head of the trolley table, his feet taking on a life of their own and touched both his palms on the temple of the cadaver, mumbling words that made his lips tremble as he spoke and sending a gossamer sheet of folding condensation that met the warmer air and twirled into oblivion.

The heat knowing it had no place here skittered away from this masquerade of an autopsy like vermin fearing extermination. It wasn't just in his head either but a physical crackle of charged atmosphere began as dark forces convened and gripped the Voudon in an almost hypnotic trance leeching life-giving heat from around him. The fingers of his right hand began to flicker with anticipation and his eyes fell on the equipment table and the gleaming tools of a traditional post-mortem examination. His ten fingers lead him almost to the insanely sharp blades, spiked ended calipers, saws with fine set teeth, forceps, punches and chisels but as his digits strolled over the implements like they were choice chocolates he decided on a stainless steel hollow tube which he balanced expertly over his knuckles, rolling it into the palm of his hand, feeling its weight and balance.

Without further thought controlled by the psychic eddies guiding his hand, Enoch levelled the point of the needle over the collapsed larynx, finding its spot like a dowsing rod and then suddenly slamming it through the neck and into the windpipe. The gases in the distended stomach immediately sought release issuing a putrid stream of decomposing stomach content and the vile by-product of the softening of tissues. He made no attempt to step away instead Enoch's nostrils flared as he deeply inhaled the noxious fumes that carried something of its host, brief snippets of his past life intertwined in corrupted DNA but not enough. He needed to unravel his memories, his secrets that were locked into the code of every cell in his body, even this dead carcass.

Retrieving the hollow spike from his neck, the Darkman's fingers were dancing eagerly over the tools settling on a glinting dissecting knife. Deftly he cut the stitches of the Y incision previously made by the coroner - V at the neck and a straight incision from below his throat to the pubis. He dug his fingers into the sutures and spreads the flaps of his stomach open wide, foul smelling mucous dripping from his hands and he peered into the body's cavity.

The words of invocation bubbled from his mouth as he threw his head back to the ceiling, his arms outstretched, rhythmic sounds that alter the tapestry of reality while you looked on, each word stripping away at what kept the sleeping masses grounded and sane, bringing him to places few people have seen and lived to speak about. Enoch swayed from its effect, anticipating an arrival telegraphed by the invisible waves lightly buffeting him, then nothing. A palpable silence descended. Then a screaming invisible someone that echoed from a dark dank pit, someone being flung forward, catapulted or discarded from where he rested and unceremoniously dumped into the stinking dead thing that was Omar Smiley.

Enoch breathed easily covered in blood, bone fragments, mucous and gore. He opened his eyes and grinned down at the carcass.

"How yuh like yuh new resting place, Omar?"

The blood curdling scream in Enoch's head was for his senses alone.

"Tight fit nuh true? But it was yours five days ago boss an' mi nevah hear yuh a complain." He chuckled amiably. "I guess you were fine where you were, in between places, wondering; eternal darkness or eternal light."

Enoch shook his head with mock sorrow and said slowly. "When yuh get dead fucking wid deh side of darkness because of stupidity there is no rest feh yuh. Do you understand?"

Enoch listened amused that Omar felt he could escape him even in death.

"I don't want to hear deh weeping and moaning star, I will leave your eternal soul trapped amongst the remaining rotting cells a dis body for ever, yuh si mi?"

Enoch nodded.

"Didn't I warn yuh? Did I not tell yuh, to see an' blind, hear an' deaf? Work hard and keep our business, our business. But yuh red eye an' bad mind against deh man who feed and cloth yuh. How you can do that? Fuck with an Obeah man of my talent and expect I wouldn't find yuh bomboclaat in this life or deh next. Only a few man have earned the ability to walk both sides of deh divide. To your detriment, I am one such man. Suh just picture yuh spirit bound to yuh bones an' when you bones crumble to dust, yuh spirit bound to where the dust remains. My voice will be the last human contact you will ever have. You will be a dead, decaying inconsequence, walked on and pissed on. Eternal silence, eternal lockup, unless..."

Enoch lowered his gaze for a moment and said nothing. He breathed with controlled ease, condensation pluming from his mouth, eyes closed, the hairs on his body standing on end.

"Deal?" He asked, opening his eyes. "Yuh want to deal wid mi now yout? Don't fancy the tight fit or sharing the stinking confines of yuh own body, wid deh blow flies and maggots? Well before we talk about sending you back from whence you came, I have some questions I need answering. And depending on how yuh cooperate will depend on how and when I fling yuh rass back to damnation.

"We have deal."

The pause, although only seconds in duration, was pregnant with threat and desperation.

"Ah, mi bwoy. Yuh are coming around to my type of tinking. Mek wi reason nuh."

Whitmore Private Cemetery
Tuesday, July 17th
12.35

Spokes had to see it for himself but even then, even when he knew how sick and perverted Darkman was, even when he convinced himself that this mad man - who had no right being free on the street - would go to any length to regain what was his even then this level of depravity would leave him speechless.

Cebert had called him, sounding scared and breathless. The Barbadian pensioner was spending his last two years working amongst the picturesque gardens of Whitmore Private Cemetery, tending the plants and lawns, his loving care keeping the place in perfect order, enjoying his passion for gardening before he moved back to his house and land in St. Joseph. He had known the old man for nearly four years and he had kindly promised to look after Jimmy's tomb with extra special care. He had lived up to his part of the bargain, making sure the memorial to his friend was the focal point of this pleasant place to spend an eternity. For his help Spokes made sure he regularly contributed to his retirement fund and it was at times like these that he was thankful he was such a generous soul. Spokes stood with his hands in his pockets, his comfortable Tod's loafers set comfortably on the manicured lawn looking over to the mausoleum, set into a background of an explosion of horticultural colour. And still with such beauty in his midst gooseflesh erupted along his arms and crawled languidly up his back. Cebert stood with him shoulder to shoulder reluctant to move even a step closer.

"You can go." Cebert encouraged.

From what Spokes could see from his vantage point the mausoleum had been violently breached. The gate had been flung open with great force and the metal of the wrought iron lattice had melted to such a degree that the molten droplets stretched by gravity, had hardened into the shape of bared fangs.

"Yuh touch nuthin', since... since yuh find it this way?"

The cemetery attendant shook his head.

"Just how I found it this morning. But I'm going to have to let my supervisor know what happened."

"Dat cool, what I have to do won't take a moment." Spokes surprised himself with that burst of bravado but it was slurped away by the sponge that was the reality of the moment.

Spokes bunched his two fists at his side steeling himself for what came next.

He smoothed down his goatee and walked over to the entrance expecting the familiar multi-sensory perception warning from his serpent head ring that would stop him in his tracks and compel him to seek safety but that did not happen. He took clumsy, hesitant steps, his lizard brain beseeching him to let someone else investigate this. He could be in the safety of his yard allowing his imagination to fill in the blanks where he could not corroborate the truth, but instead he was here. Just the site of the ornate iron gates, melted and ripped from there hinges made him feel scared and inconsequential.

He had to see what Darkman had done.

Spokes stood at the entrance his heart pounding in his chest and he peered into the murky interior. He turned to look for Cebert but he was way behind him, arms folded, with a look on his face that said, 'I'm happy just where I'm at thank you very much'.

"Yuh have a lighter?" Spokes called over.

Cebert dug into his overalls and rummaged through his multiple pockets. Triumphantly he lifted a copper flip top lighter and threw it to him, not proceeding an inch more than he had to. Spokes plucked it from the air, his reflexes not dimmed from days as a slips man in his local cricket team, he rubbed it between his fingers like a good luck charm and smelt the whiff of butane on its case. Cautiously he stepped into the gloom, his breath pluming even though outside the midday sun was at its highest and most intense. He snapped the lighter open and watched the flame flicker from a steady cold zephyr where none should be. Taking a deep breath, a musky damp aroma kept in step with him like an insubstantial doppelganger as he walked into the darkness. The immediate shadows flitted away like rats, the darkness held at bay only just as he stopped about four paces from the entrance, his mouth open as he moved the lighter from left to right.

Jeeesus Christ.

The crown of his head prickled immediately and his mouth became as dry as an arid desert.

The scene was one of chaos.

Spokes moved closer, one tentative step at a time, gently moving debris under foot and held the lighter high.

The crypt was smashed open from the top, as if a giant fist had pummelled it into submission, scattering Italian marble everywhere. Then something - he just couldn't imagine one scrawny black man could have done this on his own - had pulled the aluminium coffin that had spent four years in the cold embrace of the crypt, up to a standing position, denting and nearly ripping the casket flaps off its hinges, revealing the plush blue satin that lined the interior.

But there was no sign of the mortal remains.

Then a creeping certainty burrowed its way into his thoughts like ravenous maggots and with it a swooning wave of nausea and repulsion. Spokes directed his flickering light to the ground and the full horror of what he saw took some seconds to register. The debris that had threatened to twist his ankle was masonry, marble and desiccated human remains. The remains had been torn asunder and literally scattered to the four corners from fury or sheer madness.

If he was not seeing this for himself, he could have so easily discounted this nightmare, somehow turned his back to it but even Spokes' legendary skill of burying his head in the sand could not deny this.

The sweet almond smell triggered in the olfactory region of his brain was his ring's way of telling him there was more to see, yes sir.

The lighter extinguished and the twilight - his eyes getting used to the darkness - closed in on him. A moment of panic flared up in the pit of his stomach but with two tries he flashed the lighter to flame again and raised it over his head. The red smears on the wall became self evident.

Blood.

And he could not reign in his galloping mind from wondering whose blood had been sacrificed for this message.

"Yuh got to be playing wid me," he murmured.

Not smears on the wall but human scrawl.

His hands trembled violently threatening to drop the lighter to the floor but he managed to grip it with both hands, steadying it to read what was written on the wall of the mausoleum.

This was not Jimmy, very smart but you will be surprised by what the dead, hear. He told me everything he knew.

A pump of gastric juices lurched into his stomach like a punch to the gut and his undigested food mixed with the adrenaline of panic. The combination began rising up in his throat. He stumbled backward his hand over his mouth but even as he frantically escaped this horror house he could not help but see the other message written on the adjacent wall.

You have something for me Mas Spokes and I want it back. I will have it back.

Red Ground Estates
Surrey
21.15

Spokes sat in a room you could easily class as sterile,
sweating in a terry gown and slippers. It was a space that
was not far removed from what satellite engineers or
bacteriologists would use, it would not meet their exact-
ing standards of cleanliness but it was close enough for
what he required. This clean room did not concern itself
with microbes or microscopic impurities. Its purpose
was to protect its users from mystical eavesdroppers,
something he had picked up from a Native American
shaman in Minnesota with a love for Bob Marley and
gambling. Having the area built deep in a basement
complex under his seven bed roomed Tudor Mansion,
it's existence known only to him, was an exercise in
white magic and good old ghetto trickery. Thinking
about it now, it was a slick move on his part. He brought
in the engineers from Hong Kong, who constructed the
basement complex to the highest spec. Then he had a
young talented witch he was sleeping with briefly, destroy the paperwork and data referring to the planning
permission at the council and then hypnotize the engineers into forgetting the job they had done. And with
his rudimentary skills on a sex spell he had been working on for months, Spokes was able to manipulate her
grasp on reality and dreams at the moment of her orgasm, making her believe the favour done was an errant
fragment of a dream looping in her subconscious. Not
bad for a novice.

Spokes sat on a stool looking down on a plain aluminium table with an ancient ceramic bowl filled three
quarters with water. On either side of him were two

thick red candles, their length marked with inscriptions, crackling softly with an intense orange flame. The rest of the open planned gallery was shrouded in ever increasing shades of darkness; that made your eyes search for the outer fringes but found none while Spokes worked under a halo of light provided by a halogen spot above him.

In reality he should be much more careful with this piece of Gaelic prehistory. The reprobate Professor Angus McCracken had estimated it to be about five thousand years old and Spokes paid for his expertise as well as his silence. It was fashioned with a seer in mind, a kind of battery to help the prognostication talent see a clearer snapshot of the possible future. It came with an ancient how-to manuscript in Celtic cuneiform etched into a set of rune stones discovered with the dish. And these were the stones that Angus had translated. Thanks to extensive notes written by Darkman's thieving ancestors reaching back for generations this was one of the very few items that required no prior magical experience and luckily for him proved to be useful.

He had used it about three times and the results weren't always conclusive but that was more due to the inexperience of the wielder because truthfully any snatches of the future are an advantage. Winning a fortune on an accumulator bet for the Cheltenham Cup, winning a tasty wager on a knockout in the World Heavyweight Championship and losing a Premier Cup tie punt. Disrespectful it might be, especially after knowing its heritage, but this time its use would be for a more noble cause; his self preservation.

Spokes grinned to himself, amused by how effortlessly he had slipped into this other world of spells, spooks and sorcery. One he had not known even existed but now accepted as a part of his everyday life. And what was he about to do as nonchalantly as if he was taking a walk in the park had become uncomfortably normal. He was going to catch a glimpse of the future from his sweat and tears.

Literally.

He needed to meet those warrior princesses from the club; his ring-heightened intuition told him they were important. The ring had reacted in ways he had never felt before, ways he intuitively knew meant their destinies were to cross sometime in the future. What he had no idea of was its importance until an internal compulsion to meet them again started to build in him like a steam turbine, a throbbing yearning that he could not shake and one that had kept him awake at nights. Whether he understood it or not, he just felt his life depended on recruiting them to his cause, so he needed to find them first. Where would they be in the immediate future? And that was a question Spokes was about to answer.

It was now twenty three hours and fifty seven minutes after he had said the words, he dropped a newspaper clipping of that faithful night with the girls snapped up by a never say never paparazzi and watched it soak and sink in the bowl. He let the ripples settle. Spokes stared into the contents and watched his reflection and saw it distort into incoherence from his breathing and he let a sweat droplet hit the crystalline surface. Now he needed a tear drop in two minutes, for the spell to take hold.

He thought of Jimmy dying in his arms, thought of his mother dying of cancer in Jamaica and not being at her bedside as he had promised and in moments the tears came.

11.

Mixtapepage.com DJ Awards
After Party
Tuesday, July 17th
00.40

The Club Sodom lit up the Streatham skyline with an explosion of light. This was all reminiscent of the huge Hollywood opening nights of the Forties. Three huge spot lights glided across the under belly of the clouds overhead while the smaller versions irritated the patrons who preferred to be incognito as they crowded for entry.

Optimists every last one of them.

The DJ Awards after party had traditionally been an invitation-only affair which everyone knew and sponsoring radio stations also made it abundantly clear but the crowds still turned up. It wasn't totally a lost cause because once the high rollers were inside whatever cubic metres of space that remained would be filled by the lucky few who had started to charm the bouncers from early. Cordons ran from the entrance to the curb side. The unusual sight of a phalanx of valets ushering the arriving glitterati from their cars was another association you linked with the US. It was a stark testament to the growing power of the black British music scene and its popularity. Some publicity-shy stars ran the gauntlet along the red carpet, others stopped and bathed in the attention, flanked by excited onlookers, television interviewers and the blinding flashbulbs of the paparazzi.

A gleaming white open top nineteen forty Oldsmobile was next to pull up to the curb. Three women stepped out of the road legend and handed the keys to a valet who had shuffled into the leather driving seats as their fitted brogues touched the concrete.

Prohibition Chicago had just landed in South West London.

The three women drew the wolf calls and the cameras immediately.

Their invitations were taken and they strode up the carpeted path decked out in very provocative variations of the classic grey, pin stripe double breasted suit with matching trilby's. To the onlookers they were stars whether they knew who they were or not. For the paparazzi they needed to know more and as the trio walked past the cluster of hacks chomping at the bit one desperate journo poked a microphone through the arm pits of a suited security man.

"Are you Mecca Records' new signing and are you performing tonight?"

A tall elegant figure approached his microphone. Her jacket was open up to the level of her bra and the material hugged her breasts almost jealously. The reporter's eyes seemed to be trapped in her substantial cleavage and the multicoloured tattoo of a nine millimetre on her right breast. He looked up shakily and took in air. She took the trilby off her head revealing her corn row styled plaits framing mischievous brown eyes.

Patra smiled.

"We independent artist's, baby. And that means we free from the corporate bullshit."

"So what's your group's name?"

"You all ain't heard of us yet but you won't forget us in a hurry. Me and my sisters here are Bad II the Bone. Rememba dat. Aiight!"

She rejoined the group in a flurry of flash bulbs.

Their laughter was drowned out by the rising buzz of Club Sodom's growing revellers.

Those few minutes of interest from the paparazzi outside threw a totally different slant on tonight. The 'star' effect seemed to follow them into the club's interior. The looks and nods of acceptance, the smiles, the respect. It was, as if they had passed a test of initiation at the door and could now be accepted into the interior.

And an impressive interior it was too.

The major companies had dug into their coffers to sponsor food and drink and also made sure they used every possible inch of the decor to plug a DJ, artist, album or some related product or other. But even with their over-the-top need for promotion the plush venue shone out.

Once inside you could see the four corners of the building, there were no hidden crevices, no one could hide except amongst the revellers and VIP's who demanded privacy would be cocooned in huge glass spheres that were elevated above the dance floor, suspended above the dancers like ants trapped in a soap bubble, their antics observed but their words lost to the music.

Forming a crescent to one side of the oval dance area was the chill out zone. The colour of choice was red. It looked as if the carpet had been kissed by huge ruby lips and a probing scarlet tongue but instead they were groups of two semi-circular leather couches with a scarlet table in the middle. The Gravity bar just behind this looked as if it had been lifted, physically stuck to a whole section of wall and then tilted forward at a precarious angle. The bartenders skilfully prepared their cocktails and served drinks with the aid of harnesses like high-wire performers. Lunatic punters collected their drinks on cushions of air as they levitated down a line of short glass tubes.

You could see Patra's eye light up as she collected three shots and handed them over to the rest of the posse. Suzy's usual composure slipped away in very unlady-like squeal of delight when the dark skinned soul crooner D'Marko slid over to their position and whispered his hotel and room number in her ear, brushing his lips on her neck in parting.

Y had never seen her sister struggling to control herself from screaming and grabbing the poor boy. She had to hold her hand, remind her celebrities don't do that kind of thing and hint at her long suffering boyfriend who was at home pining for her return.

Even if it was just for tonight, they were stars. Mr Patel's promotional machinery was in full swing too as they partied. And on instruction, they were to relax and enjoy themselves. All in depth questions from interested parties should be directed to the GP Public Relations company if they required details – another one of Mr

Patel's subsidiaries. He had furnished them with the appropriate business cards and marketing material

"No matter the consequences, follow your heart and do what you do best, tonight and every other night." Mr Patel's words resonated with them as they armed their purses and clutch bags with business cards. At the venue eight gorgeous models both male and female wearing T-Shirts with the moniker Bad II the Bone emblazoned on it in silver lettering - the Roman numeral II was glimmering bones – engaged professionally with partygoers and handed out goody bags and flyers.

A Gappy Ranks track had just finished playing and Suzy and Y had left the dance floor to join Patra who was being chirped by two music exec types. They couldn't have left her no more than five minutes and already her near empty brandy and coke had magically transformed itself into an elegant crystal flute filled with bubbly and a sweating champagne bottle lay nonchalantly in a silver bucket filled with ice.

She saw them approaching and filled two empty flutes.

"Compliments of Paradise Records, girls," she said brightly.

Y shook her head in amazement and Suzy just reached for her glass, clinking it with the others.

"These two high rollers like our swagger and want us to send them a demo tape." Patra continued.

Y spluttered on her drink smiling weakly.

"They think I'm tripping when I say music is not our business."

The sigh of relief came from Suzy's obviously amused face.

"So what is the business of three ultra fit fillies, then?"

The voice that had appeared behind them had caused the two Paradise company men to blanche noticeably. The girls turned together to look into the pierced and tattooed smouldering good looks of Elektra Blue, female rapper and celebrity hell raiser. Her voice was brandy and nicotine cured, slow and considered as if she had burnt a blunt before entrance. Her dress sense was all street and not contrived either, Suzy saw that immediately. Her demeanor was ultra masculine and if she had to guess Ms Elektra Blue knew how to look after herself in a tussle; just how she moved her six foot frame spoke volumes. Like a boxer devoid of an opponent - The Natural Disaster was her musical moniker and that Suzy could believe was her personality too. She needed no assessments from music journalists on the truth of that, she pronounced it loud and clear.

"Our business is pleasure." Patra said grinning gamely.

"Now that is a fucking coincidence," Elektra Blue said and glared at the two Paradise execs just beyond watching how this developed, nonchalantly giving them the finger. They turned their backs to her unspoken threat. "Where you from girl?"

The question was directed at Patra.

"Atlanta, Georgia, born and bred." She said.

"Damn, I'm from Philly and I love you Georgia corn fed bitches but London, London is where it's at."

"Amen to that." Patra confirmed.

I could just tell you princesses were looking for a good time, man." She leaned closer to Y and in conspiratorial tone said.

"When it comes to pussy, I have a nose and a tongue for the job." She licked her lips, showing the length and thickness of her tongue. She laughed throatily. Elektra then lowered her voice and said. "I don't know but you just look like a woman who can scissor the fuck out of me. Am I good or am I good."

Y glared at her, for just a second amazed she was meeting one of a few artists that brought a sense of immediate consternation to her mood. Why this couldn't have been Usher was obvious, mush too easy. Instead she had to deal with Elektra's well documented reputation as the l'enfante terrible of the UK hip hop scene. Her antics had always seemed to rub Y up the wrong way. To her Elektra Blue was spoilt, misguided and dangerous and she didn't give a shit about her talent. Her example was toxic.

"You don't know me from Adam, why do you think I'd do anything with you?" Y asked.

"Chill, I'm Elektra Blue baby and I get what I want."

With a practised flick of her fingers she called over her ever present aides who were standing within ear shot.

Y shook her head in disbelief.

Maybe it was the shock of realising that the papers had not exaggerated their numerous accounts of her behaviour that had struck her into silence. Or was it, how tenuous her hold on reality was after being force fed her greatness by records exec's and encouraged to live up to her Natural Disaster catch phrase.

"Mek we leave dis idiot gal yah. She is trouble." Suzy said.

Patra folded her arms patiently, her sense of humour still intact and made eye contact with Y.

"She likes the shit outta you, though sugahh." Patra grinned.

"Don't...." Y threatened.

"What did Mr P say?" She cleared her throat and gave a passable impersonation of Mr Patel's accent. "No matter the consequences, follow your heart."

Out of earshot Elektra playfully hugged her two bodyguards around their broad shoulders. A haze of Armani V aftershave rose into the air as she patted their backs.

"I've scored again and you scroungers get to taste the sloppy seconds." She leant on both their shoulders and spoke the words only for their ears. A maniacal grin spread on the lower half of her face like a time accelerated rash outbreak.

Then Elektra turned to face the girls again both hands outstretched, her business face on as she approached.

"My limousine is out front, the engine is running and inside I have four bottles of chilled Cristal and enough nose candy to keep you wet and willing all night."

She held on to Y's hand.

"Let me show you my London, hood London."

Patra's response was snap back sharp and decisive.

"Not my scene Elektra but I'm sure you have a more than willing audience to choose from."

Elektra shrugged.

"I'm an equal op. kinda chick but they ain't you, though."

As far as Elektra Blue was concerned a choice had already been made and she strode off with Y's hands in hers, fully confident she would follow.

Complication number one happened rapidly.

Y's hands slithered out of hers, making Elektra stumble forward, saved from embarrassment only by a pillar in her way.

The rapper didn't turn around until she had composed herself. Then with an easy swagger and crooked smirk she approached the dark skinned warrior, again.

"No she ain't?" Patra asked incredulous looking over at Suzy. "She ain't going to do what I think she gonna do."

Suzy's eyebrows arched

"No way." Patra croaked.

"Way." Suzy said calmly, just as Elektra Blue grabbed for Y's arm.

"Let's try that again, bitch," she snarled, her big hands whipping out.

Complication number two unravelled.

Y held her ground and swung her torso right, Elektra's hands plucking at thin air. Angered she swirled trying to back hand Y but she ducked low and stepped back out of harms way, the movement as graceful as a fifteenth century courtesan dance routine. Elektra simply did not see the finer points of combat she grunted, lips curled and eyes piercing and started swinging in Y's direction as she approached.

"You don't run from me. You don't duck me," she murmured, the force of the fists cutting through the air with whoop, whoop, whooshing sounds. "You fucking do what I tell you or you get hurt."

Y stood her ground, blocking the clumsy bombs being thrown her way and hearing some of her carefully applied sculpted nails snap and ping off.

"You bitch," Y spat, looking at the destruction of her masterpieces.

Pissed, Y got in closer and started slamming her knuckles into Elektra's meridian points with speed and power. Each blow sending seismic vibrations through Elektra's muscles and sinew. Imagine hitting a charging rhino with a tranquiliser and watching it lose control due to the quick acting drug.

Same way, Suzy would have agreed.

In the dimness Y had dropped low and delivered two more furious blows in rapid succession to her thigh and a point to the left of her groin. Elektra Blue let out a strangled yelp. Her eyes were wide as a wave of pain rippled through her shutting down her motor functions in stages. Struggling to maintain her body in an upright position and failing, she succumbed to gravity and fell under a long spouted drinks table.

Even with the blaring music her bodyguards still heard the body hit the carpet and turned to see their charge writhing on the floor in a heap of elbows and knees.

They turned only to see Y bent down beside Elektra Blue's crumpled body. Incensed and startled at the same time they rushed over to investigate or deal out retribution for what had been their failing. Suzy wasn't having that and blocked the attack with her slight frame deflecting the first man using his weight and momentum against him but miscalculating the nimbleness of the second man.

The bald, tubby bodyguard was quick on his feet for his size and instead of committing himself drew back at the last minute then lunged forward, grabbing Suzy by the neck, propelling her off her feet. All her breath exploded from her lungs and she willed herself to go loose. Expecting a struggle Tubby tensed but Suzy did the opposite. She let gravity take her and fell forward out of his grip as he tried to compensate for her slackness, landing on her hands and knees. She swirled, her back to him and stared into the contorted features of Elektra, who had failed the eight count miserably and waited. In two heart beats, Suzy gracefully let her left leg swing back and up, the movement looking like a yoga posture, her heel slamming into her attacker's crotch. Tubby reacted as all men do and reached down to protect his prized possession from further injury. Anticipating that, Suzy pushed back and rose up, the back of her head slamming into his nose and lips.

Tubby staggered back stemming the eruption of blood with both his hands and spat out some shattered teeth as well.

"You fuss..king bi..sstch!" He bellowed just in time to see and momentarily experience a flying round house kick from Suzy that was a thing of beauty.

Medallion man hadn't had time to intervene in his colleague's 'ass kicking' but thought better of delaying his involvement any further.

Taller with more defined muscles and a dumb stare, Medallion man felt Suzy was fair game and was hurrying over to make his point, not seeing Patra who loved to be the centre of attraction as much as Suzy did, heading on an intercept course.

A mild discomfort at the back of her right ear that she was so familiar with, a prick and a tingle that indicated her Luck Factor was in play did not slow her down. Patra readied herself for whatever would hit the fan as probability distorted a single inconsequential aspect of this conflict tipping the outcome to her favour most times anyway.

She focussed.

And. There. It. Was.

Medallion Man tripped on a portion of carpet the size of a hand that had nudged free from the otherwise neat uniformity of the floor.

Patra braked and saw opportunity fluttering her way.

Medallion Man only knew she had grabbed his tie when he was brought to an abrupt stop and only just saw what happened next. Patra wrapped the tie around her hand and before he could break free, took to the air. Gravity took her weight to the floor and so did Medallion Man's head. He would have followed her down in a perfect trajectory if it wasn't for the drinks table which his forehead hit with such force the glasses that had sat there, rose a good two inches off the surface on impact.

The casualties numbered three, with Elektra still squirming from muscle paralysis, Tubby still trying to stem the flow of blood from a possible broken nose and Medallion Man was as unconscious as an unconscious motherfucker.

Just like in the movies the cavalry came when it was all over.

"She was groping my tooshy, Mr Officer. What could a girl have done, sir," Patra gushed, batting her eyelids and then breaking out into peels of laughter.

"The security guys believed every word that came out of your lying mouth," Y said.

"And damn, did that feel goooood!" Patra whooped as the girls held their glasses for a boisterous toast.

"Yuh know I've always wanted to do that," Y said evenly. "But thought it would stay on my wish list never fulfilled, like shagging Denzel Washington. But sweethearts," she kissed Suzy and Patra on the cheeks, "you made it all possible."

Suzy smiled.

"Normally mi would feel ashamed feh letting guh like dat. But that was deh sweetest buss ass, mi give in a long time."

"Amen," Patra said.

"Punany power," Y pronounced, attracting a mock look of incredulousness from Patra and Suzy. They raised their glasses, clinked them and flung the sparkling wine down their throats, laughing.

Weirdly tonight had reinforced the rightness of what they were about to embark on. The word was out thanks to Mr. Patel but more importantly they experienced a sense that there was hope for them and whatever problems they faced they would overcome with their unique brand of determination.

Everywhere they stood they became the focal point, the men gravitated towards them and the women made them the subject of their discussions. The message had been sent out that wherever these sisters went danger and excitement followed and the night was still young.

A solitary applause approached them from a thicket of dancers in a compulsory clinch brought on by a Beres Hammond track.

"Nice, nice, nice," the man said approaching them, his palms slapping against each other sharply.

He was an older gentleman, handsome in a rugged mature way with broad hands that obviously were used to hard work. Dressed immaculately in a tuxedo, brilliant white shirt and a felt hat, he was obviously inspired by the same era the girls had decided to model tonight except for one blaring difference.

The man was wearing black snake skin boots.

"Daughter," he took Suzy's hand and kissed it, his Jamaican accent thick. "What you did to that blouse an' skirt gal was beautiful, absolutely beautiful." He shook his head as if to shake the fading mental image of the incident back into clarity for his continued amusement. "And you warrior princess," he looked at Patra and shook his head. "You sister, are a dangerous woman to know, dangerous. Kiss mi neck," he laughed out. "Where can three little bit a gal like you three learn dem moves deh?"

Suzy looked at him a weak smile forming, not sure wether to be gracious or cautious.

Her trepidation evaporated as the stranger's adoration for her skills kept growing. She was forced to listen to him without being able to squeeze a word in edge ways.

"Excuse my manners, sisters." He handed out some fancy gold embossed business cards to all three of them. "My name is Rupert Dobson but my close friends call me Spokes." He grinned broadly. "I have a proposition for yuh that I think you'll want to hear."

Y moved forward and Spokes surmised correctly that Y, the dark skinned beauty with the athletic physique was their spokeswoman. He must have also surmised she was a no-nonsense type of *gal* and any chance of holding their attention would depend on how she responded to him. He raised his hands throwing off her focus and spoke directly to her eyes.

"Pardon deh presumption ladies but I was checking yuh out as soon as I saw you walk in." Patra leaned her head onto her thumb and forefinger and pouted.

"Don't get me wrong," Spokes added quickly. "I'm not in deh habit of voyeurism, if I like a daughta or three," he grinned. "I will say. I saw what you did to that Elektra gal and her flunkies with my own two eyes. This is strictly business."

He cleared his throat.

"Anyway from what I could work out, you're not involved directly in the music or entertainment business which is strange for girls wid your profile. You must be connected to get into here in the first place, so mi figure you're looking for exposure, some excitement."

He looked at Y.

She responded with a tight lipped, "Maybe."

"Then I was handed a goody bag with your promotional bits and pieces. Yuh keep on impressing me sisters. Yuh just keep on. Bad II the Bone, wicked name."

Spokes lowered his voice as he got to the point.

"Okay, hear what I'm proposing. Be my girls, like Spokes' Angels." He stopped to consider it and chuckled to himself. "That has a nice ring to it, nuh true? I want you to help me promote my dance in two weeks time and I will pay you ten thousand pounds each plus all expenses and I promise you won't have to take a piece of clothes off, sell your body in any way shape or form or get into bed with me, unless yuh tink it is absolutely necessary."

He grinned at his own joke and then at the slack jawed expression on their faces from incredulity.

Y had folded her arms, her face impassive, then she looked at the card he had handed her again.

Patra started laughing

"You wouldn't try to shiest my crew would you...Spokes?" Patra asked glaring at him.

"Shame on yuh." He shifted his felt hat from his right hand to his left and opened his arms in symbolic innocence.

"Hear what! Check out my website an mi Facebook profile, ding me tomorrow at my offices, we'll link up, I'll present you with further references, the itinerary, sign a non-disclosure contract and pay you five thousand pounds each in cash, as a down payment then we can do some shopping on me."

Even in the dimness their eyes lit up.

"We're going to have to think about this," Y said. "Look over that contract you're talking about."

"Think about it as much as yuh want daughta but due to the urgency of this project, I can only give you forty-eight hours and then the deal is off the table."

"Dat wil be fine," Suzy jumped in with a hard-to-conceal eagerness.

Patra tried on her game face but wasn't convincing anyone.

"Yeah! That's more than enough time, Slick." She said.

Y's voice of reason on this matter seemed to have been drowned out.

Spokes grinned.

Hook, line and sinker ladies, he thought. Hook, line an sinker.

12.

Metal Works Gym
Wednesday, July 18th
10.45am

Bad II the Bone sat excitedly in their lair at the Metal Works Gym with reams of letter headed paper, compliment slips and boxes of stylish metal business cards. The girls' excitement was a stark contrast to three weeks ago when they seemed to be at the lowest point in their lives. So much had changed and you got the impression they did not yet want to admit they were strangely drawn to this unknown territory.

Mr Patel was not happy about their decision to take on a job so early into their development but to their mind this was a straight forward gig, with the least risk possible, or so they tried to tell themselves.

Y played devil's advocate as was usual, lounging on a massive bean bag. Suzy was sipping on a steaming hazelnut hot chocolate, legs crossed, lotus position on the carpeted floor while Patra sat on a traditional chair tapping away at her laptop with her back to them.

"What do we know, about being bodyguards?" Y asked.

"Close Protection Operatives," Patra corrected.

"Okay what do we know about being CPO's?"

"Enough," Patra continued eyes still on the screen. "We're skilled more than most in protecting ourselves, that we know. Can't see why we can't use those skills to protect others and get paid, too."

"I could name one reason, at least," Y said.

"Uh-huh, I bet you can. What you got girl? Lay it on me."

"Experience," Y said simply. "We may be able to look after ourselves but if we factor in other lives how effective can we be?"

"Better than most, sugah. We gifted, you forgetting." Patra added without a hint of pretension.

"An' with some training, who knows, maybe we could be deh best?" Suzy added smugly.

"Training?" Y questioned.

"Damn, I forgot to tell you about the training."

Patra laughed and so did Suzy.

"What training is this?" Y asked.

"Yow, sis we got this all covered. Mr Patel has our back, on all things legal. Of all things, we need training and a license to work. Isn't that a bitch?"

"When was I going to be told?" Y folded her long elegant arms around her chest.

Suzy was chuckling to herself and sipping on her hot drink, savouring Y's surprise at being the last to know for once.

"You've just been told so chill." Patra teased. "It was on a need to know basis sugah and you didn't need to know."

"We knew yuh had concerns so we wanted to have all deh facts ready. Patra is just pulling your chain, sis."

"Great to know I can be a source of fun for you two."

"We glad too girl, believe me."

"Ha-ha!" Y glared at Patra signalling an explanation with her fingers drumming on the corner of her mouth, locked into that sexy stance she had.

"It starts in three weeks and it's a ten weeks full time course approved by the SIA and held by the foremost CPO training group in the world. It will qualify us for the industry and give us the finer ass details of being professionals. You feel mi?" Turning away from the laptop for the first time Patra extracted a folder from one of the draws in the desk and handed the white envelopes contained in it, to Y and then Suzy.

"It covers law and legislation, surveillance, armed, unarmed protection and everything in between. From a freshman's point of view it looks pretty damn good to me."

Y looked through the paper work and nodded with approval.

"But can we do this? Are we meant to do this?"

All eyes were on Suzy as the silence wasn't filled with her words of wisdom yet. She had placed her mug beside her and was twining her pony tails between her fingers contemplatively, her eyes off to the middle distance somewhere.

"I tink we looking at this opportunity all wrong."

"Here we go," Patra teased. "You got this shit worked out right, Suzy?" She looked over to Y triumphantly. "It's in the cards, baby. We got no choice but to follow the path." Patra said grinning from ear to ear. "Ain't that the truth?"

Suzy ignored her fake passion for her gift, shaking her head and wrinkling her nose at Patra.

"I know where you're vibing from Y. And you gal," She set her gaze levelly on Patra. "Don't fake your bravery because I know you have yuh doubts too."

"I ain't gonna front," Patra said. "I do have my doubts but not about whether we can pull this shit off. This I know we can do."

Point taken. Suzy looked at Y.

"We are at our best when we righting some wrong inflicted on us or inflicted on others. Deh only times we can truly say we are happy is when we are in the midst of crisis and working towards solving a problem with our fists or minds. Check yourself Y because that is the God truth. If we want any kind of stability or peace of mind we have to tek the path shown an' embrace deh gifts we have."

"How do we deal with Mr Dobson?" Y asked. "He needs our help now and we're not really prepared or ready."

"Then shit girl, prepare. We being offered ten thousand pounds each for two weeks work, do the maths."

"All we gonna do is keep him close an mek sure no harm comes to him," Suzy said. "I sense he's a good man, serious about what he wants."

"I kinda feel the same way," Y said. "But I get a feeling he isn't telling us everything. Not outright lying but keeping some vital details to himself. What do you think Suzy?"

"Yuh could be right but the vibes him a give off is not getting me concerned or edgy. So he is either sincere in his actions or him believe whatever he's doing is the right thing."

"You had a good talk with him before we arrived. What is your gut telling you?"

"He was harmless enough, checking out my backside every opportunity he got."

"Can't blame a nigga for looking." Patra said.

"I suppose," Y grinned.

"He was sincere and reminded me of a horny uncle from my mum's side. He was an old school gentleman, ladies man, my dad's generation with the same principles about keeping your word."

"He is kinda cute." Patra said nonchalantly.

"Gal he could be yuh daddy."

"I know and I could be his mammy." Patra laughed.

"Don't even go there P, this is all about business."

"Chill, I'm just saying." Her hands raised in mock submission. "We might talk after bizniz is complete, though."

Suzy rolled her eyes.

"What we need to rememba is that this is not a formal arrangement. Everyting has been handled with a handshake an' our word. He's just a man who tink him life is being threatened by some bad minded competitors and we can put him at ease. If he delivers on the money he promised then..."

"We in bizniz," Patra completed.

"So okay we going to have to keep a low profile now that we are minor celebrities and just hope nothing leaks out."

"Underground." Suzy responded to Y's statement.

"Under wraps." Patra elaborated.

"Pick our fights with care next time." Y added.

"Amen." Suzy said

"I guess you want me to put a plan of action together then?" Patra asked.

"That's what you do, sugah."

"Yeah that's what I do. But until then?"

"We wait and see." Suzy said sagely.

"Well while we're waiting and seeing, I've got something that can keep you focussed. Yuh gonna lurrrrve this!"

Patra went back to pecking away at the keyboard, leant back into the chair and then suddenly sat up. Y came over and stood behind Patra resting one hand on the back of the chair and the other gently massaging her neck.

Patra gently pushed the chair away from the table to give Y some space.

"What do you think?"

Y was looking at a blog page with the words Bad II the Bone emblazoned at its head in stylised fonts, all sexy curves, moulded into what looked like a kind of glistening molten platinum. The motto of their fledgling enterprise - We got your back - was under all that with a glamour group photograph of all three of them that Y had almost forgotten they had taken a few years back.

"Don't even ask." Patra said seeing Y's eyes glare down the page then softened as something resonated with her.

"We have a Facebook Fanpage and Twitter plugin linked to it. I've written three test blogs that I haven't posted to help your creative juices but this is for you, baby girl. Give me your stamp of approval."

Y looked at the screen and depressed the page down button to have a better look at what Patra had written.

It was very good.

The prose was filled with her energy, wit and optimism but it was the third entry that interested her the most. A picture is worth a thousand words they say and the photograph of Tyrone, set in a frame that was reminiscent of the FBI Most Wanted page said it all. The police style bulletin was asking subscribers to keep a look out for him, explaining what he had done and that he needed to be brought to some girl power style justice. Even Y found herself being caught up in the punchy but sincere plea for help.

"This is great Ms Jones. I love it." Y kissed her on the cheek.

"It's about us, the things that we do and what made us who we are. Interesting shit for whoever wants to know."

"Makes sense."

"I just thought that you always have the most to say. Why not have an opportunity to say it to someone who gives a shit?"

Patra's eyes glinted mischievously as she said her piece with the straightest of faces. Y squinted as if she had just been sucker punched but mellowed unable to mask her amusement and they both cracked into peals of laughter.

Stockwell Locks
Housing Estate
23.40

It happened so quickly.

One moment Sandra had walked into her bedroom and had stood watching Chips so totally engrossed in rummaging through a personal shoes box overflowing with papers that he had not realised she was standing behind him. Then next she was staggering backwards from the savageness of his slap. It was the kind of attack that was fuelled more by surprise than by genuine vehemence.

Surprise that she had just caught him rifling through her private stuff and knowing there was nothing he could say to explain it away. She dabbed at a trickle of blood that had pooled at the corner of her mouth and glared at him for a moment. The welts on her cheeks from Chips' coarse fingers raised and with them her reflexive rationalisation of his crass behaviour.

"What the fuck are you doing, going through my things?" Sandra snapped.

She surprised herself on how controlled she was.

Chips brushed past her with no remorse.

"None a yuh pussyclaat business."

Sandra followed him out into the hallway, her fingers rubbing against the indented wallpaper as if it was helping to slow her down. This situation would not end at Chips' request, not this time. All his lip service about moving his operation elsewhere so Sandra could regain some normalcy in her life was a lie. He was still using her and the convenience of the setup that had been Enoch's idea to make a small fortune at her expense.

Under Enoch's protection she had little to do and the poker games that were played Friday and Saturday nights produced an income that covered her monthly expenses easily.

Not so with Chips.

She was literally a slave in her own home from Monday to Sunday and if she protested he beat her. His obsession with Enoch and his lost valuables was like a dark cloud that hung over everything they did. Chips was becoming obsessive and she was watching the transformation before her eyes. How could a sane man believe that she knew the whereabouts of Enoch's collection and yet remained in this shithole with him and the others like him?

But he did.

She had warned him that it was a fool's preoccupation that could cost him his life.

Warned him to have nothing to do with it, forget it because although Enoch was in prison he had ways of hurting people that were not myth but fact. Ways he had directed at his enemies with devastating effect in the past.

But the lure of a possible fortune hidden away in Enoch's things was too much for Chips to control. He had conspired against the man she loved under the pretence of being a gambler, helped to plan the failed robbery against him and with his cohorts fabricated evidence against her baby father that sent him away for twenty five years.

His gambling and 'drugs juggling' was not sufficient anymore, the lure of Enoch's treasure was just too much to ignore.

The television had been turned on and the baby was asleep on the sofa. Chips was staring intensely at a football match with his feet on the coffee table and was tapping away at the remote control, raising the volume at each jab.

Sandra came in, whisked the baby away to her bedroom, closing the door behind her. She then headed for the kitchen, opened a few draws and then walked back into the lounge. The grating clamor of TV speakers not used to high volume, was annoying but filling the gaps of uncomfortable silence to Chips' satisfaction. Sandra walked purposefully up to the television set and stood in front of it, blocking Chips' view completely. From her position she switched the set off and glared at him, maybe awaiting a reaction.

The dread did nothing.

"I want you to go. Pack up your shit and just leave us alone. How long has it been since you destroyed my life? I'm a prisoner here amongst the worst of the worst London has to offer. You've taken everything from me and I don't care anymore. I'm tired. Tired of you, tired of your friends and I want my life back." Sandra looked around nervously as if she had just realised the power of her own words.

Expecting no response, no smart qualification of the facts, he would normally ignore anything she said anyway. Sandra, on the other hand, was surprised by how she had expressed herself. Chips was taken aback too at what would usually result in him ignoring her completely, he raised his head off his chest and turned in the deliberate and dramatic way of his.

"What's got into yuh today, gal? You losing yuh fucking mind? I don't answer to anything yuh say. Leave?" His laugh was throaty, Ganja soaked. "You will learn dat there is no knight in shinning armour coming to rescue you. That bwoy from Croydon, the one with the hot's for you, he can't save you. And that batty bwoy Roland who can dress but not much else. Forget him. I am your salvation and when you come to realise that you will unwrap that pussy from its velvet box an' let it off."

It was her time to laugh.

"If you haven't figured out, I'm nothing like your other women, then you are stupider than I thought. The chance you had with us if you had handled yourself differently has gone. You fucking squandered that opportunity, long ago. Too bad for you, though." She paused as if to rally her thoughts then said abruptly. "I want you out."

Sandra's words seemed to be issuing from someone else's mouth. She was listening in on herself with a sort of detachment a professional observer would make as they paid attention to the psych evaluation of a client. Her voice and the content of her dialogue seemed strange to her, prophetic even. Neither was her surprise confined to herself; Chips sat with his mouth partially open, his eyebrows had formed a gnarly 'V' and he too was struggling with the transformation that had come over her.

Sandra's collapse outside her door and the unexplained reason that had overwhelmed her senses that night must have altered her perspective.

Since then, since thinking she had sensed someone who should be in prison with a playing card as the only evidence that this supposed duppy existed, everything had become plainer. Her GP had said it was a mental episode caused from stress and depression but it had left her with a gift. Enoch was reaching out to her.

Scary and improbable it may be but such words were more than fitting for the enigma that was Enoch Lacombe.

Chips's voice forced its way into her thoughts and it was only when it reached a crescendo of anger that she focussed on his ranting.

"...You are mine an' if I have to beat yuh bloodclaat everyday to put some sense into yuh head, I will. You are not going anywhere, until I am good and ready to release you. You an' yuh ugly face yout are my security if deh witchdoctor show himself before him time an' want to tek tings personal. Me an him."

From her stance and that determined look that was stamped onto her features, Sandra could see the shift in his opinion of her, a glimmer of fear that a day previously did not exist. She was no longer the compliant and docile woman he could push around. But she did not forget for a moment that his ego was being challenged and men like him would fight to the bitter end to maintain their credibility.

Stalemate sat uncomfortably with him.

As he stood up from the sofa, the persona she had become so comfortable with sloughed away with his faint shadow like a disused jacket and the real man, the real conniving, vile opportunist that he always was, stood up with him.

"I shoulda realise that a bomboclaat country gal like you could never play amongst toppa-top. Yuh a guh rot away in this council estate, wid yuh bang belly pickney, dependant on the government for sustenance, for the rest of your worthless life. Yuh think you can get me to leave. I'm here to stay gal an' the sooner you come to realise that, the better it will be for both of us."

He kissed his teeth sweetly.

"Yuh know what the story is out a street? Let me tell you; I have been appointed by the witchdoctor himself to look after you while him rub him time in jail. Which pussy will test that theory? You are tainted. Better the devil yuh know than the devil yuh don't, nuh true?"

Sandra shook her head in disgust and walked to the door, leaning on it weakly. She hesitated then turned to face him again.

"Enoch told me that I would get pregnant on the 14th of January and you know what, I did. He told me I'd have a baby boy on the 19th of October. And guess what he was right. But what worried me the most about Enoch was he insisted he had to take Rowan away from me, teach him in the ways of his destiny, and return him when he was older. What that meant I don't know but you learn to respect what he said whether you agree with him or not. We argued but he insisted my baby had a destiny to fulfill. I had many sleepless nights wondering when Enoch would leave me and take Rowan and I was almost relieved he went to jail, I'm not proud to say. But now I find myself wishing he would come back for little Rowan, give him what I can't."

"Him welcome to try," Chips spat. "But you Sandra, you are on yuh own."

Her lips blossomed into a confident smile, its rich almost overpowering everything Chips had just said.

"Will you pack your shit or should I?"

"Who will mek me, you?"

Sandra's eyes shone like glistening twin pools in moonlight and then her lips parted.

"Enoch will make you." She said simply.

Chips snorted his nose flaring, as he swallowed and his Adam's apple bobbed along his long neck like an erratic elevator. Chips opened his mouth to speak and as his rebuttal formed behind his teeth he decided on saying nothing.

The witchdoctor was in prison. That much he knew.

Her sense of certainty had shaken him, though.

He bit down on his lips and pointed at her threateningly, his dark face flushed by a growing sense of uncertainty. Sandra stood with her hands in front of her, she exuded not a glimmer of doubt and her unwavering confidence in what she was doing, disarmed him even further. The picture he saw in front of him contrasted so starkly with the weak and helpless victim he strived to create.

"Yuh know what? Mek me leave you to think about the craziness you talking before I do something stupid."

He stormed out of the room and slammed the door behind him.

Almost immediately the world seemed to take a breath and hold it.

Mere seconds later, a sense of accomplishment shot through Sandra like adrenaline pumped into her system. Head lulled forward, chin resting on her chest, the world of the sitting room became less corporeal and swam before her eyes. She lost control of her legs and fell backwards, her back slamming against the door and almost comically she slid down to the floor, mentally and physically exhausted.

Funnilly, Sandra welcomed it because with it came a sense of certainty that her situation had dramatically changed. And she would not swop that all over glow of achievement she felt for anything.

South London
Thursday 19th July
14.25

The reinforced black Bentley GT slid down Streatham High Road effortlessly; its occupants far from relaxed but comfortable. Unknown to the girls a protective spell sparkled briefly around the car as errant starlight broke through the light pollution. The promoters ride was protected corporeally – bulletproof glass - and mystically but he was still restless. Spokes was getting used to being driven around in his favorite ride by a chauffeur. He loved the idea of having the girls around but his loner sensibilities, made him strangely resistant to their instructions.

It had nothing to do with how capable they were either. For all intents and purposes, this was the safest he had felt for many months and his snakes head ring could attest to that. The bachelor life had molded him into expecting his freedom could only be compromised on his say so and in tolerable doses. But these were extraordinary times and yet still the conditioning was strong even with the insistence from the snake head ring on how important they were to his survival. He just wasn't completely open to the idea of sharing his plans with strangers. But for all that conditioned recalcitrance, he would do what he must.

The girls were pros - at least that's what it felt like to him - and they insisted on delving into aspects of his life he had only shared with a handful of people. First he had to divulge his itinerary - something that was more of a mental intention than something he wrote down. They became familiar with his yard too - the amount of rooms, hidey holes, attics, basements that his house possessed. The security and surveillance arrangements for the place were of interest to them also. Even his girl-friends and associates were scrutinised, so Bad II the Bone weren't playing.

Wrapped in that aura of safety they provided and with the guidance of his ring, Spokes still couldn't disclose everything he was up to. They knew what they had to do and if the powers that be were looking down on them favourably with their gifts and his protection they would come out of this alive. And no one needed to be the wiser.

The statuesque American chick who he clicked with immediately handled the Bentley with a familiarity that was almost scary and cut short his musings with a question.

"So who did you say we gonna meet at this pirate station?"

"I didn't baby," Spokes said his expression obviously needing coaxing.

"No secrets," Y said.

"No secrets, sista. He's a good spar of mine, the director of the radio station."

"Didn't realise pirate stations had directors."

"Well let me just say that Flex FM is no ordinary pirate radio station. Let's jus' say that Flex has used his ill gotten gains an' a head feh technology and done very well for himself. If you want your promotion talked 'bout on the street den Flex is deh place to do it."

"How is he involved in your dance, outside of his promotion work I mean?" Y asked.

"Him have so many fingers in so many pies you would think he was a sea puss. He's helped me out from street teams, flyers to internet promotion and a dedicated website."

"So you up for the technology then?" Y asked.

"Isn't dat the only way to go forward in deh future, sista?"

Y nodded.

"Anyway, today's visit is a more down to earth running's. We're just finalising the security arrangements. Making sure his street teams and security units know what is expected of dem."

"You seem worried?"

"Flex runs a tight ship. His street teams are all marketing graduates and sales people head hunted from stiff Fortune Five Hundred companies. His security unit are all ex-military. An some Yard shootas, to spice tings up a bit."

Spokes laughed.

"Nigga sounds like an OG?" Patra said.

"A reformed street soldier, sista."

"Do you know any law abiding citizens?" Y asked. Patra took her eyes off the road for a second to give Y the glare.

"A few but those are my circles. But don't judge me yet, there is much more to me than what you see."

It was Patra's time to laugh as she slowed the top marquee to a crawl.

"You still haven't answered my question though, Spokes," Y persisted.

Spokes paused, rewinding the conversation in his head, then said.

"If me nevah worried sistah Y, I would not have hired you to protect me. I'm just being careful." His focus shifted to Patra immediately after answering Y's queries.

"Laugh agen for mi Cleopatra, you brighten up deh place wid it."

Y shook her head at the blatant flirting and could swear she saw the black woman in the driving seat blush.

Patra's cheeks turned rose and she said.

"Satnav says we here D."

"Irie, irie. Just pull over here and turn up that radio deh. I love dis tune."

Dennis Brown was crooning the Reggae classic, 'Money in my pocket' from which Spokes croaked out a few bars before the song ended.

"Dis is one of the things that makes this radio station so popular. Deh play list is second to none and the DJ's are nuh bathroom disc jockeys but artists. And DJ Justine is one of the best."

DJ Justine's silky voice reminded her captive audience how good these classics make you feel. Bringing you back to your childhood if you were old enough or just cloaking you in the warm embrace of timeless reggae music. But what came next had no warmth to it at all. No quaint memories of the good old days.

DJ Justine screamed on air.

Unable to contain her joy, maybe?

She screamed again.

And this time if anyone was in doubt of her emotions, they were assured her song of panic came from primal depths where darkness and terror were real. A silence that was almost deafening followed. Everything in the car seemed to have stopped, frozen in place only the panic in the studio broke the spell. Spokes shot up in his seat as if the temperature had risen sharply under his ass, forgetting where he was, a surge of nervous energy galvanising him. He sprung towards the dashboard his flight impeded by the sturdy headrest in the front seat. Patra and Y just stared at the Blaupunkt in-car system with their mouths open. The screams shrank to the background and there was this uproarious laughter, guttural, obscene and outrageous, rising to a crescendo as if it had been recorded in the depth of a dank pit. The voice - deep, booming and unintelligible at first like the words were being spoken backwards and slowed up at the same time, began making sense to their ears. The world around them wasn't following suit. Spokes peered outside, his eyes wide. No traffic, no pedestrians and an almost cloying silence that had substance enough to envelope them. Spokes reached for the door handle then hesitated, his fingers fluttering at the prospect of escape but the Bentley had other plans and engaged its central locking. The promoter decided against even touching the polished walnut veneer or the silver coated door release. He just let his panic rise like bile in his stomach looking for release.

Patra was almost stooped on the driver's seat, staring intensely at the digital player trying to be as far from it as was possible. Y had wedged her back into a juncture between the seat and door her eyes still wide with disbelief, a heart beat away from panic. Spokes reaction was far less subtle and his usual cool demeanour had given way to ill fated attempts at smashing his way out of the car.

"Mas Spokes?"

The voice was so alien, so otherwordly sounding you got the impression it was an unfamiliar way of communicating for this *ting* but still its bass range was that of the vocal chords of a tyrannosaurus, carrying with it rumbling power, an unearthly chill and an auditory psychic rankness that smeared your mind and made you shiver uncontrollably. Everyone in the car reeled back from the mental halitosis as it stank up their thoughts.

"My sponsor wants to send yuh a little message, partner." The God awful voice taunted.

Y shrank further into her seat shaking her head to clear it of the corrupted static making the crown of her head tingle.

"DJ Justine is yuh favourite, dat right?" The hell thing asked. "Tasty bitch I must agree. What do you want me to send you? Her head or her guts? Maybe send her to you as kibbles. Niiiicccceee and sweet she is! You choose Mas Spokes one or deh other."

"Goddamn yuh rass to hell. Leave her alone," Spokes spat.

"Hell is my home partner. Chose one or the other."

"Why don't yuh come for me, instead?" The promoter beat his chest. "Yuh tink yuh bad. Come test me face to face."

The words dripped from the Blaupunkt speakers like raw sewage.

"Take the snake head ring off, cancel the hex around your car and separate yourself from the three protectors an' we can arrange feh dat. But as yuh are charmed amongst the charmed and as old time people seh, if yuh can't ketch Kwaku, ketch him shirt. The good will have to suffer for deh bad."

Spokes was shouting at the top of his voice. Droplets of saliva vacated his mouth with white deposits gathering at the corners of his mouth.

"Send deh rassclaat bwoy Darkman come then. Mek him deal with me, man to man. No demons, no coolie duppy, no Obeah just me an him."

"But that is why my sponsor sent for me. You are protected from him but my kind is not so easily dissuaded. And which one of us could turn down the opportunity to acquire a tasty hu-Man soul."

"Justine is an innocent."

"Isn't that the sweetest kind?"

"Yuh a guh suffer feh dis God know."

"Him," the hell thing kissed it teeth, like it was sucking the innards of a poor living thing guts, bone and all. "His hands are tied, pardy. A little something them call free will."

It chortled grossly like it was having trouble adapting to human speech

"Time up pardy." It announced. "Me and Justine will just have to surprise you."

The gales of laughter began and the screams continued with it. A throaty gurgle, a wet tearing sound, more uncontrollable screaming, splashes of life giving blood maybe and the thump of a body falling to the floor, pieces at a time.

The screaming stopped and so did the Flex 91.1 FM horror show.

When Deacon summoned you from his ivory tower, you immediately began to retrace your actions in your head and what you could have done inadvertently or blatantly wrong. If you had the slightest doubt, change your identity and leave the British Isles. Chile was good this time of year. If on the other hand you were confident your actions were honorable then don't just finish what you were doing and leisurely make your way to the meeting place with a savoir fare attitude. No, that wasn't the type of man that he was even for a bonafide operator like Chips.

Deacon demanded strict attention to his demands if you were under his protection or in business with him.

He had a fearsome reputation amongst his peers and a more than healthy respect from his enemies. But from his snitches you were next to nothing, a cockroach at the bottom of his special edition Nikes, a necessary inconvenience that could be replaced by a throng of other unnecessary inconveniences at a snap of his fingers. Being one step up on the evolutionary ladder did not make Chips any more secure in Deacon's presence and for a grown ass man that was very disconcerting.

Why make life even more difficult for himself? When he got the call on a Friday evening - one of the busiest times at the Spot - he had to leave Tricky to look after Sandra and keep things level while he made his way to Green Park. Traffic had been a bitch coming into central London but as he pulled into the private parking bay underneath the illustrious Imperial Fitness Centre it was not a good idea to carry his seething annoyance in with him. Instead he checked his ego in the parking bay. He wouldn't want Deacon to think his bad mood was directed at him. That would not be a good idea, and although Chips was two rungs up from the bottom of the food chain as classified by Deacon - street zoologist, he had moments. They were infrequent flashes of inspiration that catapulted him into heady realms of Boss but they did not last long enough for him to get comfortable or get noticed. He had to keep his aspirations for power close to his chest - for now anyway.

Chips slammed the door of his Range Rover, taking a cursory look around his well lit surroundings. The smell of motor oil permeated the air with the smell of new metal and freshly vulcanised rubber. Admiring some of the tasty motors, he saw a cadre of Deacon's soldiers hanging around the entrance to the elevator in the distance. He made his way over to them. As soon as he cleared the obstruction of the massive concrete support pillars that spread across the floor plan, they spotted his approach. The shottas didn't show their weapons but Chips knew they were strapped and from the fluttering fingers in their jackets they were ready to use them at a moment's notice.

"Deacon sent feh mi," Chips made sure his hands were high when he approached them.

"What's your name then?" one of the men asked.

"Dem call mi Chips. He's expecting me."

The man nodded as if to say I've heard it all before and motioned to another man.

"Call up for authority then frisk him."

After a rough assault and personal probe that they deemed to be a body search he was directed to the interior of a stationary lift already filled with three large men for padding, he presumed. One operated the door - using his manicured but thick finger to press for the fifth floor - while the other two took turns in scrutinising him inch by uncomfortable inch.

An unexpected march of gooseflesh trotted up Chips' spine alerting him to the excessive nature of all this and perceiving the possible reasons why. When they arrived on the fifth floor and the door opened a clearer understanding of what was going on revealed itself to him.

The atmosphere was electric. The smell of frankincense, bitter wood, some exotic plant and possible animal extracts perfumed the plush area ahead of him. He stood on the threshold and took in the scene, pinned in place for a moment too long maybe, feeling the reassuring poke of a gun to his back, coaxing him forward. They had not changed the foyer much, burning incense pots scattered around the furnishings. The marble floor was covered in symbols and vévés of protection etched by charcoal or lined with cornmeal. He strode as confidently as was possible for him, his eyes on the focal point of a steam room fifty yards dead ahead, issuing steam like an old Dutch pot on a cookout.

An arm sheathed in white, obviously part of a white shirt, came out from behind a massive Jabba pot that housed a huge coniferous plant and stopped him dead in his tracks. Chips looked down at the gnarly fingers and the dark skin with venom but controlled his ire commendably. The owner of the arm came out from behind the large vessel, like his movements were buoyed up by his disrespect for gravity. Bare footed, dark skinned and scrawny he was all in white, Panama hat, shirt, trousers with a pendant swung around his neck strung with unknown vegetation and desiccated animal parts. The witchdoctor blew a stream of liquid in the opposite direction to Chips, his five finger tips still on Chips' chest keeping him in position and making sure the chicken foot he had in his right hand was doused in the liquid.

Chips fidgeted nervously.

"Stand still," the man commanded in his Caribbean twanged, French accented English. Slowly he traced the chicken foot around Chips' body, every meridian he stopped at he murmured a mantra or chant. When he was done he called out to another contingent of men.

"He is real and free from any dark charms." He said to them.

The men parted, leaving his path free from obstruction, not directing him but assuming he knew where he was going. The door to the steam room was slightly ajar and plumes of steam were escaping into the foyer. Chips pulled it open and walked into the tiled room and there was Deacon lounging on one of the steps alone, his area made more comfortable by scented pillows stuffed around him. He had his eyes closed and was naked accept for a large beach towel that covered his mid section.

Chips started sweating immediately, a combination of heat and nerves.

"Suh you made it?" Deacon opened his eyes and swung his legs down to a sitting position.

"I reach as quickly as the traffic would allow mi to." Chips answered.

"Mi feel yuh, it's a Friday night and deh roads can be fuckery at this time."

Chips nodded and wiped sweat from his forehead.

"You're looking good Chips. Gambling treating you well it looks like."

"Times tough but yuh know the hustle have to continue. We all need to eat food, don't it?"

"Can't fault a man feh dat but you seem to be as successful as me in surviving the tough times while others aren't as skilled at the games as we are. I wonder why?"

Chips didn't know what to say in response to that he was not sure where this was going.

"In the space of two weeks I've lost eight good men." Deacon paused. "Well okay five good men, the others were expendable but yuh get mi drift. Twister, Cockal and Spider were virtually eaten alive. And Minty..." His voice trailed off absently. Then he was back.

"Forensic reports tell mi dat Spliff Tail and Morgan died of massive pulmonary distress. You know what dat mean?"

"Heart attack," Chips said emotionlessly.

"Suh yuh were paying attention in class, good. Yes my yout, they were frightened to death and here you are, fit and well without a care in the world, unaffected as deh rassclaat world goes to hell in a hand basket."

"You don't think I...? Listen I don't flex dem way deh, star."

"I know yuh not capable. But I did have my doubts because after all you were the one who suggested the job on Enoch and even come up wid the plan feh rip him off. You even helped me to frame him when deh plans went south. But Enoch is locked away in prison and all the players involved in the original game are dead except me and you. I know why I'm still breathing but you had me concerned for awhile, den it clicked."

Chips felt rivulets of sweat trickling down his back and into the crack of his ass. His dreadlocks were itching and his scalp tingling. But as uncomfortable as that was, it would not look good if he started scratching his back and head nervously. Of course, that was what Deacon wanted. The only reason behind meeting in a Mickey Mouse location such as this was humiliation and dominance. His vest was soaked and it was just a matter of time before his shirt then his jacket was saturated too. Salty perspiration stung his eyes and he wiped them with the sleeve of his jacket. This was turning out to be an exercise in endurance that was proving stressful.

"My theory is Enoch knows yuh a fuck him woman and doesn't want the yout to get harmed if him retaliate."

"Yuh talking like you think Enoch is walking street?" Chips asked.

"What do you bomboclaat tink? Duh you think what you passed outside, to get through to me was for deh drama, rude bwoy. If it's not Enoch it's someone him send. And whoever him send has been instructed to seek revenge on the men that put him away."

Chips listened and Sandra's episode re-enacted in his mind's eye - her collapse, the ace of spades playing card left beside her - but from how this conversation was heading, that memory would stay solidly in his mind. Deacon was getting paranoid and grasping at straws for answers. Chips couldn't help him with facts, just rumors.

"Nothing has come on mi radar 'bout Enoch being released from prison. Him would be spotted by someone and dat nuh come to my attention."

"Would you tell mi if it did?" Deacon asked.

"Of course..." Chips said.

"Like rass you would. Yuh an me know deh value of deh Darkman's treasure. Wid me out deh way, what would stop you from gaining what we both have been looking for. But I run dis shit for a reason. And becah me is like a junkyard dawg with a bone, I don't give in at the first sign of trouble. My dominoes are turned down, I've played my hand and you have just passed."

"Believe me Deacon, if I knew anything you would be the first to know. I've gone through every inch of that flat, there is nuthin in deh that would point to the treasures whereabouts."

Deacon sniggered and continued as if Chips hadn't spoken.

"But if for whatever reason my plan fails, now that I realise the Darkman does care for something other than himself, Enoch's girl and deh pickney will be used as bargaining chips in this drama. Whether he is on street himself or him a work him Obeah from prison, he will know mi nah play, when I start murdering dem rass, one by one."

Chips didn't realise he was kneading his hands in front of him but Deacon did. He tightened the vice with pleasure.

"Dat won't be necessary boss, a man like Enoch cares feh nothing but his family. A move like that will just make him even more out of control."

"Is that real talk or are you just bloodclaat begging for the life of Enoch's woman and pickney?"

"I don't care what happen to dem." He snapped. "They are tools but I don't think fucking with his family is a good idea."

"Well den, we a guh test that theory. And we will see if you come out of this as smoothly as yuh have so far."

Chips grinned nervously looking down at himself dripping wet and his clothes elongated and baggy from being water saturated. Suddenly his actions against Sandra, the intimidation, the insults and the sporadic beatings came to the forefront of his mind with such force he felt faint. Before he didn't care but now the prospect of inflaming the wrath of the Darkman did not sit well with him. And whether he believed he was roaming the streets or still locked up in jail, a malevolent wraith doing his bidding, some part of his consciousness had switched on to the belief that it was all possible. A neural pathway had been laid and as time passed it would be reinforced completely evaporating any doubt he had that Darkman was alive and well in London city.

13.

Hyde Park
Thursday, July 20th
11.40am

A sunny day never failed to make Y introspective. Throw in a shady tree, the smell of green grass, a bit of privacy with a few home comforts and she could idle the day away easily.

And she was tempted to but she was still on the clock as it were and this moment of tranquillity was just a brief respite from bodyguard duties. She had deposited Spokes at the only place he trusted to get his hair cut – Lenny's Hair Emporium in Notting Hill - while she took some much needed 'me' time.

Y sighed.

Look at this place, straight out of someone's fairy tale but so few realised it was a buffer helping to protect you from the realities of the other side.

She shivered.

The girls had discovered the gardens by accident and because it was a stone's throw away from the Underground they had decided it would be an ideal meeting point while in London.

Y had got here early for the express reason of some quality thinking time before Patra arrived. And she could do that without worry. There were no playgrounds built here and it was far enough from the traffic to make you think you were isolated. No animals were allowed in its confines so no worries of treading in unexpected mounds of dog shit. Whoever created these grounds definitely had solitude and beauty in mind. The grass was like the green velveteen, uniform in height with not a blade out of place, as if barber Carlene was vexed with doing human hair and decided to take her trusty shears to the turf instead. A wrought iron fountain with some mythical seafaring beast spewing massive jets of water to the sky was set dead centre while interconnecting walkways criss-crossed the area like a spider's web. Then set in concentric circles like the patterns of ripples in a pool were the startling colors of planted flowers. Y found herself admiring the ground-man's skill.

You'll never go hungry, Mr. Grounds-man, she thought.

Lying on her back with her legs drawn up and her head propped at an angle by a folded towel, above her the sun sat regally on a soft mound of pale blue sky as the few remaining clouds drifted ponderously out of sight. In the distance frisbees were being thrown, footballs kicked, lovers cuddled and the only blot on the picture perfect landscape was the filthy looking hobo muttering to himself in the immediate distance. He slithered about the park his clothes slick with dirt, a grimy bag that seemed like a coal sack with a thick rope like pull string on the top. She didn't know why but the thought popped into her head that he was some kind of anti-Santa some perverse version of St. Nick from some other place that instead of finding out who is naughty or nice when he slid down the chimney it was with a skinning knife to eviscerate your family with a guttural Har!Har!Har!

Y shivered again at her flights of fancy and closed her eyes the image fading. She took in a lung full of the fragrant air and adjusted the earphones on her MP3 player. The music of Eyrikah Badu formed a seamless backdrop to the calm.

A sweet musical score for how life should really be.

For long moments nothing mattered. All the pain she had been through was a hazy memory that could so easily have never happened and her contentment while it lasted in the here and now was all that existed.

Not for long.

Already, the darkness they had been exposed to was grating on her perceptions of the world she had spent twenty five years understanding. To be introduced to another aspect of existence that was hinted at in religions or popular culture but never truly accepted by the majority was scary, almost impossible to comprehend.

"Wake up an' smell the goddamn roses," the voice of reality whispered in her ear and she sighed. Opening one eye she looked up to see Patra blocking the precious sunlight and grinning down at her. "Wha's happenin' bitch?" Patra was obviously in a boisterous mood and having a dig at her for good measure.

"I was great before you turned up," Y said as she raised up on her elbows. "How did you get here?"

"I rode my baby. And I must have shaved at least ten minutes off the time it took me the last time I was here."

"Orgasmic?" Y said sarcastically.

"Hell yeah!" Cleopatra looked around. "Where's Suzy at?"

"She bought her roller blades with her so she's skating through the park somewhere."

Patra nodded and took her iPhone from inside her leather jacket. She punched the touch screen and bought it to her ear.

"Alriiight," she began. "Where here?" She nodded pointing to the floor. "Waiting for you girlfriend. So bring your big balloon ass over."

Y shook her head and laughed.

"You sleep with it, don't you?"

"Nothin' gets past you, girlfriend. This is dual function shit, right here." Patra held out the smartphone in the palm of her hand as if she was a shop assistant about to go into a preamble on the benefits of the product. "It keeps me connected and is a cleverly disguised dildo too," she laughed, girlishly. "I'll get one for you on your birthday, aiight?"

"Thanks." Y said.

It didn't take long before Suzy was whizzing up the path towards them. Her movements were a blue and black blur with her dark hair flowing behind. Swerving past obstacles with a fluid grace and leaping over a park bench as she approached.

A sharp bank and she was standing in front of them in a cloud of dust and Chanel.

"Everyting criss," Suzy said brightly.

Patra high fived her.

Y nodded.

"So, let mi guess," Suzy said breathing evenly and looking at Y's unconvincing show of impassiveness. "Yuh couldn't tell us over the phone, suh it must be serious."

Patra looked over to Y questioningly and then to Suzy.

"So what's this about?"

"A development." Y said cryptically.

"Goddamit, Y man! This is a good gig," Patra blurted. "No, this is a great gig. You're not going to fuck it up with some deep analytical shit are you?"

"It's not about Spokes, this time."

"Well, cool," Patra sighed, relieved, her voice lowering. "If it don't affect my paper, I'm peachy."

"It's Tyrone."

"Damn," Patra blurted out. "Why didn't you say it was about that cocksucker?"

"If I knew it was about him, mi woulda come sooner." Suzy said her voice more urgent.

"Well our friend has been sighted. The response from the blog has been incredible. The sisters out there are as pissed off as we are about our money."

"How many subscribers we get so far?" Suzy questioned.

"Two thousand, one hundred."

"Goddamn in four days. The sisters got our back, man." Patra said.

"Feh real," Suzy sounded incredulous and then the canvas of her face altered to a blank emotionless stare. She was looking beyond Y and Patra but couldn't seem to look away. Her focus was in the middle distance which became a blurry netherworld of past and future, cause and effect, filled with the uncountable threads of possibility stretching into an unknown horizon then image faded. Suzy was gripped by a compulsion that tightened the muscles of her neck, holding her sight squarely on a hobo in the distance. This was the first time the derelict had come to her attention and must have taken a circuitous route, around and around the park, in ever diminishing circles, gibbering, dragging his lace less boots - that had become almost slippers - picking up detritus that was fascinating to his eyes only.

For every nugget his crazy mind conjured out of thin air and he popped in his mouth, he let out an almost sorrowful mewling sound and continued on his way. And his way was ever closer to where the girls sat.

Patra looked around briefly at the sound but turned back to the conversation.

"He's been spotted three days ago in Croydon," Y said evenly.

Suzy turned back to face her, pale.

"You mean dat son-of-a-bitch nuh have the decency to leave London at least. Him bold nuh rass?"

"Nah that nigga ain't bold, that's his way of telling us to kiss his black ass." Patra shook her head and planted her left hand on her hips. "In other words that jiggaboo thinks we can't touch him, he thinks he's in the clear."

Suzy cracked her knuckles combatively, getting back into the conversation.

"I know how you guys feel and that's why I felt I better break the news in person." Y said.

Patra and Suzy sat on the grass.

"I just feel like I want to go and stake him out inna Croydon, right now," Suzy said. "Just check out his coming an goings."

"I'm with that." Patra said.

"Me too," Y said. "But we've got enough on our plates to deal with so leave that dawg for now. I got something special for Tyrone, trust me."

"Suppose he skips town?" Patra asked.

"Well if your theory is right and he thinks that he's got one up on us then he'll stay and gloat."

"An' we have him." Suzy rose up gracefully from a legs crossed position all thought of Tyrone drained out of the discussion. Instead her eyes were on the bag man, head down coming their way. Suzy flowed into a wushu form her stance solid and ready but it was her eyes that gave her away. Her eyes that made Patra ask.

"What's up Ms Wong?" Then she looked back herself and scrambled to her feet.

Y was able to have a better look at the derelict and it did nothing to improve his standing in her eyes. Instead it made her sense of disquiet much worst. His hair was brown shoulder length matted and caked with grime. He sported a substantial beard that was flecked with saliva and fragments of his last meal. Persistent gnats swirled around him in a cloud of which he was the centre.

He muttered as he dragged himself closer.

"Be careful Y." Suzy's said the words with considered emphasis. "Him is not what him seem."

Those words reverberated in her head discordant and chaotic. Y reached out to Patra and both pulled themselves up to standing, turning to face the hobo who was shuffling towards them as if they did not exist.

"Let's just leave this crazy motherfucker. He can do his strange shit on his own, it's a big park."

"London is not big enough for you to hide from me, girlies." The hobo said, his voice roared like the flames in an ancient hearth stoked with a bellow of air.

The girls took a step back.

The bagman that earlier was engrossed in his own sick world was suddenly present, in the here and now, aware and curious. A cold intelligence inhabited his eyes, where a vacant one had been. His posture snapped rigid in a crouch, his movements almost feline prowling. As he circled his prey, his focus steadied on them with an almost furious heat of anger or hunger or something, that ignited in him.

A monstrous smile unfurled from his lips.

"Jesus." Patra said. The girls were fixed to where they stood in rapt amazement.

"I'm going to enjoy tearing you apart. Who will be first, first ,first?" His voice boomed with otherworldly sibilance and he licked his lips with an impossibly long lizard tongue. The tip was forked, the body a mottled, meaty protuberance, black, pink and grotesquely prehensile.

"Oh,Christ!" Y rocked back, reached behind her and snapped the latch of her Versace monogrammed sword bag on her back. She gripped the handle of the katana and pulled it free.

"You can try." Suzy said her face losing colour in degrees, her voice carrying horror instead of intent.

The hobo thing laughed its shoulders rising and falling, exposing a dirty flannel shirt and an unzipped body warmer every time laughter gurgled repulsively from its mouth. The flesh under it rippled and contorted. A barley audible hum and buzz of insect intelligence, moved under his shirt with the hive mind of a swarm. The hobo thing shivered deliciously. Cockroaches and Black Beetles fell from under his shirt and scurried away. He caught one, an armored beetle and looked at it inquisitively. He then popped it in his mouth, where it proceeded to burrow into his cheek, travelling under his skin to his neck and disappeared. The hobo thing rolled his neck in satisfaction.

"You I want first," he pointed to Patra his finger nails dirty thick talons."Ah!" He sniffed the air like a hound."Juicy, tender and bloody. Somebody's nasty." He said in a sing song voice.

Like a cell from an old film reel stuck in a dilapidated projector, an instant in time that hitched in her memory cold and clear, Patra could feel her adolescent embarrassment flush over her again, tears pooling in her eyes

"Somebody's nasty." Her class mates had teased as her first ever period left it's bloody mark on her grey metal chair. Patra caught herself drifting under the hobo things spell and shook her head, swearing under her breath.

It had burrowed into her mind, kmowing it was her time of month and purposely picked the trauma from her past, using it against her. Fucking with her head, fucking with all their heads. Patra composed herself and instinctively took back control and slammed the trapdoor of her mind shut to his intrusions.

"Didn't know we could do shit like that, ain't that right motherfucker." Patra gave a weak smile and snapped into a Thai form, fists up, poise loose. "He trying to fuck with our minds girls don't let him."

Suzy stepped forward composing herself with effort rubbing shoulders for reassurance and said.

"Jus fuck off and leave us alone. Wi nuh frighten that easy."

"No fun in that," the hobo thing said.

"Let me hear you scream. Now or later. Your choice. Always your choice."

His grin was broad, impossibly so, almost splitting his face in two and that inhuman tongue flickered behind the prison bars of black and rotting teeth that held as much menace as the slavering canines of a vampire.

"Tangling with us will not be fun peckerwood, I don't care which satanic hood you're from. You maybe gangsta down their but up here, so are we." Patra spat the words a dark resolve eclipsing her features.

"This will be fun, fun, fun. The legion know of you, you are celebrity meat in the pit. So I want to be first to gut you, to taste you. I want to be the first, first, first." He raved like child in a tantrum.

"Not today," Y said calmly. "Today you go back to where you came from."

Y stood with the glowing katana pointing towards it. She slid smoothly into a kata, locking each move, each breath, the anger maybe or the horror intensifying the umbra of power emanating from the sword. Patra and Suzy stepped back.

"Walk away or get carried away."

The hobo thing flinched noticeable at the sword, its focus reverted inwards for a moment, the infernal brimstone glow in its eyes dimming, as if it was consulting with someone or something not of this world. Then as if its fears were confirmed it snapped back to lucidity with a feral grunt. Its smile was impish, eyes calculating as he absorbed them as if their image would become a mental keepsake for him. This time he stepped back tentatively.

"Next time you won't see me coming. Next time will be fun."

He took a longing look at them and scurried away, his manic laughter trailing behind him.

"Neeeext time will be fun," he screeched. "Next tiiimeee!"

14.

Docklands Cargo Bay Ltd
South East London
Friday, July 19th
11.40

The tinted smoke from the Monte Cristo cigar rose lazily from the searing tip. Enoch Lacombe savored the taste by turning it around in his mouth and then pulled almost lovingly on the Cuban, sighed, tilted his head back and let out a stream of the aromatic smoke to the zinc alloy ceiling.

"Do dare dedi datum vita." The words spoken gently had the power to alter the laws of matter and bending it to the wielder's will. He blew out another small twirling maelstrom from his mouth that suddenly decided to disobey the laws of thermodynamics and form into a flying vulture looking as if it was preparing for landing. His mind drifted over the blood that had been shed these past weeks and with a mental shrug he was as focused as a laser beam again. His eyes settled on the space on top of the antique bureau and he recalled the importance of what was missing from it. Invariably a deluge of pain and urgency overwhelmed him. Darkman stretched in the Celtic throne chair thought to have been charmed by Merlin himself and now housed in his makeshift home, a sixty foot trailer modified for habitation and containing some of the curiosities, charms, amulets and talismans that he had collected in his travels. Every item in his menagerie of arcane culture spoke of where he had been on the globe and the people and organisations that had willingly or not, shared their knowledge with him.

Home away from home, until such time.

But amongst everything around Darkman that was of obvious value and significance, two designer paper bags stood dust free, pristine and totally out of place beside the Celtic throne chair. With the cigar in his right hand, he leaned over with his left and rummaged inside. He plucked up a trouser and shirt set suited for a three to four year old, dangling it on his fingers as he observed it.

A scowl darkened his face.

His father died cursing his name for the stone that was bound to the Lacombe family had not returned in time to save his land. But of equal importance was his son, his sole bloodline and heir to the family traditions who was suffering with his baby mother under the heel of his enemies. He promised himself he would take him home, restore self worth to his woman and keep spilling the blood required for retribution by the dark god's until the balance was restored.

He dug his nose into the fabric of the baby clothes and inhaled a lungful of newness and innocence. Enoch had never seen his child in the flesh but he had projected himself to his bedside many nights and he sensed much more than a flicker of the Lacombe talent in him. He would be strong and significant in a world that did not realise his kind existed. And although his offspring and his mother where under the yoke, a situation he took full responsibility for, he felt no guilt, no shame, just a ice cold conviction that they were pawns in a celestial domino game, characters created from a genetic lottery, given free will when it suited the players or they lost interest. His duty was to maintain the integrity of his character and be who he was meant to be - a vicious, vindictive, vain, vengeful son-of-a-bitch who believed in family first. If the act of manifesting the duppies and demons that were his storm-troopers in this war sucked him dry as a bone, he did not care because he had been the cause of all this. He did not care that for every higher order demon, every creature from the pit he dragged fourth it drained him significantly. He needed to take respites like this to recuperate drawing on the almost endless supply of negative energy that the city of London emanated, continuing to unravel his scheme in his head but he was still only human. What he had lost he would never regain but what he was short changed in longevity he would gain in pride.

A sharp astringent smell broke his reverie and he leaned forward to exit the chair, carefully placing the baby clothes in their place. He walked past a stuffed dodo bird into the area he used as a kitchen and watched the simmering demon weed in the distillation glass bubbling heartily. Enoch added a solvent to the mix and returned to his throne.

He never thought it possible but his time in prison had taught him patience, soaking up his brashness and his compulsive need for adventure and tempering it with calculation and cunning.

Deh bwoy Spokes, who he knew held the remainder of his treasures and more importantly, the John Crow stone, had himself prepared by accident or device a powerful artifact even he could not penetrate. Then, as if this country man was taunting him, he had acquired the services of a group of the Watunza Mwanga – the cares of the light, reincarnated warriors his forefathers had run into on their numerous travels in Africa. They were wild cards thrown in amongst all the conflicting forces that made up human existence to maintain the balance and fairness of the domino game. His side had been chosen by his family many centuries ago and so by their very nature he was physically unable to be within a hundred Talmudic paces of them.

How Spokes knew his way around the mystical landscape was a mystery.

But he was no Voudon, that he knew.

He dusted the ashes of his cigar into a copper dish balanced on the arms of the Merlin chair and smiled fleetingly.

What was his once, would be his again.

The precious drops of distilled demon weed fell into the ceramic beaker and as he procured the required quantity, he too condensed an idea to spill blood, a lot more blood.

"Every knee shall bow ...."

Red Ground Estates
Surrey
02.30

The girls sat on the large bed in one of Spokes' many spare rooms, but this one, large enough to hold two double beds comfortably, acted as a command centre. Y was applying nail polish to Suzy's toes and Patra had her chin propped up in her hands watching the flat screen television. Surrounding them were ten monitors with CCTV camera feeds that were situated at the many vantage points around the mansion, sitting on tables that they checked regularly and backed up with a five man unit who were also securing the grounds. They were in constant communication with the roving security teams and so their short distance radios went everywhere they went in the grounds. That fact alone made the burgeoning fashion accoutrement a candidate to be accessorized. When Patra had finished with them they were bedecked in diamantes, lanyards representing Jamaica, UK and the USA and blinking LED's on the tips of the antennae. Sufficiently pimped they were slung around necks or hips. On their recommendation – Y had Googled perimeter security - Spokes had wired the estate with state of the art motion and pressure detectors on her inexperienced recommendation but in his eyes it had been given by a security professional with an unblemished track record of countless years. Now getting into the estate without being detected required a full tactical assault team and resources that Deacon could not marshal in a million years. So the flesh and blood intruders were dealt with.

Check.

The other types would not be so easily deterred and that concerned Suzy.

How could you grow up in Jamaica and not have an affinity for the supernatural? Rich or poor, sufferah or risto, out of many one people as the country's motto proclaimed and you at least appreciated the unseen powers that condemned many an unsuspecting Yardie. Christianity had tried it damndest to convince its mainly African descendents since the fifteenth century that their power resided in heaven and with one God. Forced indoctrination could not wipe what had been written on the collective consciousness of generations of Africans and the Holy Spirit had to coexist with the spirits of the mother-land. Not all the ancient traditions where of a benevolent nature though and where there were Pocomania meetings celebrating life, there was black magic seeking to destroy it.

Suzy knew there were few children who had not been scared by the twilight stories of the Darkman in the same breath as the Three Foot Horse, Rolling Calf and Coolie Duppy. He was an urban legend back-a-yard. The bogeyman she was referring to was known even by her grandmother who used the stories as a threat to way-ward children scaring them onto the straight and nar-row.

Believing he was real was straining on the elastic of her convictions. But Suzy had witnessed his power and his demonic connections. She had seen the effect of Darkman, on her waking world and she couldn't help thinking that they were completely and utterly out of their depth.

If they were normal people they'd be buckling under the enormity of the revelations but being who they were the world they thought they understood shattered at their feet and the remnants shoved under the proverbial bed, to be cogitated on at a more convenient time.

In the immediate future Y was annoyed. Spokes had misled them. And she would be damned if their services would be prostituted because they were in need, if they were to be fucked, their eyes needed to be wide open. So Spokes was walking a groove into the floorboards in the study next door preparing for a oestrogen fuelled inquisition. And the girls waited patiently.

Y started laughing and in her crossed legged position bounced in one spot with the hilarity of it all. Suzy looked over to Patra who shrugged her shoulders at the corner of the bed, engrossed in some Extreme Makeover programme and rolled her eyes. The laughter was contagious and in seconds all three were chortling, uncontrollably. Between splutters Suzy asked.

"Will sumbody please tell mi what is suh funny?"

With aching cheeks Y tried to compose herself. She screwed on the top of the red nail polish and placed it in her utility tray with the cotton balls and the acetone.

"Life is funny," she said finally.

"I wouldn't go as far as saying that this son-of-a-bitch we call life was funny. Challenging and sometimes a pain in the ass but funny no," Patra dried her eyes.

"Not funny ha-ha but funny strange." Y explained.

"Strange just doesn't explain what we're going through right now. This is some outright bizarre shit."

"And my is telling me, this is just the beginning.

"I was afraid of that," Y said. "Remember how I used to moan about how life was passing us by. I could only look forward to the infrequent scrapes we got ourselves into, our training sessions and partying. It was driving me crazy."

"How could I forget your bitchin'? Then the mother-fucker Tyrone came into your life."

"Our life," Suzy corrected.

"Smoothed you the fuck out," Patra observed.

"So smooth, all my defenses were down and he ripped us off of everything we had. But look at us now. Excitement, mystery, danger and some money. And I'm beginning to think we've bitten off more than we can chew."

"No shit." Patra laughed.

"Getty, getty nuh want it, wanty, wanty cah get it." Suzy recited the Jamaican saying stoically.

"Be careful what you wish for." Y murmured as if she regretted that dreams did come true after all.

"Amen." Patra focussed on the television for a moment. "You know what I wish for?" She looked at her freshly pedicured feet and wriggled her toes. "I want to live to see next week. But as that is uncertain I'm going to squeeze the good shit out of every moment."

The girls went silent with that shared and succinct assessment of their situation; the horror and mystery trickled back into the moment as they stood on the edge of darkness. A cold chill descended.

Were they trying to protect a man who did not deserve protection?

The room door pushed open and in swaggered the man with the answers. He slowly closed the door behind him, grabbed a chair, swinging it around and down so he could straddle it like a cowboy.

"Mek wi reason." Spokes said

Spokes stretched out the five fingers of his right hand as if he was testing the strength of his nerves and let the ceiling lights catch the blue jewel being devoured by a dragon that encircled his index finger. The scaly gold skin etched on the rings surface by a master artisan glinted reptilian like and was very old or was made to look so.

"Is this for real?" Patra asked.

"I researched it thoroughly. Had it corroborated by an Iraqi professor of antiquity," Spokes said. "It cost me an arm, an a leg too, the back door business don't come cheap, mark my words."

"Mesopotamian, you said," Suzy repeated. "Four thousand BC?"

"Roughly, used by Babylonian priests also to protect their order from back bitters, thieves and murderers who wanted to do them harm. The spell was cast in Sumerian by my pardy. Yuh believe dat, a country bwoy from Mobay, speaking a long dead language and casting spells? The ring is linked to my soul or life force."

He lifted his hand up to the light again and admired it.

"Enoch collected magical objects with power from all over the world. My guard ring is from his collection and kept mi invisible from his prying eyes all this time. My spar Jimmy, knew the importance of it and made sure in his dying moments that I wore it." Spokes suddenly said nothing, he swallowed hard, his focus drifted and his eyes glistened. "I found out that he can't personally come too close to the wearer so that is the only reason why we have not faced him personal like. That alone is saving my life." He paused. "And you of course."

"Why does it feel like we're being set up? You need protection that only we can offer?" Y asked. "And yet that demon thing disguised as a derelict in the park. It was saying the same thing about us. It was almost scared of the three of us together."

"I didn't intentionally set out to mislead you sista Y, believe mi I had no choice. You are ordained, the Watunza Mwanga – carers of the light - only you can keep me safe. You walk both sides of deh spiritual divide and all deh evil Darkman has pulled forth, knows dis."

"Don't get it twisted OG," Patra said. "We convinced this shit is real, we just not sure, you for real."

Suzy sighed.

"Deh thing is, you weren't as open with us from the beginning although your intentions were honourable."

"Would you have believed me in deh first place?" Spokes asked. "I had to drip feed you the information."

"Ok, we were doubtful but that was your job to convince us." Y said flatly. "Now we feel like we want to pull out, leave you to handle this ... situation yourself."

"I wish it was that simple, sista Y."

"It looks simple enough from where I'm sitting."

Spokes shook his head.

"The Darkman legacy has survived for a few hundred years on guile and ruthlessness. If I know who you are, he will too. Him a guh put two an' two together and conclude rightly you are with me. For him to get what he wants, an' for us to be the wiser for it, a plan had to be put in place.

"What does he want from you?"

Spokes smile was a patient one but his eyes shone his determination.

"His collection. Money and magical booty, he and his family plundered all over the world. My best friend was murdered because of him and I was dragged into dis world wholly unprepared. I should have had nothing to do with dis rass if not for my idrens memory."

"Why now?" Suzy asked. "After all dis time. Why him come after yuh now."

"Them bind di beast." Spokes laughed, his booming voice echoing off the high ceilings. "His enemies were smarter than he thought and Darkman was held in the Queens prison, trapped with three life sentences over him head. I became the custodian to his treasures from then on."

"The motherfucker broke out of prison, right?" Patra asked.

"Dem couldn't hold him forever, that's why these four years, I was preparing. Making sure I had an exit strategy."

"Now he wants his shit back and he thinks you are a part of the problem."

"Correct, Miss P. Anyone he feels is responsible for his incarceration is dead meat, me, you, we all included."

"Great, so we are a part of this exit strategy?" Patra lamented.

"It seem suh. The ring found you and the higher powers set the way."

"So you have a choice and we don't." Y sat up from the bed, her body language combative.

"If reaching out to help a bredrin, in need was a choice, den maybe. But I feel destiny had already set out the pieces in the cosmic draught game and you ladies are a part of its game plan."

"So we are supposed to just go along with all this. Accept higher power, your story while we risk our lives protecting yours."Y said flatly.

"Yeah man, that sounds about right. That is why you are, who you are. You have a bigger purpose and I am just a part of it. The higher powers have taken a personal interest in your schooling." He shrugged. "I'd be flattered."

Y kissed her teeth like a seasoned Jamaican.

Suzy listened but was almost enamored to the ring on Spokes' finger. She wondered how much of their lives were preordained, how much knowledge it contained and if it knew what path they should take.

"Can I touch it?" Suzy asked. "See if I can feel something of what you're telling us."

Spokes looked down at the ring on his thick fingers and then held out his hand like a Cardinal expecting it to be kissed.

"Do your ting," he said.

Suzy reached out and touched it.

15.

Clinton Recreational Centre
Friday, July 19th
9.30 am

Her scream echoed off the glass walls, an almost orgasmic release of pleasure as she stretched herself to the limit and realised that wasn't enough.

It was the cry of a woman who had made a play that should win her this very competitive set. A cry that relieved the levels of stress she had to maintain that most people would buckle under. And boy, did she need it. The girls were back at the mansion covering Spokes while she was given the opportunity for some much needed R&R.

The ball exploded off the net of Y's racket rebounding from the front wall and then losing a fraction of its momentum as it bounced off the side wall on its way to the ground. Grunting Shaft was at full stretch and being tugged by gravity as he glided through the air. The ball bounced once and he caught it in the middle of his racquet, just on the Wilson logo for a return that should have been impossible.

A frantic sprint on Y's part couldn't regain the lost point as the ball bounced three times before she was anywhere near it. To add insult to injury her tired legs finally gave way, throwing her to the floor in a giggling heap. Bursting into full blown laughter, Y sat where she fell and watched Shaft who was on his back all this time shaking his racket over his head in triumph, pumping his arms and legs, giving it his best Des Lynam in commentating mode and providing the crowd-going-crazy sound effects at the same time.

"They had counted him out, ladies and gentlemen. The boy from the Streatham estates had done the impossible. They thought that he couldn't beat the world champion, they thought this would be a formality but Winston the Sex Machine McFarlane has done it. The under-dog has done it and the crowd goes wild!"

"Lucky shot," Y shouted, her chest still heaving from the exertion.

"The only lucky thing about this whole game is that I didn't thrash your little backside three sets to nil." He jumped to his feet and started to reproduce his match winning play in slow motion.

Y was shaking her head with a broad grin on her face.

"First thing is my backside isn't little, see?" She rubbed her hands over her curves, playing down the mischievous sparkle that had just appeared in Shaft's eyes.

"And you're crazy do you know that?"

"It takes one to know one."

Shaft walked over to her, took Y by the hand and pulled her up.

"A cold juice to soothe the pains of a loser"

She nodded.

"Enjoy it while you can Mr Sex Machine. Remember we meet again next week Thursday. And I know it will be a different someting then."

Shaft gulped audibly and said in his best Clint Eastwood impression.

"I love it when you talk dirty."

Y was still laughing as they left the squash courts hand in hand.

The refreshment area of the sports club overlooked the Olympic size swimming pool and above that was a massive skylight that made sure it would be bathed in sunlight for the better part of the day if the weather permitted.

No one else seemed to be taking advantage of its comforts and the bartender had a hungry look in his eye when he saw them walk over. After ordering they had to feign tiredness to get away from him as he unsuccessfully tried to pull them into some long-winded and totally meaningless conversation.

"Now that is a man who is dying for a listening ear," Shaft grinned.

They came to a cosy table as far away from Desperate Dan the barman as possible. Shaft pulled out a chair for Y then took a seat himself.

Ceiling fans ran noiselessly and the area was comfortably airy and warm.

He put his palms flat on the table as if he was going to use it to lift himself into a standing position and said.

"Have you decided to make a formal charge against your boyfriend yet?"

The atmosphere between them chilled noticeably.

Y crossed her legs and focussed over his shoulder. Shaft saw her neck muscles tense as she squeezed her hands together under the table.

"I'd prefer if you didn't refer to that piece of shit as my boyfriend. It's bad enough coming to terms with the fact that I actually cared for him once upon a time. I guess that I should want the police to lock him up and throw away the key."

"Just for old time's sake," Shaft added.

Y shook her head.

"The idea that he's going to be in jail, eating food and learning a trade from my taxes makes me cringe. Let him roam free, we will meet again."

Involuntarily he shuddered.

His mother used to say that to him when he was in line for a good whipping and no matter what his scheming mind could concoct to evade her, she would catch him sooner or later. Young brash UK cunning against an old world Jamaican Machiavellian.

Spokes lost every time and he felt genuinely sorry for old Tyrone.

Shaft gulped his frothy cocktail and licked his lips.

"Ah!" he sighed, stifling a belch. "I needed that."

Y looked at him slyly as she too took a swig from her own drink.

"If I had to make a guess on what line of work you were into, I'd say you were a Financial Advisor or something. You're so unlike any policeman I know," Y said after watching him lean back into his seat. "Come to think of it you're the only policeman I know."

"Policeman?" He jibed with a fake middle England accent. "Detective Inspector."

"Don't you dare start that again." She pointed her finger at him with unconvincing threat.

"I've laughed enough today as it is."

"Do you think I'm doing this for you?" He looked at her with a confused expression, "I need to see that beautiful smile of yours. Let's just say it makes a difference to me."

"You're full of it, Winston. D'you know that?"

"But you still love me, don't you?"

Y shook her head and blew him a kiss across the table.

"Seriously though, why did you, with your personality, want to become a policeman in the first place?"

"Would you believe me if I said Starsky and Hutch, Steve McGarret and Quincy ME? I even wanted to have a snitch like Huggy Bear, when I grew up."

"That's it? Television?" Y said with mock disappointment. "I was expecting some profound and honorable tale of making a difference in society or being a role model to the kids."

"Sorry but Blaxploitation cinema informed my career." He cleared his throat with fake embarrassment. "John Shaft, Superfly and Truck Turner."

"Your parents must have been the open minded sort?" Y asked.

Shaft nodded.

"I guess my old man's hero's became mine."

"And school? Did you find the time for it?"

"You kidding, me right? I was a geek. All glasses big feet, big ears and buck teeth. Cute though."

"I can just picture it," Y said, grinning.

"My favourite biographies were of Mathew Henson, Bas Reeves and Washington Carver. Growing up I never saw myself as being anything else but an adventurer, when I grew up. I obtained a Masters in Anthropology and Criminal Psychology. I did two years research in

Africa for my doctorate, which I didn't complete and returned to London. I joined the Force soon after that. Training was an eye opener though."

Y shook her head, understanding exactly what he meant.

"The type of person I am, they'd kick me out for insubordination in no time. I have a thing against authority and Police training camp seems a bit too much authority for one person to handle."

He nodded.

"You don't know the half of it." He spun his glass in a pool of condensation recalling the past. "I've had to deal with the fucked up perceptions of 'every black man looks alike', our inferior intelligence, our laziness, indiscipline and lack of commitment. And I took every one of those bullshit preconceived ideas and turned them on their heads. Sometimes my back was against the wall, pressure from all sides and still as a grown man I'd be asking myself how would Superfly handle a situation like this? Kick some honky butt and ask questions later, or use my determination like the explorer Mathew Henson to outmaneuver them and then kick some honky ass?" He laughed heartily, "Stupid I know but it got me through. I guess if you want to blame anybody for me being here, blame the director Melvyn Van Peebles."

"He has a lot to answer for," Y said under her breath.

He nodded his head then lowered it for a contemplative moment, emerging with a wide toothy grin.

"Enough of me, how are you managing? How is the world of celebrity handling you?"

Y paused and thought of where to begin or if she could even explain it at all.

"Holding on, I suppose. I think we've finally decided that this is something we can do and do well, getting the business side arranged through Mr Patel and also preparing to get licenced."

Shaft moved his chair closer to her.

"Busy bees. One thing missing, though."

"And what's that?"

"You've forgotten to ask me how I can help."

"Just being here is help enough for me, truly." Y said

"But if you need anything, anything at all you will let me know, right?"

"You will be my first advisor."

"You make it sound like you convened a war council in the time of King Shaka."

"It feels like we did."

"Come on then, don't keep me in suspense. What is the rest of the posse doing for the war effort?"

"Well, about now they should be with our client, making him feel all loved and protected. We got offered jobs!"

"In personal protection?" Shaft asked surprised.

"Yep."

"A paying client?" Shaft asked again, incredulous.

"What other kinds are there? Of course, paying."

The detective should be amazed but he knew that when it came to the girls if it was right for them all the elements would fall into place. Seeing how they maneuvered the pitfalls with a kind of effortless ease was a truly uncanny thing to witness. He reached over from his seat, nodding his head as he hugged her.

Shaft wasn't sure why he did it but he kissed her on the lips and held her close.

There was no resistance.

"You're a bitch," he said breathlessly to her.

"Is that anyway to talk to a lady," she said with her cheeky smile. "I'm a queen bitch."

"Touché!"

After the celebration he asked.

"So what is this gig? Can you talk about it?"

"If I tell you, I'm going to have to kill you," she laughed but she was wrestling with the idea of telling him everything but how did you explain the dark fantasy she was experiencing with her sisters? This was the realm of insanity that involving Shaft in may not be a good idea.

And this was going so well.

"Not much to say, really. Our client is a music promoter with powerful enemies and wants our protection up to and including the night he holds a big dance."

"It seems basic but I could check him out for you."

"We did our due diligence but if you could check him out too then that would help."

"I'll get onto it for you."

"Be careful. The Met won't appreciate your extra-curricular activities if you get caught."

Trying to make light of her comments, he peered at her keenly as if he was examining her for fleas.

"What is really on your mind? There is something more I'm missing or you're not telling me."

Am I that easy to read? Y thought.

Y's response was swift and laced with misdirection.

"I'm just uncertain if we can do this. Have we met our match with this celebrity thing? I'm proud of whatever we do but I want this to work. I'm not sure I could suffer more disappointment."

What was meant to be deadly serious made Shaft laugh.

"Welcome to the human race, Y. You can be phased by life like the rest of us mortals but hush." He took her hand and stroked it gently, "You're too hard on yourself.

If there's one lesson I've learned it's that a bit of uncertainty in life is healthy. Nobody likes a smartass who unfailingly knows where they're going from one moment to the next. It makes them a boring liar and a potential candidate for a good kicking. Delving deeper, and quoting my brotha Confucius, 'only from uncertainty you will find certainty'". He gave his best voice of wizened authority. "It's going to work out, just be cool."

"Did Confucius actually say that?" Y asked.

"Not exactly," he said flatly. "But if he was here, he would."

"So, I'll just take your word for it then," Y said.

Shaft threw his hands in the air.

"Now you're getting the hang of this." He grinned then genuflected, kissing her hand on his way down.

"Fool!" she said and started laughing again.

16.

Red Ground Estates, Surrey
Friday July 19th
22.20

The men who had been stationed outside of Spokes'
country residence were getting used to the cold
hard facts of slipping personal hygiene, twelve
hour shifts, unpalatable coffee and indigestible food, but
that was what was required of them. The money was
good and no one in their right mind would question
Deacon's orders without having a well armed regiment
in reserve for the backlash.

In the meantime they prepared for a possible opening
in Spokes' battlements on the off chance you see. Deacon was adamant and obviously a firm believer in providence awaiting any possibility, whether mundane or
supernatural to breach Spokes' defenses.

Team Bravo were five hours into their shift and the
five man crew in a BMW SUV hidden in the leafy copse

out of sight were preparing to send a two man reccey unit to see what they could see. Robert and Stevo were dressed in dark overcoats packing enough heat to engage an equally armed crew not a millionaire promoter who had no experience in the world of violence they occupied.

Deacon's desperation was showing.

Stevo reached for the door release when someone rapped on the tinted glass.

"Shit!" he said, hearing weapons cocking in the background with the swiftness of seasoned assassins. Stevo calmed their nervousness and his with a gentle to and fro of his hand, knowing that suburbia threw up these situations from time to time, switching his facial muscles to neutral and placing the pistol behind his back, he opened the door.

A tall dark skinned man, dressed in light khaki slacks, Clarkes shoes with white shirt and Panama hat of which he tipped in his direction while smiling grotesquely.

"What?" The man in the van asked gruffly.

"I need your van, pardy." Darkman said evenly.

Stevo glared at him and then laughed.

"Are you fucking retarded or something? Walk away before I hurt you." He tried to slide the door shut and it wouldn't budge.

"Don't be like that, star. What if I promise not to kill yuh."

Darkman placed the cricket bag he was carrying on the ground beside his leg and with one hand on his waist, a smile creeping slowly across his lips. Stevo was yanking on the door perplexed as to why it still would not close when it dawned on him that this strange Jamaican was threatening to kill him.

"You what?" Stevo glared angrily at the man who had not moved and was watching his ineffective efforts with amusement. "Kill me? Are you listening to this lad's?" His head snaked inside. "This wanker want's us dead."

Laughter erupted in the vans interior.

Enoch shook his head in a gesture that almost looked like remorse for what he was about to do. He reached into his pocket, popping a small bundled up parcel of vegetation in his mouth like gum. He chewed heartily on the unprocessed leaves of the demon weed, his salivary glands pumping mouth water into the cavern of his mouth. Enoch was careful not to swallow any of the masticated contents. He puckered his lips and prepared to squeeze the liquid through his tongue and upper palette. The incantation unraveled in his mind rearranging the form and function of the liquid in his mouth as he forced it out. His spit vaporised explosively from his lips filling the interior of the van with a powder cloud of tornado force that obscured them into silence. Moments later the hoarse wheezing of five men overcome and bent to his will whispered out to the cool air like the slow leak of a bike tyre.

Slowly Darkman entered the SUV, casually checking over his shoulders to see if he was seen and closed the door behind him.

Surrey Heath, Victoria Park Nature Reserve
Saturday July 20th
22.15

A dark uneasiness crept in time with the girls as soon as they wandered through the gates and into Victoria Park and only Suzy Wong felt it.

It had been a spur of the moment decision which they had discussed and decided Spokes could be on his own while they got some air and down time. The house as large as it was and sporting every amenity a reclusive millionaire could ever want still was unbearable after forty-eight hour stretches. Y had come up with the idea of a walk in the park. At the time it felt like a good idea. The boss was asleep and the floor surrounding his bed was marked with Mayan sigils of protection for his peace of mind. If it was triggered he had an hour worth of mystical defence. The grounds were covered as usual with his personal security detail, the park-cum-nature reserve was twenty minutes walk away and his ring should afford him enough time to contact them if he was being threatened. So here they were walking arm in arm, shooting the breeze with at least two out of the trio enjoying the vast greenery even in the darkness.

Suzy subtly excused herself from Y and Patra's discussion and fell back. The deeper they got into the reserve's winding pathways and open expanses the more her disquiet increased. She watched her sisters proceed in the distance oblivious to the waves of menace, that had her emotions in a tangle. She stopped feigning interest in a blooming bougainvillea and tried to settle herself.

Moments later Y sensed Suzy's absence and stopped to look back only to be reassured by her easy wave in the distance. They stood their ground and continued their conversation waiting for Suzy to catch up.

Suzy focussed but her five senses detected nothing. It was her intuition that was expecting the rows of foliage to transmute into a monstrous plant with a taste for human flesh. But a warm breeze ruffled their leaves and nothing more sinister emerged from their branches. Suzy could not shake the feeling though so on a whim she left the safety of the foot path and moved silently into the shrubbery. She inhaled a heady mixture of humus, sap and chlorophyll as she nestled into the dense branches and crouched to wait.

After five minutes she was beginning to feel silly then that feeling of foreboding returned with more intensity.

Something appeared.

It came as an almost imperceptible grating murmur that she couldn't distinguish if she had heard it or if it was extrasensory in nature. Her temple prickled immediately and her ears tingled as minute forces of some kind ran up and down her earlobe stretching it as if they were becoming elfin. Suzy shifted in her crouched position wanting to sprint away from there but fear and curiosity held her fast. That God awful murmur was behind her, so she spun to face it and saw nothing. Then at the periphery of her vision something swooped out of eyeshot, through the leaves, silent and ethereal, large enough to be human but with no definition to speak of but ink black with many tattered and flapping edges. The figure moved through the air like a demented vulture trailing its substance behind it as if this world had some effect on how it moved, dulling its power but not its inquisitiveness.

It was looking for something, looking for Suzy.

She crouched; transfixed then with the cold hand of dread gripping her spine she stood up and walked out of the shrubs.

"You wanted me?" Suzy growled up into the night sky.

The spectral bird of prey swooped again at the edges of her perception responding to her voice. It twirled with satisfaction when it realised she was still in the park, almost whooping with delight from its aerobatics, it shot upwards merging into the trees, leaving behind a sense of foreboding that Suzy now knew had to be acted on.

Enoch's essence returned to his body seated in the SUV, sans its original five passengers with such displeasure, his corporeal self spasmed and gasped for breath as he became one with himself again. He slammed the door to the astral world like a teenager slamming his room door shut with vexation and kept swearing. He uncrossed his legs and leaned back into the passenger seat, his five senses re-aligning themselves to the here and now. The euphoria of being unfettered from his body disappeared and what returned were the emotions of flesh and blood.

Deh Chiny gal can see mi to rass. He thought.

He had been right to not take them for granted and from what he had read about them, there talents could manifest in different forms but a warrior sensitive, now that was different. The plan to track them to where Spokes was holed up was an inspired one but what was genius was the vévé he had planted at the entrance to the mansion. It was a work of voodoo art if he said so himself using the skin of a deer as the canvass and his paints were black sand, cornmeal and human blood to mark out the delicate patterns that would subtly nudge his targets to a particular way of thinking. He was not used to the delicate strokes, and the spider web energies it would influence, his diagrams were more heavy handed in their construction and effect but this was almost beautiful in its function. The spell was so unencumbered with the usual trappings of bending the will of it's subjects that the three bitches thought the idea of walking to the park was their own. That's why this trap he was about to spring would prove pivotal.

He had read accounts of the Guardians interfering with the scheming of his great, great grandfather on one of his frequent jaunts around the world. They were immune to overt magic and reveled in conflict so to distract or destroy them required subterfuge and cunning. Grandfather Pierre was in Costa Rica when it happened and he circumnavigated the issue without shedding any blood and still getting the Tabernacle Moth that he seeked. Enoch thought it was a good strategy but bad for his ego. And when he sat to write his memoirs, he would recount how he trapped and slaughtered the blessed Guardians with his ego intact.

No back dung, an no compromise.

They would die, Spokes would be alone and although he couldn't face him directly he would instruct the demons from hell's Seven Circle to rip off his ring finger and gut him open from ass to gullet. Another chunk of Enoch's soul forfeit to the darkness but it was worth it.

"You don't bomboclaat keep secrets from Darkman," he muttered. "Then try to keep me from what is my birthright, pan top a dat." He snorted derisively. "Death for you will be the easy part, my friends. Trust mi."

The threat hung languidly in the confines of the van, as if waiting for its activation into the real world was dependant on tonight's outcome.

As far as Enoch was concerned the night was pregnant with promise and his concerns could be unnecessary. He closed his eyes and let the anger maintain its grip on him and waited for his puppets to do his bidding. Soon his minions would be returning with the severed head of one of the Guardian bitches and he would be one step closer to what was his.

Surrey Heath, Victoria Park Nature Reserve
Saturday July 20th
22.35

"Hey ma, you aight?" Patra directed the question to Suzy who had materialised beside them from a jog.

They had left the nature reserve and were heading across another small park that would connect them to the main road and Millionaires' Row.

"What were you doing back there?" Patra asked. "Find something interesting?"

"Something found mi instead. We were being followed," Suzy said flatly.

Patra stopped in her tracks.

"By whom?"

"Don't stop," Suzy insisted as she dragged her to pick up pace. "Let's just get back to the yard now and we can talk there. Oh, an' it's not a who but a what."

"You spooking the shit out of me girl. What do you mean a what?"

"Nuh time feh no long explanation P, I'll tell you everyting when wi safely inside. Just keep moving."

The message understood, they picked up speed, start-ing to jog across the low grass when just on the verge separating nature from asphalt the shadows congregated, the figures looking hazy and bent as the light from the street lamps diffused through the heat being exuded from the ground. Then ever so slowly five, ten, fifteen rambling figures joined the original set. The girls slowed their pace but did not stop. Instead Suzy turned back dragging Patra and Y with her. They slid down the hill and once they hit the bottom they took a sharp left and headed deeper into the shrubs.

The thought that they could out-run them kept Suzy focused but so far they were everywhere. The park was a big place and the shambolic shuffling of the shadows stalking them could not or were not inclined to follow for very far. But soon it became clear that what Suzy was feeling was Darkman's attempt at destroying the threat they posed to him. He had recruited a horde of malcon-tents drugged or under his dark magics to coral them in the park and then take them out. So far every escape route they had tried was compromised with unexplained energies that were vibrating high on Suzy's psychic Richter scale. She was trying not to have to explain Darkman's plan to her sisters, just get them to safety as quickly as she could. Suzy didn't want to explain how she was receiving a multitude of echoes from the figures stalking them. Ugly, oily, empty and hungry. A ravenous hunger that emanated off them and was smearing and clogging her headspace like a mad painter throwing ex-crement onto the canvas that was her mind. Movement was good, taking her attention away from the emotional onslaught battering her mental defenses. This was not the time to be stopping but Patra had something to say and she could be very forceful when she wanted to express herself.

Patra suddenly brought them to a stop, holding there hands and dragging them to their knee's

"Now is not the time, sis." Suzy said. "Trust mi pan dat." They breathed heavily.

"I do trust you Suzy. It's not that but I want to see these motherfuckers. Who are they and who sent them?" Patra paused. "Don't answer that I know who did this, I just wish he would show his punk ass. I get antsy with the idea of being trapped."

"We'll get out, I promise but we have to keep moving." Suzy said.

"Why aren't we taking the fight to these crack heads? You ain't telling me you think we can't breakthrough these assholes?" Patra said he voice a harsh whisper.

"That's not what your saying is it Ms Wong?" Y asked. "You don't want to try, do you?"

Suzy didn't confirm or deny Y's observation.

"Let's just keep moving, ladies. I don't like what I'm feeling and I don't want to find out I was right to be afraid, yuh understand mi?"

Patra nodded her lips stretched tight and her eyes wide.

Y intervenes with a calm tone that belied her concern for Suzy's weird behaviour.

"Ok, lets keep trying to get out of here without any contact with these people. But if were cornered......?

"We taking niggas out!" Patra spat.

They kept moving on a track that wasn't so well used, an alternative route cut from necessity or convenience by the feet of someone who required change on his own terms. Overgrown foliage encroached on the path but it didn't much matter to Bad II the Bone. They followed it where it led using Patra's smartphone as a light source. Suzy was being guided on instinct alone and nothing was making sense except the overriding impulse to get home. They kept pushing forward. The ground was hard from the drought that had been news in this part of Sussex for a while. The smell of sappy green and soil was pungent as they disturbed the air from their movements, movement that was brisk at first but slowed as they burrowed deeper into the thicket, a foreboding mental fog shadowing them like a rain cloud. But just as suddenly the bushes became less dense and more easily traversed and shafts of light bore through from what they hoped was civilization.

"Damn do you smell that, shit?" Patra asked bringing everyone to a stop as if an invisible wall had suddenly erected before them.

"Like something died, man." Y concluded. "Lots of them."

Then the moans floated up into the sweetness of the night air, amplified by the silence.

Suzy grabbed Y's arm, like vice grips, her hands trembling, her heart thundering in her chest.

"We can't go any further sis, there out there, all a dem."

"Them who?" Patra snapped.

"I don't understand Suzy." Y absorbed some of Suzy's fear her voice shrill. "Who's out there? We can't keep doing this all night. We got to face them."

"She right, sugah. I'm done running around in circles while these crackheads spook the shit out of us. We are the Guardians right? We ain't scared of no man and anyway hiding just ain't our style." Patra grabbed her crotch obscenely. "If they think their scare tactics a gonna keep on working, they can suck my dick."

"You nuh feel what mi feel." Suzy said. "An emptiness I want to shake but can't. A kind of hunger where every part a yuh a scream feh food. A nastiness countless showers nah guh cleanse."

"We're together," Y reassured her. "Whatever it is that's making you feel like this, you won't face alone. Do you understand me?"

Suzy nodded and all three held hands.

"For all this drama, I think I need to give them a piece of my mind or my blade, whichever works better."

"Preach!" Patra encouraged with a nervous grin."

They kept moving through the smell of death and decay that hung languidly like an ethereal dirty curtain. It stuck in their throats and soiled their clothes, adding a note of urgency to their step. They hurried through a copse of trees at the bottom of the small hill and headed up a slight incline that quickly plateaued. Ahead of them is an open field and beyond that the glimmering lights of the main road and cars traversing the country lanes.

Sweet escape.

Then they paused, their focus now on the immediate distance, their hands falling to their sides, staring on with an unexpected awe.

Suzy's face looked like a cold granite frieze of an ancient warning etched into some Roman temple. Her mouth was moving but her words were heard by no one.

Patra flinched, a nervous tick suddenly manifesting as her mind tried to understand what she was seeing but the jigsaw puzzle of images shattered from the initial shock were having difficulty forming a cohesive whole she could understand.

Y is shaking, her spine goes cold, her heart pounding behind her ribs, only her grip on the sword slung on her back kept her from discounting she was a part of a waking nightmare.

It was real.

"Duppy." Suzy said.

"Say what?" Patra exclaimed.

"Walking dead." Suzy expounded in a deadpan tone.

"Motherfucker!" Patra whispered, her mental clarity returning. "You got to be fucking kidding me."

Together the tableau they saw would be fire branded into the confines of their memory for some time to come.

A throng of dead things were materializing from the wispy mist on their left and right flanks, their stench carried in the air. A riot of moving corpses, thirty or forty of them maybe more were dragging their dead asses towards the startled girls. The walking dead were in varying degrees of decomposition. Their clothes caked with mud as if they had clawed themselves out of fresh graves, gooey splashes of decrepit body fluids stained them, shit stained and bloody, fresh blood as if something warm and alive had got in their way and paid the price with their lives.

A lumbering cadaver dressed in a green soiled and ripped shell suit led the ponderous charge. Another that looked like a school teacher in an advanced state of decay, black drool dripping down from cracked lips, the side of her head caved in and body parts falling from her. Some of them were clad in their Sunday best, shirts untucked, hats still atop heads, innards exposed and dragging. Some of them dressed for more leisurely pastimes but lacked arms and legs. Slivering and hopping their way towards them, blackened teeth chomping at the prospect of life giving flesh. Milk white eyes gleaming in the moonlight devoid of all intelligence and overcome by an insatiable hunger. The thought had occurred to Y to go back to where they had come from but the rustling of the bushes at the bottom of the incline put paid to that idea. Suzy looked back to where they had come from longingly too, knowing with an uncanny certainty that trouble was on its way from behind also.

Y had her samurai sword unsheathed and was gripping it in both hands, a nervous tightening and relaxing of her fingers around the hilt between her digits. Y let reason fall like a stone in a pond, watching the ripples in her mind's eye, spread and diminish to nothing.

Y charged the fifty yards between them, the sword singing through the air and in a heart beat she is amidst the shuffling hordes in a controlled frenzy of violence. The katana was a silver blur, cutting through mouldy neck and spinal cord, putrefied sinew and rotting muscle, hollowed bone and poisoned marrow that should not be able to accommodate life – no not life, anti-life – but did. They kept coming and Y kept hacking, hyper aware of her surroundings.

Separate the head from the neck, because nothing else would do.

The remainder of Bad II the Bone stood their ground.

Patra eyed a broken tree limb that had been snapped by excessive weight or overzealous swinging. She ambled over and picked it up. With a flick of her wrist, she spun it in her hands nimbly and then swung it both sides of her with a fierceness that could break bones. Her show of aggression done she let the weapon rest easily at her side.

Suzy took off her light jacket and slipped out of her blouse ripping it in two. She got back into her windbreaker and then bound her fists with the torn blouse. After minutes of controlled slaughter Y backed away from the horde, rejoining Suzy and Patra. She wiped the blade on her sleeves, her movements lethargic from sore muscles, her chest heaving from the exertion of battle and her clothes drenched in black blood and guts.

"I can't get through...them alone. We have to do this together."

Y nodded.

"You stink," Suzy said to her, all three with their backs to each other.

"If we get out of this alive, you can chastise me for my slipping personal hygiene later, okay."

"Deal," Suzy said.

The atonal moan of the zombies approaching them suddenly swelled and Bad II the Bone looked on with a mixture of puzzlement and fear.

The shuffling mass of figures parted.

A group of five men approached. Covered in white dust from head to toe streaked with their own blood seeping from their eyes, nose, mouth and ears. If they were the living dead, their demise was recent because they looked intact, free from corruption to their flesh and their clothes lacked age or deterioration. But whatever covered them was luminescent and seemed to provide a gross attraction that kept them close together like clusters of single cell bacteria and as they came closer motes of dust sprang up as they dragged their feet. Murmurs trickled from their lips in a strange unified groan from a collective awareness.

Stranger still, as they drew nearer moonlight glinted off swords and machetes they carried loosely between stiff and gnarled fingers. They shuffled towards them in a tight group like stroke victims, movement spastic as if control of their limbs was inefficient but still capable enough to hold on tightly to the sharp edged weapons they carried.

The walking dead held their positions like blood splattered AWOL soldiers trapped in a force field, watching.

Waiting.

The crooked silhouettes shuffled towards them.

Suzy smoothly moved into the praying mantis stance, her fists up and clenched.

"Could do with my butterfly swords right about now." Suzy muttered. "Not looking forward to putting my hands on dem."

Patra nodded an agreement and as if to say that's why I have this, grabbing the tree limb with both hands and swinging the wood back and fourth to test its suitability for what was about to come just for reassurance.

Y marked the air with her samurai sword and held her stance.

"Never leave home without it, Ms Wong?" Y said.

Their banter fell on deaf ears.

"What's the deal, motherfuckers? Y'all never hear of us before?" Patra asked. "Well you sure as hell gonna find out now." She paused seemingly considering her response. "Tell that asshole, Darkman from me, he can kiss my ass. You know what scratch that, I'll tell him myself, up front and personal."

Their eyes showed a deep emptiness as if their souls had been sucked from their bodies and what remained could only take care of locomotion and nothing more. But Patra's provocation seemed to spark something in them that suddenly spread like wild fire. It was almost as if an invisible puppeteer was pulling on their strings and stoking them to a white hot frenzy. Only when they reached boiling point the tether of spell or suggestion was snipped and the men with new found energy, ran at the girls screaming like banshees from hell.

Red Ground Estates
Surrey

Several hours later Patra stood naked, being bombarded from a multi nozzle Shangri-La of lilac scented steaming water. The shower was mirrored on every side and combined with the shower head's LED mood lights she felt as if she was in a surreal disco for swingers. Naked wet swingers. She admired herself in the mirror through curtains of steam with the tired expression of someone who had had just experienced a jump in initiation for some South Central gang bangers and she had come out the worst for it. She looked exactly how she felt – exhausted and beaten and covered in cuts and bruises. Her fingers came up to gently touch her shoulder that was nicely scrapped, a lucky deflection from a blade. Even hovering over the area with her fingers transmitted a warning of pain to come.

She was lucky, she had no broken bones or gashes especially to her face. Patra protected her looks fiercely. The bruises on her body would smooth out and the battered blood under her skin would dissipate. And in time her body would repair well but she wasn't so sure about her mind.

Her gift had turned up to maximum against tonight's threats and she was glad. Her Luck Factor was like an old dog she had back in Atlanta when she was growing up. Old Grover did things in his own time, whether it suited you or not. He had to go do his business according to his needs and if you wanted to come along for the ride – be his pooper-scooper - then that could be arranged too. But Grover could surprise you and would bite your ass if you jangled a mean streak in him and usually that was a reflection of the meanness in you. So tonight the quantity of meanness was of such a degree her gift came out to compensate.

She winced.

The most significant throbbing came from both her thighs and she could see the discoloration from the bruising showing through her caramel skin. She had to beat off some sly attempts from that disgusting desiccated, nasty smelling, and ravenous cock sucker with no legs that had crawled up in the frenzy to take a chunk out of her thigh. Maybe opening up its head like a dry coconut on an anvil wasn't a good idea after all because she was paying for it now.

Thai boxing used the thighs a lot in attack and those things they had been up against earlier may have seemed insubstantial, rotting, facsimiles of humans but they were tough like old leather, meat fossilised to rock, bone ossified, unyielding and hard.

But she had given as well as she took from those motherfuckers and they had led her down a road she never knew she would ever take. Patra shivered. A quake starting from the pit of her stomach, radiating outwards and feeling like it resonated bluntly with the gold piercing in her clitoris. Shivering even amidst the steam, Patra let the water wash through her cornrows and sluice down her body carrying with it blood, dust and chewed up gore.

No woman and especially a black woman after having her hair 'Did' the way she liked it would allow the elements to taint it. Rain, showers even vigorous lovemaking can flip the switch from good girl to crazy bitch because it was important to keep the myth of female perfection alive. Patra propagated that belief but tonight was different.

Tonight she was washing away blood from her skin some hers, most others', watching it flow from her and swirl away down into the sewers, not caring about her coiffure.

She braced herself on the mirror, looking at her hands and her cracked and shattered nail extensions and swore. She needed as complete overhaul, hair and nails. And then she wondered about her state of mind. Patra's eyes caught a wash puff made from some kind of mildly abrasive synthetic material folded into itself to form a cute ball and thought this wasn't the kind of thing Spokes would use on himself. Then she saw the store label and smiled weakly. He had tried his best to make them welcome, his angels, Spokes Angels. Maybe taking the job in the first place was a mistake? Things weren't going so well and yet Patra had felt truly alive through it all. If her risk free attitude could possibly be ramped up then knowing Spokes had done just that. It was just the consequences of that rush she had conveniently decided to not think of. No biggy, life had chosen to show it to her anyway. She plucked it from the sucker attached to the wall, soaked it in liquid soap and began to scrub herself.

Patra started from her face, then her chest, arms and breasts down to her stomach and her legs. What started casually became more frantic as the horrors of tonight stood before her accusingly and she continued scrubbing as if she wanted to buff through skin, muscle, cartilage to clean white bone.

Working her way back up to her shoulders, Patra started to massage her biceps in turn, trying to ease the soreness from them, hoping the force of the water would help too but they remained stiff. That hefty tree branch she had been swinging offensively at first and then when shit got real, as a tool of extinguishing life had taken its toll. Not that these walking dead cocksuckers didn't deserve it but they weren't all that way. Darkman had thrown in some wildcards in the mix to mess with their heads, play on the weaknesses they possessed.

Taking life did not come naturally to them even under the circumstances and he knew that. What he had done was to be his little 'go suck my dick' message and they received it loud and clear.

The Darkman had snatched a piece of them tonight, leaving the wound purulent and infected but his septic mind games would not take hold in them, she just knew it. In her case it was a small piece but significant enough to have her question what she did tonight. Making her believe that a dark cancerous corner of her psyche enjoyed thrusting the jagged points of the broken tree limb into the zombies throat, watching him flap like a fish out of water. Remembering how surprised she was at the feeling of its warm arterial blood arcing onto her arms and face and the guttural gasping for air from a shattered larynx of a man not a reanimated corpse. Then watching in horror that malevolent spark depart him – that thing Darkman had used to hold him enthralled - and then his humanity returning to his eyes, sparking them alive again just before he died.

The few seconds looking down at his pale face and those piercing blue eyes felt like an eternity. Patra shivered although the stinging droplets of hot water bounced off her skin, gooseflesh marched up and down her back.

Yep, Darkman had taken a bite and it would leave a permanent mark. And she knew there would be more to come but a sparkling sense of certainty punched through the dark clouds. It was the words from her father of all people, Pastor Ignatius Jones, that God fearing, pulpit preaching and family loving hypocritical mo'fucker who couldn't look her in the eyes ever since he knew she was bi-curious, heteroflexible, AC-DC. The worst kind of heathen there was in his books. It's going to be all right, he said in her head with biblical conviction. It's going to be aaaalright!

This time she believed him.

Brixton Police Station
Sunday July 21st
10.45am

Shaft looked at the circular coffee stains on his wooden desk and blocked out the drone of activity in the operations room at Brixton nick. He leaned back on his favorite chair - the one with the busted back rest he had bound together with packaging tape - and massaged his lumbar region into it until it creaked lovingly.

He had mentally pulled himself out of the frenetic activity taking place around him. The other team was in the last stages of a sting operation that was hopefully going to apprehend a gang of armed robbers targeting Farringdon and its jewellery district.

His small unit was sharing space with the Flying Squad and he observed their certainty and high levels of optimism.

They needed to take a walk in his world and see how the lines of reality and fantasy blurred.

Twenty minutes away, just to refocus.

Contrary to what his superiors thought about his legendary laid back attitude, these moments he took to think of other things, other interests, hadn't affected his crime busting record at all.

In fact, when the rank and file were doped up and tanked up from job related stress, his mental health would be intact.

He checked today's menu in his head.

Shaft had two mouth-watering choices to occupy his short time.

Y had left a voice message on his mobile and it sounded like she wanted to talk. And damn, he was not too proud to say even her voice was a turn on for him. So in effect he'd be enjoying twenty minutes of extremely sensual verbal foreplay.

No contest, really.

Except for mouth-watering choice number two.

The neatly compiled manila folder sat tantalisingly in the middle of his desk, its recycled paper showing through its grooves like a busty woman would her assets.

Okay it did not have an ass that brought tears to your eyes, or long dark sculpted legs that he would willingly volunteer over his shoulders in a steamy evening romp. But it was work and the weak man that he was, Shaft succumbed to the pile of folders' immediate charms and the possible secrets it held over Y for the minute.

Men, weaklings.

He pulled the files along the table towards him and opened the top one reluctantly. Shaft took more time than usual to observe the blue Manila folder with the colorful elastic binder. He wanted to handle the coroner's report with forceps and a Hazmat suit. Just the thought of the contents made his hands go clammy and an immediate animated knot of pain twisting into his gut accompanied with that sense of cold sweat and creeping flesh. Justine Dorset - murdered. No suspects and about a thousand witnesses. Modus operandi was similar to Enoch Lacombe's sadistic viciousness - the poor girl was evaginated - on live radio. The Scotland Yard forensic teams were having a field day with this. Impossible, unprecedented, inexplicable, bizarre were all words being thrown around to describe something no one could explain. Shaft hadn't been able to attend the post mortem but the photograph's said it all. Her body was turned inside out, all her internal organs, hanging outside of her skin suit like gross body ornaments. Now, how the fuck do you affect the human body in that way? What in God's name, can harness the kind of forces required to turn bone and muscle into itself like you unfurled a sock from your foot. If it was machine generated, the Metropolitan Polices' brightest and best knew of no such technology that could affect the body in that way. While the other option was equally ridiculous and the conclusion unavoidable. It was caused by a antagonist who had the ability to bend and brake every physical law at will, leaving no signs of entry or exit, just a degree of bloodthirsty sadism seldom seen in London crime scenes. Shaft closed it and tucked it in at the bottom of the pile, his hand shaking.

Calming himself, he picked up a covering letter that had been written by DI John Dawson and set out to make the contents even more appealing to him. He closed with an ominous message.

Having read these documents under no circumstances keep them on your person. Destroy them immediately.

The man was on a Mission Impossible tip but could you blame him.

DI Dawson for all his eccentricity had made it possible for him to follow this case more closely than he would if he was researching it solo. If truth be known this could present itself as a sweet opportunity to earn the move from DS to DI. Career advancement aside, and ignoring Dawson's hard-on for its historical value, it meant something to him personally. This case was his first ever as a DS in Black Book and, although long and bizarre the main suspect was eventually caught but the artefacts and historical heirlooms were never recovered. Officialdom had the case retired while he had developed his seventh man theory. When the snickering of his superiors had died down, his line of enquiry was blatantly ignored. But Cold Case file FS13877 was never forgotten.

It came to his attention again when one member of Darkman's crew had testified against him and Deacon's thugs who had joined the witness protection scheme began to be murdered in inexplicable ways and it was then Dawson contacted him.

Only one man out of this situation of robbery and murder came away unscathed and that was the gangster Deacon himself. Shaft knew he had orchestrated Enoch Lacombe's life sentence and made three soldiers in his firm go down for him. Two of his men never had the opportunity to plea bargain and were given full sentences for armed robbery and murder. The other, a self assured psycho whose claim to fame was his looks and his legendary thirteen inch dick, was locked away in Belmarsh Prison, serving a reduced sentence of five years because he had helped in the investigation. Shaft had the benefit of all the current facts at hand but it still read like a tale of the fantastic. He wondered how the three erstwhile crew members who were banged away for their crimes had reacted to the news. Four of your mates had been murdered in the space of a month by an unknown assailant, who is able to kill by unknown means and leave without a trace. The prison grapevine was a very effective link with the outside world but even if you did know what had happened, three killers like that wouldn't be worried. Why should they? Deacon's men were untouchable on or off the streets and in the nick they were respected.

Well that's what they thought.

Thomas Gatling Gun Gardener was found on the recreation grounds after a late evening exercise session. He died from massive unexplained body trauma. The other two were attacked and almost eaten alive by rabid animals - rats it was thought - in their cells. Preliminary forensic notes showed the MO was identical to the other murders linked with this case. Dawson had made a footnote explaining that all forensic reports that involved the case had been transferred to another department. He seemed worried and concerned.

"Jesas," Shaft whispered to himself. "What the rass is going on?"

He made a note on his smartphone to call Wormwood Scrubs again to book an appointment to see Enoch Lacombe. Only he could shine some light on this situation.

Or could this be the doing of Jimmy Éclair who they had thought had been killed but had acquired a new identity? Appearing now from wherever he was to settle old scores.

But why?

Shaft's theory had Jimmy Éclair being the recipient of a treasure that the Darkman had stolen and murdered for. If a failed robbery attempt by Deacon's men as Jimmy was transporting the booty to a safe holding company had not brought this situation to the police's attention then none of this would be an issue. Just another unknown network in the tangled web of the London underworld. But a shootout in North London tended to pique Scotland Yard's attention. Jimmy had escaped the ambush and the empty truck was found in a scrap-yard with his blood all over the front seat.

If he survived this, what kind of lingering grudge would he harbor for men who tried to kill him and with the kind of money at his disposal, the creative ways for revenge would be myriad.

Murder just did not seem like one of the things on your mind if you were living it up in South America.

And committing murders that could only be achieved if you were the Amazing Spider man, Jack the Ripper and some mutant with teleportation powers all rolled into one just was not sensible.

He was missing something here, something crucial.

And that bugged the hell out of him.

He closed the file and stuffed it in his drawer. Looking up from his task to check out what was happening around him, he started rummaging through his tray. A pin stuck him in his finger tip and he swore. Being more careful this time he waded through rusty paper clips, furry magnets and a myriad of exotic stationery items until he pulled out a flaking black combination padlock.

He secured the draw.

At that moment he thought of Y and strangely how she and the girls could be inadvertently involved in this case. How a random fact he discovered had their new client actually knowing Jimmy Éclair.

Now, wasn't that a coincidence?

Shaft was experienced enough to know that a break in a case could come from the most off centre of sources. So why not the girls?

Stranger things have happened.

17.

Crypt Nightclub
Central London
Monday July 22nd
13.11

Spokes was drumming his fingers on the ornate desk, waiting impatiently for talks to reconvene on the subject of essential renovation that he needed to do before the Council's Building Enforcement office closed down the nightclub for non-compliance. Little did the blood sucking, South American, *blouse an' skirt* he called his business partner realize that it was an elaborate sham.

The Dance was a week away and Spokes had to set some well placed lies in position to facilitate his permanent exit from this rat race. His frustration was real though and that came as a natural consequence of being in spitting distance of his partner.

You work dat out.

They had been business associates for four years and promoted some of the most profitable music promotions in London together. Carlos' love of money above all else never sat well with Spokes but it had been a marriage of convenience. This is what Carlos thrived on and Spokes encouraged him along so the illusion that things were as always was reinforced. But Spokes wanted out and this was a part of his exit strategy. The story was he wanted the revenue from the bar and the door, altering the usual way things ran between them. And Spokes didn't care that Carlos sensed a change in his attitude, this would be his swan song.

He had obviously come on too strong in the initial negotiations because Carlos - the leech – suspected that something was not quite the same about this promotion. Spokes was too intense about it and from experience his Jamaican partner did not do intense. Spokes promised himself to tone down on the melodramatics.

When he met Carlos four years ago, the man from Sao Paolo was in serious financial difficulty but he had a creative mind and ambition and with his promises and big plans he convinced Spokes to work on the night-club's structure and redecoration at a substantially reduced charge. Both their lives changed around about that time in ways Carlos would never truly understand. What he did understand though was that they had been on a winning streak for the last four years, every promotion a smash hit and their partnership seemed to have the Midas touch.

All good things mus come to an end, pardy.

Carlos Velors - who had been called away from their discussion for the fourth time by the phone - was not the easiest man to hold down. And even when you did have his attention, every sentence was punctuated by his incessant questions or the ring of the phone.

Why even go through this shit?

Well, it was this thing Carlos had about the etiquette of behavior between business partners. This was a gesture of respect that was being exploited by the trumped up little Napoleon for his own self aggrandizement. So Spokes felt it was his duty to make the exercise as uncomfortable for him as possible.

He rose himself off the leather seat slightly, grimaced and broke wind.

"Irritable bowels," he muttered as a means of apology.

Velors looked over to him from the phone and Spokes smiled brightly, trying to wrinkle his nose at the stench and seem unaware at the same time.

Velors smiled back, brushing air from his nose.

A combination of stress, the red peas and pork tail soup did not help his constitution.

He belched next.

Damn.

What the hell was he doing on the phone for so long?

The goddamn man was like an eel, unable to sit still for a moment without some erratic movement on his part. From a twitch of his eyelid, to suddenly jumping up out of his seat scattering whatever was in his way to the carpet.

He was like some uncoordinated puppet unable to control basic movement. Spokes had to have his wits about him to not be pummelled by flying furniture or a flailing arm. Thankfully a metre of wood separated them but still it was an exhausting exercise to watch him.

One more week of this to endure and it would all be over.

He reached into his attaché case and slid one of the promotional flyers, a list of advertising sources and the fake Building Inspector's report over to where his business partner was seated. The dummy Building Inspector's report he had had done by a girlfriend in the council just as a smokescreen for Carlos' attention. Not that he would question his need to smash through the wall in his office, that was his trade after all, but he just felt better covering all bases.

Even showing him the flyers and the promotional pack was just a courtesy because Carlos had nothing to do with marketing and wouldn't know the first thing that was required to arrange an event like this successfully. He just counted the chips and accommodated his requests. What made their unlikely pairing even remotely possible was steeped in the power of magic, witchcraft and Obeah. The Brazilian was sitting on top of forces that consistently bent and broke scientific laws and commonsense. Ancient trinkets and oddities collected by an Obeah man from around the world, stored below where they sat in a Roman crypt he had accidently stumbled upon while renovating the place four years ago and which he used as the perfect hiding place for Darkman's ill gotten gains. He had used some of the more obvious wealth himself and made sure Jimmy's family was looked after. The remainder he had buried, recorded and studied. He used his new found wealth not just to make himself comfortable but began to research and consult experts who could identify and unravel their secrets. Darkman returning to the scene had altered his plans but the results would be the same - a new life.

And something as important as this could not be left to chance. The date of the dance just hadn't been guessed upon but had been divined by men and women who knew these things.

Finally Bagga John, Father Fowl, Diamond Ruff and even Anthony Gee would be able to regain their positions that had been taken from them by his secret treasure trove in the basement.

This would all be over soon, once he got the key to Carlos' office - the only entrance into the Crypt through the walls. He could work without disturbance getting in and out with the treasure and nobody would be the wiser.

Make no mistake, this was a courtesy extended to Carlos because with or without his authority or help he would be demolishing his wall to get into the catacombs.

The phone slammed down on its cradle and Spokes looked up from his thoughts.

Velors had finished his conversation finally and was grinning in his direction.

"Señor Spokes, apologies for the interruptions. Where were we?"

"Someting to do with why the figure we agreed on keeps going up," Spokes said sarcastically.

"Ah yes. I'm happy with what we've finally agreed on. Your proposal is a good one don't worry."

"Mi looked worried to you, rudy?"

"You do actually. What can I do to relieve some of that stress?"

"Feh starters you can reconsider changing our sixty forty deal to fifty fifty. Then while you're at it give me access keys and magnetic cards to all the rooms so on the night I can give deh council surveyors access to every nook and cranny."

"Sure. I'll have them ready for you," he said. "And let me sleep on the profit split. Nothing should come between us and the healthy profits we're making, right?"

His face lit up with the wattage of his greed at the thought of the profits to come.

The phone rang.

Spokes kissed his teeth.

But Velors flashed his veneered gnashers, his jaw angled to profile his good side. His eyes twinkled artificially, savoring the sense of importance it made him feel, he paused before answering.

"Have a drink, relax," he pointed to the drinks cabinet, "I've been expecting this call," he said. "Two minutes, tops."

Spokes stood up and unruffled his linen suit. He made his way out of the office where his protective angels would be waiting for him. The door sucked shut behind him and the only thought that made him feel good was him being out of the picture and a crazed Velors, having spent thousands on a party standing in the middle of the venue thinking he had the Midas touch and realizing that he was alone and useless. All the greedy, gravoliscious, vindictive, tight-fisted son-of-a-bitch deserved.

He smiled fleetingly and played the mind movie in his head again.

His smile broadened.

Westfield Shopping Centre, Shepherds Bush
Tuesday 23rd July
12.51

Shaft inhaled the aroma of his cappuccino as it waft-
ed up from his cup and continued to massage Y's feet
under the table with his free hand. A grin, surgically attached to his face by a skilled Beverly Hills plastic surgeon, stood triumphant for all to see as he contemplated
how great life was, amidst the Tuesday scrum of intelligent shoppers.

They were sitting in one of these conveyors belt type
restaurants with staff who by rights should be mucky
while preparing the food but pranced about in immaculately white smocks and with eager grins only he could
appreciate in his present good mood.

And this good mood was fuelled by the adolescent
exhilaration of being around not just one but three pain-
fully sexy women, who made him feel as if he was P
some Hip Hop mogul on a video shoot. A sigh of contentment came from his lips like an inadvertent belch.

Why women thought men were a Rubik cube-type
puzzle to be solved with nagging and tears was a mystery he couldn't understand. Men were simple creatures.
Feed them, stroke their egos - and anywhere else that
needed attention - and you would have a friend for however long it took him to get bored.

Strangely enough though, he never did feel out of
place around them. And the subject of boredom was as
alien to these three as work to a benefit cheat. Bad II the
Bone's exploits were nudging precariously close to the
excitement levels of the Flying Squad in his opinion.
One or two gun battles over a few months and they
would nearly be there.

Y looked over her magazine with a little smile on her face after reading her horoscope. She caught Shaft either reading the front page of the Pride or looking at her through the magazine. Her eyes didn't linger with his for too long but that did not stop her from trying to figure out from his expression of total cool and his delightful thumb movements over her feet what was going on in that handsome head of his.

Carefully, she closed the magazine and placed it on the table. It was time to give up the struggle, having skimmed a sentence four times and still not understood a word she had read.

"Let's go and rejoin the girls at Prada," Y said suddenly.

"Not when I'm getting into the swing of tings," Shaft's voice had taken on the chocolaty undertones of Barry White, "I can still feel areas of tension, here, here and here." He pointed.

Y shivered deliciously as he trailed his finger up her calf.

And if you continue doing that I will not be held responsible for my actions, Y thought. Then she swung her legs out from under the table and picked up the bunch of designer named shopping bags beside her chair.

"What is it about men and shopping that gets them all jittery and frightened?"

Shaft slurped the remainder of his coffee as he stood up and glared at her, a smile not too far from his lips.

"I resent that generalization," he said with his corny voice of authority. "But I can briefly say by way of explanation, that a man's aversion to shopping is a primal response that is triggered when the male of the species back in the day saw the imminent collapse of his tribe through his mate's carelessness. Translated into layman's terms shopping equates to possible bankruptcy, collapse of a man's tribe. You see?"

"Do you know, you are a chauvinist dawg?"

Shaft howled and grinned broadly.

"I prefer to see myself as a wolf, baby. A chauvinist wolf."

Shaft and Y walked down the busy shopping mall arm in arm. She was chatting away about how predictable most men were while the detective was occupied with a strand of information left over from the discussion they had the last time they met.

He wished he didn't have to bring it up now but he felt it important enough to run the risk of placing a damper on the fantastic time he was having. And for a detective there was nothing worse than having unresolved questions lurking around in your head.

Y preferred the direct approach anyway, so he laid it on the line. He stopped, squeezing her hand gently and pulled her in to face him.

"Remember I said I'd look into the client you're working for, some background stuff that could prove to be useful? Well I found something peculiar."

Y maintained her smile but her body betrayed her deep seated worry by the tautness exhibited in her neck and shoulders. Shaft pulled her in closer.

"You okay?"

"I'm good, let's talk here." They shuffled over to a length of balcony and made it their own; the exquisite perfume of savory crepe teased them from the restaurant across the way. Shaft leaned on the cool brushed aluminum tubes and looked down at the milling shoppers below. Y leaned her backside on it with folded arms, ready to hear what he had to say.

"Your man Spokes has no criminal record but had a minor traffic violation seven years ago. He was driving a car that the motor patrol bobby thought had been stolen but turned out to have been loaned to him by a friend, Jimmy Éclair. They were buddies back in the Caribbean."

"I know this is going somewhere right?" Y asked feigning impatience.

"There's more," Shaft continued. "At the time Jimmy Éclair was working with a self professed Obeah man from Jamaica called Enoch Lacombe who was running a gambling den with a few close acolytes around him as he begged, stealed and murdered for certain types of antiquities. Years later Éclair disappeared and his murder, along with three other people working with this psycho, was pinned on him. Spokes has never showed up on our radar since. Until now."

Y stroked his arm.

"You're beginning to worry me. You don't walk around with these facts bouncing around in your head as a matter of course, do you?"

Shaft laughed then got serious staring intensely into Y's eyes, his voice lowered.

"Normally I'd say no but on my desk right now is a set of murders linked with this sadist Enoch Lacombe. In the last four weeks eleven people have been slaughtered. Some of these victims deserve everything they got but there are other casualties who have been caught up in a struggle I can't explain. Decent people torn from their families. That's when the facts aren't just mere facts but people's lives. And it sticks with me, everywhere I go. The thing is this killer has been in prison for the past four years of a thirty year stretch. He is physically incapable of committing these crimes but they are happening. Then there is this niggling feeling I've got, that's prompting me to ask you if any of this is related to your client."

"So why haven't you asked this Enoch Lacombe guy to give you his take on the situation?"

"Funny you should ask that because I've been trying to book an appointment with him in Wormwood Scrubs for five weeks and as far as I can figure out it's been denied from the top. First my Governor wouldn't have it and when I tried to sidestep him the Prison Governor literally laughed me off the phone. It's pissing me right off but until I can find out who is copycatting his methods, I'm guessing."

"So you presuming it's copycatting."

"What else could it be?"

Y shrugged.

"Is there anything you want to tell me?" Shaft asked.

"I have a question, first," Y said.

"Fire away."

"Do you believe in Obeah, magic and things that go bump in the night?"

"Ah, the supernatural," he grinned. "What a question, to ask me on a first date. Luckily for you my incomplete anthropology doctorate was on African Urban Mythology. And yes some people think so. But the theories tend to attribute those kinds of belief systems to our need to believe in something greater than ourselves. God, witchcraft, magical powers and that kind of thing are archetypes that have followed us into the twenty-first century from when we huddled around camp fires, telling horror stories. From my experience of tracking these urban myths in Southern Africa, I've been unable to categorically prove the existence of anything overtly supernatural but I did generate a shit load of unanswered questions.

"And your mind is made up?"

"I'm a detective and a scientist. I'm open to the possibilities."

Y pursed her lips in contemplation at his answer.

"Who is Darkman?" She asked bluntly.

Shaft looked at her. He spoke slow and deliberately.

"Where did you hear that name?"

Shaft's Adam's apple rose up to under his chin and stayed there.

The words fell out of his mouth with more haste than he could conceal.

"Hey, if you don't want to talk about this, I understand babe but ..."

Her eyes flashed trepidation and fear. An almost imperceptible change in Y's stance said she had just physically reinforced herself for a conflict that only existed in her head. She held onto his upper arm, her grip tight and stared into his eyes.

"I think your man Darkman is trying to kill our client."

Completely out of context he kissed her on the lips and held her close.

There was no resistance.

He would figure out why he did it, later.

"Yow, yow, Y! Cut that shit out, man!" Patra shouted out to them with her solid cheeks glowing. "You got your grubby hands all over a nigga, damn. Crushing up his shirt and putting lipstick, all which ways over his shit."

"Yeah, just cool, nuh." Suzy added, promptly making parting movements with her arms like some overzealous

Catholic nun chaperoning her girls at a mixed ed. dance. "Wi like him jus' as he is. All neat and smooth."

Shaft unclenched and looked at the two women approaching sheepishly. Y had left his embrace and joined her sisters over the short distance.

Patra pulled up beside him and placed the bags at her heels.

Suzy looked appraisingly at Shaft and locked her arms in his, speaking over her shoulder to Y.

"Yuh told him, nuh true?"

"He is as good a detective as we thought," Y said, sounding apologetic. "But all the juicy bits I've left for you two to fill him in with."

"Only fair," Patra quipped and she took up her position on Shaft's free arm.

Y called after them.

"I don't think he believes me, so you may have more luck convincing him than I did."

Shaft felt that familiar school boy flush when he was around them returning, he wondered how long he had to know them to be completely comfortable.

"You're gonna dig this," Patra said to Shaft excitedly, dragging him into a bistro and directing him to a table. Spokes sat loosely in a wicker chair, his fingers fondling the black trilby on his knee and an empty plate in front of him.

"Detective Inspector McFarlane, Spokes." Patra introduced them then without further fanfare began her story with Suzy filling in the gaps. Shaft still could not bring himself to believe what he was hearing.

They had been talking to Shaft for the last twenty minutes and the warmth of Shaft's kiss still lingered on her lips. Her heart felt languid and a spark of fuzzy heat exploded in her stomach as she savored the strong chemistry between them. But soon her mind was on other things and Y began hoping Shaft would be an ally in this craziness.

It felt like Patra and Suzy had accepted this situation more easily than she had and after Sunday night's clash with the undead, sleep was at a premium for her and nightmares showed no sign of abating either.

They had killed that night.

Their assailants may have been drugged and bound by some spell, bent on taking their lives but having to kill did not rest well with any of them.

Maybe the reason why she was so keen to see Shaft believing in what they were going through was the importance of a shared experience from the perspective of someone with no vested interest in their weirdness.

A sceptic.

Spokes was paying them well but it had become much more than that now. Y craved for a point of view outside of their trinity something or someone that could keep her balanced. Because the more situations they were exposed to in this brave new world the more the boundaries between the normal and incredible would wear thin.

And how much more of her beliefs about the world could she see shattered? Maybe she would finally give in to the raging battle inside and fully accept it as part and parcel of her world.

Maybe.

It was these thoughts that occupied Y's mind as she intercepted the girls, Spokes and Shaft as they left the bistro.

"We taking him home," Suzy announced and Spokes accepted the verdict with a nod of his head.

"His head is all fucked up with the truth, our kind of truth."

"I'll walk you to the car." Shaft had his hands on Y's shoulders and mirrored her uncertain steps playfully.

"Had enough from the tales of the Twilight Zone?" Y asked as they walked through the sliding doors to the car park.

"If I didn't know you better I wouldn't be wasting my time listening to this but..." he corrected himself. "You ladies are the most level headed people I know. Making head nor tail of this is difficult."

They walked out onto level three and headed to section AF to where the limousine Spokes had hired was parked in the distance. Spokes, Y and Patra were just ahead as Suzy fell back beside Shaft.

"If I was yuh, I guess I wouldn't believe it either but lucky for me I have my sisters. If dem convinced of anything then I'm a believer."

"That can be dangerous, don't you think, relying on a second party's opinion and not the facts as you see it."

"Normally I'd agree with yuh." Suzy shrugged. "But I have an advantage. Anyway if you've seen some of dis evil with your own eyes, fought it with your hands and when you have a second to confirm it was real, yuh know yuh not going crazy."

He nodded.

"Me an deh girls have dis connection ting. Hard to explain but when we decide to use it we can feel deh truth in most situations."

"Why am I not surprised, by that?"

"There is hope for you yet, then Mas Winston," Suzy said.

John-John the chauffeur jerked up from his newspaper as he saw the group approaching through his rear view mirror. Folding it self-consciously he neatly squeezed it into the glove compartment and jumped out of the luxury car, using the keys to close it remotely.

He was a very courteous lad, who took the responsibility of giving his passengers the best customer experience he was capable of. As he straightened his ill fitting jacket around his thin frame, he walked briskly up to meet his passengers some way from the limo with extended hands to greet them all and relieve them of some of the baggage.

"Ladies, Sir." He took as much as he could carry and without looking around, pointed to the Cadillac and pressed the door release.

There was the characteristic bleep sound and the car shuddered violently as if a massive force was struggling to get out from under the hood. Everyone stopped and stared as a roar erupted from the interior. The big car bucked and twisted, the undercarriage screeching with the strain. There was an almighty boom and the car lifted from the ground engulfed in hungry red flames and bellowing black smoke. Another nerve shredding screech like a pterodactyl from prehistory and the nebulous smoke and flame formed the outlines of a hideous giant bird of prey. It emerged from the limousine like it was disgorging from a metallic egg, head first then wings. The dark phoenix screeched, and a geyser of car parts and concrete rose up with it, forming its body while its massive flapping wings were all flame and smoke.

Shaft's mouth fell slack as the flame bird birthed itself in all its savage glory. The scorched and mangled limo fell apart like the shell of a giant misshapen egg. The bird of prey conflagration fixed them with its soulless lava red eyes. It flung its head back again and shrieked angrily, its massive wings span catching an easy rhythm over the chaos, attempting to detach itself from it's source – the burning car. It flapped its fiery wings to keep itself aloft, sending waves of baking convection currents over the distance to them. The heat was intense and stank of cooked meat, grease and molten metal.

"Jesuuus." Shaft murmured, stepping back.

It shrieked its frustration of being held in place to its source and in a huff the dark Phoenix suddenly shrunk back into the remnants of the vehicle, letting off a sonic boom of ear splitting proportions. Car windshields in the surrounding area cracked or exploded. The security alarms blared over the confusion, soon to be joined by the screams of human panic. Nobody could make sense of what had just happened. Even the bystanders who had seen it all would put it down to some elaborate hoax or reality TV for special effects experts. By the evening the reasons for it happening would be completely rational and sane.

For most people at least.

As the smoke cleared, Bad II the Bone, Spokes and Shaft, stood up from their crouched positions, ears ringing, nerves frayed, unconsciously standing their ground, for fear that this was not all over.

Y held onto Shaft's shoulders unsteadily from behind and he reached up with his trembling hand to touch hers.

"Seeing is believing, they say, right." Y murmured.

Shaft could only nod.

18.

Tuesday July 23rd
Red Ground Estates, Surrey
21.40

Spokes' 'batty' was clenching involuntarily hours after witnessing the fire bird destroying the limousine. For some reason even with the precognitive power his guard ring afforded him, it did not make him feel protected at all. His usual confidence had departed and look as he might through his mental rolodex, there were no sugar-coated platitudes he could pull forth to make him feel better.

This is war, Iyah.

Darkman knew who and where they were and from now on his supernatural lackeys would transform their lives into a constant state of fear.

The girls sat silently watching Spokes uncomfortably twisting one moment and the next eyeing the more heart racing performance of LL Cool J on the Blue Ray player. Spokes kept getting out of his seat with that pained expression on his face and pacing. The small motes of dust from his movements made it seem like friction was burning the fibers of the rag pile. His eyes darted over to four Louis Vitton cases that were packed beside the bay doors that overlooked his one acre garden. An overcoat was thrown neatly over them like the completion of some Turner prize exhibit with a deeper significance that was not apparent to your five senses.

Not so in this case.

His eyes made an awkward orbit as horrible images took on their own awful life for a moment. He settled on the girls for much longer and shook his head. A tangible air of relief that they were fine washed over him.

Look at dem, all cool and sexy, and they've saved mi rass life three times already. How many more times?

"Suh, everbody alright den. Yuh want another drink girls?"

"For the fifth time," Y said testily, "We're fine."

Spokes frowned.

"Don't sweat it, Slick," Patra consoled. "We made a deal to complete the job and we won't welch on our promise."

"Jus' cool, Mas Spokes, we trying feh understand all dis. We are unprepared; not that anything could ever prepare us for this but wi have yuh back."

He looked at Suzy fleetingly and smiled.

Y wasn't so forgiving.

"Have you ever thought of us through this whole fucked up situation?"

"Tink of you?" he asked incredulously. "Widout you I'd be six foot six!"

"I mean your plan. Have you considered our escape strategy in all this? How do we handle any backlash from you disappearing?"

"Y have a point king. We can't just apologize to the Darkman," Suzy added.

"Motherfucker doesn't look like the forgiving type." Patra said.

"You sista's have me all wrong. But that is not your fault. I never mek all the information forthcoming as I should have. Wasn't sure you would appreciate it."

"Slick, baby. We appreciate the fuck out of this situation, trust me. There isn't a goddamn thing you could tell us now that we wouldn't believe."

He smoothed the skin under his chin with his little finger, scratching the small shoots of grey bristle there.

"Ok, ok." He began. "I've explained to you that I hold dat dog Enoch responsible for my Idren Jimmy's death. You already know his treasures are buried under the nightclub but there is something that he wants more than anyting else."

"I don't even want to guess what dat could be," Suzy said.

Patra simply groaned.

"So you're saying amongst these objects under the club we have something to leverage or protect ourselves from him."

"See it deh sister Y, you have it," he said triumphantly, slapping his hands together. "Mi nah leave you swinging in the wind, baby. I've had four years to research these things that lay hidden in the club and I tink I know what he wants. Dat will be my bargaining chip that will protect you from him. I've looked at this from every angle I know how."

"What about just cancelling the dance, going in and taking what you need under the cover of darkness?" Y asked.

Spokes laughed, shaking his head and rubbing his fingers through his curly greys.

Y glared at him and Patra was infected with the giggles.

"I was like yuh years ago, naive to the real world around me. Jimmy's death and everyting surrounding it drew mi into this and I've had to learn the hard way how to navigate this journey."

"So what are you saying?" Patra asked.

"Now Darkman has found me, we are under his watchful eye. The only way is to throw him off deh scent. He's at a disadvantage because physically he can't be close to me because of this." He pointed to the ring on his index finger. "Him also loses his full potential around deh gifted like you ladies."

Y laughed nervously, not sure if he was exaggerating or serious.

Spokes kept on.

"He will send his agents of night, no doubt about dat. And they come with their own set of rules but you sisters are mi key card."

Spokes chewed on his lips nervously.

"You have been chosen by the powers that be to fulfill some works on deh earth plane. How or why, I don't know but I'm gonna guess it will be revealed in the fullness of time. Deh ring goes a good kind of crazy around you but your true power is in the trinity - you three together. Yuh si me?"

Suzy nodded and Spokes cleared his throat.

"Darkman is at his worst around you so we have to use that to our advantage. Then there are the crowds, deh bigger the better. Darkman will have to use his black magic in deh middle of all that spiritual static. I'm making it so that he has to stay away or his powers will be curtailed. The dance is necessary."

"So we are truly your guardian angels?" Y stated.

"The muscle and the magic," Patra added.

"Spokes' Angels, as I've always said," the promoter grinned. "Right now, I'm more concerned with the flesh and blood threat than anything else. Just help me through this and yuh can return to your lives much richer and free from repercussions. Dis will be over soon."

The LL Cool J concert on the tube had been relegated to the background as once again another layer of this mystery was peeled away and another part of this nightmare world they lived in opened up revealing its horror and majesty in equal measure. The girls did not have a clue where Spokes' plans would take them. They only knew that they would hold up their end of the bargain to the bitter end.

"It seems like you've become an OG in this mystic shit Slick," Patra said.

"Believe mi Sister P, I wasn't one for reading. The Bible sometimes and the racing section of my newspaper but all dat had to change when I found out what had been left in my care. I had to start again. Suh I went on my journey feh knowledge. I bought books and chatted with the experts and acquired a few tings on deh way to further open mi eyes."

He paused considering what he was about to say or do next as it would immerse them further into the rabbit hole. Involving them so deeply there was no hope of ever turning back.

He sighed.

"Oh, by the way Y," Spokes said matter-o-factly. "Deh ring picked up something foreign and dark, when we met for the first time. I nevah said anything but as we are being honest, let mi start, how mi intend to continue." He paused recalling a memory. "Not much of it was left staining yuh aura but it was obvious enough."

"Staining my aura?" Y asked slowly.

"I mean someone placed a powerful glamour spell on you. I'm sensing a smell of honeysuckle and cedar wood from the ring." He paused. "It was a breddah that did it, someone who spent a lot of time with you. Not too bad feh an amateur it looked like he realised you ladies are immune to long term magic. He had to stay close to top it up from time to time, to prolong deh effect. He used music, a guitar to reinforce the spell."

Y looked on bemused and Suzy's eyebrows raised but the penny dropped elsewhere in the room.

"Son-of-a-bitch," said Patra slowly looking at them. "You mean Tyrone is Harry Potter?"

A stunned silence descended on them as the door of clarity was flung open.

Moments later Spokes kept the surprises coming.

"Let me show you someting."

He motioned for the girls to follow him and he led them out of the room along the immaculately set white landing that looked down into the entrance hall two storey's down; bypassing the concealed lift and heading down the vast marble stairs with Bad II the Bone in tow.

"I've never shown anyone this before. Never been able to let anybody in feh fear they could get hurt. There isn't anyting much you girls have not seen and you have

kept your wits about you. I don't think there are no better people to show dis to."

Y looked at Patra ominously making the American
shrug. Suzy was eager to see what the revelation would
be but maintained that cool demeanor. They continued
down to the lower ground floor, passing the steam
room, massage rooms and the well equipped gym on the
way. Then the house's whole aesthetic changed and
there was no doubt at this juncture that they had come
face to face with their intended destination. This hallway
was more hi-tech than the rest of the house, lined with
frosted glass and sanded steel, the lighting was subdued
and embedded into the concrete supports activating like
a runway as you passed them. At the end was a reinforced door, glinting dully from two spot lights shining
down on a keypad and a menacing Omni cam attached
to a stalk like a poisonous black fruit.

Whatever was behind it was meant to be protected
and concealed.

Spokes shouldered his way to the front and steadily
punched in a six digit code, the edges of a chrome pad
lit up and he placed his thumb on it. He waited for an
affirmative beep, beep and heard the heavy cylindrical
bolts retract. He pulled on the vault door to open it, ser-
vo motors assisting his efforts to swing it open and the
ceiling lights inside the room flickered on. Patra peered
over Spokes' shoulders and whistled. He stepped to the
side and motioned them in. Without hesitation Patra
strode forward.

The inside was reminiscent of a surgical theatre with
a temperature that suited its look and feel.

Chilled.

Chrome book shelves lined the walls, filled with con-
trasting tomes on metaphysics and magic, sorcery, voo-

doo and occult history. Like an art exhibition dedicated to all things mystical. There were photographs encapsulated in chrome frames attached to the ceiling and floor with wires and oil portraits hung on the walls with magical scenes possibly painted by grand masters. Set centrally around a glass tube that skewered the room was a three quarters circular marble desk, forty inch monitor, keyboard, printers and a Wrexham executive chair. Behind his work station and inside the tube was an chrome and glass constructed lift that could barely accommodate three people and serviced some levels below. One end of the room ended in a wall of glass from floor to ceiling and that seemed to attract Patra's attention. She wandered over while Suzy and Y were looking at books and stared intrigued at the photographs and items housed in glass cases. Spokes stood with his hands in his pockets and said nothing, letting them discover for themselves what had lain hidden here ever since their arrival.

"Motherf..." Patra sprang back from the glass wall and looked over to Spokes with a perplexed wide eyed stare.

Obviously expecting a reaction sooner or later, Spokes ambled over to where Patra was, Suzy and Y behind him.

"This shit you got to see," Patra said to the others, who both plastered their faces onto the exceptionally cold partition peering inside. Moments later Y stepped away with a look of disgust on her face and turned her gaze at Spokes accusingly.

"He's dead. Well in deh clinical sense, so don't get jumpy," Spokes said. "Let me introduce you to my pardy Jimmy Éclair."

Spokes' hand hovered over a light-switch and the gruesome exhibit sprang to life from the subtle ceiling lights.

Y shivered involuntarily and for some reason the frailty of her existence buckled in on her and the simple pleasures of ignorance evaporated with every new revelation. She wanted to return to what she knew before but couldn't.

"He's at peace," Suzy said, her face still close to the glass, condensation smearing it. "I can feel him."

"I'm feeling him too, he's a handsome nigga," Patra nodded and put her forehead to the glass again.

"He's so well preserved - almost as if he was alive." Y said.

Most of the body was enclosed in a jump suit made from some aluminium type material that was punctured by hundreds of leads that looked electrical and others that were liquid carrying capillaries. His face was the only part of him that was completely visible and that was slightly frosted from the cold inside.

"He's in cryo freeze," Spokes began. "I just couldn't leave his body to the Babylon, dem to make his family suffer more than they had to. They would investigate and mistreat him to find answers, I couldn't tek that." He shook his head forlornly.

Only Suzy responded with a nod.

"It cost mi a small fortune but what could I do? If he was going to be with me I couldn't just let him rot away, so I did what I could. I paid for him to be refrigerated then contacted a hot shot yout studying cryogenics, short on money but big on ideas. The design of the machinery, now that was something else entirely but the long an' the short of it is I got deh job done."

"You got some freaky shiiiit goin' on here, Slick."

"It was necessary, Miss P believe me. An Obeah man worth him salt could extract information from even a dead body, up to the bones if dem skilled enough. In all conscience I couldn't put my spar through that and I didn't want anything leading back to me or his family."

"I feel you." Patra answered.

"Nothing can stay hidden forever, though," said Suzy.

"True word, so that is why I had to make a choice. Take back what I can an' just disappear, making sure no one I care for gets hurt. Didn't count on deh gangster Deacon still being involved or Darkman finding out where I live. That's why we go ahead with what I have planned and outsmart deh whole rass a dem."

St Jude's Catholic Church, Chelsea
Wednesday July 24th
18.40

"Hiiiiyaah!" The shrill voice of youthful exuberance echoed off the community centres ceiling.

The reverse round house kick was genius and had snatched Tenisha's little legs from under her in a flash. Still dazed from what had happened, lying flat on the impact mat, Tenisha looked up as Michelle glared down at her with braids flying everywhere delivering the killing stroke – metaphorically speaking - like a seasoned wushu professional.

Suzy held back a smile and nodded towards the two young combatants who had jumped to their feet and were standing with heads bowed.

Give deh one Michelle she, four more years an' that gal a guh hot like any bonfire.

The rest of the class came together from the fringes and bowed in unison.

"Teacher!" they shouted together and formed a circle around her.

Suzy Wong sat in the centre of a circle formed from subdued and disciplined bundles of pubescent energy in the shape of eight year old girls and boys. The physical aspect complete, now was their time to relax and meditate. Suzy welcomed these moments too. Being exposed to the incredible and the horrific had her emotions and thoughts in ragged tatters. These sessions helped to centre her, absorbing the psychic energies of optimism and innocence they exuded. She only wished there was more time with them but the parents would be waiting.

So their five minutes up, Suzy bid them farewell and in no time the church hall was quiet and she was alone with herself.

Y and Patra were in Surrey at the mansion looking after Spokes and she had taken the day off to help out here and briefly placate a love-starved boyfriend. She wasn't quite sure she understood the need to prepare herself but just knew that what lay ahead wouldn't require just physical strength but spiritual and sexual energy too. Her focus wouldn't be on him and that wouldn't be fair. Even here, her mind had immediately started looking for solutions, connections and explanations to the myriad of questions posed by this gig from hell they had acquired.

Explaining what she was going through to Steve would be difficult but he would respect her need for abstinence even if he didn't understand why. She had been blessed with a good man but eventually he would want answers and she was obligated to tell him the truth.

The whole truth.

And how was she going to do that, when the tamest thing right now in their crazy lives would make your hair stand on end.

The silence in the church made Suzy think back to touching the guard ring Spokes had on his finger. The memory was so poignant the emotions associated with returning to wherever she was transported on touching it, vivid.

Suzy found herself disembodied and in a dimension of complete and utter darkness which seemed to recognize a change in its state and burst into a constellation of lights that reminded her of looking into the night sky of the Jamaican countryside. Suzy's very presence in this place sent a ripple of warmth through what was cold desolation, like a spark of ignition, that kick started its function. And as she looked on admiringly a still small voice was telling her that these were not stars in the astronomical sense but the lights of life.

Every human soul living today was represented and spread across the panorama in their billions. The blue of birth and the diminishing red of death sparkled in the firmament. In this place thoughts were things, brought into reality as they were conceived and all the emotions that made us who we are blew through this eternity like solar winds. Nothing remained hidden, everything was open for her to see, past, present and burrowing into the rabbit hole of the future. From time of birth to present and beyond every detail recorded with five sense clarity ready for access at a thought. As ideas came to Suzy's awareness they played out for her to see and feel as if she was an omnipresent observer. She thought of their situation, events replaying instantaneously with details she could never ascertain in the waking world. Then Suzy pondered her past in Jamaica and before her mind settled she was reliving how she received the dragon scars on her arms. The fire at the wushu School in Constant Spring, trapped students screaming for help, how she freed them by clearing fallen debris and pushing into the burning studio, searing the impression of the dragons embossed on the copper gilded Chinese doors into the skin of her forearms. Suzy smelt her skin burning again, felt the pain then slung forward in time where she was making the decision to intricately tattoo the burn scars in glorious colour and take ownership for something that could have been a deformity but which she made into a badge of honor. Suzy's heart lifted with a sense of certainty that meandered its way through her soul. Her life and the life of her sisters had been ordained with a deeper purpose and Spokes was a part of that. This she knew with crystal clarity because this place had told her so. The girls had said, she had gone deathly quite for no more than two minutes, but in that two minutes, Suzy felt as if she had lived a lifetime.

Was her life suddenly clearer for it? Not that she could draw on what she had seen from the ring, she just knew it was accessible when the need was required. Have faith, even when she felt she was balancing on a line that separated the irrational and rational world her talent of seeing and feeling things on the other side of the line was becoming more pronounced. As the dark clouds gathered around them, she had to be clear headed enough to help her girls navigate the hidden and the dangerous. Suzy needed time to calm the static and to hear the message because against Enoch Lacombe and the others who were after Spokes rass they needed every advantage possible.

This helped.

The smell of incense, dust and wood.

Suzy said a thank you as she walked out of the church hall into the main reception, her movements echoing around her. The small walk between the reception and the church brought back flashes of Jamaica and walking bare-foot on the grass. Suzy entered the impressive modern architecture of St. Jude's through huge oak doors that were always open and welcoming. She genuflected in the aisle and sat on one of the pews for a moment.

She wasn't a practicing Catholic but ever since attending Immaculate Conception Girls' School in Kingston, the church building more so than anything else in her experience, trapped the essence of calm and all that was good and true in the very brickwork. Traditional Catholicism didn't impress her but she knew one truth and that was the essence of good, God, the universe or whatever you conceived it to be, resided here. She stood up and walked closer to the altar and stood staring at the detailed structure of a dark skinned Christ nailed to the cross.

Pain.

They had promised themselves Bad II the Bone would be their final port of call. No more dead end jobs, just a single minded effort in making their dreams work. And although this was a far cry from what they had planned this felt so natural, so right.

Suzy looked up at Christ on the cross for one last time and knew this could be their-own crucifixion scenario. She bent to her knees and took a moment.

Docklands Cargo Bay Ltd, South East London
Thursday, July 25th
21.40

Darkman observed his surroundings with a keener eye than usual, knowing he would not be here much longer. If it was at all possible to develop affection for his temporary home and command bunker, the events of the last month would endear him to this sixty foot container. But he made it as comfortable as was required, making sure that only the essential tools of his campaign against these cattle was evident.

Outside protection and concealment were laid in an area close to the entrance to the trailer. Drawn from the ash of six murders the complex vévés took him forty eight hours to map out. An intricate design that bent the boundaries, shifted realities and opened up a gateway to hell itself and provided the anonymity he required.

Inside he had cordoned off a space for his distillation plant which was constantly bubbling as it extracted the active ingredient in the demon weed essential to most of his concoctions and spells. Extractor's whirred around the perimeter, balancing the internal atmosphere and protecting it from excess moisture. He moved around the container like a man at peace, immaculate white wife-beaters, khaki slacks and sandals but he was focussed. The natural oils made his dark skin gleam but there was no sweat. The rudimentary spells that created the internal eco system kept the temperature comfortable whether outside was cold or hot.

Darkman stopped his pacing and folded his arms, looking at a plastic shopping bag hooked to hanging vegetable baskets that held what was left of the demon weed. He would require every ounce of his remaining plant samples for his final push.

He eyed his humble bunk bed and discounted rest for now. Darkman had too much to plan for his departure. Jamaica was calling him with its sweet Mento melody, leaving the London war zone he had created in his own image behind. Taking his heir, his only son, a blood splattered reputation that would not be equaled and the John Crow stone.

He looked at the empty cradle with it's Yoruba markings and imagined the powerful ancient artefact back in its place.

He smiled.

A smile that was wide and menacing like the smile of a shark. Murderous yet assured of its purpose.

Deh best was yet to come, pardy.

All the players were in place and once he had enough reserves of physical and dark spiritual energy, he would carry out his final plan.

This entry into the Lacombe history books was to be concluded soon and a situation that seemed hopeless would begin to be amended.

That was his promise to the Lacombe forefathers.

The best was yet to come.

19.

Dance Night
Lunar Street, South East London
Friday 26th July
22.15

The Bentley GT pulled up into the open plan car park and so did the A5 Audi that had been following them for the last ten miles. Normally, with Patra at the wheel nothing short of a drive-by would get her to lose focus or concern herself with a motorist engaged in vehicular stalking but these dudes were insistent. As the miles diminished to the club their tail became more brazen. So as soon as an opportunity arose they pulled up alongside the GT, windows down and pointed automatic weapons at them threatening to fire if they did not pull over.

As always Bad II the Bone interpreted the challenges that life threw at them through their unique perspective and relished the conflict. After a drawn out pursuit either to infuriate or confuse them they slowed down and turned into a parking area of one of those cut price supermarkets whose ethos was stack 'em high, sell 'em low. The car parking wasn't as isolated as you would think at this time of night but the Bentley came to a stand obscured slightly by vehicles beside it and to its back. Cautiously, the Audi followed and stopped facing the vehicle about a hundred or so metres away, argon lights on full. The occupants stayed put, trying to intimidate but this time it did not have the desired effect.

It took Patra the personification of braggadocio to step out from the driver's side with a lighter in one hand and a cigar in the other. Lil Wayne was pumping through the Blaupunkt speakers and an obscured figure in the back seat watched in silence the unfolding drama. Patra was the epitome of ice cool sexiness. Dressed in a tight fitting cat-suit, hair braided tightly to her scalp, subtle makeup and hoop earrings, Miss P brought the cigar to her lips and flared the lighter to its tip. With legs slightly apart, she took a series of long puffs and blew smoke in the Audi's direction. To herself she whistled the theme song of the Sergio Leone western the Good, The Bad and The Ugly.

Patra didn't give a shit.

That sense of panic or controlled fear she used to experience when she was about to embark on something extreme or risky was gone. Instead her preternatural instinct tingled at the back of her skull, shifting the laws of possibility ever so slightly. Before her experiences with the supernatural, apprehension would have influenced her actions, although she would discount it most times but these days were different. These wanksters were real men, mature gang-bangers who graduated from drive-bys to contracts. They could bleed and they could die.

After experiencing what lay beyond and seeing what damage these forces could unleash in the world of men, these motherfuckers merely piqued her interest. What they didn't realise was that given the opportunity confronting flesh and blood was always a pleasure.

She took another pull on the cigar and gave them the finger.

The car park lights threw criss-cross shadows across a surface that after years of usage was stripping off its original top layer and in parts was cratered from the meteor shower of age. Swamps of darkness that would never experience artificial light due to illumination that had never been fixed, lay like chasms in an imaginary landscape filled with dangers. The area had seen better days too. The perimeter was edged with trees and some cars left overnight or abandoned dotted the giant sized checker-board. The Audi had its headlights on full beam almost as if they wanted to pin Patra to the spot or compensate for the flickering bulbs from the faulty car park lamps.

The Bentley sat there, lights out, almost contemplating its fate while a defiant Patra stood her ground.

The men in the Audi dimmed their headlights and stepped out into the beam of light they made, approaching Patra with weapons drawn. The lead goon, five foot ten, sporting a Gucci t-shirt and non-descript jeans, shoots his mouth first.

"Where's the old man? Where's Spokes?"

The other two men either side of him, revolved their shoulders as if the guns were too heavy for them.

Patra took another puff on the cigar and shrugged, giving them the sign of submission, arms outstretched to the side with palms up. He obviously wasn't convinced as his whole body language transformed like a method actor taking on the persona of a vicious character he had rehearsed for. He swung the Glock up with his right hand and steadied it with his left, the business end of the weapon pointed to Patra's chest. The rest of the goon squad followed suit but targeted the Bentley instead. Suddenly the two men were finding it strange that both passenger doors were open, where moments before they were closed.

A lone figure still sat in the back seat.

They looked over to each other quizzically and gripped their weapons, eyes furtive.

Guicci T-shirt saw nothing; his focus was on Patra and her lack of respect for him and his gun.

"Bitch, don't let me ask you again," he hissed. "Hand him over."

And that's when the blur hit him.

The pain from years of experience of these things was uncomplicated and direct. No signature feel to it, just the shredding of flesh or the breaking of bones. The pain in his wrist was sharp and intense, making the muscles around the carpal bones spring open as the gun flew from him into the darkness. He grunted dealing with the agony and showing his anger at being taken completely unawares and still being unsure of who or what was the source of his attack. He swung viciously with his right hand, hoping to use his clenched fist as a battering ram but instead his attack went whistling through the air in an ineffectual arc. All he could think of to protect himself was to keep moving but his efforts were clumsy and inept. Another series of small explosions of pain at the back of his legs, stomach and chest lit up his nervous system in quick succession, each erupting into miniature geysers of blood from the points of impact. His clothes were ripped and bloodied and his skin marked with tracks from something razor sharp. He had been hit at pressure points that had him on the ground trying to convince the muscles in his legs to respond but they wouldn't. A swelling to the side of his face was throbbing and from his position he looked up without moving his head after seeing a pair of black leather boots beside him and in the distance through pain dimmed eyes his colleagues at arms being beaten severely by a petite oriental girl. He eventually managed to look up to the dominatrix-like black chick standing with a samurai sword with his blood dripping from it, glaring down at him.

He shuddered.

She deftly whipped the blade to his throat as if she was about to decapitate him, stopping inches from his throat. There was no contact but the keenness of the sword must have magically transferred across the short distance because he could feel his skin break and a bead of blood - or was it sweat? trickle down his Adam's apple. He flinched from the discomfort of his position and that infernal humming of the crafted metal pointed at his neck made him tingle all over. His legs were weak, his wounds were gushing and he was acutely aware of the contents of his stomach gurgling. But he was under the control of the wielder of the blade so he dared not move only finding himself looking at the Japanese inscriptions on the blade and then to the woman. Steely determination met his stare and he knew the next thing he did would determine whether he lived or died.

"How we a guh duh dis?" The female with the Caribbean accent held a gun to one man's head while the remaining gunman, dazed but unhurt aimed at all three women in turn, unsure who posed the most threat to his captured colleagues. The lone gunman looked indecisively at each situation until the black chick, obviously interpreting his indecision as stalling suddenly jerked the blade upwards against the throat of her captive. He grunted at the added pressure to the soft folds of his neck, eyes wide with terror.

"You've been taken motherfuckers. Accept it and walk away." Patra had casually walked over from her vantage point and joined the intimate standoff, dusting cigar ash into the proceedings as if it was a sacrament. Defying his dumb look, the lone gunman went against his instinct and dropped his weapon. Patra retrieved them pushing one in the small of her back and one in both hands.

"One more thing to do before we leave you wanksters." Casually she walked over to the Audi and fired two rounds into each tyre. "Yeah!" Patra said, turning to face everyone. "Hand over your mobiles gentlemen, 'cos you don't want me rummaging through your shit to retrieve 'em."

Reluctantly mobiles were handed over and smashed one at a time. "You know, this feels good but not as good as if I buss a cap in your boss's punk ass. You tell that country boy, he better see me, before I see him because if he doesn't, there will be hell to pay. He fucking wid the wrong bitches."

They sashayed back to their ride and drove off.

Stockwell Locks
Housing Estate
22.15

The door buzzer chimed out a tacky rendition of Bob Marley's *So Much Trouble in the World*, just as Chips reached out to scrape up his winning from the middle of the velvet poker table, to the certainty of his own corner. The door buzzer went off again and in a remote part of his mind Sully was loudly undoing the latches and bolts after looking through the peephole to identify who was outside.

A drawn out silence.

That's when the commotion began.

Sully yelled out and then grunted, followed by raised voices and wild shuffling of feet. Gravity's merciless pull was evident as a body hit the door, bounced off it and then met the floor again on rebound with the force of a two hundred and fifty pound man of which Sully was. That caught the attention of the men sitting solemnly around the poker table but there was no need to investigate because the men who had entered brashly walked through the hall and into the lounge unannounced. Chips flicked his chair backwards with his calf and made the authority he held over this little piece of London real estate felt.

"Yow! Don't you know this yard is under Father Deacon's protection? The aggression ting is bad for business champion. Talk to the man yourself, feel free..."

Chips took out his Blackberry punched a few buttons and passed the smart phone in his direction. The man ignored him simply watching Chips' show of control trickle away, replaced by a dumb gurgle from the back of his throat as he heard a phone ring in the small hallway.

A Movado ringtone. Deacon's favoured dancehall artist.

Chips' eyes bulged incredulously, as a man stepped out of the hallway dressed in a long black Burberry raincoat, hands in his trouser pockets. Almost shielding his eyes was an Adidas flat cap on his smoothly barbered head. Beside him was a dark skinned man whom he had encountered at Deacons Gym, neat straw hat on his head and around his neck were links of herbs and flowering plants. He carried a khaki bag around his shoulder and he was bare footed. He observed the surroundings with a furtive stare and mumbled to himself.

"Father Deacon," Chips stammered. "Good feh see yuh."

Deacon nodded as the room filled with large men all bearing weapons.

"Weh she deh?" Deacon asked.

Chips looked confused but Deacon's stare was unwavering.

"She....." Then it dawned on him. "Yuh mean Sandra? She's in the bedroom with deh yout. Problem?"

Deacon closed his eyes and bowed his head slightly.

"The problem is that nothing useful has come from you shacking up wid dis gal. I'm no closer to finding the obeah man's treasure than I was four years ago." He paused and considered his next words. "Before, I would happily play deh longtail but as of now rude bwoy, time is an issue."

"But dis has been a success." Chips sounded bemused, motioning around him. "I've produced good money for you."

Deacon laughed throatily, a gold tooth flashing.

"Money is only a measure, star. Power, now that is the new currency and Darkman's treasure and its secrets are power. The obeah man has a weak link and although him try to play gangster with a real gangster, him have feelings feh him little family. He will tell me where the treasure is or sacrifice life of what he holds dear. Guh get her."

Deacon directed his question to his men and then pointed at Chips.

"If this rastaman overstep deh mark, bag an tag him bomboclaat."

Chips flopped back down in his chair, defeat tugging on the slit of his eyes and twisting his lips. He folded his winnings with a resigned certainty that the poker game was well and truly over.

"Yuh look disappointed star? Don't blame me if you didn't get deh pussy, you had ample time?"

Deacon grinned made the mobile phone sign with his fingers and glared at the soldiers left in the lounge.

"Keep her here until I call with further instructions. Enjoy yourselves but keep her alive. Nobody leaves. Yuh si mi?"

The men grunted responses and Deacon ambled out of the room with his Haitian Vodun beside him and two other thick set men who valued his physical welfare above their own. He suddenly stopped in his tracks, his entourage mimicking his abruptness and watched him close his eyes as if he needed to focus. Sandra's screams echoed behind him and only then did he smile and proceed to the front door.

Sandra's piercing screams did not hold the exquisiteness to the ear for Chips that they had for Deacon. The uncertainty of this situation and the calibre of men Deacon had left behind to do his bidding did not bode well. Every whimper, every wail, bruised the atmosphere that before was expectant with profit but now only served to set Chips' nerves on edge. No matter what he thought of Sandra and her little brat, he wasn't sure if he could sit back and allow them to do this. The men around the poker table had already retrieved their meagre winnings and had been corralled into a spare room. Everyone witnessed their hostess being unceremoniously dragged by her legs, kicking and screaming into the lounge and everyone kept quiet. What would his rep be if he followed suite and did nothing? He would be a laughing stock, if the streets recorded this story and his essential role lacked his resitance or protest.

Sandra's flailing hands and kicking feet were knocking over all that she had lovingly displayed to try and make her surroundings homely.

"You don't hafe do dis." Chips spoke evenly and stepped towards the men as he did so but the slap of leather that accompanied his plea for compassion said none would be given. Five guns were pointed at him with safeties off.

"We do have to," Bookworm said - slight frame, almost the antithesis of gangster dress, glasses with a psychotic stare. "And if you keep questioning Deacon's orders I'm going to take it you want to challenge what I'm going to do next."

Chips raised his arms in defeat and backed away humbly.

"Mi just a seh."

"Well it's duly noted that you disapprove. I'll give the boss your feedback." He scoffed.

Chips wasn't sure he could stay to endure this but what choice did he have? Sandra was still screaming and thrashing, her wild eyes fixing his with panic beseeching him to help but never directly calling out for him. Was he waiting for that to happen?

Maybe.

He tended to speak to her disrespectfully, even slap her a few times but no one else would dare touch her except Deacon himself. He listened as baby Rowan, next door, feeling his mother's distress, began crying too and the hard hearted gambler that Chips aspired to be began to melt away and it made him angry. Deacon may have been right about his feelings for her but Sandra did not deserve this.

Chips buried those feelings for her as deep as he could.

Now they were past the point of no return.

The three men that held Sandra in the air like a human sacrifice slammed her down on the table. She grunted, saliva exiting her mouth, a rictus of pain as her face cracked on the table, the effect causing her eyes to twirl in their orbits with disorientation.

"Wha deh fuck rude bwoy, easy?" One thug entreated.

It was like these bastards had been given the order to hurt her before killing her.

Chips didn't think.

Instead he dashed forward attempting to tackle one of the men pinning Sandra's left foot to the table. In that drawn out second it took him to gather momentum, his breath hissing through his teeth, anticipating the impact and knowing he had to do something, it all went wrong.

Bookworm needn't have worried.

A split second of restraint saved Chips from being shot by a dude whose ancestry was an unfortunate coupling of Neanderthal man and a mountain gorilla. He was light on his feet too and stepped into his path as he barrelled forward, smashing down into the Rasta's skull with his ham fists and spinning Chips to the ground in a mound of arms and legs.

"Stupid must be your middle name moron," Bookworm spat. "Dump him rass in the room with the others."

Dance Night
The Crypt Nightclub
South East London
22.40

The velvet rope unhitched from the Swarovski encrusted posts and two huge shadows parted to allow Bad II the Bone entry with Spokes huddled between them like a prize boxer being escorted to the ring. Y led the way on the red carpet and her every step was followed with hungry eyes and gasps of surprise. She was an imposing figure in a black tight fitting strapless jump suit with her katana slung around her shoulders in a custom made sheath emblazoned with the Gucci logo. Suzy and Patra were similarly attired but with some slight variations to the theme. Patra wore her padded driving gloves and Suzy's design had one arm sleeveless showing the fire breathing tattooed dragon scars stretching the length of her arms. Sexy and practical. All had communication earpieces set to club frequency. They were being asked for autographs.

"Damn," Patra said, signing a flyer that had been thrust at her with a pen. "The party's jumping G."

Spokes nodded.

"What you expect with the magic touch." He turned to have a better look. "Check it out?" He pointed to the snaking queue stretching into the distance. "I will miss deh old place but tonight is a fitting tribute to it and my departure. New start." The grin on Spokes' face was getting wider as they entered the Crypt to the overwhelming presence of hundreds of partygoers letting loose.

He knew it was time but he would miss it.

The serendipitous events of finding the crypt and being bequeathed stolen treasure had set up a whirlwind of unexpected adventures for him. It had taken him to places he would never have imagined and altered his perception of the world forever. Even the inspiration behind the design of the club - Spanish Inquisition torture chambers - was something he stole from a film he loved by one of his favourite classic film stars - Vincent Price. The six cages were hung from the ceiling and contained two male and four female dancers. Like the furnaces that the real house of horrors had to brand its prisoners, the lighting rigs caught dancers and revellers in splashes of red and orange simulating the purifying flames from the Grand Inquisitor himself. The world famous Stone Love Sound System from Jamaica was spinning the hits and the excitement level was seismic.

His relief that he was here, relatively incident free was hard to mask.

Both he and Carlos had enjoyed unparalleled success at the club but that would end tonight. There would be no charms or spells that would attract the club goers week in week out. He would disappear start a new life away from England, protected from esoteric attack by his ring and live a normal life. Jimmy's remains and his family would be looked after, he would see to that.

Spokes looked around his surroundings nostalgically.

"Let's get dis done," he said and pointed to a network of gantries above that led them to the far side of the club without the inconvenience of wading through the revellers. Y took point, leading them over to the scaffolding type structure. She clambered up the rungs quickly, Spokes behind cushioned between Patra and Suzy.

Stockwell Locks
Housing Estate
22.40

Bookworm was acutely aware of what was going on and what he needed to do next. He took centre stage finally without any further interruptions and watched the Rasta man being dragged away. His advancement in the organisation depended on how he handled this situation. The men respected decisiveness and showmanship and he was about to give them both.

Sandra was held fast, mouth stuffed with a bathroom flannel, muffled moans of desperation ineffective as he looked down on her. She wore a black and white house dress with buttons to the front. Her chest rose and fell with the panic this situation brought with it and her skin glistened with the perspiration of fear. The Harry Potter reject ran his index finger between her breasts.

"We are going to keep you entertained for a few hours so relax."

His cronies leered, trying to keep that professional detachment but unable to ignore the potential excitement to be had from this. There were times when Bookworm despised his job and was able to take nothing from it that could edify him in any way. But today was one of those rare occasions that made up for.

Beautiful black woman great figure, smooth chocolate skin.

No, this would be a pleasure.

The thought trailed and before he took control of his hand it had already reached under her cotton dress, the tips of his fingers feeling the warmth of her flesh and the sheen of her skimpy panties. He gripped on the material and ripped them off.

Sandra couldn't see exactly what was going on at her feet but knew what was about to come. She railed and kicked, her screams ineffectual through her gag but that did not stop her from trying.

Baby Rowan could sense her panic and was screaming at the top of his little lungs, losing volume at times but making up for it as he caught his breath.

"For fuck sake hold her steady," Bookworm hissed and in that moment Sandra could only think that for a gangster his hands were smooth and warm. Like a teenager fumbling in the dark at his first intimate tryst, he finally grabbed onto the waist of her silken underwear and ripped it from under her.

Sandra's mind was a tableau of fear and panic, tears were streaming down her cheeks, the fear for her baby, the fear for herself, it gave her crazy strength but it wouldn't be enough. Her captors were impressed with her fight but the novelty didn't last and a pile driver of a right hand from an impatient Bookworm put paid to any further struggle.

Sandra looked peaceful with a trickle of blood at the corner of her mouth but the baby continued screaming with an unearthly sibilance.

"Will someone shut that fucking kid up!"

When Chips regained consciousness he was being dragged by his arms, like he was a side of beef by the two goons who had put him in the position in the first place. He dug his heels into the carpet to get their attention and turned to look back at Sandra struggling on the table then braced himself. Waves of anger swept through him. His fists clenched so tightly, his nails bit into the life lines of his palms and he could feel trickles of blood running over his fingers. He wanted to get back there and *swat deh fool dem* from her but he did not have the strength against the men who watched him. He could do nothing but close his eyes and groan.

And that's when he felt the cold. A numbness, that at first he thought was shock, his body rebelling against the punishment metted out to him. But no nausea followed, no light-headedness just the plummeting temperatures. His breath plumed from his lips and the men in the room began to feel its effect too.

"Hey, what the fuck?"

"You feeling dis?

The windows crackled as a formation of ice slid across the double glazing in every room.

Then darkness followed.

A deep darkness, that made Chips think his eyes were closed.

He blinked and could see nothing still. A reaction of panic made him gasp at the depth of night that had descended on them. It was a primal darkness, impenetrable and bone chillingly cold. It was absence of light like a tangible blanket of dark stuff that had been scrapped from the guts of a dead star and then unceremoniously flung over everything.

Chips had his arms around his shoulders shivering and questioning his sanity in the same breath, not giving a shit about the grunts of exasperation and confusion from the professionals who had held him captive.

His eyes were shut tight. He shivered and mumbled to himself, only moments later did he figure out that he was saying a prayer.

Jah knows, he had not prayed in years but whatever was on its way to them demanded a cry for help from the highest authority he knew of.

"Sandra, I've come feh deh yout!" The voice reverberated around the room with the force of its bass and still Chips couldn't tell if it was in his head or sensed it from his ears.

"They can't hurt you again but my son is coming wid his father, yuh hear mi?"

Someone didn't care about his demands and opened fire.

An immediate grunt and somebody went down.

"Hold your fire wanker!"

"Moron!"

"Easy nuh!"

A single flame jumped into prominence in the darkness.

Someone in the heat of the moment felt a lighter flame would dispel the confusion but instead it escalated it into absolute terror.

A man stood with his hands in his pockets, a billowing cloud of darkness flowing not just around him like a sentient mist but protecting him like an extension of himself. Chips had not seen him for five years but the distinctive features were unmistakable. Darkman stood looming, his face war painted with a grotesque white skull, his own eyes and mouth forming the mask and looked down on the men with unshielded venom.

"Yuh shouldn't have done dis to my family but mi glad yuh did. Letting go is going to feel real good."

They opened fire again and multiple muzzle flashes lit up the room in the direction of that horrific image of the Obeah man. Chips should have taken his own advice and kept his eyes closed but he didn't and that image above even what he was witnessing now would remain with him, burnt in his unconscious to torment him for the rest of his days.

"Yuh ready fi dead?" Darkman's voice was low and sibilant, like the growl of a tiger that was able to speak. Its force filled the room. "Tek dem, leave no guilty man standing." He commanded. " Tear dem rass asunder."

Chips could only see in second intervals that corresponded with flashes from some of the weapons' fire but it was enough, too much. Darkman's command agitated the writhing nimbus that had surrounded him to a frenzy. Diabolic tendrils of pitch black sprang forth, becoming flying, slivering, crawling abominations with a taste for human flesh. They sprang claws, fangs, horns and tore, shredded and pierced. Some were greedily swimming through the air like black mambas through water tearing through stomachs. Others descended like hawks, gouging out and popping eyeballs. And still others entered rectums and mouths, eating their way out with spectacular effect in a frenzy of carnage. He tried to block out the sounds of screaming, flesh being torn, the splash of blood, the splatter of gore hitting the ceiling, floor and walls but he couldn't.

How do you stop yourself from smelling expelled bowels and steaming viscera, even with your arm over your mouth and nose?

You can't

He closed his eyes, whimpering, as the smells of the human abattoir were thick in the air but his mind recreated the horror for him with equal verisimilitude. Chips prayed for his life to be spared.

Prayed like his life depended on it.

20.

The Crypt Nightclub
22.55

The bouncer protecting the door to the main office - all six foot four of him - nodded as the group approached.

"Mr Patterson sir, what's good?"

Spokes and the big man shook hands vigorously.

"Yow, Ricky, I'm irie partner. How's dat pretty little girlfriend of yours doing?"

"Keeping me happy."

"As she should, rude bwoy. As she should."

Spokes turned to motion to the girls behind him.

"My ladies will man this point for the rest of the night and Duncan should reassign yuh to another position. Cool."

"I'm there," he said and turned to go.

"Ricky?" Spokes called after him. "Watch yuh head back, rudie."

Ricky looked back at him quizzically for a moment.

"I always do, Mr Patterson."

"Nice guy," Patra commented on his departure.

"Decent yout, from New Jersey," Spokes said, opening the door at the same time and switching on the light in the office. "Give mi a minute sista's. Make yourself comfortable."

Immediately Y moved with him, his personal shadow until this was all over, but he ambled only three doors away. He fished in his pockets for a set of keys and opened up the room. He then disappeared inside, coming out with an aluminium tool box on wheels, overalls slung over his arm, a rugged torch and battery powered lamps. In a moment he was squeezing past her with the stuff.

"Need to keep mi Jasper Conran suit criss, don't it?" He grinned. Fully in the office, Spokes waited for Y to step in and closed the door behind her.

Bad II the Bone knew how this was going to run and were conversing about trivia as they moved into position. Spokes became background while he changed into his overalls. Suzy laid palms on the girls' backsides and silently took to her post outside the door. She had now become the first line of defence. Patra and Y quietly watched Spokes prepare his tools, move furniture and then snap on his protective goggles. He twisted the torch in his hand and slapped the headgear firmly on his head, looking like a miner, with hard hat, knee and elbow pads, and gloves.

The promoter rapped on the wall. The sound it made gave away its hollowness. Spokes watched their reaction.

"Prefab ladies. I did feel I would be doing dis soon, suh I made sure it easy to cut through. I haven't been down here in almost two years but before mi wall it up I had enough time to plan." Spokes tapped his temple sagely.

Y wrinkled her nose a question emerging on her lips.

"How are we going to navigate the darkness without knowing a layout of the caves, even with lanterns?" The question stirring up a dormant fear for enclosed spaces.

Spokes smiled again.

"Don't fret sistah Y. Deh candles that were left by deh original owners still burn, can yuh believe that? Deh Romans knew how to build to last, trust mi. When I light the way I'll let you come down and see wah gwan."

"Yeah, now that would be cool," Patra perked up.

"If we have to," Y muttered under her breath and nodded.

Spokes hefted another hard plastic case out of the wheelie case - two feet by two feet - with the name Pal-ette emblazoned on both sides with orange and red flames shooting from the letters. Patra and Y looked on quizzically.

"My Ex," Spoke said, pointing to the name. "Don't ask. Let's jus' say I won't forget her in a hurry."

He pulled out the mean looking circular saw and plugged in the lead. Switching it on, it almost protested in his hand at being tethered to the outlet and roared irritably, barring its sixty five titanium carbide teeth.

Spokes grinned with it.

"Dis will only take a minute," he shouted over the din.

Deacon, two of his best men and Monsieur Remy had no problem entering the club with guns and the voodoo oddities that were required for tonight's performance. A basic spell the Haitian had cast blocked the habitual motor responses of the bouncers. So instead of their usual vigilance, they now exhibited an overwhelming lack of concern for duty that revolved around Remy & Co. access without search or question. In a heart beat they had fallen back into their familiar groove feeling they may have slipped up on something but just could not put their finger on what it was. Deacon's small group had already merged into the melting pot of nubile flesh. Armed with the tools of the trade in destruction unbeknownst to the partygoers they were hell bent on getting what they came for, come what may.

VIP area - The Crypt
23.15

The music was just how he liked it and the punters were hyper, a stark contrast to what he was forced to work with at Black Book. He wasn't sure the comparisons between crime fighting and entertainment were justified but it felt good ganging up on his bread and butter. Dancehall, reggae, hip hop, r&b and rare grooves, all being played in one spot, he felt like going home for his duvet and making this place his permanent residence. Old habits die, hard.

Shaft sipped on his Courvoisier and wondered if a copper ever truly took time off from being a copper. Your sense of inquisitiveness just doesn't switch off because you're not on the clock. It's much more than work or commitment but hardwired into your character. And if you're relaxed, your eye for patterns is even more acute.

Relaxation, interesting word.

He'd heard that term before but that wasn't something he was really familiar with, especially in the last few weeks. Shaft savoured the mellow yet strong texture of the top class brandy and grinned to himself.

If the truth be known, tonight he felt like a stalker and it was not the kind of look he was going for. But it couldn't be helped. Y was here working and that meant he would have to be here too. When they talked last, Y's excitement was tempered with the fear of the unknown. If you throw in the almost impossible factor of Darkman wreaking havoc on the street then you have a possibly explosive concoction that he would not sit back and read about in the dailies tomorrow. Y tried to convince him they were safe because Spokes rationalised away any concern they may have with the guard ring he wore and the spiritual connection the girls had together. All that would make the Obeah man stay away long enough for them to do what they had to do.

He shook his head and reminded himself to smile at a young lady on the opposite table.

That explanation may reassure the ladies but he had a more distinguished track record on the foibles of psychotic personalities.

Enoch Lacombe was relentless and would find a way to get what he wanted. If it was painful for him, you can rest assured it will be unbearable for you. That's where Shaft came in.

What could he do against the forces Enoch Lacombe could call upon at will? Now that was an entirely different issue. But he would be here. Shaft just hoped the Obeah man didn't decide to make his move while the DJ was playing his rare groove selections. Better yet he could just decide to stay away. And while he was at this game of What Would Be Better? it would be great if all this was a combination of good dream and a bad night-mare so after some tossing and turning in bed he would wake up with a feeling like he had lived through days but in actual fact it was one night.

Shaft pinched himself and waited.

Nope.

He was still here and the threat was still immediate. He sipped on his brandy and waited.

Main Office - The Crypt
23.15

Y checked her watch and looked into the twilight maw of the ancient crypt for the fourth time, pacing to and fro nervously.

"He's been out of radio contact for more than half an hour." Patra nodded and conjured up an expression on her lips that Y could not read. "It just doesn't feel right. He was talking to us, all the way down there. Now, nothing."

"Maybe he dropped his radio and he just can't get in contact."

Y raised an eyebrow.

"You don't think Slick fell and hurt himself do you?"

"I just don't think so. He's careful and quick on his feet. That alone has me concerned."

"He did light his way down there, so I figure he knows where he's going. Shit he could be having a good laugh at our expense."

"I don't think so. It's just a feeling I've got."

"Sugahh, don't go all Hollywood woo-woo on me now. Suzy's got that base covered. And she's good at it."

"Thanks."

"Keeping it real, is what I do." She paused for thought. "I think we should go down there," Patra said ignoring the barbs directed at her and carefully observing Y's response.

Cool exterior as always.

Y was the strategist and her mind was best suited for planning and considering possible roadblocks before they came into being and this scenario was considered and expelled from her mind in quick succession. Y smoothed down the non-existent crinkles around the waist of her designer suit. Deep down her fears of darkness and closed quarters were shrieking inside her but the bushido training kept them at bay. Y licked her suddenly dry lips.

"Let's go, but Suzy needs to know."

"I'm on it."

"I'll try and reach Spokes again."

Patra gazed down into the cavity of the wall before she opened the door and left the room for a moment. When she returned, Y had just placed the handset down on the teak desk and grimly shook her head in the negative.

"She's not there," Patra said matter-of-factly.

"What?" asked Y.

"I checked the corridor and there's no sign of Suzy."

Y touched the earpiece, keying the radio and calling for her over the radio waves.

Static responded.

"Call her mobile," Y instructed.

Patra flipped out her smartphone phone like it was a deadly weapon and voice dialled Suzy.

Suzy's phone rang with no answer.

"Voice mail kicked in." Patra pronounced.

"Can you feel it now?" Y asked.

"I don't have to, I know something ain't right."

Y swore and stormed over to the entrance and threw open the office door, stepping outside into the corridor and briskly walking its length, calling out for Suzy as she went.

No sign of a struggle, not as much as an indication that she was ever here. Even the smell of her perfume was absent. Y turned to head back to the office when she sensed her surroundings sway, as if God the DJ had touched the disk of Earth's movement as if preparing to rewind a cosmic track.

The music stopped.

Human chatter died away.

The club was dead quiet.

A sudden chill quaked through her body and Y's legendary composure vanished. She reached behind her and pulled the katana out of its sheath. Her senses ramped up four notches. Her breath was coming through her mouth in raspy spurts as she backed into the office, the katana tracing figure eights in the air, her eyes straining to catch any movement. Patra knew what was coming next.

"Oh man, I'm not dressed for this spelunking shit." Y moaned.

Without looking back she spat.

"Let's find Spokes."

"We can't just up an leave her." Patra said. "She may need us."

"Remember when Suzy's Security van got jacked, a year ago, an that idiot armed robber tried to shoot her. She received a flesh wound and she broke his arm and his ten fingers."

Patra smiled.

"Yeah."

"Can you remember how you felt?"

"I just knew the Ms Wong was hurt but ok. Yeah I knew. Weird shit."

"What do you feel now?"

Patra closed her eyes for some seconds and nodded licking her lips.

"Nothing." Patra said.

Y kicked the door shut, felt the temperature in the room fall some degrees and scurried down into the crypt.

Dancefloor
The Crypt
23.15

This was one of the very few occasions that Deacon allowed himself to be led into a situation that he had not stacked to his advantage with subterfuge or violence before-hand. Standing behind the Obeah man Monsieur Remy Jean-Philippe smelt the air like a shiny brown cocker spaniel, attracting the attention of some of the more curious revellers not occupied in dance and drink. When they became too inquisitive at the peculiar man dressed all in white, totally out of sync with accepted fashion trends, he would skewer them with dark emotionless eyes, drawing them in for a second into his diabolical world and then discard them.

Soon enough they scurried away to some other part of the room where the sense of threat wasn't so acute. The Vodun was on a mission that involved pride and power in a similar vein to Deacon's search for the artefacts. Monsieur Remy wanted to be known as the most powerful living Vodun while Deacon wanted a more corporeal prize.

Run the street uncontested.

A little yout from Trenchtown, boss of all bosses.

From Papa Remy's excited murmuring and galvanic spurts of movement, that possibility was becoming apparent with every moment.

They moved through pockets of dancers easily, the Voodoo priest's eagerness or enthusiasm cutting through the gyrating bodies, leading them across the dance-floor to the other side of the expansive room. Deacon had a feeling they were not being led to the open areas but the zones that were restricted to staff only, areas that he could see from here, were heavily guarded. They were tooled up but this wasn't to be that kind of mission, at least not amongst so many witnesses. It would be interesting to see how Remy would surmount that obstacle from his bag of tricks. The Vodun himself was being drawn by a burning desire which was tugging him to the seated area and a darkened cubicle in particular where a velvet rope hung with the words *Reserved* attached to it.

"Sit." Remy unhitched the rope and motioned for Deacon to enter. He slid in after him and immediately placed his satchel on the table and flipped up the flap. The witchdoctor rummaged through it and eventually pinched a white powder and then some blue crystalline granules onto the table. He opened up a pocket knife and used it to combine the two compounds.

They immediately reacted and started issuing streams of fluffy white plumes of smoke. Deacon attempted to get up but Remy had already placed his nostrils over it and he was inhaling deeply, sucking it through his nose and mouth.

Without further delay the Haitian was back on his feet, bag over his shoulder, on a course for the 'Staff Only Beyond This Point' sign ahead of them.

Deacon was wondering "What next?"

Although he had faith in his powers, in a strange way he was waiting to be surprised like a child anticipating a magician's next illusion. Except in this circumstance it was all too real. The gangster was doing his own assessments in the meantime, confirming what he had expected, that all the staff entrances were covered by security personnel except this one which most likely allowed access from the inside only. For all he had seen, all the incredible and sometimes downright scary stuff he had performed, he waited with bated breath especially for the surprise he would be experiencing any moment. CCTV cameras hung like the trophies of a hunter of mechanised Cyclops, only a red blinking light indicated that they were alive and surreptitiously monitoring all their movements in its zone of influence, its masters thinking it could replace the intelligence of a man. Never in a million years would they have thought it would be monitoring the movements of a sorcerer.

Remy walked up to the cameras, looking up at them as if he didn't understand their function. He inhaled deeply and blew out a stream of smoke from his mouth and nose that kept coming. Seconds turned into minutes.

Without a breath.

The hoarse sound from his throat accompanied by the whoosh of the smoke got louder and Remy's mouth was at full stretch, like a boa constrictor's jaw dislocating to accommodate its prey.

Deacon stepped back with his men fearing Remy was going to spontaneously combust and watched in rapt awe as the substance that looked like smoke had acquired coherence and a semblance of life. It became a writhing mass, sprouting tentacles hungry for discovery or mayhem. It crawled over the electronics, frying microcircuits and melting plastic, rendering the cameras ineffective in its path. It oozed its way through vents and cracks leaving a caustic trail of destruction on its way to do the Obeah man's bidding.

Yuh hafe tek bad ting mek laugh, he thought.

Amidst the horror Deacon pictured Papa Remy going 'boom' in his mind's eye and just couldn't stop himself from chuckling. Even as the security door opened on its own accord and Remy boldly stepped through, the hilarity stuck with him as he followed him in.

Guard Duty Outside Main Office
The Crypt
23.55

One moment Suzy was settling into the waiting game, enjoying the music but aware of her surroundings and the next she could feel the sticky tentacles of something other-worldly encroaching on her normal world. That itchy sensation inside the back of her head was creeping along her spine, laying eggs that hatched into more creeping things along the way. Suzy swung around, checking her zone but her perception felt odd as if she was onstage and the backdrop had changed subtly. Something was different. She took in a calming breath and realised the other security guards that she could see from her vantage point had disappeared. Suzy stood on her tip-toes and still she could see no one securing the other entrances or exits.

Then, peculiarly the music stopped suddenly with no protests or consternation.

The hum of human merriment just went dead too and for no particular reason Suzy checked her digital watch.

It had stopped.

Gooseflesh migrated along her back and chest, making her nipples and clitoris tingle. Not a good sign. Suzy reached for both the suntetsu on her waist and gripped them in her fists, trying to ignore the hairs on her back standing on end. The suntetsu was a weapon adapted from the ancient design the ninjas used in feudal Japan. It was a small metal spike with a ring attached in the centre of its length for your middle finger to thread through and was easily concealed in the palm of your hand. It was an assassin's tool, inconspicuous but deadly in the right hands. Of which hers was perfect.

Suzy waited, her heart thumping like a trip-hammer in her chest.

Nothing materialised.

She put her back to the office door and rapped on it three times with the tip of the suntetsu.

"Girls someting a gwane."

Suzy rapped on it again.

Her head snapped right and then left expecting something to materialise from the shadows but nothing did. She turned the door handle, leaned her back against it and looked in quickly to see what was happening.

The room was empty and all she could see was the gaping hole in the wall and the flickering of candlelight beyond.

"Y! Patra!" she called.

Her voice echoed hollowly in the room and the cavernous crypt beyond.

"Rass!"

Suzy gripped the door handle from behind and gently pulled it shut but didn't let go. Her arms were trembling with an unseen pressure or just sheer nervousness. She soon understood why. Something was forcing its way through the cracks with the arachnid manner of a predator, expanding into her space with a menacing ponderousness melting anything synthetic in its way. Wispy caustic smoke with animal intent bellowed down the walls. Gasping, Suzy backed into the office. The entity reeked not just from her sense of smell but in her mind too. A psychic revulsion that left a dirty impression on her life force that would need some meditative cleaning to wipe. Spokes' office was literally a breath of fresh air as she swung in and closed the door behind her. The image of the smoke thing making its way towards her, was still sharp in her mind. As an after thought she quickly removed her back from the door and stood instead at the neatly cut entrance that had been fashioned into the wall and which led down into the crypt.

The door wouldn't stop it.

Then what?

She felt the eddies of heat from the candles streaming up from the caves on her back and the smell of burning vegetation like the dry breath of ancient skeletons.

The door stood unbreached.

Suzy hoped this was the end and whatever it was outside had decided to move on. She needed to keep the girls protected from the rear.

Silence.

And the feeling that she had imagined it all was creeping up on her slowly.

A powerful knock at the door startled her.

"Jesas."

Suzy scampered backwards and drew both suntetsu in her fists, heart pounding, mouth dry, ready for the inevitable.

"Open the door bitch, I haven't got all day." The voice demanded.

Whatever that was behind the door, sounded exactly like Patra's irreverent tones. Suzy knew it couldn't be her. An icy finger crawled up her spine and gripped her insides. Whatever it was on the other side of that door, whatever evil thing that was lurking outside, needed her permission to get in, that was a fact.

"Guh fuck yuh mumah," Suzy spat. "Yuh tek me fi fool?"

"Is that anyway to talk to your sister?" The voice boomed, its true malevolent self revealed.

The laughter that issued after that outburst made the hairs all over her body stand on end. Suzy shivered, imagining if she could put a voice to insect infested excrement that would be it. The thing slammed and rattled at the door as if it wanted to tear the door off its hinges.

"Open the fucking door you bitch!" it bellowed.

The urge to flee into the crypt was intense but she kept her composure, every muscle tense.

We need you to cover our backs.

Suzy would hold her ground until such time as she couldn't.

Absently she pushed the desk closer to the door and then wedged the executive chair under its handle. Returning to the desk Suzy swept the accoutrements to the floor and sat on the table cross-legged with both suntetsu in front of her. The pounding at the door had stopped but that itch inside her skull that she couldn't scratch remained.

21.

The Labyrinth under the Crypt
00.10

Both women hurried deep down the slope and along the path cut by hands that probably suffered and died down here. The route felt like they were walking into their own graves, their footfalls echoing off the damp walls. Dusty rocks littered the crypt's floor and they took care evading them and each other. Still, it was an ample space allowing them to stand upright - the ceiling clearing their heads by a good five feet and with enough breadth that three of them could stand shoulder to shoulder. They were amazed at how light it was aided by the torches and natural phosphorescence of the walls but beyond that portions sank into gloom, completely engulfed in darkness. The walls and large portions above them were covered with pictograms and ancient writing etched into the bare stone. Patra ran her fingers against the smooth slightly moist rock and watched the route ahead wind its way deeper into this place. They navigated the path easily, their breath pluming with condensation in front of them, the temperature having dipped ever since they had come down here. The torches were set at the appropriate distance, trying not to allow even an inch of footpath to be free from illumination. They kept close and alert, overwhelmed somewhat with what they were doing and with the alien surroundings. Y rotated the katana in her palm, the sword felt like an extension of herself while Patra feeling her own heartbeat, the stones crunching under her feet, the long drawn out silence and the smell of the ancient while she clinked the brass knuckle dusters together in time with her steps. Both concentrating in their own way and visually mapping all the features that stood out for them in case they could prove useful.

No breadcrumbs for them.

"One way in, one way out," Patra said in a whisper.

"I noticed. No chance of confusion if we need to get out quickly, then."

"None."

"Why you whispering?"

"Not sure about any stray bad guys hanging around. Why the hell you whispering?"

"Does this place fill you with the need for girly chit chat?"

"You damn right it doesn't, it gives me the heebie jeebies."

Y shook her head as they pressed on with renewed respect for Spokes' sense of adventure. Discovering this place by accident was one thing but exploring its confines, researching its origins was something completely different. Y wondered how a place like this had never been stumbled upon by civil engineers, archaeologists or exposed by a World War II doodlebug. How many other places like this existed protected by their own kind of magic?

Y shrugged to herself.

They walked for some time without a word exchanged between them. They could both feel a pervading sense of foreboding descending on them with every step of the way. Instinct was tugging on their deepest fears and the evolutionary trigger designed to preserve life was trying to do just that. Turning back was not an option, so the relief they felt was palpable when their stone corridor opened up into a much larger chamber with three darkened passages ahead. They walked in cautiously, thankful that Spokes had lit six torches that ran the circumference of the chamber, saving them from the choice of which passage to take next.

Their way was lit.

Then came a blood curdling scream that slashed the silence into ribbons.

The harsh sound echoed off the walls followed by a barrage of Jamaican expletives with an equally nerve shredding shriek from something they dared not put a name to. The girls picked up the pace. They chose not to think about what was beyond the opening and sprinted towards the end of the stone corridor.

The Crypt
Dancefloor
00.10

Shaft had a smile on his face when he sat back down at his table and took a sip from his brandy. The DJ had played a tune from soul balladeer Eric Benet that he hadn't heard for so long that he had to get up and dance. Well not strictly dancing, that usually involved moving from the spot you came to rest in but he did look good doing the Lean Back though. That was a proper dance for a DI, masculine with a bad bwoy edge to it. He smiled at the thought of meeting one of his superiors here while he was shaking his thang.

Not in a million years.

Leaning back into the leather he looked across the dance-floor and up at the dancers in the torture cages above the heads of the revellers. His gaze shifted back to the immediate area around him and especially where people stood chatting or dancing. He wondered how the girls were getting on and was glad the conclusion of the night had been uneventful so far. That was before the scream.

His stomach twisted.

Short, sharp and shrill.

Shaft's neck snapped to the direction of the commotion and saw a young lady flashing her limbs in disgust. You know the kind of reaction to vermin some women have.

Exactly that.

He relaxed for a second and the untrusting soul that he was, he looked deeper into the gloom beyond where she had stood.

Damn.

Shaft stood up leaned forward, squinted and looked against the darkened wall and floor again. Someone screamed, a man jumped away, someone shivered and another kicked out in revulsion.

There were hundreds of them. They were hard to distinguish and seemed to perfectly blend with the darkness, scurrying in the umbra between the floor and wall. A procession of rats so black they absorbed the scant light, rendering them almost invisible.

Shaft shivered and he was not squeamish. Something more was at work here. That niggling feeling persisted and the conclusion of a sudden vermin infestation on such an auspicious night did not wash well with him.

Darkman.

Partygoers were moving away from the walls in clumps looking down at it with puzzlement, knowing something was there but unable to see exactly what it was.

Human nature at its most inquisitive wanted to know more even if there was a risk to life or limb. And that need to know was approaching at a break-neck speed for everyone to witness. Some big dude was sitting on his ass against the wall, a human bottleneck. Obviously he had too much to drink and was resting from all that dancing. He was about to get the scare of his life as the rodents with an uncanny sense of purpose scurried all over him in their hundreds. What else was bothering him about this other than the strangeness of Darkman being a pied piper figure summoning these critters at will?

Something else, though.

Shaft jumped up, took a swig from his glass and started to frantically make his way through partygoers to get to big bwoy's position on the floor. He felt odd and expectant at the same time, wanting to get over to him and yank him to his feet so the rats could be on their merry way without his reaction of surprise.

Through a haze of perfume, Shaft burst through the last picket of bone, gristle and breast. He leaned forward with outstretched hand to the man on the floor.

"Let me help you up," Shaft said.

Big bwoy looked at him as if he had seen a ghost, broke into a smile and then started to shake his head as if it was going to fall off.

"Who died and made you scout leader?" he slurred.

"That honour goes to me. I'm a bit of an egotist you see. Now take your lard ass up, shit for brains."

Shaft reached down and tried to drag him from the wall by grabbing two fistful of his shirt and pulling but his weight held him in position.

Shaft glanced to his right and saw the dark blur skirting the perimeter of the wall with urgency, their approach unchecked.

"Get the fuck up," Shaft shouted at him but this was much too funny a moment for big bwoy not to laugh at.

And he did, heartily.

Soon he wasn't laughing and neither was Shaft. Big bwoy's eyes bulged and his body jerked to a grotesque merengue sending waves through him like gelatinous surf. Blood erupted through his mouth and nose explosively and trickled through his ear. All his organs were pulverised to make way for the rats burrowing through him. Chunks of flesh and body fluid erupted over his ample chest, his white shirt dark red with oxygenated blood, his mouth open and drooling. The wall was a spray of crimson.

"Jesus H!" Shaft jumped back, horrified, catching sight of something. A tail, rows of razor sharp chitin daggers for teeth in a wildly exaggerated mouth, stumpy ripping claws glinting white and the eyes.

Christ Almighty, no eye balls, no lids, more like an open wound, smouldering red, like a furnace from the pyres of hell itself.

Safe to say these fucking things were not rats.

Panic followed.

The Labyrinth under the Crypt
00.30

Y and Patra sprinted out of the passage into a cavern, skidding to a stop as they tried to make sense of their surroundings. Patra poised in Thai boxing stance, gold knuckle-dusters up and Y with the katana an extension of herself, tense as a coiled spring. Zephyr winds were twirling about the interior with no obvious means of origin. The cavern was huge. Above them was a unique honeycomb structure of stalactites that made you think it had been secreted by a spider as a means to trap human sized prey and was not a natural occurrence. The interior was lit by an eerie phosphoresce from up above, casting pools of shadow on the ground as the light passed through the reef of stalactites above them. Fifteen torches were set around the perimeter with Spokes close to the cave's rough hewn walls, condensation trickling down to their right and disappearing further into the ground. He was on his knees in the middle of a hurriedly drawn circle with a crusty wooden box beside him. He was rocking to and fro, mumbling to himself as if he had suddenly contracted autism but could multi task at the same time. He ponderously sprinkled a white dust into the gaps left around the circle made by the swirling winds. With tilted heads and blank stares, it was obvious that this scene had not been processed at all. Patra maintained her stance and Y kept her sword raised, unmoving. Then ever so slowly a realisation of what this was and who they were up against started to needle into their consciousness.

This was it. The final confrontation but what were they fighting against or what were they protecting themselves against?

The spell broken, fascination transformed into a cautious saunter to where Spokes was genuflecting, still the need for urgency not foremost in their minds. The twirling winds literally approached them screeching, miniature dust devils twirling between them with a playful flourish and then heading towards the make-do circle with malicious and considered intent, erasing Spokes' hard work. They were acting like pack animals, letting out howls of excitement obscuring him in fine dust, frustrating him to insanity.

The girls picked up the pace.

"Slick!" Patra called out a warning to him, not sure what the hell she was alluding to. "They coming from behind you."

Spokes, startled, spun on his reinforced knee pads to face them, his eyes wide with terror as the whirl-winds attacked the circle en masse. They were snarling, howling, threatening like ethereal wolves or the spirit of wolves. What they lacked in teeth they made up for in the ferocity of their wind speed.

"Don't stop walking towards me. Keep coming. Keep coming, yuh hear mi?" His fear transmitted across to them like a jolt of electricity through a vacuum and that galvanised them into a sudden burst of movement his way.

"Dem will try to suffocate yuh, overcome you if they can, don't let them," Spokes barked.

Y saw two break off from the pack, gleefully screeching their way towards them. She spun to her knees and let the momentum bring her back to her feet before she could complete a full circle. Her blade slashed through the twirling winds, once the then twice and the dust devils shrieked like dying things, a red tinge colouring the whirlpool of their innards.

"Stay in the circle whatever yuh do. The circle is our protection, yuh understand?" Spokes shouted.

The girls stopped suddenly maintaining balance by grabbing onto each other so they didn't fall out of the five foot diameter circle. Spokes unceremoniously dumped small handfuls of white dust into their hands.

"They are ancient Mesopotamian dust demons," he pointed to the twirling winds. "Keep the circle whole, nuh matter what dem little rass try to duh. While I try to suck dem powers with this hex."

Now they knew that Spokes' insane mumbling was him chanting, completely alien words to them, but they could feel the power as he repeated the mystical stanzas over and over. For every mini tornado that dissipated into the darkness another one took its place, much weaker but still hell bent on obliterating the circle and the one thing that could keep them alive it seemed.

Patra and Y worked ceaselessly, looking over to Spokes who was sweating, his overalls dusted with debris and his mouth rapidly spitting words of power.

Suddenly the winds shrank back.

Dust devils were either reconsidering their next strategy or losing power from Spokes' incantations.

The girls caught their breath with a frantic stream of questions.

"What the fuck is going on?" Patra spat out. "What is all this?"

"He's here," Spokes said with an attitude of inevitability. "Darkman." Spokes pouted and pointed his lips to the ceiling as if he could not bring himself to point.

Reluctantly they looked up.

At first it was a blanket of black velvet. Nothing could be made out until your eyes started to discern patterns then depth and tone. A pin-prick of red light at first and then more and more until there was a sea of red specks blinking off and on.

The connection wasn't made immediately, not until Spokes whispered to them.

"Dem a watch you, an' me a watch dem."

"Eyes," Y murmured.

"Son-of-a-bitch," Patra whistled with what sounded like admiration.

Hundreds of eyes greedily looked down at them from their perch in the ceiling.

"Bats," Y said not sure if she was asking or stating, having no knowledge of bat habitats to call on.

Patra wiped condensation from her arms.

"They are like no bats me ever see." He shook his head wildly. "Dem ting deh aren't designed by nature, sister. They are dark pickney summoned by Enoch from below. They are scavengers with a taste for human flesh, fully under his control. The only reason why we're alive is because of the protection diagram. Oh, and baby girl, that dripping on you is not water, dem hungry."

Patra shuddered and wiped her arms.

Spokes opened the top of the alabaster jar to show the dwindling measure of white powder.

"We got to think of something quick beacah when it done..."

"... our ass is grass," Patra completed.

Spokes groaned when he felt the slow rise of the wind again and watched disheartened as the dust particles languidly gave in to the twirling currents, manipulated by the dust devils.

Spokes wished for a miracle but amongst such evil wishing for miracles was ineffectual. There was no balance in this place, just shades of rottenness. Yet the intricate patterns that weave the tapestry of life can be unpredictable at the best of times and fucking sardonic too. In that moment Deacon, two goons and his pet Obeah man came bursting out from a corridor on the right, guns drawn and grins of triumph on their faces.

Not quite a miracle but beggars can't be choosers.

"Spokes, mi breddrin," Deacon boomed. His voice gathered resonance as if he was speaking through an amplifier.

"Finally we meet. Mi nuh too late for deh party?"

Deacon stood in the middle of the cavern, his gun pointed at the three huddled in the circle. The two men with him moved out to his left and right surveying the place suspiciously.

Remy stood behind them, not venturing as far into the cavern as the others. He had his fingers in his shoulder bag tensed for a quick protective spell at any indication of threat. He looked up and then looked around nervously, retreating slowly as his head did a three hundred and sixty degree orbit. The bravado he exhibited earlier was leeching away with the seconds. Uncertainty, like a tick burrowing into his flesh had replaced it and more uncertainty was hatching. The forces of dark magic that were thrumming through the air reacting with everyone and everything, subtly changing ordained outcomes, tainting them in imperceptible ways, was startling. Remy trembled with a mixture of fear and awe. He could feel the power he had available to cast spells had improved ever since being in the employ of Deacon but nothing he had at his disposal could challenge the man who had created this display. Manipulating the Chinese girl's sense of time and space, as elaborate as he thought the incantation was, that exhibition paled into insignificance in comparison to this extravaganza. This was an overwhelming act of voodoo craftsmanship that he had no answer to. Being as far away from this place as he could was his plan of action. And while Deacon and his men were focussed on the prize, Remy intended to slip away.

"Yuh not talking to mi, boss? I'm hurt," Remy heard Deacon say absently. The Obeah man's focus was more on survival than the inane banter taking place between the other two men. If they knew what he did they would be more concerned although the other man on his knees with the haggard look of horror and incredulity said he knew something Deacon ought to.

"I understand, my yout," the gangster continued. "I'm not in a talkative mood either. I just want to know one bloodclaat ting. Where is deh treasure?"

Remy hesitated at the words because his heart had been set on acquiring some of those magical artefacts for his own practice. The advantages he would have, the respect, the money.

Whatever his heart desired.

His life meant more to him.

Remy edged back into the darkened corridor.

Deacon grimaced.

Just a few things gave away the fact that there was something very unsettling about this scene. Not the subterranean location because that was expected for such things and not the fact that a bad man of his calibre was about to add his own rare breed of craziness to the mix.

Nah, that was a obvious.

His senses were screaming out caution although for the life of him he could not detect the threat. Okay, the breeze was weird within a cavern but weird wasn't dangerous. And the danger was here as solid and unassailable as a twenty foot brick wall. Spokes and the two bitches, huddled together, riveted with fear and subdued panic flashing in their eyes, was puzzling enough. Consider what lay beyond them in the shape of a stone hewn altar or ceremonial table stacked with rare books, artefacts, scrolls, old boxes and good old fashioned currency and jewels was what perplexed him. If they had made an attempt to acquire it before he had arrived, he had no indication of that now. Something or someone had stopped them from completing what they had set out to do.

The dark skinned gal kept looking to the ceiling nervously. Deacon's eyes followed hers but the darkness above him meant nothing.

"I don't know what deh fuck is going on but I want all three of you to approach me very slowly. Yuh si me?"

No one reacted.

Deacon fired two shots into the earth, feet away from where they stood. The slugs threw up chunks of clay with the sound of the report echoing in the cavern.

"Yuh tink mi a play?" Deacon forced the words through clenched teeth.

"We look like we having fun to yuh?" Spokes shot back. "Can't you feel it? There is more happening here than meets deh eye. Ask yuh Obeah man if this place feels like play time to him."

Deacon turned to see what Spokes was referring to, keeping his gun hand in his direction and his eyes met Remy's backward retreat.

Deacon cocked his head and smiled grimly.

"You going somewhere, bwoy?" Deacon asked evenly. His weapon was now firmly aimed at the Haitian and from that distance he could not miss him. "You should be standing beside me. Walking in the valley of the shadow of death, in my footsteps," He entoned sarcastically.

"This is suicide, Deacon," the Obeah man blurted out with a grating French patois lilt, his right hand already in the bag around his neck, his finger tips pinching grains of potions that he started sprinkling at his feet while murmuring words of power and ignoring the gun pointed at him. "I'm telling you this cannot be won. Come with me, lets walk away from this..."

He didn't finish. Didn't have time to finish.

A heel caught him with a perfect roundhouse kick to the jaw, cart-wheeling him to the ground. Suzy stood over him a bit worst for wear but with a playful gleam in her eyes as if she understood this cosmic joke was at her expense and decided to do the mature thing and laugh along. She stood in combat stance her senses attuned to her environment. Suddenly everything was amplified and the cavern was acting as a huge echo chamber for every sense, not just sound.

Her eyes, hyperactive, already the positions of all the players in this drama branded into memory. Her skin prickling from the eddies of the mystical and natural forces at play, she took in the waft of excrement, sulphur, earth, sweat and fear. The coppery tang of that latter emotion, she tasted sharply in her mouth.

Suzy looked down on Monsieur Remy's bloodied face and crumpled body and looked up defiantly at Deacon as if asking, *Yuh got more? Bring it come nuh!* Slowly she took her long plaited hair and wrapped it around her neck Manchu style and realising what was to come, she took the ends of her pony tail and bit down on it, anchoring it with her teeth. She moved effortlessly into wushu dragon form and beckoned them forward with her fingers a la Bruce Lee.

"Yuh still alive Chiny gal?" Deacon bellowed. "The last time I see you," his tone more measured as he recalled the memory. "You were diving off a gantry about fifty...sixty feet high. Don't know how yuh did that an' survive but it don't matter." Deacon grins looking over to his hench men. "Chuck, Rog. Dead dis pussyclaat gal for me please." He pointed to Suzy and returned his focus to Spokes and the girls in the circle.

"Now some one betta start walking towards me or I will empty mi clip in somebody rass tonight."

The men opened fire on Suzy without hesitation.

They acted with the randomness she fully understood. The goons and Deacon wanted her dead. Off the cuff preparation and a hammered down strategy was not for a situation like this. This required chaos thinking and Suzy had a sneaking feeling Deacon was an 'A' grade student in that. In seconds, Suzy Wong was the centre of attention and the time it took her to inhale deeply, the men had taken aim and were firing copper jacketed death her way.

As battered and bruised as she was from the last encounter with these two gorillas, adrenaline injected into her blood stream like a fuel injector, she was tumbling and somersaulting out of harm's way like a gymnast. The nine millimetre ammo chewed up a route behind her as she skittered away behind a carved rock formation. Suzy placed her back to the moist cavern wall, breathing heavily, and used the only opportunity she would ever have to observe her surroundings properly. Not that there was much to see from the vantage point behind the rock but she just had to hope quick glances would not end with her head being blown off.

She had no choice.

The men were approaching cautiously, firing as they came and walking in the light as if they were men of virtue. She already had a snapshot of what was behind the structure and still the picture made no sense to her. The girls, Spokes, Deacon - he had told her that much before trying to kill her, the two gun men and that witch doctor she had dispatched. What concerned her, even more than not knowing what she was looking at, was that the scene was dynamic and would not remain in place for her to take action based on what she had seen seconds earlier. But whatever action she did take it would involve evading bullets and disabling pro killers. Deacon was shouting at the top of his voice, Patra and Y were calling out to her, the goons kept coming and that god awful wind was gusting without let up.

Under the circumstances she should be cursing the day Bad II the Bone was ever conceived; instead she felt a gruesome exhilaration. She felt as if she had been dipped in a malevolent night and was infected by it. For the first time she understood it completely, bypassing mere senses for a whole body experience. Her reasonable and sane self wanted to get away and have nothing to do with this place. But that part of her was not in ascendency tonight.

Escape wasn't an option.

She was feeling the dark powers being focussed into the cavern like an infernal magnifying glass, feeling the wind whip through the cavern, the air pregnant with menace. A storm was on its way and she could sense it as certainly as she knew it was going to rain when she was back in Jamaica. Suzy felt almost relieved, as if everything had led up to this moment. She looked up to the darkness above her; she sensed the movement. Even above the din of the wind it reminded her of thousands of puppies' feet, their claws tapping on the rocks as they moved. Her mind constructed a picture of twisted Chihuahuas who were imbued with the darkness and a taste for human flesh scurrying above her. Then as if in response to her macabre musings black teardrops started falling to the cave floor with the sound like a coming monsoon. The deluge was like something had struck oil from above. Greasy precipitation fell with droplets the size of fists, some of which instead of forming puddles, some grotesquely merged together like molasses with instincts for self preservation. Others kept their terrible individuality of teeth, claws and savagery. Suzy shuddered to her bone, the effort of deflecting the almost overpowering presence of darkness weakening her.

The decision was made in those desperate moments.

Suzy jumped up, a half baked plan forming in her mind as she ran for the closest torch on the wall expecting bullets to her back but the suddenness of her dash had caught her assailants unawares. When they realised what was happening Suzy was air-bound, leaping up to the torch and snatching it out of its holder and throwing it to the floor, dousing the flames in the dirt.

Her plan, if it worked was supposed to produce a wide enough line of darkness between herself and the gun men. A moat populated with the flesh eating demons which would keep her corralled from the gunmen.

OK, the plan wasn't perfect but it had to do for now.

Suzy was on the move again, deftly springing to the cave wall, using it as purchase to launch herself higher and yanking another torch from its holder, dousing it again and falling to the ground in a crouch. She took in four deep breaths, sprang to her feet again, readying herself to explode from where she stood but she faltered and that's when time slowed. Suddenly, another force had been introduced into the equation of motion, totally disrupting what her mind told her she should be doing now. In an agonisingly long second she was flung to the floor in a dirty, uncoordinated pirouette as the world around watched her fall with ponderous disinterest.

A pain that was distant at first became more personal and like a bubble of time dilation bursting the full symphony of agony hit her in discordant waves followed by the Doppler effect of the guns discharge.

Suzy cried out in pain and went down.

"Noooooo!"

Y's scream came from across the cavern like the crack of a whip. Her anguished face twisted in shock as she saw the shot fling Suzy to the ground. Without thought Y was sprinting towards where Suzy fell.

All around them was pandemonium. The sky above continued to rain these creatures. The twirling winds persisted with their mischief still obliterating the circle of protection and steadily extinguishing the torches, slowly spreading the domain of shadow if not for the luminescent veins of rock.

Y moved so quickly out of the circle that Deacon reacted a second or so too late but as the Browning bucked twice in the gangster's hand, his slugs connected with rock. Whipping his weapon back to where his intended targets had been a moment ago, he was welcomed by an empty space.

Patra had rugby tackled Spokes to the ground out of the circle and shielded him momentarily from the threat of bullets. Deacon barked an order and stormed after Patra, leaving the security of the light to step across the band of shadows, but he didn't get far. A tar like mound of reconstituted creatures flowed in front of him like the surf from a massive oil slick, blocking his path and defying gravity. He could literally feel its heat and the stench was almost unbearable. The air was ripe with rot and decay, an almost solid thing that rammed into his nose like a fighters left hooks. Deacon stepped back repulsed then horrified as it began to morph into the form of a man. A patch work man, who was an irreverent construct of these creatures, stuck together in haste and with a lack of respect for the aesthetic of the human form, in a kind of fuck you to nature.

Deacon started firing into it, the report of his weapon deafening, the smell of cordite permeating the air. He tried to move back, flee into the light but the man thing generated tendrils with gruesome popping sounds, shooting tentacles around his ankles, his waist and arms. He screamed pathetically, his voice cracking, a memory of which he would not be proud if he ever had a chance to recall it. He squirmed and thrashed the touch of the creature reminiscent of millions of maggots foraging through decayed flesh. Deacon stumbled, fell on his ass, swearing as he kicked and clawed, but could not break free. He was being dragged on his back, his fingers grasping for purchase, his gaze fell desperately on the upside down visage of Remy who was just picking himself up from the floor behind him

"Hey pussy," he screamed. Yuh tink mi pay yuh feh yuh good looks, amigo? Yuh need to deal with this."

Remy looked at him with bleary eyes, gaining some degree of focus with the confusion around him. His horror was unshielded and it had the power to prop him up somehow. He looked around like a frantic man planning to flee but was not sure if he could. Beginning to chant, he walked over to him with stumbling steps, simultaneously thrusting his hand into his pouch. Remy slung a cloud of dust over Deacon and the man-thing as if he was sowing seeds in a field. Every individual grain burst into incandescence, like a multitude of fire flies, lighting up what once was darkness, sending the thing shrieking for the cover of the element that had birthed it.

The crime boss scurried in Remy's direction on all fours, all pretences of invulnerability lost. The witchdoctor couldn't help thinking how weak and pathetic he looked when he came up against the real supernatural forces of the world.

Already the power of his spells had dissipated and the darkness was creeping back into dominance. Remy admitted to himself there and then that he had been outclassed, outdone had humiliated. A fact that became clear to him at the most inopportune of times.

Y made no effort to conceal her approach and with so much happening at the same time, the element of surprise was easy.

Reaching Suzy was an entirely different proposition.

Y had to be walking through portions of shadow and light with every band of darkness teeming with the unspeakable things, tearing at her from all sides. The katana was a blur, the metal humming sweetly and an iridescence emanating from the blade's surface. She hacked and sliced her way through the hell spawn, dark blood, or what these things classed as such, splattered her from top to toe. And Y's blood mingled with theirs, as the chitin daggers of their claws and teeth, slashed her flesh, through leather, slowing her down but not stopping her. She was deftly skipping from one band of light to the next, screaming from the pain but pushing forward all the time. The things were scurrying underfoot and she pounded some of them with her boots but they simply shook themselves off and continued to patrol their domain. The men who were with Deacon began to understand how important it was to stay in the light and they were winding their way to Suzy with that important fact in mind, firing as they went focused but unaware of Y's approach. One of the men was changing clips frantically, his nervousness unusual for a man who had dealt with human threat innumerable times before but now was faced with the very bedrock of his beliefs disappearing before his eyes down the rabbit hole.

Y dashed towards him, maybe sensing his indecision, the katana gripped with both hands holding it away from her body while she moved like a classical samurai from the flicks, teeth gritted and a cry rising from her diaphragm and spitting out of her mouth.

When his highly tuned sense of danger alerted him and he spun with the magazine firmly in the butt of his semi, Y was on him, samurai sword flashing and a bullet exchanging, blood splatter and the dull thud of metal hitting the cave floor. The man staggered back gripping the wrist of his gun hand, crimson spurts erupting from the stubs of his fore and ring finger. The blade had sliced through the gun metal, severing the Browning in two and the tips of his fingers with it. Anger, surprise or both made him charge her with a wail like a wounded elk. Y was quick on her feet and took flight, twisting away from him but able to use the hilt of her sword to strike him to the back of the head. His own momentum threw him further into the shadows.

"Oh, shit!" He said.

Y landed hard on her feet the pain pierced her like jagged spikes of electricity from her toes to the crown of her head. She didn't look back there was no need to.

Dark pickney swarmed him like a wave of black piranhas his body erupting into a cloud of red mist and what was left of his corpse shuddered with the ferocity of it being torn apart. Changing direction slightly, Y headed for the other guy, dashing through the shadows at speed, enduring the vicious snapping of the creatures at her heels. Going with the flow but ending up where she wanted to be. Y estimated being five strides away from where Suzy had fallen and where the second gun-man had taken aim.

I'm coming baby.

Y mounted a stone hewn plinth at full tilt and hurled herself from it.

A gun went off, then another.

Too late?

Gravity held her descent or so it felt and when it resumed its effect she smashed into the back of the gunman, only a split second choice saving him from a severed head. He stumbled forward trying to keep himself upright but failing. Y skidded to a stop, steeling herself for what she would discover.

Suzy was not there.

What remained was a blood trail that meandered to another area of light which was obstructed with another rock.

A wave of relief washed over her.

Y turned away from the blood trail just in time to see the gun man regaining his footing, standing just on the edge of shadow and light. His relief was palpable. Even if he had lost his weapon in the shadows he knew he could take this bitch.

Y watched him keenly.

He revolved his neck like a bare knuckle fighter and bunched up his shoulders. He started bouncing on the spot, using the fingers of his right hand to call her into conflict.

"Lose the sword, bitch. Let's party."

Okay, Y thought. let's, play.

Y sheathed the katana and drew a stance, checking the demarcation of the light and the shadow around her floor area. This was to be her arena and she was bound to its dimensions. The goon grinned and began to weave his way towards her like the bell had rung and he was leaving his corner.

Deacon and Remy stood back to back in an oasis of light that they both knew would not last forever. Boss man Deacon looked forlornly at what could have been. The altar was hewn from a boulder and covered with

boxes, crates, old scrolls, trinkets, oddities and bejew-
elled treasures, not to mention many bundles and stacks
of fifty pound notes unable to fit into the cases already
bursting at the seams with money. It might as well be a
million miles away. Everywhere that shunned the light
was filled with the tiny burning red eyes of the creatures
that unnaturally blended with the darkness that bore
them.

On the side where the treasure lay were Spokes and
Patra in what seemed like a similar predicament. Sardonic laughter echoed in their minds like a psychic call-
waiting you had no choice but to accept and that left you
feeling unclean and soiled afterwards.

The voice's amusement continued for a while longer
and slowly a modicum of recognition slivered out of the
hatched eggs of confusion like lizard spawn.

"Who feh kill first, eh?" it said, words dripping with
menace. "Eeny, meeny, miney, moh, catch a begga by
deh toe, if him bawl, den yuh know, eeny meeny, miney,
MOH!"

The final word boomed in the heads of everyone present, making the receivers grit their teeth, hold their
heads or massage their temples such was the force.

A wave of darkness erupted from the scattered pockets of shadows like a tsunami. Dark matter coalesced into a force that was much more than the sum of its parts.
The anguished screech it made was ear splitting, like a
painful birth that was forced upon it by its new master.
Everyone shrank back from its suddenness. The wave of
hell stuff rolled over itself, ignoring the searing lances of
light, its bulk compensating for the damage as it flowed
like a wall of oil, excrement and debris all rolled into
one. It reared up as soon as Deacon and Remy were in
its sight, a roaring mew from something that should not

have lungs but the horrific insanity did. It had many gaping mouths too, many staring red eyes that bore into you, all burning slits, dripping saliva and chomping teeth like guillotines.

Remy's eyes bugged but he was in survival mode, his mouth working away in concentration like he was chewing his cud. He let the spell fly, like a baseball pitcher, the incantation made physical as a fire ball streaked towards the creatures. But impact was as anticlimactic as a cigarette being doused in a mud bath. His hex of fire lacked purity, fuelling the hell spawn instead. Remy flinched as the darkness morphed into something resembling a giant cloven hoof and slammed down onto him with a sickening crunch. His screams made Deacon try to back up but his left leg was pinned under Remy's broken body. The gangster tried to keep panic at bay but his wild struggling to free himself spoke volumes of his fear. Remy tried to lift himself up on his hands and knees, bones broken, muscles crushed, tendrils of congealed blood hanging from his lips.

"Yuh bring a rachet to a gunfight, bwoy?" Darkman cackled in everyone's head just as the creature slammed down on the Haitan again, transforming into something else the human mind could not completely comprehend and devouring the body in a frenzy of teeth and claw.

A squeak of despondency escaped from Deacon's chapped lips. He was paralysed with terror, his mind grinding to a stop as he helplessly watched the writhing flesh devour his last best hope.

Darkman seemed to consider the pathetic figure of Deacon stripped and powerless.

"You didn't tink I would forget yuh. No, no, no. Because of you I spent four years in lockdown. Because of you I'm still recovering what is mine. Yuh tink your organisation was a match feh me? I don't need an army to vanquish you, I have deh hosts of hell at my disposal. But don't fret Deacon, I've been promised a special place in deh pit for a bad man like you. So hush, you will have to wait while I speak to my breddrin' Spokes."

Y grunted from the fist to her ribs, her body buckling in with the force but just managing to twist her torso minimising the impact.

He was strong.

And strength for strength, she didn't stand a chance against him but conflict was more than raw strength. Y braced herself. His upper cuts came thick and fast and Y kept deflecting his energy with her sore arms. He roared his frustration aggravated; he wasn't inflicting the kind of damage he was expecting. He leapt up, hurtling towards her with his knee extended like a seasoned Thai boxer.

Y read him too late.

His knee smashed into her chest, lifting Y off her feet with the force and depositing her some feet away. She skidded to a stop at the edge of shadow and light, glaring at him, from her knees, a sharp pain stabbing into her chest, stars popping before her eyes. Unsteadily she stood up.

His grimaces seemed to say, why won't dis gal go down?

Y flexed her chest and flashed her arms, a routine that was meant to erase the pain of their last tangle.

This time she came at him.

His reach was long so he swung at her from a distance and followed up with a straight thrust kick that she side stepped and parried with her forearm. Close quarter combat favoured small narrow frames and Y fitted the bill. She got in close and personal ramming her elbow and the heel of her hand into his pressure points. His body language switched from confidence to uncertainty. He tried to counteract the flurry of blows but Y just kept blocking his awkward attempts and hurt him, her anger rising a notch. He was gritting his teeth as the pain started to eclipse him. He was unable to move backwards as the shadows were nipping at his heels and unable to move forward as the bitch was on him like a rash.

He was losing energy, stability and his self control dwindling.

He roared again, kicked out with a last ditch attempt to take back some advantage but Y caught his leg, pivoted it upwards and toppled him on his back. He was up on his knees quickly but Y had already sprung up on his torso, both feet smashing into his chest and using it like a springboard catapulting herself away from him. Y landed clumsily from tiredness but she didn't care. The force sent him tumbling away from her like a disjointed hay bale and that's where he came to rest.

The sigh of relief whistled through his teeth, when he realised he was in the safe zone. He relaxed and his arm flopped in the shadows and that's all it took. The darkness snarled to life like a shapeless velociraptor, dragging him into its embrace. He thrashed violently. A mist of crimson like an aerosol spray tinted the air and screams like his body and soul were being ripped apart rose up into the vault above. The chorus of his agony was celebrated by the caverns acoustics.

Then there was silence.

The grotesquery that stood in the shadows was doing its best at being a corrupted facsimile of Darkman but even in the gloom it was struggling with keeping the form together, swaying slightly, its balance wavering from time to time. Spokes watched it with the intensity of a man whose life depended on reading its body language, watching as the creatures struggled to maintain the illusion of the Obeah man. An arm would fall off, quickly replaced with more minions moulding themselves to replicate the limb but lacking the same coherence every time they had to reconstitute themselves. The telepathic connection Enoch had established between everyone in the cavern was waning too because his words of anger had become a whisper until they ceased to be sensed altogether.

Spokes knew without the guard ring he would be dead and even the awesome powers Darkman wielded, his favours to the evil Gods, could extend so far. He was flesh and blood after all. But the promoter did not for a second take him for granted. Their lives were a precarious balancing act right now that still favoured Darkman's decision to slaughter them or offer them a reprieve. Spokes had a feeling this would be his most important negotiation to date.

Life and death.

Acidic bile rose up in his throat, a nervous tick tugged on the corner of his mouth and clammy sweat drenched him. He swallowed erratically, trying to keep the contents of his stomach down but he had to focus elsewhere, he had to build a most convincing case in this pressure cooker moment. Spokes let the facts and figures, pros and cons, indications and contraindications of everything that had happened and everything he had observed soak into him. They started making connections and links in his mind. He thought of Jimmy and how he would handle this and tried to channel his friend's gift for negotiation into the present situation.

Tentatively Spokes and Patra stepped away from the cover of the boulder, hand in hand like nervous children and made their way the short distance to what was left of the circle and the box that sat in the middle.

It had to be now.

Spokes could feel it.

He forced authority into his voice.

"So we at a Tivoli Garden standoff den?" Spokes boomed. "Well I think it best we don't waste each other's time, pardy. This is what you want, don't it?" Spokes bent and flipped the latch on the old wooden box that had been at his feet all this time and reached into it. He hesitated.

The thought crossed his mind that he had never actually handled the artefact inside. With care borne of fear and inquisitiveness, he scooped his fingers under the rock and lifted it up. It never dawned on him to examine it closely. He just knew the effect it had but gazing at it now, it was a beautiful thing to behold and it was heavy too. His fingers tingled pleasantly as he became comfortable with it in his hands. The geode looked like an ugly sandstone coloured rock from the outside but a portion of the exterior shell was split open to reveal the crystals inside. The crystalline structure was layered with deep purples, blues, clarets and whites each segmented area twinkled seductively like natures attempt at a Faberge egg. The interior was riddled with twinkling miniature stalagmites and stalactites erupting from the crystal bed, that bent and refracted light in the most exquisite of ways.

Spokes stared into its shimmering depths, transported into another dimension of stars, galaxies and univers-

es and he was suddenly imbued with a sense that anything was possible.

He held the John Crow stone over his head.

The weight was uncomfortable; its surface rough and
pitted. A steady pulse of incandescence radiated from it's
interior and you knew this was power of a kind modern
man rarely came across. The powerful African totem that
had kept the club successful had also kept lands perpetu-
ally fertile and bountiful for centuries. Darkman had tak-
en it from his home in St Thomas to replenish it in
Ghana where legend says it was forged. For five years it
remained here, providing the club with a glittering reputation but dooming his lands back home for lack of it.
Spokes knew all this and felt a pang of regret and sorrow.

"Jimmy died protecting your secrets." Spokes said, his
voice hollow. "Up to his last breath, he wanted these
treasures to be safe an' dats what I did. Me nevah involve
in yuh downfall. You did that yuself. You an' dat
pussyclaat bwoy Deacon."

Deacon flinched as eyes fell on him.

Enoch Lacombe's dark copy cocked its head. It was either losing coordination or reacting to his words, Spokes
didn't know which.

"Try to kill wi and I drop it and you have nothing. All
gone," Spokes boomed.

Enoch was motionless, his dark skin formed from the
hell creatures blending more and more into its habitat of
shadow around him like rain clouds. And around that
was the host of unblinking red luminescent eyes, waiting
for the command to overcome them.

"If we hafe dead, so be it. But you go home with
nothing. Without this, what do you have?"

Dark Pickney completely surrounded them and every slither of darkness was bristling over with them. Patra moved closer to Spokes, feeling the confinement and the smell of sulphur and excrement.

"Rass!" Spokes swore, feeling something scurry over his foot and explode passing through the charmed ring. Patra kicked out at something that skittered past her feet and it too exploded into dust.

Spokes looked down and realised what they were doing in amazement and horror.

"Goddammit."

They were sacrificing themselves and for every dead demon a gash was left open in the circle of protection, a way in.

"Damn it!" Spokes shouted. "Do yuh think I won't smash this rass to pieces? Test mi again," as he backed up raising the stone high over his head, the creatures kept their distance. One of them screeched its impatience and then the others joined, in a strangely grating but rhythmic chorus that echoed off the high ceiling and into the tunnels.

"We not dying without a fight, you know that right?" The voice rose sweet and confident into the confines of the cave. Spokes shivered at the sheer optimism of Y's voice projected and was looking around to see where it was coming from. It was Patra who directed his gaze to the right place with a point of her finger. Then he saw the light coming towards them like a beacon and the scurrying, almost panicked retreat of the hell creatures. The blue tinged light became brighter and a path was being made for the wielder of the light as they came forward. In moments he saw them more clearly. Suzy had her arm around Y's neck for support. She hopped on her good leg and crooked her injured thigh, high enough from the ground to facilitate easy transport. Y's left hand held Ms Wong's waist tightly and her right hand held the katana straight ahead, glowing brightly like it had been pulled from a blacksmith's hearth.

Dark pickney scuttled away from it in waves and Y and Suzy hobbled towards the refuge of the circle with faltering steps. Half way to them and once a path had been cleared Patra came running. Taking up Suzie's unsupported shoulder, they moved as one to where Spokes stood. The katana grew more intense as Patra joined them and the power of three was almost blinding. With Spokes in the middle, they huddled together and the glow cocooned them all. Their audience, although cautious, crowded in on them, keeping a safe distance from the light but even with this unexpected mystical advantage, the sheer numbers of the monsters would easily overcome them.

"Jesas Christ man, I have a way we can all leave here satisfied. You get what you need and I get what I need." his voice was filled with tremors as the night creatures flowed forward from the surrounding darkness. Thousands of eyes ringed them with thousands of voracious appetites.

"How we doing?" Y rasped.

"Mi have dis." Spokes cleared his throat dramatically. "Let us go man, you take your treasures including the John Crow stone, the trinkets and I keep some of the money for Jimmy's family."

Darkman turned away and started to head back into the catacombs. Spokes was feeling the weight of the stone over his head but he kept it ready to be destroyed before they overwhelmed them.

The facsimile of Darkman was turning away from them.

"Face me when I'm fucking talking to yuh, obeah bwoy!" Spokes screamed at Darkman's departing back. "Jimmy left two boys fatherless because of you."

"They are going to grow up without the man who loved them the most in this world. How dat make you feel?" A bone shuddering chill racked Spokes as the hell things, mimicking muscle fibre, nervous system and circulation in the pseudo Darkman, pulled the body to a stop in response to Spokes angry outburst.

Darkman drooped his shoulders despondently and turned to face him. But there was something different about him, his demeanour skewered. The familiar Frankenstein image of him composed of these hell creatures disappeared for a moment and he seemed to be sheathed in a phantom image of his real self, his human self. It looked like he was cradling something in his arms. Spokes focused and was taken back as his eyes discerned the figure of a phantom infant snuggled protectively to his chest and him with a repetitious hushing movement that was reminiscent of any loving father and their child.

Fatherless, Spokes thought. *You care about deh youts. So you're not completely heartless after all.*

And then as if to reaffirm to him his anger was brutal and remorseless he casually swung a spectral severed head dripping blood and gore in his right hand. His movements were reminiscent of an old reel projection from the nineteen-twenties accompanied by ethereal scenes of a distant sitting room that had been reduced to a slaughter-house. You almost felt like it was an image of something taking place somewhere else. It was like a glimpse of a place where the corporeal body of Enoch Lacombe resided, all safe and sound.

"Kiss mi muma," Spokes said under his breath watching the hell things fall away from his torso and arms leaving a ghostly silhouette of the real man behind. The ghostly Darkman stared at them for a long while, watching what was being done with interest.

Spokes lowered the stone from above his head and gently placed it at his feet, never taking his eyes off the phantom shape of Darkman in the distance.

"I'm a man of my word." Spokes said. "My word an' my balls, is all mi have."

The Obeah man nodded and Spokes swore he saw a red gash across his lower face, a gruesome parody of a smile, maybe? Darkman made a sudden sweeping gesture with his shadowy right arm flinging the head away and hefting the child further up his shoulder with his right. He started walking away from them again but this time the host of burning crimson eyes that had surrounded them extinguished, he was now nothing but a blur smudged into the grey tableau of rock and there was a whoosh of movement as a scurry of thousands of claw tipped appendages followed him out to the passage like a dark tidal wave controlled by a hellish Pied Piper.

Spoke collapsed to his knees, a physical and mental wreck.

It felt like many years before they took a breath in the dimness of the cave. A silence descended as if it had been waiting for the situation to disappear so it could resume its morbid fascination with quiet. Their minds were trying to make sense of the insanity. Patra's eyes were fixed into the middle distance, shaking her head still in disbelief, her chest shivering in spasms, coming to terms with a kind of fear she was acutely unfamiliar with. Y and Suzy were on the ground hugging each other, while Spokes was on his knees still trying to control his panicked breathing, unable to believe he had convinced the Obeah man. A cold bone-numbing aura hung in the air and so did the more real stench of sulphur and excrement. Patra looked over to where Deacon had lain grovelling.

He was nowhere to be seen but he left a trail of scuff marks and finger scratches of a desperate kind. Signs of a terror filled man who did not want to go where he was being taken.

Patra patted herself down for damage.

"Better that motherfucker than any one of us," she said looking down at the marks.

"What if Darkman never took deh deal?" Suzy asked grimacing. "What if him wanted to play rough?"

"Rougher than dis?" Spokes asked pushing his hard hat up on his forehead, a shock-generated smile appeared on his face, taking even him by surprise.

"Yuh tink mi born yesterday? If we were to die and that was a distinct possibility that I meditated on long and hard, then Darkman would get nothing, leaving wid him two long hand, an hurting to rass. I've been brewin' a special spell that would mash up everyting, including the stone."

"Nice." Y said sarcastically.

"I don't know 'bout you ladies but right about now I need a neat shot of J Wray and Son, to calm my nerves," he held out his hand and it was shaking.

"You mean Nephew," Y corrected impulsively across from them.

"For an occasion such as dis sister J Wray's nephew just can't fit deh bill."

He didn't smoke but Shaft thought this was as good a time as any to start. He stood at one of the five emergency exits at the Crypt surveying the damage done. A fine mist hung at ankle height. Mobile phones, shoes, handbags and even some soiled underwear – what the hell happened there? - were strewn over the floor from the stampede that had ensued. By rights this situation should have resulted in major casualties but miraculously the mortality rate was in the single figures. Two fatalities inflicted by these creatures was unbelievable. If their focus was not elsewhere, this would have been a blood bath.

We were lucky bastards.

And how the fuck would he have explained that anyway? He wasn't concerned about the otherworldly events themselves, after all that was the remit of Black Book, where reports were expected to be strange. But actual corroborated proof that demons, duppies and voodoo actually existed was something else completely. The question he had to ask himself was, what else was out there?

Shaft watched the vermin control guys looking around puzzled and the forensic team sifting through the mess, the bodies covered but unmoved. As an eyewitness to what had gone down, he could put his spin on the chain of events, namely sticking with the maneating rats theory. Nothing else remotely resembling the truth would do, even for his department of weirdness.

This time he was afraid the truth would not set you free but could possibly land you in the asylum.

Absently, his view caught a young lady sitting on the steps leading up to the surface wrapped in aluminium heat retardant material and talking animatedly to a fellow officer. Right about now Shaft wished he could take over proceedings and finding Y and the girls would be priority but he had to adhere to police protocol and allow the investigating officer to do his thing unless he

was invited. And he had to remember his story of being
a bystander who happened to be a detective with no clue
at all of how this happened. His impassive demeanour
and his concerned nods to his colleagues as they passed
about their business hid his frustration. He was counting
down in his head the moment he would suggest helping
and as he departmentalised his thinking worked out how
he would commence the search for the girls.

"You looked worried."

Why the voice chilled him to the core, he didn't
know.

"Y...?" he said turning around slowly to see the delectable bodies of Bad II the Bone approaching uncharacter-
istically worse for wear. Y and Patra were helping Suzy
along, a makeshift tourniquet lightly strapped to a
wounded leg. They were all splashed in green muck and
splattering of blood. Y, who had to go a step beyond,
looked as if she had immersed herself that much more
into the gore for a greater sense of relish. They were battered, bitten and bruised and their designer gear was
hanging off them from the violence of their encounter
but with enough material left to protect their modesty.
The girls still radiated this inner strength that magnified
when they were together.

And suddenly he realised he was looking at the future, his future. The traditional roles of the male hero
had been reversed and shattered. From now on he felt
they would be saving the day and he'd be the dude in
distress. Shaft wasn't sure if he should laugh or cry.

He resisted the urge to run over to them. The man
code prohibited that and it wouldn't be cool, anyway.

"Why would I worry?" he said smiling. "You're a big
girl who can look after herself, right? I'm more worried
about the damn fool that gets in your way."

Shaft called over a two man paramedic crew who immediately took over the task of carrying Suzy. Only then did he hug all three together before allowing medical aid to do their jobs.

"What the hell happened?" Shaft asked.

"Hell happened," Suzy said still including herself in the conversation, grimacing as the paramedics removed blood soaked cloth from her wound.

"I think I get that part."

"I'm not sure if you do, I'm not sure," Y said.

"Well shit I'm sure as hell," Patra added sitting on the floor beside a concrete column. "And I've got a partially chewed ass to prove it."

His voice lowered he asked, looking away from Patra to Y.

"Are you okay?"

"I'm not sure if I'll ever be ok again," Y leaned on him and Shaft circled his arm around her waist, taking her weight. She stank of sulphur and the vile green gunk that they all had smeared on them.

"The one thing I do know is that I've found my calling. This, whatever this is, just feels as if it was meant to be."

"I got to say, you don't look..." he grinned sheepishly, "or smell like someone who has found their calling. But you got this shine in your eyes. Maybe I missed you or it's the Courvoisier talking but something is humming underneath all that shit you're covered in."

"A melody," Y said.

"So Bad II the Bone is a reality?"

"As far as following our mission goes yeah."

"Mission?"

"We were told a few things to look out for," Patra added. "Some crystal ball shit."

"Interesting. And Spokes?"

"He'll be on his way to a new life by now," Y said. "Can you believe he left it all behind for us to manage? Lock, stock and barrel."

"Just like that?" Shaft asked.

"Just like that," Y sighed wearily.

"Call me paranoid but how safe is that place?"

"I'm not sure but you can help us with that, I'm guessing?"

Shaft nodded thinking through his next question and not believing he was going to ask it.

"Are you secure...mystically?"

"That," Y said confidently. "I'm more sure of."

Shaft's eyebrows rose.

Y continued.

"I'm starting to realise how smart the old guy was. He explained to me that the mansion has one of these blue plaques at the gate. The ones the heritage society awards to residences of historical importance. Well it seems this place was one of the summer homes of a Rosicrucian in Sir Isaac Newton's cabal. He was a distinguished inventor and alchemist, code for sorcerer, he told me."

Shaft laughed nervously.

"Sir Isaac Newton was a magician?"

Y shrugged weakly.

"Spokes said the place came with mystical protection, that's why he bought it and all it needed was a top up once every fifty years. We got forty five years left on the clock."

"Ok," was all Shaft could muster.

"I hope he got a contingency plan for cleaning that crib," Patra blurted out. "Cos if Slick thinks we gonna do it he got another thing coming."

"Relax," Y said. "Your nails are safe. Spokes thought of that too and lady is coming over in a weeks time, her name is Nanny. Other than that he was a bit mysterious."

Patra sighed relieved.

"What else is new?" Slapping her back to a wall, lowering herself to the floor.

"I'll explain later P, right now I'm exhausted and worried about Suzy."

"Well don't be," Shaft added. "I'll find out which hospital they're taking her to and I'll take you ladies there. You may want to have a check up yourselves while we're at it.

"If you leave with us who is going to help explain all this?"

Shaft shrugged then laughed.

"A hundred eye witnesses, who won't be able to explain head nor tails of what happened. I'm an innocent bystander remember. Why complicate issues anyway? Once the nature of this is recognised, it'll be on my desk in no time."

Patra stretched out her legs on the floor, her head propped back on the wall and her arms to her side, breathing heavily. Suddenly the muffled ring of a mobile phone startled them, piercing a brief moment of contemplative silence. Patra jumped to her feet suddenly enervated and starts patting herself down for the offending sounds. She dug into her jump suit's utility pocket and pulled out a dented, shattered smartphone, which had no right being in one piece much less ringing loud and clear.

"I see your other ear is still in good nick then?" Shaft teased.

Her middle finger went up and without the slightest show of apprehension or surprise Patra answered, pressing the speakerphone icon on the ruined screen.

"I take it your assignment went well. Is everyone okay?" The cool Bombay accented tones of Mr Patel added the final surreal element to this night. One more miracle added to a night filled with the incredible and the impossible.

How did he know? Y mouthed over to her but Patra was already over the shock.

"Great timing Mr P but we a bit fucked up right now. Don´t worry though, we gonna live, we made to last, remember?"

"It seems," Mr Patel's voice smiled at them.

"Y, I have a feeling your destiny was made clearer tonight."

It was now Patra´s turn to mouth, What the fuck! He knows?

"Look after Suzy for me and call me when you recuperate. I worry."

"We will Mr Patel," Y called over. "I promise."

Patra cut the call and looked at the phone quizzically.

A tall dark skinned paramedic rushed over to her as she leaned back on the wall. Suzy by this time was on the collapsible stretcher being pushed out to an awaiting ambulance, explaining on the way out that her injuries were not as bad as they seemed.

Y pressed her head into the crux of Shaft's neck.

"Do you know what I could kill for now?" Y asked.

"No, what?" Shaft inquired.

"A rum and raisin ice cream!"

"Near death experiences give you the munchies then?"

"I wouldn't know. This is my first real brush with death. I feel strangely sexy though. Weird right?"

Shaft gulped.

"Let's see what happens next time." Y ruminated.

"Next time?" Shaft asked. "That sounds ominous. Is there going to be a next time?"

"I've just got a feeling we're not done yet."

"So about feeling sexy and the ice-cream?" Shaft asked sheepishly. "On our way back from the hospital, we can attempt the impossible."

Y nodded.

"Let's make it interesting. If you can find rum and raisin ice cream, you can tuck me in tonight."

Without thinking further Shaft blurted out.

"So this night has not completely gone to hell in a handcart. You have a deal, madam."

Y grinned.

With a new found spurt of energy, Shaft helped Patra to her feet. She leaned on his left side and Y on his right and like wounded soldiers they hobbled through the debris, into the emergency exit to the sanity of the world outside.

Epilogue.

Hanger Lane gyratory has been known as Britain's scariest junction for good reason but tonight it was eerily quiet as a panel van pulled into a parade of shops – flung out from the orbit of the roundabout. There the filming started:

The naked man, eyes and mouth bound, forehead marked with the chalky symbols of an inhibitor spell, squirming in an office chair that he was tightly strapped to with packaging tape, was being bungled out of the van by two balaclava clad figures. Tyrone – tonight's victim - had obviously gone through all the stages of being a captive in his mind. First there was disbelief, acceptance and then he was now occupying the zone of sheer terror. Well that was what his facial expressions were saying because elsewhere on his anatomy was a whole different story. Baby boy had a raging erection that poked through his bounds and either the turn on was to come or it had occurred previously and the memory stoked his passion and his fear. Whatever it was he was a man in conflict as he thrashed and swore. The mobile camera footage was a good resolution capturing the abduction clearly but with the instability many experimental directors tended to use for its realness a la Blair Witch and Paranormal Activity movies. They pushed him along a strangely deserted sidewalk and then onto the gyratory. High pitched grunts accompanied the chair being lowered onto a four lane roadway, precariously pushed and then left on a pedestrian island in its centre. The picture became blurred, a frenzy of motion and sound then after some minutes, clarity.

The final shot showed the bound man's gag removed, his mouth so wide as he screamed his uvula was dangling at the back of his throat, lips in a pretty shade of cock sucking red and plastered all over his body were flyers of his face with the heading 'Most Wanted Thief And Scum'.

Pause.

The YouTube link was sent to approximately fifty thousand women across the globe, avid subscribers to the runaway success - Bitches & Ballers blog. Outside of its uncompromising title it struck a chord with its users to such an extent that the numbers rose steadily as women everywhere – and some men too - wanted to vicariously experience the ups and downs of the phenomenon of Bad II the Bone. Today was special.

Today their blog had a triumphant air to it and a thank you to its enthusiastic subscribers and a fuck you for all who thought they would be pushovers.

It read like this:

Dear Sisterhood

In our very first blog 3 weeks ago we introduced ourselves, began sharing our life with you and, without knowing you as we know you now, we asked for your help.

You heard what we had to say and felt our pain by lending us your blessings and support. After everything we've been through - I won't spoil next week's thrilling issue - ours and your patience has paid off.

The snake thought he could get away with ripping us off. Trying to destroy what we worked so hard to achieve and then find another unsuspecting candidate and wreck their lives too. You saw this was a righteous cause as much as we did and for all the messages of sightings you pinpointed his whereabouts, thanks. But our mystery benefactor didn't just find him but went the extra mile, presenting us with a gift that was more appreciated than chocolate under the Christmas tree.

We have attached a video file for your viewing pleasure and let us just say thank you to all the friends, homies and spars, who backed us. And to the cocksuckers, feisty whores and wanksters who condoned his actions and thought he would bounce back, better think again. As we speak a viral smear campaign has been launched against him with his identity completely wiped from government records courtesy of the world famous lady hacker Sexyprincess1. Before it can be pulled by YouTube the footage above has been played over a quarter of a million times.

Ha-ha!

So for now all is well in the world. Spokes has left us his Sussex mansion to oversee – our new headquarters – while he experiences pastures new. Whether you believe our stories to be true or not, whether we are on the up and up or just full of shit, we are just glad you are taking the journey – fact or fiction - with us.

We are magnets for the weird, creepy and unex-plained it seems but if we can use our knowledge to help then this is all worth it. Keep sending your requests, questions and support.

And remember what is strange to you, is straight business to us. We wouldn't have it any other way.

Time 2 Get it Poppin
Y, Patra and Suzy Wong
Bad II the Bone

THE END

ABOUT THE AUTHOR

Anton Marks first novel began a trend of bestsellers that would transport readers to the ghettoes of Kingston Jamaica in **Dancehall**, futuristic London – **In the Days od Dread**, government agents in **Bushman** and the futuristic world of vice in – **69**.
His next offering will be a yound adult fantasy novel entitled – The Last Prince of Alkebulahn. Expect great things as the Marksman continues writing the most creative and exciting novels in the new Urban Fantastic genre.